STEAL BIG
THE BIG CAPER

Lionel White

Introduction by Nicholas Litchfield
Afterword by Cullen Gallagher

Stark House Press • Eureka California

STEAL BIG / THE BIG CAPER

Published by Stark House Press
1315 H Street
Eureka, CA 95501, USA
griffinskye3@sbcglobal.net
www.starkhousepress.com

ISBN: 978-1-951473-31-0

Book design by Mark Shepard, shepgraphics.com
Proofreading by Bill Kelly
Cover art by James Heimer, jamesheimer.com.

First Stark House Press Edition: May 2021

STEAL BIG

When Donovan is released from prison, he has a plan, and he brings his cellmate Barker and a few old acquaintances in with him. Now he's got all five of them ready to pull off the bank job that will have him set for life. There's Jo-Jo, ex-boxer, punch-drunk, ready to do anything he asks. And Barker, of course, an ex-con with nothing less to lose. Then there's Mamma, the ruthless lady who owns the hideout, and her son Clarence, a bank teller with a fascination for crime. And Carol; young, blonde Carol. Carol's dad is in prison for life, unless she can get the money to free him. For one reason or other, they all need this heist. And Donovan needs them all to pull it off. It seemed so simple when Donovan put the plan together—if only it had stayed that way.

THE BIG CAPER

Flood has got it all figured. The Florida bank in Indio Beach is ripe for the picking. All he needs is a crew. First he sends Frank and Kay down to pose as a couple and set up residence. Then he sends Kosta, his arsonist, to join them; followed by an old-timer to blow the safe, a couple of strong arm killers, and two guys to cut the power. He's got the perfect team because none of them are part of the syndicate— they've got no ties to screw up his plans. But Flood doesn't figure on Kosta getting drunk and setting a fire ahead of schedule just for the fun of it. He doesn't figure on one of his killers bringing along a woman. And he sure doesn't figure on Frank and Kay falling in love, and wanting to get out of the caper.

LIONEL WHITE BIBLIOGRAPHY (1905-1985)

The Snatchers (1953)
To Find a Killer (1954; reprinted as Before I Die, 1964)
Clean Break (1955; reprinted as The Killing, 1956)
Flight Into Terror (1955)
Love Trap (1955)
The Big Caper (1955)
Operation—Murder (1956)
The House Next Door (1956)
Right for Murder (1957)
Hostage to a Hood (1957)
Death Takes the Bus (1957)
Invitation to Violence (1958)
Too Young to Die (1958)
Coffin for a Hood (1958)
Rafferty (1959)
Run, Killer, Run! (1959; orig mag version as Seven Hungry Men, 1952)
The Merriweather File (1959)
Lament for a Virgin (1960)
Marilyn K. (1960)
Steal Big (1960)
The Time of Terror (1960)
A Death at Sea (1961)
A Grave Undertaking (1961)
Obsession (1962) [screenplay pub as Pierrot le Fou: A Film, 1969]
The Money Trap (1963)
The Ransomed Madonna (1964)
The House on K Street (1965)
A Party to Murder (1966)
The Mind Poisoners (1966; as Nick Carter, written with Valerie Moolman)
The Crimshaw Memorandum (1967)
The Night of the Rape (1967; reprinted as Death of a City, 1970)
Hijack (1969)
A Rich and Dangerous Game (1974)
Mexico Run (1974)
Jailbreak (1976; reprinted as The Walled Yard, 1978)

As L. W. Blanco
Spykill (1966)

Short Stories
Purely Personal (*Bluebook*, May 1953)
Night Riders of the Florida Swamps (*Bluebook*, Jan 1954)
"Sorry—Your Party Doesn't Answer" (*Bluebook*, July 1954)
The Picture Window Murder (*Cosmopolitan*, Aug 1956; condensed version of *The House Next Door*)
To Kill a Wife (*Murder*, Sept 1956)
Invitation to Violence (*Alfred Hitchcock's Mystery Magazine*, May 1957; condensed version of novel)
Death of a City (*Argosy*, Jan 1971; condensed version of novel)

Non-Fiction
Sports Aren't for Sissies! (*Bluebook*, May 1953; article)
Stocks: America's Fastest Growing Sport (*Bluebook*, Nov 1952; article)
Protect Yourself, Your Family, and Your Property in an Unsafe World (1974)

The Learned, Bookless Master of the Big Caper
by Nicholas Litchfield

Though popular in his day, with major publishers after his stories, newspapers like the *New York Times* ardently promoting his "distinctive and often startling" books (Boucher, 1967), and renowned directors eager to adapt his work to the screen, biographical details about Lionel White (1905-1985), bestselling author of 35 books, are surprisingly sparse. Oughtn't there be more written about the man whose fiction helped inspire luminaries like Donald E. Westlake and Quentin Tarantino?

In recent years, writers Rick Ollerman, Brian Green, and Ben Boulden have written informative essays on White's novels and characters and the various movie adaptations. Each of these writers has trawled the Internet and numerous literary databases, managing to uncover nuggets of information about White that give a clearer understanding of his personal life, including his career, his marriages, and real-life events that inspired some of his stories.

As someone who needs no excuse to dig through news archives for tidbits on authors, I took up the challenge to see what I could find on the master of the big caper. I was curious to see what was written about him during his lifetime, especially at the height of his fame. Of the modest treasure trove of news stories, gossip columns, and book and film reviews that emerged, the impression I gleaned of White was that he was a hardworking yet flippant promoter of short fiction, as well as a highly articulate, outspoken, charismatic figure, able to motivate and delight those he encountered through intuitive opinions and jokey, droll humor.

Curiously, when you explore White's substantial canon of work, which comprises rough and tough tales of criminal outfits and the violent heists they commit, the stories are sober and the characters humorless. For a man with an abundance of epigrammatic expressions, his writing doesn't seem to reflect his jocular personality.

Through newspaper columnist Dale Harrison, who provides many good examples of his friend's sharp wit, you get a better sense of White's playful character. "A gent who writes should never read. It puts ideas into his head," White said to Harrison. "Writers should never have ideas. It makes an editor's job too difficult. Editors can't digest ideas. They choke on them. I think all editors should choke, don't you!" (Harrison, 1938).

White's adroit, delicious sarcasm was, seemingly, something to relish—something Jill Maas of *The Courier-News* noted in her assessment of a well-attended 1959 book and author luncheon in Bridgewater, New Jersey. Observing his "wit and sharply analytical qualities," she quotes White as saying, "I have tremendous sympathy for the woman who has the courage to marry an author." (Maas, 1959).

Harrison, a troubadour of letters, offers further fine examples of White's amusing, provocative humor, repeating his friend's outrageous remarks in his newspaper column. "I am the only citizen of New York with any pretensions of being erudite who hasn't a volume of any kind in my apartment," White claimed, recalling having read many books, including a dandy one with "the prettiest red jacket on it you ever saw," but, alas, forgetting the authors and the titles. Shakespeare, the one exception, made an indelible impression on him. "What a crime story writer!" White allegedly said. "Boy, could he sure slay 'em!" (Harrison, 1938).

This was in 1938 when White was working as the editor of *Crime Detective*, a magazine based on sensationalistic true police stories. White had spent the past fifteen years working his way up the literary markets, beginning as a police and general assignment reporter in Ohio (writing for *Cleveland Press*, *Cleveland Times*, and *Canton Daily News*) and progressing to sports editor and copy editor in New York (writing for *City News*, *Bronx Home Star*, *Women's Wear Daily*, *Poughkeepsie Star*, and *Schenectady Union Star*). (CA Online, 2001). In July 1932, he started publishing "Short Shorts," a magazine devoted exclusively to short stories of less than 2,500 words, with Paul Anderson serving as editor. (*New York Times*, "Books and Authors," 1932). In the fall of that year, G.P. Putnam's Sons published fifty or sixty of these in a collection titled *The Best Short Shorts of 1932*. (*New York Times*, "Book Notes," 1932). White was also co-editor of another volume published by G.P. Putnam's Sons, two years later, titled *Logical Nonsense*, a hefty 568-page volume of the complete works of Lewis Carroll. Although it contained rare, lesser-known pieces and an introduction, a biographical sketch, notes, and a bibliography, it was criticized for not having illustrations. (*New York Times*, "'The New Editions," 1934).

Later that year, he was working on a biography of Henry L. Mencken, an influential journalist, editor, and critic known as the "American Nietzsche." (*New York Times*, "Books and Authors," 1934). It's unclear what progress was made.

After his employment with newspapers and a literary agency, he held positions as a magazine editor, overseeing several detective journals. His buddy, Harrison, contributed fiction to at least one of these prior to *Crime Detective*, murdering characters with (according to White) "an artistic bluntness that left no doubt about the matter." (Harrison, 1938).

By April 1941, White had left *Crime Detective*, with George Scullin taking over the magazine editorship. He is listed as working as the "publisher of fact detective magazines" throughout the 1940s, including *World, World Detective*, and *Homicide Detective* (CA Online, 2001), eventually moving away from editing other people's work and devoting his time to finding a home for his fiction. Magazines like *Cosmopolitan, Alfred Hitchcock's Mystery Magazine, Murder, Redbook*, and *True Detective* printed his work, and, in 1952, Rainbow Books published his novel-length effort, *Seven Hungry Men!*, about the aftermath of a violent million-dollar robbery in New York City. Avon reprinted a slightly revised version, seven years later, under the title *Run, Killer, Run!*, wherein the original fairly happy ending had been transformed into "a more typical White ending," becoming "both romantic and noir and delivered with a subtle and bittersweet touch." (Ollerman, 2017, p.20).

Notable publishers like Fawcett Publications and Dutton scooped up White's subsequent tales, and screen adaptations of a handful of his books followed, including big motion pictures with directors like Stanley Kubrick, Jean-Luc Godard, Burt Kennedy, and Hubert Cornfield at the helm, and featuring heavyweight actors like Marlon Brando, Sterling Hayden, Glenn Ford, Rita Hayworth, Elke Sommer, and Joseph Cotton.

The Big Caper, included in this twofer from Stark House Press, is one of those novels that had a life beyond the bookstands, becoming a 1957 American film noir released by United Artists, with Rory Calhoun as the lead. *The Los Angeles Times* erroneously reported that Oscar-winning screenwriter James Poe (screenwriter of hits like *Around the World in 80 Days, Cat on a Hot Tin Roof, Lilies of the Field*, and *They Shoot Horses, Don't They?*) was writing the screenplay

(Schallert, "Margaret O'Brien Will Resume as 'Glory' Star; 'Big Caper' Purchased," 1955), and that popular 1940s leading man John Payne would star (Schallert, "'Bonjour Tristesse' Held Probable for Hepburn; New Joust for Taylor," 1955). Payne was the lead in *Bailout At 43,000*, the first of a Pine-Thomas productions double bill shown at Philadelphia's Stanton Theatre. (Martin, 1957).

The movie version of *The Big Caper* received mixed reviews. "Suspense filled scene piles upon suspense filled scene in one of the most gripping motion pictures ever filmed in Hollywood," raved one film critic. (*The Anniston Star*, 1957). *The News and Observer*, which called it a slow, "moderately engrossing crime story that builds to a fairly satisfactory climax," criticized the forced screenplay as part of the problem. (The News and Observer, 1957). Meanwhile, Dorothy Masters of the *Daily News*, critical of the movie in general, was especially disapproving of the henchmen, condemning a couple of them as looking and acting like absolute "morons" to the extent that it ruined the picture. (Masters, 1957).

By contrast, the novel, published by Fawcett Publications in March 1955, was an unquestionable success. The *Albany Democrat-Herald* marveled at the perfect timing of the violent, powerful "taut story," calling the book a "shuddery preview of what modern crime might try to be." (*Albany Democrat-Herald*, 1955). A few days before the book's release, two robbers pulled off a major heist at a branch of the newly merged Chase-Manhattan Bank, making off with $312,219, which was "probably the biggest cash bank robbery in the country" (*New York Times*, 1955). With newspaper headlines still carrying news of the great New York bank robbery, the release of *The Big Caper* couldn't have worked out better.

Set in the sleepy, fictional town of Indio Beach, on Florida's west coast, White's heavily-peopled, slow-burn tale concerns the meticulous plotting and execution of a large bank robbery by a team of crooks led by James Xavier Flood, a vicious, highly feared racketeer. The diverse individuals who form his little group include the old and notorious Hans Paulmeyer, a safe-blower who, despite having stolen more than five million dollars in his time, looks like he should be in a poorhouse. There's baby-faced thug Roy Cluney, and his tough, reckless partner, Wally—an imprudent lookout man who unwisely gets his vulgar, trampish girlfriend, Doll, involved in the scheme. There's affable ex-Marine Frank Gerald Harper, Flood's chauffer and messenger, who poses as a reputable business owner, and Flood's moll, Katherine Jane Garner—Kay—who pretends to be Frank's wife. Then there's the obese, sickly Kosta, an alcoholic pyromaniac who can't be trusted to be left alone for five minutes, as well as a couple of slick saboteurs, George Candle and Shorty.

White maintains a very measured pace throughout, padding out his narrative with profuse minutiae about the main characters and the townsfolk. The plot is sparse and the prose unembellished, but White pays particular care to characterization, ensuring a natural flow to the story and authenticity to the characters.

New York Times book critic Anthony Boucher respected White's prolific output, remarking that his novels were always "tense, cogent, convincing" (Boucher, 1958). He was somewhat cooler toward *The Big Caper* than some of White's previous efforts, feeling that White's writing lacked the complexity and literary finesse of works like *Violent Saturday*, W.L. Heath's heist crime-noir from earlier that year, in which the emphasis is on the town's inhabitants rather than the criminals. Nonetheless, Boucher conceded that White's writing was definitely "more exciting and convincing" than *Violent Saturday*. (Boucher, 1955).

The other novel in this collection is a gripping tale from May 1960 that was also first published by Fawcett Publications. While it shares patent similarities with *The Big Caper*, in terms of story setup and character blueprints, the style, shape, and quality of the texts differ. Though not quite as successful, *Steal Big*, the more ambitious and absorbing of these two tales, is a brisk-paced, character-focused caper that hooks the reader from the start and doesn't let up until the exciting, action-packed finale.

Though well-populated, there are no extraneous characters or redundant scenes. The author also provides a detailed visual rendering of seven key characters, each different, distinctive, and pertinent to the story. On one side of the law, there's the klutzy, luckless Patrolman James Francis Gallagher. Inept but honest, he makes a habit of disappointing his precinct captain and has done little to deserve his imminent promotion. On the other side, confined to a house in Yonkers while they organize a bank heist that will propel them to a better life, are six dishonest, money-hungry individuals who all want something for nothing and are unwilling to earn cash the honest way. There's the landlady, Mamma Pachel, a nasty old woman who would steal pennies from a dead man's eyes, and her psychopathic sadist son, Clarence, a bank teller with inside knowledge of banks and protocols. There's Jo-Jo, a brawny, menacing punch-drunk moron, and the getaway driver, Bill Baker, who's a decent college boy whose life took a wrong turn. There's the young, beautiful, misguided Carol Jane Hardin, who thinks money can help spring her father out of jail. And then there's careful, wise gang leader, Donovan, a hardened criminal with a bitter hatred of society and authority who's devoted to accomplishing the biggest bank robbery that ever occurred in midtown Manhattan.

Rick Ollerman once observed that White mainly defines his principal characters through exposition. "He relates their backstories, their dreams, their past failures, almost solely through his succinct yet detailed and poignant portraits and descriptions." (Ollerman, 2017, p.12). And that's the case here. Through a combination of knotty interactions, character analysis, and background context, you learn much about these disparate people brought together in one place. And as White dovetails plots and maneuvers his motley crew toward a thrilling, explosive climax, you marvel at his expertise in building fear and animosity and almost unbearable tension.

Boucher wrote favorably about *Steal Big*. Despite having read better by White and wishing the author had explored the rather "unlikely" band of criminals a little more deeply, he appreciated the fresh, innovative scheme and the fast-paced, methodical plotting. (Boucher, 1960). Other critics called attention to the astute plotting and multi-layered characters. For Irving Kravsow of the *Hartford Courant*, *Steal Big* was "another of those clever novels about the planning and execution of a million dollar bank holdup with some memorable characters." (Kravsow, 1960). The *Brooklyn Record*'s Charles Richman echoed those sentiments, referring to the characters involved as "fascinating." (Richman, 1960).

Unquestionably, White succeeds not merely in fleshing out his characters so that they have individuality and sufficient complexity, but additionally to the extent that they pique one's interest. As with *The Big Caper*, even though these violent stories feature a large assortment of heinous characters, few readers will want to close either book without witnessing the masterfully orchestrated, elaborate capers or discovering the fate of these dedicated, audacious crooks.

—January 2021
Rochester, NY

Works Cited:

Albany Democrat-Herald (1955, Apr 9). "The Great Bank Robbery." *Albany Democrat-Herald*, p.7

Boucher, A. (1955, Apr 24). "Criminals At Large: Criminals." *New York Times*, p.BR26

Boucher, A. (1958, Aug 10). "Criminals at Large." *New York Times*, p.BR16

Boucher, A. (1960, Jun 19). "Report on Criminals at Large." *New York Times*, p.BR16

Boucher, A. (1967, Jan 22). "Criminals at Large." *New York Times*, p.267

Gale Literature: Contemporary Authors. (2001, Sep 24). "Lionel White." Gale Literature: Contemporary Authors.

Harrison, D. (1938, Aug 9.) "Dale Harrison's In Old New York." *Appleton Post-Crescent*, p.6

Kravsow, I. (1960, Jul 3). "Pick of the Pockets." *Hartford Courant*, p.94

Maas, J. (1959, Mar 31). "Motivations for Writing Found Widely Different." *The Courier-News*, p.4

Martin, M. (1957, Jun 14). "Films at Stanton: Payne, Calhoun On Double Bill." *The Philadelphia Inquirer*, p.25

Masters, D. (1957, Mar 29). "Psychopathic Element Invades the Palace." *Daily News*, p.423

New York Times (1932, Jul 27). "Book Notes," *New York Times*, p.20

New York Times (1932, Jun 12). "Books and Authors." *New York Times*, p.BR12

New York Times (1934, Dec 2). "Books and Authors." *New York Times*, p.BR18

New York Times (1934, Dec 2). "The New Editions." *New York Times*, p.BR34

New York Times (1955, Aug 11). "$312,219 Bank Theft Solved, F.B.I Says: Big Bank Robbery Reported Solved." *New York Times*, p.1

Ollerman, Rick, and Lionel White. "Crime À La White: The Work of a Neglected Noir Master." Introduction. In *The Snatchers / Clean Break*, 7–24. Eureka, CA: Stark House Press, 2017.

Richman, C. (1960, Jun 10). "Books—By Charles Richman." *Brooklyn Record*, p.6

Schallert, E. (1955, Jun 3). "Margaret O'Brien Will Resume as 'Glory' Star; 'Big Caper' Purchased." *The Los Angeles Times*, p.67

Schallert, E. (1955, Jun 8). "'Bonjour Tristesse' Held Probable for Hepburn; New Joust for Taylor." *The Los Angeles Times*, p.35

The Anniston Star (1957, Aug 13). "R. Calhoun Due In Tope Thriller

At The Calhoun." *The Anniston Star*, p.9
The News and Observer (1957, Nov 7). "The Big Caper." *The News and Observer*, p.14

....

Nicholas Litchfield is the founding editor of the literary magazine *Lowestoft Chronicle*, author of the suspense novel *Swampjack Virus*, and editor of nine literary anthologies. He has worked in various countries as a journalist, librarian, and media researcher and resides in western New York. Formerly a book reviewer for the *Lancashire Evening Post* and syndicated to twenty-five newspapers across the U.K., he now writes for *Publishers Weekly* and regularly contributes to Colorado State University's literary journal *Colorado Review*. You can find him online at nicholaslitchfield.com.

STEAL BIG

Lionel White

ONE

From where the car was parked, two doors down from the A & P and directly opposite the South Shore Loan Company office, Barker was able to look into the rear vision mirror and see the uniformed policeman as he turned into the tavern. His eyes at once dropped to his wrist watch.

"Twenty-two and a half minutes after twelve," he said. "He never misses."

Donovan flicked his half-smoked cigarette through the window of the sedan and grunted. "Twenty-three after," he said, his voice edgy. "Fix your watch."

"A half-minute." Barker was amused. "So what's a half-minute?"

"It's the time it takes that man up in Sing Sing to throw the switch," Donovan said, this time not attempting to conceal his irritation. "It's the time it takes for your heart to stop beating when you die; the time it takes to get out of the way of a speeding car when you're crossing against the lights. It can be all of the time in the world. That's what I keep harping on. You are either right or you are wrong. You win or you lose. There can't be any near misses. Set your watch. A half-minute isn't just thirty seconds. It can be the difference between waking up tomorrow morning with a million dollars—or holding down a marble slab at the morgue in Bellevue."

"Sure, sure," Barker said. "Only you know and I know that it isn't any million. Clarence said that joint won't hold more than four or five grand at the outside."

Donovan half closed his eyes and his jaw twitched.

"This is a dry run," he said tersely. "You miss on the dry runs and you don't even get to start in the main event."

Barker shrugged but nevertheless took off his glove and pulled out the watch stem and twisted it. Donovan was right, of course. Absolutely right, just as he always was. It wasn't a case of the half-minute, the thirty seconds. It was a lot more than that. It was a matter of the right way or the wrong way of doing the thing. A matter of precision and perfect timing. A matter of ultimate perfection. It was something you had to understand and believe in—just as Donovan had always insisted. The woods were filled with people who never did have that understanding. Woods, hell. The prisons and the ground out at Potter's Field were filled with guys who had never understood.

He pushed back the watch stem and then took the pack of cigarettes from his pocket. He knocked a butt out and, placing it in the corner of his mouth, twisted his neck so that he could see the door of the loan office. The thin girl with the horn-rimmed glasses was just leaving and again his eye went to the watch and he gave a satisfied nod. His hand stretched out and reached for the car's cigarette lighter.

Donovan lifted his own hand and struck Barker's wrist a sharp blow. "Again," Donovan said. "That's what I mean, carelessness. Put the glove back on if you want to touch something in this car."

Barker felt the red go up his neck. God, Donovan never missed. Even in the little things, he didn't forget. His mind was always about ten jumps ahead. And, as usual, he was right. That would have been real smart, leaving a thumb print or a fingerprint on the knob of the lighter for the cops to find after they picked up the car and dusted it.

"Sorry," Barker said. "Guess I'm a little rusty. Guess I..."

"We're both rusty," Donovan said. "That's why we are here. You get rusty when you do time. But a few more of these should add a little fresh polish."

His eye went again to his wrist watch.

"O.K.," he said. "Get started. It's twelve-twenty-eight."

Bill Barker opened the door at his side and stepped to the pavement, unconsciously reaching up and adjusting the green-tinted glasses. He wasn't used to them and they bothered the bridge of his nose. The thick rims felt strange and partially impeded his vision so that for a moment he didn't actually see the truck coming toward him, but a moment later he caught it out of the side of his eye and hesitated to let it pass. An odd thought crossed his mind. He was lucky, never having had to wear glasses. But then of course, he had always had perfect health, nothing ever wrong with him at all. He would have hated the thought of having weak eyes, or anything really wrong with his body.

The long, water-resistant trench coat was tight across his chest and he wriggled inside of it, very conscious of the slight bulge made by the thirty-two police special he was wearing under his left armpit in the shoulder holster. It seemed to press against his heart and suddenly it seemed to weigh a ton. He'd never carried a gun before in his life, and the gun was a lot more difficult to adjust to than the heavy, tinted glasses.

It was late in March, cold and windy, but in spite of that he could feel the sweat begin to come out and form damp spots under his arms and beneath the belt around his waist. He could feel it on his forehead, under the rim of the turned-down gray fedora, and he worried for fear it would form tiny rivers and drip down his face and perhaps cut little channels into the dark make-up which concealed his blond skin.

For a moment, crossing the sidewalk and approaching the door of the loan office, he had the feeling that he must look utterly ridiculous, like some overly made-up amateur in a high-school play, that no one for a second would ever take him seriously, and that when he entered the place, they would all turn and look at him and then start laughing. The wig, the make-up, the glasses—the whole getup was theatrical and unbelievable and they would know the moment he walked in....

But again he felt the weight of the gun against his heart, or where he erroneously fancied his heart to be, and something about it restored his confidence. He moved forward unhurriedly and opened the door and entered. It was going to be all right. No one would laugh. Laughter would be the very last sensation his presence was going to inspire.

He took in the entire room at a single glance, even as he stepped across the threshold, and he experienced a peculiar sense of surprise, almost of shock, on realizing that it was exactly as Clarence had described it and as he himself had visualized it from that description.

The long, waist-high counter along the left, with the big clock on the wall in the center behind it. The two opened, glass-enclosed offices at the end, one vacant and the other occupied by the middle-aged, slightly bald man whom he knew was the assistant manager. The desks attached to the wall on the right, each one holding a lot of forms in neat partitioned boxes and a ball-pen set, chained to the desk so no potential customer could steal it. God, these shylocks didn't even trust the borrowers *before* they loaned them money!

There was the fat, elderly woman behind the counter right up near the front—and Clarence had been absolutely right. She was wearing an artificial carnation on the stiff shelf of her bosom and her rimless glasses hung from a black silk ribbon. She had the tiny, bitter mouth of a hooked manatee, just as he had described it; the sharp, distrustful eyes, the flabby double chins.

The floor was highly polished, inlaid linoleum made to look like marble, and it was slippery. The walls were dun-colored and as dismal as the sad business carried on within their confines.

Barker's eye took in the barred exit door on the right-hand side, with the thin drapes failing to conceal the bars which were behind them; took in the two empty desks with their neat sterile tops behind the counter and the empty chairs. The filing cases and the water cooler, also behind the counter and very obviously not for the convenience of the customers. Took in everything, including the safe with its opened outer door in the small alcove formed where the partitioned private offices made contact with the area enclosed by the long, high counter.

He stopped in front of the woman and was opening his mouth to speak to her when he heard the sound of the door opening and footsteps. Unconsciously, he half turned. There were two of them: a tired, thin little man in a tweed coat which was too large for him, and a heavy, plodding woman with a Slavic face and dumb, washed-out eyes. They hesitated a couple of feet away, realizing that only one person was on duty behind the counter and politely waiting for him to finish his business before they intruded.

The fat woman with the artificial carnation stared at him myopically, waiting for him to speak, not wanting to help. "I want to take out a loan," Barker said.

"Have you borrowed here before?"

He shook his head.

She reached for a form, slid it across the counter and at the same time asked, "How much will you be needing?"

"A thousand dollars," Barker said, taking the form.

She looked up quickly.

"We limit our loans to three hundred dollars with new customers," she said tartly. "You have a job?"

He shook his head.

"Own a laundry," he said. "Over in Hollis. I was told ..."

Her face broke into what he assumed was a weak smile.

"Oh," she said. "In that case see Mr. Pelling. He's ..." She looked toward the office and then corrected herself. "Mr. Pelling is out for lunch," she said. "But you can see Mr. Morgrini. Oh, Mr. Morgrini."

She had raised her voice for the last sentence and Barker followed her eyes to the back. He saw the bald man look up and he turned, went to the rear of the room, and entered the private office. As he entered, he stepped a little to one side so that he was partly concealed by the opaque, pebbled-glass partition.

The man behind the desk didn't stand up, but he smiled thinly.

"Yes?"

"I'm Joseph Adiniam. Got a laundry in Hollis," Barker said. "Came in to see about a loan."

The bald-headed man started to stand up and indicated the chair at the side of his desk at the same time. Barker held his hand out, not moving, and the other man was forced to take a step away from his desk in order to reach for it. With one swift movement, Barker pushed him, knocking him slightly off balance, and at the same time his hand darted between his coat and his shirt and then he had the thirty-two in his palm.

He spoke in a quick, hard voice, just barely above a whisper.

"Reach for that button and you are dead," he said.

He could see the bald-headed man's foot as it suddenly stopped, just off the floor and not six inches from the spot between the chair and the desk where Clarence had told him the button was concealed under the rug.

"Stay frozen," he said. At the same time he shifted a little so that he was able to partly close the office door with his shoulder. He raised the gun, made a threatening movement with it. He nodded with his head.

"Over there," he said. "On the floor, in the corner. Sit on your hands. Quick!"

For a stout man, Morgrini moved with amazing agility, accomplishing the rather unique feat of sidling into the corner of the room and dropping to a squatting position and then sitting on his hands, without ever once taking his eyes from Barker. His eyes were like a pair of tired oysters, flat, round and utterly devoid of expression. He never spoke a word, either then or during the next few minutes.

There was the squeak of the outer door, which Barker heard clearly, and then a startled gasp from the other room as Donovan's sharp command reached his ears.

He stepped back a bit as the others were herded into the small private office, first the woman with the shelf-like bosom and then the couple, the thin little man and the woman who looked Polish. Donovan was directly behind them and he appeared to be almost pushing them in.

"On the floor," Donovan said. "On the floor!" The little man scrambled like a monkey, almost falling in his anxiety as he sprawled beside the assistant manager. The Polish woman moved slowly but steadily and half turned as she went to her knees. The other woman, the elderly clerk from behind the counter, hesitated and Donovan shoved her with the muzzle of his gun. She squealed and he said, "Shut up." In a moment she was squatting with the others. The four of them filled the corner of the small office.

Barker didn't wait. He was through the door now, closing it behind him and leaving Donovan there with all the others. He stepped behind the counter and as he moved he took the paper sack from under his coat with his left hand. He found the drawers under the counter where Clarence had said they were and he jerked the first one open, tucking the gun in his belt in order to scoop out the bills into the opened bag. There were three drawers and he only had time to see that most of the money was in small bills. He knew that it was the money which had been taken in that morning from people making their weekly payments.

Barker was turning to the safe in the alcove when the front door opened again. This time it was a man in a butcher's apron, wearing a cap and no jacket. He had a red, veined face and puffy cheeks and his blue, bleary eyes suddenly widened in surprise as he stepped into the room and started toward the counter.

Barker had the gun out before the man had taken two steps into the room. He dropped the sack and simultaneously put his left hand on the counter and vaulted across it.

The man's mouth opened and Barker knew that he was going to yell. He didn't hesitate, but lifted the gun and brought the muzzle down across the side of the puffy face. The man's mouth was still open as he fell to the floor. Barker took one of his feet and dragged him to the side of the room and dropped him, leaving him so that anyone entering wouldn't see him at first.

A moment later he was back behind the counter. He went to the safe, pushed the outer door all the way open. There was a thin, steel inner door and it was closed. The key was not in the lock.

He stood up and hurried to the back office, pushing open the door.

Donovan was exactly as he had left him, standing spread-legged, the gun in his hand. The others were still in the corner, all of them sitting on their hands now. Only this time, each one had a wide piece of adhesive tape across his mouth. The woman with the bosom looked as though she were slowly choking to death.

"No key," Barker said.

Donovan stepped toward the assistant manager. He raised his gun, flipping it in a tricky way to reverse it in his hand so that he held it by the barrel.

"The key," he said in a tight voice. "You have just one second."

For a moment the large, oyster eyes stared at him and the man made no movement.

Donovan raised his hand, lifting the gun.

The oyster eyes closed swiftly several times and then the man moved and took a hand from under his buttocks. He reached for the watch chain crossing his vest and jerked on it and the chain came loose, a flat gold watch at one end and a key at the other. Barker stepped past Donovan and took it.

He was back at the safe now and he opened it quickly. He had retrieved the paper sack from where he'd dropped it. It took no time at all to find the bills and stuff them in. He didn't bother with the neatly rolled-up halves and quarters and nickels and dimes.

Standing up, he whistled twice, sharply, and then, not looking back, circled the counter and went to the door. The gun was back in its shoulder holster now and he made no attempt to conceal the paper sack as he opened the outer door and stepped to the sidewalk.

He had to wait at the curb for a brief moment for traffic, and then he crossed the street, not hurrying. He opened the door of the sedan and got behind the wheel. The key had been left in the ignition and he turned it and pushed the starter.

Holding out a hand to signal, he pulled away from the curb, then drove straight for several hundred feet and again held out his hand. He made the U-turn successfully and as he approached the bank from the other side of the street, he reached across the seat and began to open the door on the right-hand side of the slowly moving sedan.

Two men were entering the loan company office as he drew even with it. A line of parked cars prevented him from pulling over to the curb, but he slowed almost to a stop, at the same time opening the door.

The two men had entered the loan office by now and the door had barely closed behind them when it suddenly burst open and Donovan came out fast. He slipped between two of the parked cars and even as Barker began to press the throttle, he had jerked open the door all the way and was inside and next to Barker.

There was a sudden sharp yell from inside the loan office as Barker pulled into the line of traffic. He resisted the temptation to look into the rearview mirror.

"Easy—take it easy," Donovan said.

He half nodded, gritting his teeth and fighting the temptation to step down hard on the gas pedal. When he came to the corner, the lights were with him and he made the left turn.

The clang of the burglar alarm over the door of the loan office reached his ears before he was a hundred yards from the corner. Again he resisted that impulse to press hard on the gas pedal.

Donovan stared straight ahead. "You have to hit that guy?"

"I had to hit him," Barker said.

Donovan grunted.

"Phew-w," Barker sighed. "The first time."

Donovan didn't know whether he meant the first time that he'd pistol-whipped a man or the first time he had committed a robbery. But he answered anyway.

"Has to be a first time for everything," he said. "Next corner, right."

"I know," Barker said.

He made the turn and they were out of the main business district of the village. He drove on straight then, for four blocks. It may have been his imagination, but he thought he heard the sound of a police siren. He shrugged and held the car to a steady twenty-eight miles an hour, stopping once when he came to a red light. He made one more turn, drove for another six or seven blocks and then slowed down and turned into the great parking lot at the Mid-Island Shopping Center, just north of Hicksville.

The cream-white convertible was parked well to the east, in an isolated area. There were a few cars nearby, but not many. Barker pulled up several spaces away. The honey-haired girl who sat behind the wheel of the convertible was smoking a cigarette and reading a tabloid. She looked as though she were waiting for someone to finish shopping and had all the time in the world.

Barker cut off the sedan's engine and was about to open the door when Donovan reached over and took him by the arm. He nodded to where a woman and two children were about to enter a station wagon parked several feet away. Several moments passed and then the station wagon moved off and the two men got out of the sedan. Donovan opened the door of the convertible and slid in. Barker followed him.

"Everything O.K.?" the girl asked.

"We're here," Donovan said shortly.

The girl already had the shoebox in her lap. She took the paper bag when Barker handed it to her and transferred the contents. It took her only a minute or so to wrap it and then she pasted on the labels which had been addressed in advance. The return address was meaningless, but the parcel was directed to a Samuel Carson, in care of General Delivery at the main post office in Long Island City.

While she busied herself scotch-taping the parcel, Donovan and Barker took off their gray fedoras and Barker removed the tinted glasses. The girl stepped out of the convertible and started for the branch post office a few hundred yards away, in the nearest of the long, one-story buildings. She had spoken not a word beyond her original greeting. The men at once removed their trench coats and reached into the back of the car where they picked up a light tan and a dark gray topcoat. Carefully watching to be sure they were not observed, they rubbed cold cream into the skin of their faces and then used Kleenex to remove the dark make-up. Donovan replaced the fedora with a narrow-brimmed, dark brown hat, but Barker left his crew-cut red hair bare after removing the black wig.

By the time the girl had returned, they had stuffed the two trench coats into an extra-large brown paper sack.

The girl got back behind the wheel as they crowded over to make room for her. She started the car and pulled across the parking lot until she came to a public trash can. She stopped the car alongside it and then Barker got out and tossed in the brown paper sack containing the coats and the fedoras, the wig, the glasses and the used Kleenex.

When he returned to the cream-colored convertible, Donovan again spoke.

"All right, Carol," he said. "Hit the Parkway."

At one o'clock on that Thursday afternoon, Patrolman First Grade James Francis Gallagher, driving a prowl car out of the Twentieth Precinct in Manhattan, had a blowout when his car hit a loose manhole cover as he was cruising on East Eighteenth Street, between Fifth Avenue and Broadway.

It was, in more ways than one, a most unfortunate accident; for Patrolman Gallagher himself it was almost tragic.

Two minutes before Patrolman Gallagher's car hit the manhole, a woman was slugged by a purse snatcher two blocks west on Eighteenth Street. The man then opened the door of a passing car, which had stopped for a light, and, threatening the driver with a knife, forced him to use his vehicle for a getaway car.

The attack was seen by a number of people and it was at once reported. When the radio call went out and Gallagher was given directions as to where the car might be reasonably expected to be intercepted, he had just finished inspecting the blown front tire of his cruiser.

The purse snatcher got away, after removing the wallet of the driver of the car he had intercepted and stealing the car, which he later abandoned at an uptown subway entrance.

Gallagher's captain summed up the entire incident very neatly that evening in the squad room.

"Sure," he said in a bitter voice, "I understand, Gallagher, that it wasn't your fault. It never is. Never. But I don't give a good goddamn whether it was or not. I am getting sick and tired of your bad luck. Sick and tired of it. Every time something happens in the Twentieth and you are on the beat, you're off somewhere having bad luck. And every time, I get hell from downtown. Change your luck—or by God you'll end up walking the asphalt out in Coney Island!"

TWO

The large-bosomed girl sitting at the receptionist's desk in Abe Kurwitz's outer office shifted the wad of gum from the right side of her mouth to the left and almost carelessly looked up from under heavy eyelids, idly watching the small, elderly woman with the dead-white hair who sat patiently waiting. Her tiny form was almost lost in the large red couch, but she sat straight, and, although her feet barely touched the floor, there was something very dignified, very correct about her.

Taking in the black, neatly tailored dress, the very proper small handbag, the quiet, unmoving hands in their white gloves holding the bag, the almost stern, unrouged and unlined face, it occurred to the receptionist that her boss, Mr. Kurwitz, certainly had some very odd visitors. She couldn't help comparing this rather elderly, dignified woman with the client who was even now finishing up his business behind the door down the hallway marked "Private."

The client was none other than the notorious Buggsy McGowan, extortionist, blackmailer, murderer. The receptionist had not been with Kurwitz and Kidder, Attorneys, very long and she was no avid reader of newspapers, but she was well aware of the fact that it was only through the brilliant legal manipulations of her employer that Buggsy McGowan was still at large, still free to ply his nefarious profession as a union racketeer and muscle man, a professional hired killer. It occurred to the receptionist that her boss, the well-known and renowned criminal attorney, Abe Kurwitz, must be a very brilliant man. And, of course, she was quite right. If anyone could keep you out of prison, it was Abe Kurwitz.

She felt, for some quite unknown reason, just a little sorry for this gentle old lady who had been waiting now for more than twenty minutes to see the great man. She couldn't help but wonder what possible business the two might have together. In a sudden desire to be kind, which surprised even herself, the receptionist said, "I don't think he will be long now, Mrs. Pachel."

The small elderly woman looked over and smiled at her rather sweetly. She half nodded but said nothing.

A moment later there was the sound of a door opening and each of them looked up as the burly figure left the private office in which Abe Kurwitz conducted the greater part of his activities. The door closed behind him and he strode down the hall and started to cross the reception room. And then he suddenly hesitated.

His eyes went to the woman on the couch and a quick smile split his hard, craggy face.

"Why, Mamma," he said.

Mrs. Pachel looked up. She didn't smile in return. She nodded her head, acknowledging the greeting, and then again looked down, almost demurely, at the carpet.

McGowan hesitated a moment and then turned and quickly left.

A buzzer sounded on the receptionist's desk and she looked again at the visitor.

"Mr. Kurwitz will see you now," she said.

Mrs. Pachel smiled her thanks and got to her feet. She walked down the hall, taking short, almost dainty steps. Without hesitation, she opened the door marked "Private" and entered. Carefully, she closed the door behind her and then she turned and looked over to where Abe Kurwitz was slumped behind the large bare desk.

For a moment Kurwitz made a move as though to stand, but then, apparently remembering his two hundred and seventy pounds, relaxed and compromised with a smile and a nod at the large chair at the side of his desk.

"Mamma," he said. "How are you, Mamma?"

Mrs. Pachel half grunted and moved toward the chair. The attorney pushed an opened pack of cigarettes toward her, his large, broad face genial, as she sat very erect in the chair.

"You look marvelous, Mamma," he began. "Marvelous. How is ..."

Quickly she cut him off, her voice deep and harsh and, coming as it did from her slender throat to issue from between thin, almost dainty, well-formed lips, in such strong contrast to her appearance that it hit him with a shock which he never seemed able to get used to.

"Cut the crap," Mamma Pachel said. "Get to the point. Did you see him? Did you see Johnny?"

Kurwitz's face assumed its usual blank, almost stupid expression. He nodded, leaning back and folding small white hands over his huge stomach.

"I saw him," he said. He shook his head, but he didn't look particularly sad. "Turned down. The Parole Board turned him down again. He won't come up for another ten years."

Mamma nodded, also without expression.

"What I expected," she said. "He'll die up there. It will upset the girl. How did he take it?"

Kurwitz shrugged.

"How do you expect? He wasn't happy but he wasn't surprised. He knows he isn't going to get out. He knows it would take a miracle. Only thing bothered him was the kid. He worries about her. Wanted to know how she is doing."

"He's got nothing to worry about," Mamma said. "My God, haven't I been taking care of her for the past five years—ever since she was sixteen? He knows that he can count on me. He knows that I ..."

"Sure he knows," the attorney said. "But he also knows you used to run a house. And so he worries. He wants the kid to grow up straight ..."

"He does like hell," Mamma interrupted. "He just wants to see that she don't go on the street. He just wants to see that she is taken care of and stays out of the clink."

Kurwitz shrugged. "So what?" he said. "He's her father, isn't he? It's only natural."

Mamma nodded. "Carol's all right," she said. "But this is going to upset her. I told her not to, but she still had hopes he would make parole. This is going to make her pretty bitter."

Kurwitz shrugged. "Everybody's bitter," he said. "So what? Anyway, tell me about yourself? What's new? How's the rooming-house racket coming? By the way, I understand you got yourself a new boarder. Donovan."

Mamma nodded.

"Yeah. Been with me for a month or so now. Ever since he got out of stir. He and a young punk named Barker. They came out together."

The lawyer nodded sagely.

"You got yourself a doozy," he said. "Donovan is a very tough boy. Very tough indeed. I defended him on his last rap. He was lucky he got only five-to-ten instead of life. Who is Barker, by the way? The name doesn't ring."

"A punk."

Mamma's normally sweet, rather wistful face suddenly hardened and there was a thoughtful look in her eyes. "Just some young punk who happened to be in at the same time Donovan was. They were roommates for two years."

Abe Kurwitz looked thoughtful and then again turned to Mamma. "Name still doesn't ring a bell," he said.

"It wouldn't. Barker isn't a pro. He accidentally killed a man during a tavern brawl. Anyway, he says it was an accident and maybe it was. The court must have believed it anyway. That's why he only got a two-to-five on manslaughter. He was drunk at the time it happened. No record before then."

"If he hangs around with Donovan, he'll have a record all right," Kurwitz said. "Anyway, the hell with them. So the rooming house is doing O.K., eh? Fine. Except I don't believe you, Mamma. I just don't, somehow, see you sitting around running a rooming house. By the way, how is that son of yours? Clarence. How is Clarence?"

For a moment the expression on her thin, almost cultured face changed and she looked up at him quickly, shrewdly, as though she questioned the sincerity of his query. And then she smiled for the first time and when she spoke there was a note of pride and of possessiveness in her hard, throaty voice.

"Clarence is fine," she said. "He's still with the bank. Doing fine. He's an assistant teller now."

Kurwitz nodded. "Great," he said. "Great. By the way, what does an assistant teller make? About sixty-five a week?" There was an amused look in his eye as he spoke and his voice had a cynical, almost nasty tone.

Mamma didn't take offense. She looked back into his heavy, fat face and smiled just slightly.

"Don't worry about Clarence," she said. "Don't worry about him at all. One of these days he is going to surprise you. Surprise you quite a lot."

The lawyer hunched his shoulders and laughed it off. "Nothing Clarence will do will ever surprise me," he said. "Nothing at all."

"He's a bright boy," Mamma said, almost defensively. "Bright. And he may be small, but let me tell you something, Abe. He's tough. Tougher than Donovan or that punk Barker or any of them. Don't you worry none about Clarence. You'll never have to get him out of the pokey."

"I don't worry about him," Kurwitz said. "I just worry about the people who know him."

Mamma moved forward in the big chair, putting her hands on the arms to help her rise.

Abe Kurwitz looked at her shrewdly.

"You come in for anything special?" he asked.

"Just wanted to hear what happened with Johnny," she said, getting to her feet. "The girl was anxious to know."

Kurwitz nodded. "You want to have a bite of lunch with me?"

She shook her head. "I have to meet the boy for lunch," she said. "He has the late shift and I'm seeing him downtown at a quarter to two. I was just killing time, waiting for a phone call which I expected to come ..."

At that moment, almost in answer to her words, the telephone on the desk rang and they both looked at it. Kurwitz reached for the instrument and said, "Yes?"

He listened, nodding his head. "Yeah," he said, "I saw him. No luck. Sorry, kid." Again he listened for a moment or so and then hung up without another word. He turned to Mamma.

"That was Johnny's girl," he said, without expression. "Had a message for you. Said to tell you everything went off all right."

Mamma nodded. "Sure," she said, not explaining. "Sure. Why shouldn't it? Clarence gave them the plans." She left then, without explaining what she meant.

The criminal lawyer sighed and after a moment or so, he spoke softly under his breath. "So Donovan is back," he said. "Well, well, well. Business should be looking up."

Clarence Pachel glanced at his gold-faced wrist watch and then looked up at the large clock on the wall at the far side of the room to double-check the time. It was exactly one-thirty. Ignoring the line of men and women standing outside the partition which separated his teller's cage from the main lobby of the building, he removed his name plate from the slot beside the opening in the glass and then pulled down the glass window.

Paying no attention as a woman with an angry mouth rapped on the window, he began carefully rifling through a sheaf of bills, making notations on a pad. He was meticulous as he counted the money he kept under the till and in the cashbox on the counter. It took him a full five minutes, and when he was through, he gathered all the currency and the coins, which he had also counted and made note of, into a large cashbox and left the cage. He deposited the money, along with the notation, in the main safe, and then went into the private washroom used only by bank employees.

Three or four fellow workers, who also took the late lunch shift, were there washing their hands and adjusting their clothes, preparatory to leaving for the one-hour lunch period. A couple of them looked up as he entered, but didn't speak.

Clarence looked at no one and spoke to no one. He was not a friendly man and his fellow workers had come to understand this.

Clarence left the bank by the main entrance at exactly one-thirty-eight, after passing through the general offices where a dozen or more girls were busy at typewriters and business machines. He had glanced over to where Mildred Shapiro sat, hesitating for a fraction of a second as he considered asking her to meet him after work for a drink at a nearby cocktail lounge.

Mildred had been turning down his invitations for weeks now, ever since the night that she had had the date with him, but that didn't faze Clarence in the slightest. He understood why she turned him down. The date had been anything but successful. He'd taken her to a movie and then driven her out to her home in Brooklyn, stopping along the way in a deserted warehouse district where he had made a valiant attempt to rape her. Mildred, however, had proved very nimble and had kneed him in the groin as he fumbled to hold her down in the seat of the car. He had screamed with pain and momentarily lost his hold on her, and she had managed to get out of the car and run.

Far from embarrassing Clarence, or frustrating any further attempts, the incident had merely served to intrigue him. He was firmly convinced that Mildred was a pushover and he couldn't believe that sooner or later she wouldn't succumb.

He took a cab and told the driver to drop him at the northwest corner of Twentieth and Fifth Avenue. Fifteen minutes later he passed through the swinging doors of the Needle Trades Amalgamated Bank and Trust Company. He went at once to the third teller's window from the front door.

The man looked up and smiled. The teller knew him. He had, in fact, been greeting him once each week now for more than a month.

"Looks like rain a bit," the teller said.

Clarence nodded, not smiling. He pushed a pass book, a ten-dollar bill, and a deposit slip he had already filled out, through the grillwork. The teller took the book, still half smiling. He was thinking that this was the kind of depositor the bank liked. A nice, steady-looking young fellow in his late twenties. Neat and conservative dresser. Serious. Thin, dark face, closely shaven. Eyes possibly a little too close together behind the thick lenses of his horn-rimmed glasses, and a rather tight-lipped mouth. But steady. In each week like clockwork to deposit his ten dollars in a good conservative savings account.

The thing which amused the teller mostly was that he knew exactly who Clarence was and what he did for a living. He knew that Clarence, like himself, worked in a bank. And he could well understand why Clarence didn't use his own firm to handle his savings. The less the bosses know about your finances, the better off you are.

The reason the teller knew about Clarence was that he, Clarence Pachel, frequently devoted his free time to earning extra money doing night work at the Needle Trades Bank itself. This Pachel was a very ambitious young man. But not very friendly. Not much of a talker.

While the man took care of his deposit, Clarence glanced idly around the bank. He noticed at once that the routine was changed. Something was different. At first it was a sort of subtle, unconscious sense that told him so, a peculiar instinct that he always seemed to have. And then he realized what it was. The uniformed guard who usually stood over near the door was missing.

It might be of no more importance than the fact that the two potted palms which stood near the entrance had been shifted and were now at the back of the high-domed main lobby. But that wasn't the point; the point was that Donovan would want to know. The way he wanted to know everything.

Clarence finished his business and turned to leave, automatically observing that there was a new face behind the number-two teller's cage, the one used for Christmas savings accounts. Again he made a mental note of the fact and then hurried to meet his mother for lunch.

He was anxious to hear how the boys had made out on the job over in Nassau. He had no interest in Donovan or Barker so far as their personal safety was concerned; in fact, hating each of them the way he did, he would almost have welcomed news of failure. But the success of the operation was essential, he realized.

Clarence had an appointment in four days to close the lease on the old vacant building on East Eighteenth Street, which had been a stable for years but which, for the past decade, had been empty while the owner held on for a good price for the property. Clarence had arranged to lease the three-story structure for six months, ostensibly to be used for storage, and he knew that he was going to need some of the proceeds of the bank holdup as a down payment.

Hurrying now to keep his appointment, his mind seethed as he thought of his plans. Yes, Donovan might be the brains and the leader all right, but where would Donovan be without him, Clarence? Where indeed? He was the key man in the entire scheme, backed by Mamma's intelligence and his own experience as a bank employee. Donovan was nothing but a cheap hood, even if he had been responsible for formulating the original master plan for the big caper which they were all plotting and working on.

Carol took the Triborough Bridge into Manhattan and drove down the East Side Drive until the turn-off at the Fifty-third Street intersection. She crossed over to Broadway and went north for two blocks and then pulled to the curb.

Donovan left the car without a word, entering a four-story building. He walked up two flights of stairs to the pool room on the third floor. Three minutes later he was shooting pool, by himself, at a table at the rear of the room.

In the meantime, Carol had driven on north and when she came to Columbus Circle, she again stopped. This time Barker got out of the car. He turned to her as he was closing the door.

"Sure you don't want me to come on up to the house with you?" he asked.

Carol shook her head, not looking at him.

"No," she said. "No. Donovan says you shouldn't get back until after six. I'll go on alone. I have to go up and let Jo-Jo know what happened."

She started to pull away from the curb. Barker was about to say something, but then he turned and walked off without speaking. He was muttering under his breath.

It took her a half-hour to cross town and get on the West Side Highway. She could have made it in a little less time, but she stopped near West End Avenue long enough to run into a drugstore where she found a phone booth and put through her telephone call to the lawyer.

Back in the car, she felt for a moment or so almost as though she were going to faint. But she didn't, and setting her mouth in a grim, hard line, her teeth biting her upper lip, she shot forward and found the ramp leading up to the overhead highway. She headed north, knowing that it would take her a good forty-five minutes to get up to the rooming house in Yonkers. She had plenty of time; Jo-Jo wouldn't be leaving for his job as bartender until four o'clock.

Carol drove slowly, killing as much time as possible. She didn't want to get there a minute before she had to. She despised Jo-Jo and was just a little bit afraid of the big man. She would much rather have gone to a telephone and called him and then stayed on in town with

Barker, spending the rest of the afternoon at a movie and just wandering around, but that wasn't the way Donovan wanted it. Donovan wanted things to look right at the house, didn't want her hanging around New York. And he was the boss.

Today, for the first time, she was really beginning to understand Donovan. Understand his fanatical hatred of the law, his hatred of society and of authority, his bitterness. It was the news she had heard from the lawyer, the news that her dad had had his bid for parole turned down, which was making her understand. It was like Donovan said—they were all rats, lice. The police, the authorities, all of them. She started thinking of her father, whom she hadn't seen in more than five years and whom she wouldn't be seeing now for a long, long time, and she felt her eyes smarting.

She gritted her teeth, keeping back the tears, and pressed harder on the gas pedal. Donovan was right; take what you wanted and let the chips fall where they may. He was right and she'd go along with him. She had nothing to lose. None of them had anything to lose—she, Donovan, Mamma, Clarence, or Jo-Jo.

Her thoughts stopped there, stopped short of Bill Barker.

THREE

He stood in front of the low sink, facing the mirror, his huge, two-hundred-and-sixty-pound truncated body almost filling the area of the tiny bathroom. He was stripped to his narrow waist, dressed only in shorts and a pair of slacks, and his bare feet were splayed out on the linoleum floor as he leaned forward, peering at the great flat face which looked back at him. One hairy paw held the big-bristled, old-fashioned shaving brush and the other held the straight-edged razor.

For a moment he merely stared at his reflection, his mind blank, and then slowly he winked one small, red eye and his narrow, corrugated forehead wrinkled. His thick lips opened over broken, yellowed teeth in the travesty of a grin and he spoke in a hoarse, guttural voice.

"Hello, Jo-Jo," he said. "Hello, killer."

He lifted the brush, began to lather his square chin, still grinning. He felt good. Felt fine. The way he had been feeling now for several weeks. Ever since he and Donovan had again gotten together. It was funny, but his mind was very clear and he was really thinking straight. Yeah, he was thinking fine.

It had been like that now for some time; he wasn't confused

anymore, wasn't all mixed up. Money—that was the ticket! Money and women. By God, what he was going to do once they had pulled the job and gotten their hands into that hard cash. He wouldn't be pushing the stick behind some lousy bar. He'd be drinking his liquor and eating thick steaks. And he'd have women. God, the women he would have! He'd find a good whorehouse and then he'd move right in.

A dull look came to his eyes and his hand stopped in mid-air. It was getting a little confused in his mind again, the way it used to be. Everything all mixed up. A great big bed and tens and hundreds of girls and steaks and liquor and ...

He shook his head quickly from side to side and, raising the hand holding the brush, gave himself a sharp smash on the side of his forehead. He was getting confused again and he wanted to think straight. That's what Donovan was always telling him—think straight.

He knew he could do it; he knew he wasn't really punchy. Nobody who could handle a sawed-off shotgun the way he could, handle his two hard fists, could be punchy. Hell, wasn't he a good barkeep? Wasn't he ...

Jo-Jo left the water running in the sink and his razor and the shaving brush lying on the side of it as he left the bathroom and, hurrying with his lumbering gait, went down the two flights of stairs to the kitchen. He opened the icebox, found a cold can of beer, and punched open the top. Beer always made him feel more clear-headed. He knew very well that Donovan would be a little sore about it because Donovan had made him promise not to drink until he was through work. But what the hell. He wasn't working now. He was only shaving and getting ready to go to work. He could handle it all right.

He was halfway through the can of beer when he remembered the bottle of whisky. It was Mamma's private bottle and he knew very well where she kept it—on the top shelf in the broom closet.

He found the bottle at once and held it to his lips.

Funny, it had seemed three-quarters full when he found it, but now there was less than a quarter left. He crossed the room to the sink and, with a sly look over his shoulder, opened the tap and half filled the bottle with water. Then he laughed loudly and put it to his lips again. When he put it down, the bottle was empty.

He laughed again and left the room, not bothering to place the empty bottle back in the broom closet.

He could handle it; he'd always been able to handle liquor. But he had to get back and finish shaving. Donovan might not find out about his drinking, but Donovan would be home before dark and if he found him, Jo-Jo, there and not at work behind the stick at the neighborhood bar, he'd be mad. Real mad. Jo-Jo didn't want Donovan to get mad at him.

He stopped suddenly, as he was halfway down the second floor hallway, and he noticed the partly opened door to the bedroom. Again a sly look came over his heavy, dull face and he turned and punched the door all the way open. He'd never been in the room before. But he knew whose room it was. Knew very well whose room it was.

He staggered slightly as he approached the dresser opposite the bed. His hand reached out and he pulled open the top drawer. He blindly looked at its contents. The scarves and the hairpins and the make-up bottles and the odds and ends which a women always keeps in her top dresser drawer.

Almost carelessly, he rumpled the contents of the drawer and then, as though he wasn't even thinking about what he was doing, he pulled the drawer all the way out with one hand and tossed it halfway across the room. He opened the second drawer and rummaged through its contents. When he lifted his hand, he was holding a dainty fragment of cloth, a pair of underpants.

He crossed to the single bed, sank down on the chintz counterpane, and then held the garment up to his cheek. His heavy head half dropped and suddenly his eyes clouded up and he started to cry.

He didn't hear the sound of the tires as the white convertible turned into the driveway and circled around the side of the house. He didn't hear the sound of the engine as Carol turned the ignition switch, cutting it off. He didn't hear the outside door as it was opened and then closed.

He sat on the edge of the bed, his great weight almost breaking the sagging springs, tears streaking down his cheeks. It was like it was before Donovan came. Everything all confused and sad. Everything all mixed up. Everything ...

He didn't hear Carol's voice as she called his name from the hallway downstairs.

Carol Jane Hardin sat at the kitchen table, oblivious of the empty whisky bottle. She had tossed off the beret she had been wearing on the side of her pretty head and her shoulder-length, honey-blonde hair was smooth and sleek as it formed a frame for her small, piquant face. She leaned on one elbow, holding her slightly pointed chin in her hand,

and her hazel eyes were steady and unwavering as she sightlessly stared at the sink across the room.

She was twenty years old and her rather slim body had already assumed the full proportions of a mature woman. She had a beautiful face and a long, slender neck and the sport clothes she wore tended to emphasize her well-developed, pear-shaped breasts, her slim waist and perfectly rounded hips which never failed to excite Clarence when he would surreptitiously watch her as she'd lean over doing her chores around the house.

Carol was lost in memories of the last five years she had spent with Mamma. The years since her father had been put behind bars and she had moved in as a sort of ward to the woman who had been his friend. She had never had any illusions about Mamma and had always known her for what she was, but in a way, Carol liked Mamma. There had never been anything warm or intimate about their relationship, but Mamma had done as her father had wanted and seen that she had a home of sorts. She had seen to it that Carol finished high school and that she had clothing and food. And she had left her alone.

Of course, there had been the business about Clarence, but even in that Mamma had been fair. She hadn't let Clarence bother her, although she had made it pretty obvious to Carol that she couldn't understand how the girl could fail to see the virtues she herself had so easily detected in her only child.

In a way Carol owed quite a good deal to Mamma, and Mamma had been fine up until the time Donovan and Barker had showed up. Donovan and Barker and then, a couple of weeks later, Jo-Jo. Carol had known almost at once that something was up when Mamma had gotten rid of the other roomers.

Donovan too had been a friend of her father's. Carol, of course, had always known about her father. Always known that he was a thief and a burglar. It was this knowledge which was in a great many ways responsible for the way she had lived these last few years. For the fact that she had almost no friends and never went out with girls and boys her own age.

Her father was a criminal and a jailbird and she accepted the fact without question and almost without resentment. For, no matter what else he might be, he was still the one person in this world whom she loved, the one person who had always loved her and had always been good to her.

That first week after Donovan had showed up, Donovan had hardly spoken to her. And if it hadn't been for the accident of hearing

Donovan and Mamma talking late one night, she probably might never have gotten to know him.

It wasn't that she had been eavesdropping or anything like that. She had been out late, on a baby-sitting job, and she had walked home and let herself in quietly, not wanting to wake anyone up. The house was dark. She was starting upstairs when she heard the voices coming from the kitchen. She saw at once that the door was partly opened; there was a dim light coming from the room.

She had been about to continue on upstairs when she had heard her name. Donovan was telling Mamma to get rid of Carol and Mamma was explaining how Carol could fit into their scheme.

Hours later, as she lay sleeplessly in her bed in the small second-floor room, she reviewed the snatches of conversation she had heard. She knew very well what it was all about. She knew that Donovan was a crook, knew that he was there planning some kind of job. She knew that it would be something big and that they would feel her out and see if she wanted to be in on it.

Two days later Donovan made his pitch.

It was early in the afternoon and they were alone in the house together. The young guy, Barker, had gone out somewhere or other and Jo-Jo hadn't shown up as yet. Clarence was at work at the bank and Mamma had gone shopping.

Carol was in the living room looking at television when Donovan strolled in and, crossing over wordlessly, flicked the switch turning off the set. The room was almost dark as Carol had pulled the shades in order to get a better picture. After turning off the set, he went back and closed the door. Then he sat down on the couch beside her. She was just barely able to make out his lean, saturnine features.

"Want to talk to you, kid," he said.

She just sat there, saying nothing.

"Let's start this way," he said. "You got a boy friend?"

"No."

"You sure? Maybe some guy you're on the temporary outs with? Maybe—"

"No boy friend," she said.

He grunted. "How are you on keeping your mouth shut?"

She half laughed; she thought, God, is *this* a stilted conversation. She began to wonder if he was as smart as she had led herself to believe.

"As good as the next," she said.

Again he grunted. He moved suddenly and she felt his arm around her waist and she sat half frozen. And then, before she could move, he had pulled her close and half pushed her down on the couch and she felt his hard lips on her mouth. She felt one strong lean hand on her breast, holding her hard, and he was half suffocating her. Even before she had a chance to begin to struggle, he released her and sat back.

"You like that?" he said.

For a second, even before she had a chance to experience shock or anger, she felt keen disappointment. Was this Donovan's idea of feeling her out? Was this the way...

"I said did you like that?" he repeated, his voice edged with hardness. She shrugged. "Not particularly."

"You like men? Do you like to make love? Do you want to—"

"If that's making love," she said, bitterly, "the answer is no."

"Maybe it's just me," Donovan said. "Maybe you would rather have someone else ..."

"Maybe I would," she said, interrupting him. "But that way, like an animal, it wouldn't matter. I still wouldn't like it."

He leaned back then, suddenly relaxed. He laughed. "No one can say you're a teaser," he said. "I just wanted to find out a little something about you, Carol."

"Well, I hope you found out."

"I was just trying to see if you were really his daughter."

"His daughter? Try me out, mister. Just try me out!"

Again Donovan laughed and there was real humor in his laugh. "No thanks. I just did," he said, and as she started to protest, he cut her short again. "Let's get serious. Your old man had two qualities that I liked and that made him, in my book, a great guy. He was, according to his lights, straight as a die. He never double-crossed a friend in his life. And he had what I call integrity. He was his own man. I guess you are your own girl."

"I'm my own girl all right and I'm going to stay that way."

"Fine. That's all I wanted to know. Now ..." He hesitated, not knowing exactly where to start, and so she helped him along.

"Say it, Donovan."

"All right, kid. You know why I'm here?"

"Yes. I think I know. I think you're here planning some kind of a caper. A robbery or something that's big."

"You're a smart kid. Very smart. And you're right. I'm planning a little more than just a plain heist or stickup. I'm planning something big. Real big. A caper which can bring in three quarters of a million or better. And I can use help."

She didn't say anything, waiting breathlessly.

"I'll go a little further. I can use your help."

"My help?" Carol said. "What could I do—"

"Never mind the details just yet," Donovan said. "Just take my word for it. I can use you. But under just one condition, that is, assuming you want to play along."

"What condition?"

"This. That after the job is over and done with and we split the dough—there will be several of us in it, but I can tell you this, my cut will be a couple of hundred G's—anyway after it's over, and we split out, you come with me."

Once more she felt that sudden sense of disappointment.

"Come with you?"

"Yeah," Donovan said. "Come with me. Now don't get on your horse. Just let me explain. As I said, there will be several of us. There'll be a monkey named Jo-Jo. You haven't met Jo-Jo yet, but he's a little punchy. There will be Mamma and that nasty kid of hers and there will be Barker. Well, when it's all over and done with, I want to take my cut and put just as much distance between them and me as I can. I never want to see any of them ever again."

"But you want me to come with you," Carol said, sarcasm in her tone. "Why me?"

"Not for the reason you think," Donovan said. "Or to be completely honest with you, not primarily for the reason you think. I want you to come with me mainly so I can keep my eye on you for a certain length of time. You see ..." He hesitated for several seconds and then went on, speaking very carefully and in a dead monotone. "You see, kid, you may think you want in on this and you will probably be able to handle your end all right. But the real pressure isn't going to be while we're doing the job. It's going to be afterward. It's going to be if the cops get a lead and pick someone up. I don't have to worry about Jo-Jo—no one on this earth could make him rat on me. I don't have to worry about Mamma, and Mamma can always handle that bastard son of hers. I don't have to worry about young Barker. He's no professional thief, but I know that boy. By God, I've just spent three years in the clink with him and I know him like I know the back of my hand. I can trust him all right.

"But I don't know you. Oh sure, maybe you'll mean all right and maybe you'll even be able to take it afterward. The worry and the fear and everything else. But then again, maybe you won't. You're just a kid and you've never been through anything like this. You can crack as well as the next one. You could—"

"I'm my father's daughter," Carol said.

"That's what I'm counting on, kid," Donovan said. "It's one of the reasons it has to be my way. I know where I'm going afterward. Know where I'll be safe. And I want you with me—for two reasons. The first one is so that I can protect you and see that you are where you can't get into trouble and no one else can get you into trouble. The second one is because I am not going to take any possible chance of you being picked up and made to talk. Now, if you want it that way, I'll go ahead and tell you a little more."

Carol looked over at him in the dim light, an odd expression on her face.

"So I go away with you afterward," she said. "And then what? Then what happens? Am I supposed to—"

"Don't get ideas again," Donovan said. "I got a hideout arranged. I won't tell you just where yet, but let's say someplace like a ranch up in the Canadian Rockies. We go there together, as father and daughter maybe. And we stay. Stay for a year. Maybe two years. Stay until things have quieted down and the whole thing has blown over. Just sit it out. By then, I am going to know a whole lot about you. I'll know if you are going to be safe to leave. Safe for me and safe for yourself."

"Suppose you don't think I'll be safe?"

He hesitated for several seconds and she could see that he was staring at her.

"Well, kid, then in that case, I'm afraid that I'd have to make you safe. That's what you have to think about. If you want in. You don't have to give me your answer now. Just take a little time and ..."

Carol reached over and took his hand.

"You can have my answer," she said. "Now. I want in. I want in bad." She sighed then and rushed on. "God, Donovan, you have no idea how much I want in. I want money. Lots of money. I want the money to get away from here, to get away from these creeps and never see Mamma or Clarence or any of them ever again. I want the money to live decently where no one knows me or knows anything about me. Where I can make friends and see people who..."

She was half sobbing then and unconsciously she had leaned over so that her head was against his chest and his arms had gone around her and he was half rocking her on his lap.

"O.K., kid. O.K.," he said. "Take it easy, baby. You're in. You're in, all right," he told her.

She lifted her tear-stained face then and her mouth found his and held it in a long kiss. Then she quickly untangled herself from him and got to her feet. She sensed the tension of him as he had held her, felt the sudden tautness of his muscles. She had felt his restraint and was grateful for it. "You're all right, Donovan," she said. "You are just like my Dad said you were. You're all right."

"You're all right too, kid," Donovan said.

FOUR

Gradually, as she sat there leaning her chin on her hand and staring at the sink, the sound reached her mind, penetrating her consciousness and interfering with her thoughts. At first she was only vaguely aware of it and tried to ignore it. She was thinking of that afternoon with Donovan and she was feeling a sense of wild expectancy now that things were really progressing.

He'd gone ahead almost at once, first buying the white convertible, which she knew would be a part of the job. But she had been very pleased. He could have bought almost any old second-hand car, but he'd gone out of his way and gotten her this one. This fancy, leather-upholstered convertible with the push buttons and everything fresh and clean and new, and she had been delighted.

Clarence had screamed, of course, saying that it wasn't necessary, and he had been right, but Donovan had shut him up with one hard look. Yes, Donovan had been fine. And he was keeping his unspoken word. Not by the slightest look or action had he shown anything but a strictly paternal attitude toward her. If anything, his attitude had been almost too standoffish.

Carol realized that her own feelings had gradually crystallized over the past few weeks. It was almost as though he really was her father.

Once again she became conscious of that odd sound. It came from somewhere in the house, upstairs she thought. It sounded like a wounded animal. A sort of half sob, half moan.

She straightened up and her eyes went directly to the ceiling.

Jo-Jo hadn't answered when she had called out to him and he had obviously left the house. A curious look, not frightened, but slightly perplexed, came to her eyes and she slowly stood up.

It was exactly as though a child or small animal were crying.

Slowly she went to the foot of the stairs and listened closely.

Once more the sound reached her. She remembered the time, a week or so previously, when she had left the window of the bathroom open and the alley cat had crawled in and gone to sleep next to the tub.

Shrugging, she started to turn back to the kitchen, when again she heard a sort of soft, muffled cry.

Quickly she went upstairs.

Jo-Jo didn't look up as Carol opened the bedroom door and suddenly stopped in her tracks, staring at him. He was hunched over, his shoulders shaking, and he held the torn piece of cloth, which had been her underpants, in his hand. It was pressed against his lips.

For a second she stood there, her eyes wide. Her hand went to her mouth and then, as he moaned once more, she spoke.

"Jo-Jo," she said. "Jo-Jo—what in the world is the matter with you? What are you doing in my room?"

He looked up then, staring at her blindly. His hand fell away from his face and for the first time Carol saw what he was holding. Her eyes swept the room and she saw the opened bureau drawers and the clothes scattered over the floor.

For a moment she stood there rooted, and then, almost too casually, she started to take a backward step. She knew that the big man was drunk and her eyes stayed riveted on him. She realized that he didn't recognize her or even know that he was there in her room.

Her foot caught in the rug and she staggered backward.

He was off the bed like a monkey, moving with fantastic swiftness for a man of his size.

Carol opened her mouth in the beginnings of a scream as he reached her. He caught her, one great arm circled behind her waist as she was starting to fall.

For a full ten seconds they held the tableau, Jo-Jo half holding her up in his arms and she leaning back, staring wide-eyed into his tear-streaked face.

Suddenly the blankness left him and he opened his mouth and half laughed. His arm tightened and he pulled her close.

"Jo-Jo," she cried, her voice a half scream. "Jo-Jo—let me go. Let me loose. Take your arm ..."

She didn't get to finish the sentence.

With one swift movement, he jerked her off her feet and swinging, threw her down on the bed. Before she could make a move, he fell on top of her, crushing her slender body under his bulk. His hands were jerking at her clothes and she felt a sudden horrible flash of pain as his teeth tore through the heavy fabric of the sport jacket she was wearing, just missing the nipple of her left breast and cutting a long gash in her soft flesh. She started to cry out then, but his great hand suddenly closed over her mouth.

She was dimly aware that he was mouthing a string of meaningless obscenities and that the slobber was soaking her as his lips crawled over her naked flesh like a pair of great leeches.

For a moment she felt a sudden lessening of pressure as he shifted his weight, pressing his knee roughly between her thighs, and then the pressure was back and one of his cruel hands was reaching down, searching.

She screamed in sudden agony.

Bill Barker walked away from the convertible without looking back. In a way he was glad to leave Carol, glad to be alone. He was experiencing one of the greatest feelings of exhilaration he had ever had. It was like being doped up, drunk to the gills. Except there was nothing foggy about it.

He'd come through with flying colors; he'd carried out his part in the stickup and he hadn't faltered. He had never thought, from the very first, that he could actually do it. That was his secret, a secret that he didn't believe Donovan or any of them had guessed. He'd been flying under false colors all along. Kidding them, and possibly himself, into thinking he was really tough, had what it took. But had he been kidding himself? Wasn't it true that he did have what it took?

He thought of the money they had stolen, the better than four thousand dollars, but quickly his mind went beyond that. It wasn't the money. The money was of relatively small importance. The thing which was important was that he'd had the guts to take a gun in his hand and walk into a loan company and pull a daylight stickup. That he had risked his very life. And the lives of others.

Somehow or other the last thought left a foul taste in his mouth. It didn't actually take a great deal of courage to risk someone else's life. But that didn't detract from the fact that he'd been willing to put his own neck on the block.

Yes, he, Bill Barker, had proved to himself and to Donovan that he had what it takes.

For the first time he really stopped and thought about the big job, the real one. The Needle Trades Amalgamated Bank. Three-quarters of a million dollars! That's what Clarence had estimated.

He thought back to the day he had first met Donovan. It was his twenty-third birthday—and he was celebrating it by being assigned a cell in state's prison after going through his six-week isolation period.

He'd been heavier then, weighing around a hundred and seventy-five. But he wasn't fat; his six-foot-one-inch, wide-shouldered, heavy-boned frame could take the weight all right. In fact, aside from having dropped some fifteen pounds during those three prison years, he'd changed remarkably little. He still had the same short red hair, crew-cut and unmanageable. The same grey-blue eyes above the rather long nose. The same finely chiseled lips and slightly prominent chin.

The three years hadn't aged him. Not physically. But they had changed everything else. Changed his outlook on life and his ambitions. Part of it was what had happened to him—that business of the fight in the barroom which had ended up in his taking the half drunk longshoreman outside and battling him. Hitting him just a little too hard so that he had fallen and cracked open his skull on the sidewalk.

An accident? Yes, in a way. But he had been spoiling for a fight when he had gone into the place. It was the day the Air Corps had turned him down because they said he had bad hearing in one ear and the disappointment had made him mean and touchy and he'd been looking for trouble. He'd found trouble, all right, and it had cost him three years of his life.

That had changed him.

But what had changed him even more was Donovan, the old professional criminal with whom he was to spend those three years, sharing a cell and sharing most of the hours of their lives.

Bill remembered a conversation he had had with Donovan one time during the first few weeks of the years they were to spend together. He had asked the older man, naively enough, why Donovan had chosen crime as his profession. Donovan had summed it up very neatly.

"It's the only business for which I have a natural-born talent," he had said. "All of the essential qualifications. You see, I have no morality, no principles, no faith. And no scruples. I'm lazy. I hate work and I hate bosses and I like luxury. I have no education, and no training. No particular talent—aside from the fact that I can handle a submachine gun, pick a lock, drive a fast car, open certain types of safes.

"I like money—for what it will buy. I have no way of making money, real money, honestly. So I make it the other way. Maybe, if I had dough to begin with, I'd gamble in the market or even in business. But I don't have money. The only stake I have to put up is my freedom—my freedom and possibly my life. That, my boy, is why I am a crook."

Bill laughed and shook his head. He couldn't help saying, "Maybe you have no talent for that either. Otherwise you wouldn't be sitting here in the clink telling me all about it."

He thought that Donovan was going to get sore, but the older man just laughed.

"You couldn't be more right," he said. "But you have to remember, even the stock-market speculator misses now and then. The businessman goes broke. The company executive gets fired. The difference between the man who is really good and the failure is that the big man makes a comeback. And that's what I am planning to do when I get out of here. This is tough, but I don't guess it's any tougher than the years an interne puts in working for nothing in a hospital. I consider it in the light of experience. Gives me time to think. And I am doing plenty of thinking."

It wasn't until at least two years later that Donovan was to tell Bill what it was he was thinking about.

Barker had been walking aimlessly as he was thinking and he suddenly looked up at a street sign and noticed that he was at Broadway and Forty-eighth Street. There was brilliant, neon-lighted marquee of a movie theater nearby and for a moment he thought of going in and seeing the picture to kill time, but then he noticed another man several feet away, watching him, and at once he spotted him for a plainclothesman or a detective. He'd gotten so he could pick them.

For a second, he felt a sudden sense of fear. It wasn't because of the stickup. It was because he realized suddenly that he was on parole. That he should be working and not loitering around the midtown section of New York City in the middle of the afternoon.

That was the trouble with being an ex-con; he couldn't look at a cop without that nasty, subtle sense of fear.

And yet he knew he had nothing really to fear. Donovan had fixed that—the very first week he was sprung. The job, the phony job Donovan's lawyer had arranged, was all taken care of.

But he still felt ill at ease wandering around, and, as casually as he could, he moved up the street from the plainclothesman, and turned a corner.

He wished now that he had gone on back to the rooming house with Carol. Thinking about that, Bill remembered how she had looked as she had driven away. God, she was a pretty kid, all right. Pretty, hell.

She was beautiful. For the first time since he had met her, Bill suddenly thought of Carol not as someone who happened to live in the same rooming house and was going to be mixed up in a job with the gang. He thought of her as a desirable and attractive woman.

And then he remembered that she was even now on her way back to that rooming house. He remembered that when she got there, she would find Jo-Jo, alone in the house. And he remembered something else which had completely escaped his mind during the wild exhilaration of the loan company job. He remembered a remark Jo-Jo had made to him less than a week ago when Jo-Jo had been a little tight after coming home late at night from his job as bartender.

They'd been sitting in the kitchen having a beer, and Carol had just gone upstairs.

Jo-Jo had said, "That kid. Someday, someday I'm going to get her alone and when I do, man, I'm going to put the blocks to her, but good."

"Nuts," Bill had replied. "She wouldn't give an ape like you the time of day."

Jo-Jo had grinned evilly.

"When Jo-Jo loves 'em," he said, "they may not like it at first, but man, they got nothing to say. Nothin' at all. What I do to 'em, afterward they're afraid to say anything."

Bill Barker had laughed it off, hardly paying any attention to the remark. It was typical of Jo-Jo's insane, punchy conversation and no one paid any attention to what Jo-Jo said.

And then Bill remembered something else. Something Donovan had once told him when he had been questioning the other man about how he happened to know Jo-Jo and why Jo-Jo had such a fanatic devotion to Donovan.

"Saved his life one time after he killed a girl in a warehouse," Donovan had said. "He went crazy and wanted to give himself to the cops. I straightened him out."

"Killed a girl?" Bill asked. "You mean he beat her to death?"

"No, it wasn't that," Donovan said. "I wouldn't have taken care of him if that had been it. Jo-Jo didn't really mean to do it. You know, he goes a little crazy when he gets drunk. Doesn't know what he's doing. No, he didn't beat her to death. I guess you could say, if you wanted to stretch a point, that maybe he loved her to death. You see, Jo-Jo is an animal. And like an animal, he doesn't know his own strength and he can't control it. With that girl—well, it was like a lust-starved ape suddenly came across a woman in the jungle. He didn't beat her. Jo-Jo just left her with every bone in her body crushed. He never did realize what he had done."

Bill Barker suddenly experienced a peculiar sense of panic. His heart seemed to miss a beat. He was again remembering the way Carol had looked as she had driven off in the white convertible, her honey straw hair flying in the wind as it escaped from under the edges of the midnight-blue beret.

He started running, heading in the direction of Grand Central Station.

Mamma and her son Clarence finished their lunch just before two-thirty and Mamma took a couple of bills from her small black bag and paid the check. They had hardly spoken to each other throughout the meal, and when they at last left the restaurant, they went to the curb in front of the place and it was Mamma who held up her arm and waved to a passing cab.

She gave the driver the address of the bank uptown where Clarence worked and a few minutes later the driver pulled to a stop and Clarence got out. Neither one said good-bye to the other.

Mamma gave the driver the address of a famous music store on Madison Avenue and ten minutes later was entering the establishment. She told the clerk who greeted her that she wanted to see a tape recorder.

The display was on the second floor and she was taken up in an old-fashioned elevator.

"My son is a divinity student," she explained, looking small and helpless and slightly bewildered, "and I have come to the city to buy him a gift. He is graduating this coming spring."

The clerk smiled indulgently and suggested that perhaps her son would be more interested in a phonograph or a portable radio.

"No," Mamma said, "he specifically asked for a tape recorder. You see," she smiled meekly and spoke in a proud voice, "you see, he is going to take a six-month tour. Around the great cities of the nation. And he will be visiting churches and cathedrals and he wants to take down all he hears on tape."

The clerk showed her a small machine, selling for under a hundred dollars. Mamma patiently listened to the instrument, then shook her head.

"Don't you have something a little better?" she asked. "Of course, I don't know anything about these contrivances, but I want the very best for him."

The clerk said he had something better and showed her another machine. It didn't please Mamma.

"Of course, we have the big professional jobs," the clerk said, trying to conceal the slight annoyance he was beginning to feel. "But really, they aren't at all necessary. Not for the sort of thing that your boy—"

"What my boy will be doing is the most important thing in the world," Mamma said. "As important as life and death," she added, smiling secretly to herself as she spoke. "He must have the very best. The best is none too good for the Lord's work."

The clerk, a little grimly, crossed the room and showed her an elaborate job in a huge cabinet. Mamma insisted on hearing it.

"The price," the clerk said, "is sixteen hundred dollars."

Mamma looked shocked. "Sixteen hundred dollars," she said, scandalized. "That's a bit high. Anyway, he will be travelling all of the time and it must be portable. I want you to show me the very best thing you have in a portable set."

She spent more than an hour and a half in the store and was finally satisfied. The set she settled on was reasonably small, no larger than a fair-sized suitcase. It was very complicated, but it reproduced the sound of a human voice perfectly. With a half-dozen tapes and the microphone, it came to five hundred and seventy-six dollars.

"The very finest instrument of its size you can buy," the clerk said, sweating a little as he wiped the back of his neck with a silk handkerchief.

Mamma took out her pocketbook, reached in, found five ten-dollar bills. She handed the money to the clerk.

"I don't have all of the money today," she said demurely, "but I will come back next week and give you the rest of it."

"Wouldn't you like us to have it delivered?" the clerk suggested. "We could send it to your home C.O.D. We have free delivery anywhere in the Greater New York—"

"Oh, please don't trouble," Mamma said. "You see, I live 'way upstate and I will be in town for the next few days anyway. I'll just come back and ..."

"Perhaps to your hotel then, madam?"

"Next week," Mamma said, her voice suddenly cold. She gave him a name and the clerk gave her a receipt for the fifty-dollar down payment.

A spunky old girl, he thought, as she turned and left. Knows just what she wants and how she wants it and is taking no back sass. It was surprising the amount of character these little helpless old ladies sometimes showed. Well, at least her boy, that divinity student, was getting the best machine on the market. Shame it would be wasted on a lot of dull sermons.

"It takes all kinds," the clerk said under his breath, at the same time mentally adding the commission he would make from the sale to his weekly drawing account.

The rooming house in Yonkers was in one of the older districts of the city on a quiet street of semi-decayed mansions with large rolling lawns surrounding them. It was a deceptive house, with its high red-brick stoop and its steep sloping roof which came down past the third-floor rooms; the rooms were lighted by a series of individual gables. Mamma had rented the place, signed a five-year lease, and, because the neighborhood was a little run-down and no longer in fashion, there was no difficulty about using the place as a rooming house.

Bill took a cab from the railway station and even before the driver had come to a full stop, he had the door open. He handed the man two one-dollar bills, telling him to keep the change.

Running up the path leading to the front door, he was able to see the end of the white convertible from where it was parked in the three-car garage at one side and to the rear.

He was in the lower hallway when he heard Carol's piercing scream of agony.

For one brief second he stood there, frozen with a sudden fear. And then he moved forward, taking the steps three at a time. He knew exactly where to go.

The door to the girl's room was partly opened and Bill crashed through, almost taking it off its hinges. And then he had his hands buried in Jo-Jo's hair and with a powerful wrench, pulled him bodily from the bed. He lifted his foot and kicked the other man full in the face, and Jo-Jo slumped to the floor, stunned for a moment.

Jo-Jo looked up at him blindly as the blood suddenly spurted.

Even in that instant Bill realized that against the superhuman strength of the other man he would be helpless. He was turning, looking for any kind of weapon, when Jo-Jo hunched his great truncated body and got to his feet, half crouching.

Bill backed carefully to the door, staring straight into those small, mad, bloodshot eyes.

Jo-Jo grunted deep in his chest and lunged, and Bill ducked out of the door, turning toward the stairs. As Jo-Jo reached out for him, he dropped quickly to his knees. Jo-Jo's body went hurtling over him down the stairwell.

Bill slowly got to his feet. Again he started looking around wildly for a weapon when he suddenly became aware of the silence below. Cautiously, he looked over the railing.

Jo-Jo was at the bottom of the staircase, out cold. Bill at once realized what had happened. The big man had struck his head against the newel post as he fell and had knocked himself out.

Bill went to his own room and quickly grabbed two leather belts from his dresser drawer. Two minutes later he had Jo-Jo's arms strapped in back of him and his feet tied together at the ankles. He went into the kitchen then and got a long piece of clothesline, wanting to make sure and knowing what Jo-Jo's strength would be when he recovered consciousness.

After he was through, he went back up to the bedroom.

She was sitting on the edge of the bed, her clothes half torn from her body. She was almost naked from the waist up. There was an ugly gash across one of her soft breasts and tiny drops of blood were dripping down on her lap. Her breath was coming in gasps. She looked at him from tear-blurred eyes as he stood in the doorway.

"Bill," she whispered. "Oh, Bill! Thank God ..."

In a second he was beside her and she was in his arms, crying as she buried her head in his neck.

"That animal," he said. "That animal. I'll kill him. That's what I'll do. I'll kill him!"

She held him tight and for a second he struggled to get up. And then suddenly he relaxed and his arms were around her, holding her and rocking her, as he whispered incoherently.

FIVE

At four-thirty Donovan stacked his cue and went over to the cashier's desk next to the entrance to the pool hall. He told the man how many racks he had shot and the man didn't question his figure. Donovan paid for the racks and left the place. He walked to the subway kiosk at Seventh Avenue and Fiftieth Street and caught a downtown local. He got out at Canal Street and walked east for several blocks.

The six-story loft building he entered fifteen minutes later was not more than a couple of blocks from police headquarters on Center Street.

Donovan didn't look at the half-dozen worn, barely legible signs in the dingy lobby of the building. He went at once to the elevator and asked for the fifth floor. Getting out of the elevator, he turned left, took a dozen steps and knocked on a pebbled-glass door. The door bore the legend, KUBRIC NOVELTY COMPANY.

He had to wait several moments before there was the sound of footsteps and then he heard a bolt being shot back and the door softly opened. Donovan entered and the small, bald-headed, round little man who had let him in locked the door after him. Wordlessly he followed the man to an inner office, and, unbidden, took a seat opposite the scarred oak desk.

The man looked at him, saying nothing.

"I'll be wanting a thirty-eight and a forty-five," Donovan said.

The man stared at him for a moment and then opened his small, cupid's-bow mouth. "What do you do, eat them?" he said. "You just got two yesterday."

"I eat them," Donovan said.

The man shrugged and got up. "I'll be back," he said. He was gone for a full five minutes. When he returned, he had the two guns wrapped up in a towel.

"Ammo," Donovan said.

The man nodded. "With the rods," he said. "Half a box for each."

"I only need them loaded," Donovan said. "I'm not going target shooting. Just fill the chambers."

"Not in this place you don't," the man said. "They come with a half a box apiece. You don't want to use all the shells, throw 'em away. You pay for them anyway."

Donovan nodded and took out his wallet.

"Two hundred," the man said.

Donovan looked up sharply. "One-fifty," he said.

"The price has gone up since yesterday."

Donovan scowled. "Don't start making it too tough, Georgie," he said. "I'm a good customer."

"You may be a dead customer," Georgie said. "The price is two hundred. I'm getting short and they are hard to come by."

"I can buy them in a dozen states," Donovan said.

"Not this kind," Georgie said. "Not without the numbers. But go ahead if you want—buy in any of eight states."

Donovan smiled wryly and handed the money across the table. He took a key out of his pocket, handing that across also.

"The north passage at Grand Central," he said. "Bank of lockers almost at the end. Number is on the key."

"When do you want delivery?"

"Next Tuesday. No later than eight o'clock in the morning. And don't use a shoebox this time. It looks silly taking a shoebox out of a locker. Spend a buck and buy an attaché case."

"You payin' for it?" Georgie asked.

"Goddamn it, no," Donovan said. "Don't the customers ever get a break?"

"O.K., O.K., Donovan," Georgie said, and smiled. "I can always try."

He moved to stand up, but Donovan waved him back into his seat.

"I'm not through."

For a second the little man's eyes widened and he looked a bit startled, and then settled back.

"Yes?"

"I'm going to want a chopper," Donovan said.

Georgie's eyes squinted and he looked sharply at Donovan. "A chopper, Donovan? A chopper is hard to come by."

"I know. That's why I came here."

Georgie nodded slowly.

"Well, maybe," he said. "But they come high. Very high."

"I didn't ask the price," Donovan said. "I want a sub-Tommy and it has to be good. It has to be very good. How much will it stand me and when can I have it?"

Georgie thought for several minutes, staring up at the ceiling. At last he shrugged and looked back at Donovan.

"I can get you a really first-rate piece of equipment," he said. "The best. But hot. Very hot indeed."

"I don't care how hot it is," Donovan said. "If I have to use it at all, it won't matter."

Georgie nodded.

"O.K. It will be two grand."

Donovan whistled.

"I could shade it a little if the equipment is to be returned," he said. "Of course, the deposit would have to be two grand anyway."

"It won't be returned," Donovan said. "O.K. Georgie, two grand it will be. But make sure of one thing. Make sure that it's in absolutely top condition. When can you have it?"

"Top condition for sure," Georgie said. "You know my reputation, Donovan. You don't have to worry about my goods. About delivery—" he hesitated, again thinking for several moments—"say a week."

"A week will be fine," Donovan said. "But no later."

"How do you want it delivered?"

"I'll pick it up myself."

"Not here you won't, Donovan. Not here. How do you want—"

"All right, Georgie," Donovan said. "Make it a messenger. In a wooden box. I'll give you an address."

Georgie nodded.

"I'll have the money sent down the day after tomorrow," Donovan said. "The man who brings the money will give you the address. I'll expect it a week from today. Next Thursday—in the afternoon."

Georgie nodded.

"A couple more things to come along with the chopper," Donovan said. "I'll want a sawed-off shotgun, a twelve-gauge. Not a double-barrel job—an automatic. And two more rods. Again a thirty-eight and a forty-five. I'll want ammo for all of them, with an extra drum on the machine gun."

Georgie whistled. "You *must* eat them," he said. "Good God, what have you got planned anyway? Are you going to try to knock off the U.S. mint?"

"Don't ask questions, Georgie," Donovan said. "And Georgie," he added, "it wouldn't be healthy to talk around about this order. Not healthy at all."

George looked shocked. "I never talk," he said. "Never. You know that. All right, I got your order. It will come, all together, to about—" he stopped, figuring rapidly on his fingers—"to two thousand, four hundred and eighty-five bucks."

"Wrapped up all together and ready for the messenger a week from today. Is that O.K.?" Donovan said.

"Done," he said. And then, as Donovan stood up to leave, Georgie put the two revolvers in a flat square box and wrapped it with heavy brown paper. He took out an oversized rubber stamp and stamped the word TOYS on three sides of the package.

"Don't let these get into any trouble—at least for the next week," he said. "I don't want to lose that two-grand sale." He smiled and Donovan smiled back and half nodded.

"They'll be waiting at Grand Central for you," Georgie added.

"I'll expect them," Donovan said.

Forty minutes later and he was on the train headed up to Yonkers.

The moment he opened the door, Donovan knew that there was trouble.

Mamma was there waiting and before he could open his mouth, she nodded her head toward the parlor and Donovan quickly followed her into the room, closing the door after him.

"Quick," he said, "what is it?"

"It's plenty, Donovan," Mamma said. "Sit down."

"Never mind sitting down," he said. "Just tell me."

"It's Jo-Jo. He's upstairs with a broken head."

"Good God!"

"Nothing's good about it, Donovan," the old lady said. "Sit tight and I'll tell you all about it. There's nothing that can be done in any case. I don't want to call no doctor into this house, and anyway, I don't care if he does die."

"Just tell me about it," Donovan said tightly. "What did he do—get drunk again?"

"That and then something," Mamma said. "He got drunk and when Carol came home, he tried to rape her. Barker came in while it was going on and there was a fight and Jo-Jo fell over the banister. Hit his head on the newel post. Barker wants to finish the job and I think he was going to, but I got here in time."

"The girl," Donovan said quickly. "Is she ..."

"She's all right," Mamma said, her voice sarcastic. "Bruised up a little and she was hysterical. But she's all right. She isn't the problem. Barker wants to kill him, and Jo-Jo may be hurt bad. I don't know. We were able to get him upstairs. He's on his bed, passed out. But that may be the booze. He got into my bottle. Anyway, you got to get rid of him. He's too dangerous. This could have been serious."

"Where's Barker?"

"He and the girl went out. I think he took her to a doctor. He didn't say so, but I think that's where they went. But she wasn't hurt. I guess it was only because Jo-Jo didn't have time. She wouldn't let me look at her, but she wasn't hurt. The problem is Jo-Jo. You have to dump him, Donovan."

Donovan slowly shook his head.

"That goddamned ape," he said. "Dump him? I can't dump him. It's too late. There isn't time. We need him."

"He's crazy," Mamma said. "Don't you understand, Donovan? He's crazy. Oh, it isn't what he wanted to do to Carol. That doesn't bother me. She wouldn't be the first girl to get herself raped. And a little rape never hurt anyone. But Jo-Jo—he isn't sane. He gets some booze into him and he goes nuts. A man like that—you can't trust him. Can't count on him."

"For what I want him to do, I can trust him," Donovan said. "I can trust him all the way. Sure, I know that he goes nuts on booze. A lot of guys do. And he's a little punchy. But I can trust him."

Mamma looked at him, wide-eyed. "Sure, you can trust him," she said. "But what about Barker? What about the girl? You think they'll stand to have him in on the job now?"

"Barker I can handle." Donovan said. "And the girl—well, I think I can straighten her out."

"Don't be so sure about the boy," Mamma said. "I think he's flipped for Carol. And he'll kill Jo-Jo. Kill him for sure if he has the chance. Unless Jo-Jo gets him first."

For a long time Donovan just sat there, thinking. Finally he took a cigarette from a pack and lit it and looked up at Mamma.

"Listen, Mamma," he said. "I have spent too long planning this thing to have anything happen now. I can't stop and I can't change my plans. My God, this is worth three-quarters of a million dollars. Do you realize that? Do you think I can pass that up?

"No, no, I'm not going to quit now. And I can't change the plans. Jo-Jo has to stay in. I can handle him and I need him. I can't dump him now. And I can handle Barker too. Hell, you said that Carol wasn't really hurt, that there was no real damage done. So I'll talk to her and I'll talk to him. And I'll go up and see Jo-Jo."

Mamma shook her head. "That bump he got on the head," she said. "He might have a fractured skull."

"He was able to get upstairs, wasn't he?"

"Yes, with a little help."

"Then he's all right," Donovan said. "You couldn't kill that bastard with a pickaxe. I'm going up and see him. And if Barker and Carol come back while I'm upstairs, keep 'em down here. Tell them I want to talk to both of them."

"Watch Jo-Jo," Mamma said. "That ape ain't human, Donovan."

Donovan laughed sardonically.

"Neither am I, Mamma," he said. "Neither am I. Jo-Jo doesn't bother me. I've handled crazy horses and mad dogs and they eat out of my hand. So does Jo-Jo."

He left the living room, slowly walking upstairs. Entering Jo-Jo's room, he saw the big man sprawled out on the bed, lying on his back and with his mouth open, breathing heavily. His eyes were closed and there was blood across his forehead. It was dried and caked.

Donovan went to the bathroom. He filled a heavy crockery pitcher with cold water and returned. Unceremoniously, he threw the water over Jo-Jo's face, drenching him.

Jo-Jo grunted and slowly opened his eyes. He looked at Donovan blankly. He blinked several times and then shuddered and closed his eyes.

Donovan leaned across the bed and slapped him as hard as he could, flipping his hand back and forth across the man's flabby, gross face.

Jo-Jo tried to turn away and Donovan spoke in a hard, tight voice.

"Sit up and listen to me, Jo-Jo," he said.

The big man struggled and swung his feet to the floor. He leaned down, elbows on his knees and head in his hand.

When Donovan again spoke, he made an effort to keep the anger out of his voice.

"You got drunk, Jo-Jo," he said. "You got drunk and you promised me you wouldn't."

"Don't get mad," Jo-Jo muttered.

"I'm not mad," Donovan said, speaking as he would to a child. "I'm not mad at all. But I want you to get packed up. We're all through and you're leaving."

Jo-Jo looked up, startled. "Leavin'?"

"That's right, Jo-Jo. Leaving. Getting out of here. You and I are through."

Jo-Jo slowly shook his head. "But Donovan," he said, his voice thick. "You can't mean that. Why, I didn't do anything. Just took a little drink and ..."

"You got drunk," Donovan said. "You got drunk and have blown your job. I warned you about that. Yes, you got drunk. You attacked Carol and if Barker hadn't come in when he did, you might have killed her. Like you killed that other girl. Remember, Jo-Jo? The girl you killed? Do you want them to put you away for good? I've told you what would happen. You know. You know when you get drunk what you do. Anyway, I don't want you anymore. I don't want you around."

Jo-Jo looked as though he were about to cry.

"But Donovan," he said. "Donovan—you can't send me away. How about the job? How about our plans? The money? And you and me— we're buddies. We're going to get the money and then we're goin' away and ..."

"It's off," Donovan said. "All off, boy. I told you that you had to stay sober; had to behave yourself. And now you've gone and done it. You've gotten slopped and ..."

Jo-Jo suddenly stood up and he took Donovan by the lapels of his coat. His voice was a soft cry as he pleaded and Donovan saw the tears come to his eyes.

"Donovan," he said. "Donovan, don't do this. Don't send me away.

Look, beat me or do anything you want. You can cut half my share. Anything. But I want to stay with you. I want to be with you. You are the only one who understands me. The only person who has ever helped me and given me a break. Honest to God, I promise. I promise that I ...”

Donovan let him talk. He spent more than a half-hour in the room with him and then finally he left and returned downstairs.

They were waiting for him in the living room. All four of them. Mamma, Clarence, Barker and Carol. The shades were drawn and the room was half in darkness. Donovan gave Carol a quick look as he entered and then he turned as Barker started to get up.

“Sit down,” he said in a hard voice. “All of you sit down and listen. I got something to say.”

Barker started for the door.

“That son of a bitch,” he said. “I’ll kill that—”

“You’ll kill nobody,” Donovan said. “Sit down.”

Barker hesitated a moment and then reluctantly went back to his chair. His face was white.

“You all right?” Donovan asked, looking at Carol.

“I’m all right,” she said in a low voice. “But you have to get rid of that animal. You have to—”

“If you are all right, then just shut up,” Donovan said.

Clarence looked up and laughed.

“And you too, you shut up.”

Donovan pulled a chair out from the table, flipped it around, and sat on it, straddle-legged.

“Now listen,” he said. “I know what happened. I know what each of you is thinking and how each of you feels. And I also know something else. I know that I have spent a long time working this deal out. I know that it’s too late for anyone to back out now. And I know that I am not going to let anything in this world interfere with what we have planned to do.”

Barker started to speak but again Donovan shut him up.

“Listen to me,” he said. “Listen to what I got to say. I told you that no one is getting out. No one. Including Jo-Jo. It’s too late. We need him. And he knows too much. What happens to him after this is over and done with and we have the money—well, that’s something we have to decide. But we can’t let him go now. It would be too dangerous. And we need him. And so he stays in. He’s not going back to his job— he’s going to stay in that room upstairs. Until I have to use him. He isn’t even going out of the room. Mamma can take up his meals and the rest of you won't have to see him at all. He'll come with me Tuesday when we pull the New Rochelle job and then he'll go back into his cage until the day we do the big one. That's the way it is going to be."

"What makes you think he'll stay in his cage?" Barker asked.

Donovan turned to the younger man. "I know he'll stay," he said. "I know. He'll stay because he knows that if he doesn't, I'll kill him. I'll kill him the very second he does a thing that I don't want him to do. Jo-Jo may be crazy—in fact he *is* crazy. But one thing he understands. He understands I'll do exactly what I say I'll do. You don't have to worry about him anymore."

"Maybe Carol shouldn't have worried about him," Barker said, bitterly.

Donovan swung to him and glared. "Listen, punk," he said. "What happened to her is her business—not yours. I'm not running a lonely hearts club. I'm planning a bank robbery. Carol is the one who has a squawk if anyone has. What happened to her is her business and no one else's."

He turned then to the girl.

"Listen, kid," he said. "I'm sorry about what happened. All I can tell you is that it won't happen again. Getting rid of Jo-Jo now would be dangerous. And we need him. We need him in on this thing. What have you got to say about it?"

Carol looked at Donovan for several seconds, her expression noncommittal. Then she shrugged.

"If a mad dog bites me," she said, "I don't hate the dog. I just feel sorry for him. But I don't want to be bitten twice."

"You won't get bitten twice."

"All right," she said. "Just see that I don't."

Mamma looked up and coughed.

"If Donovan says he can handle Jo-Jo, then he can," she said. "Let's forget about that." She looked over at her son. "Why not get down to business. Clarence, how about Tuesday?"

Clarence took the cigarette out of his mouth and spoke in a soft, almost whining voice.

"It's like I told you already," he said. "The place over in New Rochelle is a pushover. Go in at one o'clock. There will be two clerks, a teller and the guard. Maybe a customer or two. We have already gone over that. You have to be careful about the alarm. There are half a dozen buttons around but I don't know for sure where they all are located. The alarm bell is over the front door and there's a connection at police headquarters. You already know the layout and have maps of the streets. You already know the getaway route. One thing you got to be careful about. One guard is a nervous type. He could panic. You want my advice, you'll blast him right off."

"We blast no one right off," Donovan said. "Jo-Jo can knock him out and that will be enough. What do you figure we can take?"

"Like I told you," Clarence said, "around six or seven grand. No more. It's just a neighborhood branch and they won't have much."

"Six or seven is what we need," Donovan said.

"I still think the White Plains job is a better bet," Clarence said. "Why hell, they could have twenty-five or thirty."

Donovan looked at him coldly.

"Sure," he said, "sure. And they are also about two blocks from the police station, in the heart of town. The chances are there would be a real jam. And, like I said, we don't need twenty-five or thirty. What the hell good is twenty-five or thirty? Look, we got one car, we picked up about four grand today and we still have a thousand or better in the bank. All we have to have now is enough for the truck, the other car and some odds and ends. I ain't taking one extra chance. These little jobs are not for real money. They are only for expense dough. Expense dough and some experience."

"Look, Donovan," Mamma said, "why don't you take Barker there with you on Tuesday and leave Jo-Jo out of it. You two did fine today—there's no point in taking a chance on Jo-Jo!"

Donovan shook his head.

"Like I told you, Mamma, experience," he said. "Barker had his today. Jo-Jo needs a dry run."

"Hell, that ape has had plenty of experience," Clarence said. "He's—"

"Not this kind of experience," Donovan said. "I want him to know what the inside of a bank looks like. I want him to go through the sort of thing he'll be facing in two weeks. Sure, he's done a lot of things he shouldn't have, but he's never pulled a daytime stickup. Not in a bank. He's got to try it once. I have to be dead sure he isn't going to slip up anywhere when we pull the real job. Jo-Jo goes with me Tuesday. And Carol drives the switch car again. Right, Carol?"

"Right," the girl said.

Donovan pushed back his chair and stood up, facing all of them.

"Good," he said. "Good. There'll be no changes, no changes at all. Except I'll call up the bar and tell 'em Jo-Jo had an appendix attack or something. And we'll just keep him cooped up until we need him. So how about some dinner now?" He turned and looked at Mamma.

"Carol and I ate while we were out," Barker said.

Donovan looked at him curiously for a moment and shrugged. "All right," he said, "then look at television. Me, I'm hungry."

SIX

It was long after midnight and the two of them, Mamma and Clarence, had been sitting in Mamma's bedroom and talking for more than an hour. Mamma lay on the bed, wrapped up in a dressing gown, slowly sipping a whisky and soda, and Clarence paced the floor. He'd taken off his coat and tie and shoes and walked back and forth in his stocking feet as he talked.

"It's the split," Clarence said. "I don't like it. Don't think it's fair. Why should Donovan be guaranteed a hundred thousand off the top? What the hell is he doing but putting up a few bucks? After all, you're putting up some of the money too, Mamma. And the idea of the whole thing is mine. Right from the very beginning it was my idea."

Mamma shrugged.

"Take it easy, son," she said. "Take it easy. Remember, Donovan may be taking a hundred grand off the top before the split-out, but so do I. I get a hundred thousand too."

"Sure, after Donovan's," Clarence said. "But just suppose there isn't more than a hundred all together?"

Mamma looked at her son sharply.

"You are the one who told us that there is going to be well over a half million," she said. "You said you were dead sure of that. Is there any doubt—"

Clarence quickly shook his head.

"Of course not," he said. "I know. Know for sure."

"Then don't worry," Mamma said. "Let Donovan have his first hundred thousand. I get the next and then it's a six-way split. A sixth to you and a sixth to each of us."

"Sure—sure," Clarence said bitterly. "A sixth to that idiot Jo-Jo and a sixth to Carol. How come she—"

Mamma held up a thin, almost transparent hand.

"Keep your voice down," she said. "What do you care how much Carol gets? Remember, son, after we get our cut and split up, Carol comes with us. So the way it works out, I get the hundred thousand from the top and you and Carol and I end up with half of the remainder. As I say, Carol is with us."

Clarence looked at his mother knowingly.

"Yes," he said. "Yes, that's right. Carol will be with us."

For a moment he looked thoughtful and then again nervously paced the floor.

"I don't like the way she and Barker have been hanging around together," he said. "You don't suppose—"

"Don't start worrying," Mamma said. "I can handle the girl. She'll do just what I tell her to do. Barker? Don't worry about Barker. He and Carol fight like cats and dogs. Anyway, I'll be holding the girl's share of the money. She'll do what I tell her to do. I've handled plenty of these young quail in my time and I certainly have no worries about Carol. I brought her up, didn't I? She may need a lesson or two after we get through with this caper, but I guess you can handle that, can't you, son?"

"Yeah, I can handle that," Clarence said. His thin face was mean and hard as he spoke and he laughed shortly.

Mamma held out her empty glass. "Fill it up again, son," she said. "And then you better get to bed. You gotta get some sleep tonight."

"I don't need sleep," Clarence said. "Don't you worry none about me. I don't need sleep."

Mamma grunted and half turned away. "Get me the drink," she said.

The television set was turned to the late late movie special and the picture was a trifle out of focus. The sound itself was turned down low, so as to be barely audible to the two who sat side by side across the room on the couch in the darkness of the room. Neither one was watching the screen.

Carol kept her eyes on the floor as she spoke.

"It's none of your business," she said. "None of your business at all. What I do with myself—what happens to me."

"Sure it's none of my business," Barker said bitterly. "I know that. What almost happened to you this afternoon was none of my business either. But don't you ever learn? Don't you ever get smart? You play around with dynamite and you get hurt. You have no reason hanging around here. It doesn't make sense. And you have no right to get mixed up in a robbery. You're young, just beginning to live, just starting out...."

She turned to him, her hand on his sleeve.

"And how about you?" she said. "How about you? You're mixed up in it. You're going through with it. I have as much right as you have to—"

"It's different," Barker said. "Damn it, can't you see that? It's different. I'm an ex-con. I've done time. I killed a man. I have the label, the name. So I might as well do the deed. But with you it isn't the same thing at all. You're a girl. And you—"

"Sure," Carol interrupted. "I'm a girl. So maybe I don't need money. Maybe I can't use money."

"You can get a job and earn money," Barker said. "You don't have to steal it. You don't have to take the chances. You don't have to end up like your old man, doing the book—"

"Damn you," Carol said, "you leave my old man out of this. He's a better man than you or anyone else ever will be."

"Carol," he said. "Carol, listen to me. Please ..."

Quickly she moved away from him.

Donovan couldn't sleep.

That was the way it had been for a long, long time now. He would go to bed dead tired and he'd close his eyes and maybe doze off for an hour or two, and then he would be wide awake. Awake and staring up into the darkness, his eyes open and unblinking. And he could lie there for hours, thinking and remembering.

It had started when he had first been sent up and it had lasted all the nights of those weeks and months and years he had spent behind bars. He had always thought that once he was free again it would stop. That he would be able to go to bed and fall asleep and go on sleeping until he was rested and his body had revived itself.

But it hadn't been that way. He still was unable to sleep for more than an hour or two at a time.

If he could only stop thinking, it would be better. He wouldn't mind lying there in the bed, wide awake, if only he didn't have to think. But his mind never stopped working and the thoughts and plans and memories raced on and on.

It wasn't that he worried. He never worried. And it wasn't that he had regrets. Oh, of course there were many things he wished had been different, many things which he might wish had never happened to him at all. But even so he didn't regret and he never felt sorry about anything he had ever done or anything which had been done to him. He wouldn't have changed anything at all.

Of course, it would have been a lot nicer if he had not had to do the time in the state pen, but that was one of the hazards of his trade. He was a thief and thieves were expected to take certain calculated risks. You can't win them all, and he was smart enough to know that and not expect to.

You always had to expect trouble and you had to be prepared to take the bad breaks. The thing was not to regret them or spend any time feeling unhappy about them when they happened. The thing was to figure it out so that the bad breaks could be avoided in the future. To try and plan so that you ended up winning rather than losing.

The damned trouble was that there were so many unseen factors. You plan something out perfectly, take every precaution, and then something seems to go wrong.

Well, this was one time nothing would go wrong. This was going to be that one perfect job, the one which was so carefully planned and prepared that nothing at all would be left to chance.

It started with his figuring percentages. Obviously, the more jobs a man pulled, the greater were his chances of being caught. The thing to do was plan the one big job. And the next step was to have enough cash in advance to take care of the initial expenses. A bank robbery was like anything else. It took a certain amount of nut money, a certain amount of capital. The right guns, the right getaway cars, the right equipment. And they would all cost money.

There had to be a hideout arranged for in advance and a way of getting to it. There had to be a place to stay put in while getting ready for the big job.

And, of course, most important of all, there had to be the big job itself and someone on the inside to case it. That's where Mamma had first come into the picture. Donovan had known her for a long time and when he learned through the prison grapevine that her son Clarence was working as a bank teller in Manhattan, he began to get the germ of an idea. Donovan didn't know Clarence. But he did know Mamma. And so he had managed, despite the handicap of being in prison, to make contact with her. And he had managed to let her know what he had in the back of his mind. She in turn had let him know that the moment he was out, he should come and see her and talk things over.

That had been the first step. Donovan had been right. Mamma was ripe for a venture and her boy had the necessary contacts which enabled him to get the vital information which he, Donovan, would need.

The second step was organizing the group which would do the job. Again Donovan worked on percentages. The fewer persons involved, the more chance of success and the less chance of someone missing up and spoiling everything. Also, the fewer mouths to feed and the fewer persons to cut into the proceeds.

Mamma and Clarence, of course, were essential. Clarence was the finger man and Mamma had the place for them to hide out in before and afterward. Each would also serve in other ways on the day that the robbery was to take place.

Barker was the next one Donovan enlisted. Barker was perfect for the part he was to play. Donovan knew him as only one man can know another with whom he has lived for months and years, cooped up in a prison cell.

Barker could be trusted. And Barker had other assets. He wasn't a professional criminal and that was good. He was a man who had done his time because of an accident and he had a deep-seated bitterness toward the society which had sent him up. That too was good.

But it didn't end there. Barker had driven midget and dirt-track racing cars and he was a genius behind the wheel. He was an expert mechanic and he was young and strong and bright, could be trusted in a pinch. Of course he had never had experience in sticking up a bank, or, in fact, in sticking up anything. But even that was good. He would have nothing to unlearn. And certainly, after it was over and done with, the police would never dream of seeking him out as a possible suspect.

Barker's lack of professional criminal experience didn't bother Donovan at all. He knew that he could test Barker under fire, so to speak, during the two or three smalltime preliminary stickups that he planned to pull in order to get the necessary and essential capital for the really big steal.

Yes, Barker was an excellent choice.

Jo-Jo was his next choice and again Donovan was proud of his selection. It was true that Jo-Jo was punch-drunk and at best a low-grade moron. But this was good. Donovan had known the ex-prizefighter and wrestler for years. Had known him during that long period when Jo-Jo was constantly in trouble with the law, forever being arrested and sentenced on petty charges. He'd helped Jo-Jo out, given him money, taken care of him. Jo-Jo worshipped the ground that Donovan stood on, and Donovan knew this. He had, literally, saved Jo-Jo from the electric chair. Jo-Jo was far more loyal than would have been possible for a man endowed with normal intelligence. He had the allegiance of a dog. Jo-Jo would do exactly what he was told to do—no more or no less.

Once again, Donovan reflected, the police would never in a million years suspect Jo-Jo of being mixed up in a really first-class bank robbery. And if by any chance they should arrest him later on, Jo-Jo would be as safe as the Bank of England. His very stupidity would make him safe. They could beat him to death before he would ever say a word. He would follow Donovan's instructions to the letter. Say nothing, absolutely nothing. Answer no questions, not even his name. Dummy up and stay dummied up. Few men would be able to do it, but Jo-Jo would.

Yes, Jo-Jo was loyal with a dumb, unquestioning loyalty.

Stupid, yes. But his stupidity wouldn't matter so long as he followed instructions. What would matter would be his tremendous physical strength. His amazing dexterity as a rough-and-tumble fighter. His genius with a sawed-off shotgun.

Donovan's plans for Jo-Jo, after it was all over, were beautiful in their simplicity. He would see to it that Jo-Jo received a few hundred dollars out of his cut. And he would let Jo-Jo go into town, but not New York. One of the smaller industrial cities across the river in Jersey. He'd tell Jo-Jo that it would be all right for him to take a few drinks— that he had a celebration coming.

Jo-Jo would end up in a brothel and Donovan knew exactly what would happen. The same thing which always happened. Jo-Jo would blow his top, go crazy. Donovan wouldn't be there to take care of him. There would be the usual fight, the shambles and the insane battle royal and the police would come and Jo-Jo would keep on fighting. There would be only one way to stop him and that would be to kill him. No one could stop Jo-Jo any longer when he went crazy, except Donovan himself. And Donovan wouldn't be there.

Lying in the darkened room with his eyes wide open, he suddenly had a desire for a cigarette. He turned on his side and his hand reached toward the night table and found the half empty package. A moment later he had the lighter and after the second try the flame burst, throwing strange shadows on the wall of the room as he deeply inhaled.

He smiled secretly to himself. Yes, his selection of personnel had been good. And Carol was the final touch. The one he was proudest of all about. No one, no one but Donovan, would have figured the girl as a smart move. Even Kurwitz, the lawyer, would have called him crazy to have considered her. But Donovan knew exactly what he was doing.

He knew damned well what Mamma had in the back of her evil mind. She wanted the girl's cut. Figured that she and Clarence would take off afterward with the girl and that in that way she would sooner or later control that much more of the money.

But what Mamma didn't know was that Donovan himself had exactly the same idea. Yes, Donovan would have his own cut and most of Jo-Jo's cut and he and the girl would go away together. She would be doubly valuable. She would be paying her own way and she would give him the kind of front he wanted, once he started hiding out.

There was, of course, more to it than that. All along Donovan had worried about whom to get to run interference. It had to be someone, who, if questioned, would be absolutely beyond suspicion. Someone who was at once intelligent enough to get away with it and a good enough actor to carry the part. Someone with courage and someone with a perfect front. Carol had all of the qualities.

It was a small part, the part the girl would play. But it was vital. And then, once the job was accomplished, there would be just the two of them. Jo-Jo would go and Mamma and Clarence would go. Barker would take his end and leave. And there would be just himself and Carol. Between the two of them, they would have half of the loot and it could be as much as a quarter of a million dollars. If Clarence was right, it might even be more.

Donovan butted the cigarette and pulled the covers up. He turned on his side, making a final try for some sleep. He was going to need his rest; he had a busy schedule ahead. Tomorrow, early in the morning, he and Clarence had to go over the plans for the New Rochelle job for the last time. The one which he and Jo-Jo would be doing the following Tuesday. The one which would bring in the last of the money. The money which, pooled with the loot he had already taken, would go to pay for the truck, the English Ford, the warehouse rent, the tape recorder, the submachine gun and the other equipment he was getting together before they embarked on the ultimate venture.

He must spend a long time with Clarence, and then he must have a session with Jo-Jo. And he must talk with Carol and with Barker, too. He must talk with them all, keep them in line, see that everything went smoothly, now that they were so very close to reaching their goal.

By midnight Thursday, Fifth Avenue below Forty-second Street lay quiet and deserted and the thousands of windows of her office buildings, department stores and loft buildings were darkened eyes looking out on sidewalks and pavements on which almost no one moved and few cars passed. Now and then the stillness was momentarily interrupted as a lone pedestrian made his tired way uptown or down and only the twin lights of a stray taxi or cruising police car cut into the solitude of the night.

The footsteps of a private watchman resounded as he made his way from building to building, checking doors. In one or two office buildings, lights would flash on and off as scrubwomen worked late cleaning up the debris of the day and preparing for the next day. But for the most part, even the scrubwomen were now at home and in bed.

One of the few buildings which was still lighted up, however, was the Needle Trades Amalgamated Bank and Trust Company on the corner of Twentieth Street and Fifth Avenue.

The staff of the Needle Trades Bank kept odd hours. The great doors leading into the institution were only open for business with the public from nine until three-thirty, five days a week, it was true. But public banking hours are deceptive. Once the front doors closed, much of the real business of the bank was still carried on. The clerical staff always worked until five and on this particular Thursday night, a few unfortunate members returned to their desks and cubbyholes and continued working far into the night. Thursday night was very important—for Friday was payday for thousands of employees of dress firms and textile companies which had their offices and factory lofts in the immediate vicinity.

A large proportion of these firms banked at the Needle Trades Amalgamated and a certain percentage of them would send armed and bonded messengers to the Needle Trades the first thing on Friday morning to pick up the payrolls. Others, in an effort to forestall possible holdup men, would delegate the messenger tasks to secretaries or clerks or sometimes junior members of the firm, as a good many of the payrolls consisted of envelopes containing cash. The money had been appropriately proportioned and put into the individual envelopes by the bank on the night previously.

This work was done by a small staff who, each week, worked late. They did their work on the second floor mezzanine of the bank, off the main lobby. While they worked, two uniformed guards were always on duty and never left until the last cash payroll had been made up and placed safely away in the bank's great impenetrable vaults.

Marvin Kelley and Horace Grayman were, on this particular night, the only two clerks still at work. All of the others, with the exception of the two guards who loitered outside the office, had already left. Kelley was a long-time employee of the bank, a thin, dissatisfied man in his late sixties, who was waiting to retire. He had a couple of years more to go and couldn't wait until he could get away from the job which had been his prison for so many years.

At one time, long ago, when he had first come to the bank directly from business school, he had had ambitions. But he had never been very bright and he had never been good at figures, and his immediate superiors soon discovered that his only virtue lay in a willingness to work long hours at the dullest sort of occupation for extremely low pay. It took him a long time to find out that he had no hope of ever really getting anywhere with the bank, but by the time he understood, he was too old and too deadened by the monotony of his life and his job to think of making a change.

For a time he had been down in one of the teller's booths, but he had made so many mistakes that he had been taken back on the general clerical staff. As the years went by, he would receive small annual raises, but it seemed that each time he got a raise, they piled more work on his shoulders. Actually, there was no such plot afoot—the truth of the matter was that each year he became slower and less efficient and it would take him longer and longer to complete the same dull chore. The bank wouldn't fire him, but at the same time they got every ounce of labor out of him that they could for the parsimonious salary they allotted him each week.

Kelley never complained and now, as he listened to his young partner's incessant groaning and bitching, he was unable to conceal his annoyance.

"So what if it is midnight?" he said. "Where would you be if you weren't here helping me out? Where, eh? Probably down in some tavern getting drunk to the gills. Maybe with one of those young—"

"That isn't the point, where would I be," Grayman said. Grayman was only twenty-six and had been with the bank less than a year. "The thing is they have no right working us like slaves. They have no right ..."

"We get paid for it, don't we?" Kelley said.

Grayman sneered. "Paid? Sure," he said. "We get paid straight time. No time and a half, no double time. Just straight time. What we need is a decent union. We need—"

"You want a union, get a job in the dress business," Kelley said. "Nobody asked you to become a banker."

"A banker?" Grayman laughed raucously. "My God, you think sitting on your tokus here counting out money into envelopes is being a banker? Man, no wonder you never got anywhere. Anyway, I'm getting fed up. It was bad enough before, when the bosses used to bring in the outside help on these night jobs. But now they've tightened up and make the staff do it all. I've just about had it."

"Quit then," Kelley said shortly. "And anyway, who wants outside help? The Needle Trades Amalgamated don't have to call in riffraff from other banks to do its work. Now you take that fellow Pachel, or whatever his name was. Clarence something or other. The one from the uptown Consolidated National. He came in to help and all he did was snoop around and smoke his foul cigarettes and butt into everybody's business. We've had enough like him around here."

Grayman stood up and stretched.

"You've had enough like me, too," he said. "One more week and I'm quitting. The hell with this white-collar routine. I've got a job with my brother-in-law. Driving a truck."

Kelley looked at the younger man with disgust.

"Driving a truck," he said. "Like some damned hunkie. Is that what you spent three years in college training to do?"

Grayman reached for his jacket and started to tighten the knot in his tie. When he answered, his voice was again good-natured.

"I spent three years in college learning how to enjoy being a gentleman," he said. "Driving a truck will give me a pay check which will let me use some of that education. Working in this sweat factory, the nearest I'll ever get to living will be handing somebody else's money to strangers who are smart enough not to work in banks. Anyway, the hell with it. I'm quitting and right now I'm folding up and going home. You coming along?"

"Not until I finish this work," Kelley said.

He didn't say good night as the other man left the room.

Patrolman First Grade James Gallagher looked at his wrist watch and whistled.

"Jeez," he said. "After midnight. And I have to get all the way out to Flatbush. Allie will raise hell."

His friend, Sheldon Greenbaum, detective second grade, looked at him under shaggy eyebrows and smiled.

"So what, Jimmy?" he said. "So what? Let her raise a little hell. A man is entitled to a little peace and quiet and a small beer or two after a hard day's work."

"I'll tell you so what," Gallagher said. "I'm getting enough hell down at the precinct to last any man a lifetime. I don't want to start catching it at home too."

He beckoned a waiter and when the man came to the table, said, "A couple more—and bring the check."

"What's with the precinct?" Greenbaum asked. "I thought that you were in line for a promotion. Don't tell me they caught you shaking down a pushcart peddler."

"Nothing that simple," Gallagher said. "And anyway, where you been living? There hasn't been a pushcart in this neighborhood in ten years."

He reached for his glass and took a sip. "Two thousand damned patrol cars in this town," he said, "and what happens? I have to be driving the one which gets a flat at exactly the moment some mug snatches a purse and then pulls a car theft right around the corner. So I'm back in the grease again. I never saw such bad luck. The old man just about blew his top. Yes, I was in line for a promotion all right, but the way things have been breaking for me lately, I'll be damned lucky if I'm not back pounding a beat. And this time it will probably be up in the deep Bronx."

"What's wrong with the Bronx?" Detective Greenbaum asked, defensively.

"Nothing's wrong with the Bronx. Except I happen to live out at the end of Brooklyn and my wife likes it out there and don't want to move. And she likes to see me once in a while. Also she is getting a little fed up living on my salary. I could use a promotion and a raise."

Greenbaum shrugged.

"You'll get it, kid, don't worry," he said. "All you need is one good break. Knock over a stickup man, break up a riot, grab off a couple of teen-age muggers, get yourself shot."

"Sure, sure," Gallagher said. "In my precinct they don't have those things. Nothing happens—except like today when that mug grabbed the purse and then stole a car. And I had to be looking at a flat tire. I won't get another break like that in a blue moon. It happened and I wasn't there. I can tell you boy, nothing ever happens on my beat, not once in a blue moon. If I gotta wait for something big before I get that promotion, I can be waiting around forever. You know how it is in this racket—you have to be lucky. Be at the right place at the right time. I seem to have a genius for being at the wrong place. And those right times don't happen too damned often. Crime has moved out to the suburbs."

Greenbaum hunched his shoulders and his mouth twisted in a wry laugh.

"You don't know when you're well off, kid," he said. "So nothing happens on your beat—you can't get in no trouble. Be happy that things are quiet. Who wants to have someone slinging lead at them? Dead heroes ain't no good to themselves or to their widows. Your Allie should be satisfied you're on a beat where you don't have nothing happen."

"My Allie will be a lot more satisfied if I get home some time before morning," Gallagher said, standing up. He reached for his wallet, but Greenbaum quickly snatched the check.

"On me, boy," he said. "After all these sad stories of yours, I couldn't feel right letting you pick up the tab."

He laughed and shoved Gallagher out ahead of him as the younger man started to protest.

"I'll give you a lift to the subway," Greenbaum said.

"My car is parked a block away, in front of the Needle Trades Amalgamated."

SEVEN

Donovan slept badly, but, in spite of that fact, he was up at daybreak on Friday morning. He showered and shaved and then dressed in slacks and a sport shirt and made his way downstairs to the kitchen to get himself some breakfast. He was careful to walk quietly, not wanting to wake the others.

Clarence was already downstairs, however, when he pushed open the kitchen door.

Looking up, Clarence said, "Coffee's on the stove, Donovan. Pour yourself a cup."

Donovan grunted and took a heavy mug from the cupboard.

"What gets you up?"

"I wanted to talk to you," Clarence said.

"Yeah?"

"Yeah. I arranged to take next Tuesday off."

Donovan looked at the small man closely.

"You think that was smart?" he asked. "You shouldn't have done it. You start your vacation a week from Monday and you don't want them getting any ideas downtown."

"Oh, don't worry about me," Clarence said. "But do you know why I took off Tuesday?"

"No."

"I want to go with you and Jo-Jo on the New Rochelle job," Clarence said, speaking softly.

Donovan hesitated as he poured the coffee, but didn't look up.

"Why?" he asked. "You think me and Jo-Jo can't handle it?"

"I didn't say that. I just said I'd like to come along on it."

"You talk to Mamma about coming along?" Donovan asked.

"I don't have to ask Mamma," Clarence said. "I just want to come along. Got any objections?"

Donovan shrugged.

"Maybe," he said. "Maybe not. But if it is the way you say it is, we don't need you. You're crazy to take any extra chances. Me and Jo-Jo are going to be able to handle it without any help."

Clarence put his cigarette down and blew out a puff of smoke.

"Listen," he said, "I'm going to be in on the big one two weeks from today. Right? I am going in there with a gun in my hand. You are counting on me for that one, aren't you? So why shouldn't I get a little practical experience? Like the others."

Donovan turned and stared at the other man for several seconds.

"Practical experience? Who are you kidding, Clarence? Who are you kidding? You have had plenty of practical experience. Plenty. You've had a gun in your hand before. You've used one, too."

"Maybe I have," Clarence said. "But this thing is going to be different. I've never walked into a bank with a gun, never before been on a really big one."

Donovan shook his head. "Listen," he said, "the New Rochelle caper isn't a big one. You know that. I think you just want to play it for kicks. And brother, that is the one thing I don't want. I've told you before, we aren't playing games. The only reason I took Barker yesterday was because he did need the experience. Jo-Jo is going Tuesday because I need him—we need that dough. Two of us can handle it fine."

Clarence looked mean and then shrugged, forcing a half smile.

"Play it your own way then, big shot," he said. "I just thought I could help. I told you the guard may be a little nervous. Told you—"

"You told me," Donovan said. "So now I know. I know also that I am not changing my plans. If you are taking off next Tuesday, that's your business. Go to a movie or do anything you want. But leave the New Rochelle bit to me and Jo-Jo. You'll get a bellyful of experience two weeks from today when we walk into the Needle Trades Bank. Until then, do what you are supposed to do. Clean up the details on the Eighteenth Street place; see that Mamma gets the tape recorder and that it works O.K. Do the other things you got to do."

"They'll get done," Clarence said. "Just as soon as I have the dough."

"You'll have the dough. Just pick up that little package in Long Island City on Monday during your lunch hour. If everything goes right on Tuesday, we'll have the rest of the money before the end of the week. But leave New Rochelle to me."

Clarence left the kitchen a few moments later, muttering under his breath. Donovan turned to the icebox to look for eggs and milk. After he had finished eating, he scrambled another half dozen eggs, made several slices of toast and poured the remaining coffee into a pitcher. He found a tray and put the food on it, then left the kitchen and climbed to the third floor. He opened the door to Jo-Jo's room.

At nine-thirty, Carol left the house, driving the white convertible. She headed north on the Bronx River Parkway, arriving at Ossining before noontime. She had an appointment to see her father. It was visiting day at Sing Sing.

Bill Barker had wanted to drive up with her and wait for her in the town, but Donovan had vetoed the idea. He had several reasons for doing so, but the reason he gave Barker was that he didn't want him in a car unless it was absolutely necessary. And he didn't want Barker anywhere in the vicinity of Sing Sing.

It was just as well that Barker didn't go along. Carol was in a particularly foul mood on her way home that afternoon. She had been unable to see her father and the prison authorities had been very cagey in telling her why his visiting privileges had been taken away. But she gathered that he had gotten into some sort of trouble— something had happened after he had learned that his parole had been denied.

Mamma spent the day visiting an old friend in Manhattan, a girl who had worked for her at one time, but was now respectably married to the vice president of an insurance company and lived in an apartment on West Seventy-ninth Street. They spent the afternoon drinking gin and tonic and cutting up old times.

Jo-Jo stayed in his room and Clarence went to work.

Donovan got to work on the garage and Barker joined in to help him. It was a cold, miserable day, but fortunately it wasn't raining and the last snow had completely melted away.

They dressed warmly in old clothes, and Donovan did most of the planning. It wasn't too complicated a job. First they sawed off the low-hanging limbs from the trees which bordered the driveway. And then they removed the old-fashioned hinged doors from the double-car garage and cut the opening so that it was ten feet high. They took out the center posts which divided the garage into three stalls and braced up the ceiling. Afterward, they hung the huge new overhead door.

It took them all of Friday and most of Saturday to complete the task. When they had finished it, Donovan took out a steel tape and measured the new opening. It was big enough to drive a ten-ton truck through, which was exactly what it had been planned for.

Jo-Jo stayed on in his room, having his meals brought up to him. He missed the television, but Donovan kept him supplied with comic books. He couldn't read the print, but he liked the pictures. And he slept a lot. His head still bothered him a bit.

On Monday Clarence again went to work as usual, and during the lunch hour he went over to Long Island City and stopped at the general-delivery window of the post office to pick up a package.

Mamma and Donovan and Barker spent most of the day playing pinochle on the kitchen table. Carol sat with the two small children of the neighbor who lived across the street and down a couple of houses while their mother went into New York to shop. Carol made four dollars and fifty cents, which was exactly what Bill Barker lost playing pinochle.

Shortly after ten o'clock Monday night, Carol drove the white convertible away from the house. Barker and Clarence sat beside her in the front seat of the car. She took the Saw Mill River Parkway and turned off at Hawthorne Circle, cutting east. She drove on for several miles and finally stopped at a lonely place on Lincoln Avenue in Purchase, in Westchester County. Without a word, Barker got out of the car.

Clarence leaned over the door.

"A quarter of a mile back," he said. "Big white gate-posts. It's a long, circular drive and the garage is in the rear. Don't take the blue and gold job, take the black Caddie sedan. You sure you can start it all right now?"

"I'm sure," Barker said. "But are you sure about the people? That they are still in Florida?"

"Goddamn it, of course I am sure," Clarence said. "The guy's my boss, isn't he? Just be careful, especially until you get back on the road. You don't want anyone to see you leaving."

"I'll be careful," Barker said.

While Barker was breaking into the garage and short-circuiting the ignition system to get the Caddie's engine started, Carol was driving back to Yonkers. Clarence suggested they stop off and have a drink, but Carol, not answering, continued driving south.

"What's the matter with you?" Clarence asked. "Ain't I good enough for you?" His hand slid over and rested on her thigh and Carol roughly brushed it off.

"That's right," she said. "You aren't good enough. And keep your hands to yourself. This isn't a pleasure trip."

Clarence muttered an obscenity and Carol gritted her teeth, driving on and saying nothing.

She was in her room, undressed and in bed, but fully awake, a little over an hour later when Barker drove the Caddie into the garage behind the house. He didn't bother to change the plates or do anything to the car. If Clarence was right, the Caddie wouldn't be missed until the family who lived up in Purchase returned in about ten days or two weeks. Or until the car was found abandoned in a supermarket parking lot sometime within the next forty-eight hours.

An hour before daybreak on Tuesday morning, Donovan left the house. He went at once to the garage and got into the Caddie. Jo-Jo was with him.

Donovan drove very carefully leaving Yonkers and headed south until he came to the George Washington Bridge. He crossed the bridge and entered Jersey, and shortly after seven o'clock found a diner which was open. Parking the car, he and Jo-Jo entered and ordered a large breakfast. At eight o'clock, he left the diner. He was careful to check his watch.

Barker got up an hour and a half after Donovan had left and he dressed and had a cup of coffee in the kitchen. When he left the rooming house, he walked the three quarters of a mile to the railway station. He caught a train to New York and got off at Grand Central Station. He went at once to the bank of lockers on the north passage and checked the numbers. He found the one which matched the key he was carrying almost at once.

Georgie had done as he had promised. The package marked TOYS was in the locker.

Barker left the key in the empty locker as he was supposed to and turned away with the package under his arm.

At ten-thirty the stolen Caddie again crossed over into Manhattan, using the Lincoln Tunnel. At eleven-fifteen, Donovan pulled to a stop at One Hundred Twenty-fifth Street and Broadway, on the northeast corner.

Barker was waiting, and, without speaking, he handed the box marked TOYS through the open window. Jo-Jo took it, carefully avoiding Barker's direct glance. Donovan opened his door and got out and Barker replaced him at the wheel. Donovan climbed into the back of the car.

Carol left the house just after twelve o'clock, driving the white convertible as usual. She was alone. She had a little better than fifty minutes to make the parking lot behind the supermarket in White Plains.

Clarence was looking out of his window at the driveway as the car left. He laughed shortly and turned back to what he had been doing. He had been carefully taking down and oiling a Luger which he had stolen some months before from a locker used by one of the guards at the bank where he worked.

Ten minutes later, he too left the house. He left by taxi, which he had telephoned for.

Mamma didn't see him go. Mamma was in bed, nursing a particularly vicious hangover which she had acquired the previous evening while sitting up late watching a western saga on television and drinking straight gin.

Mamma would have worried had she known Clarence was leaving the house with the gun tucked into his trouser waistband and concealed by his coat and topcoat.

Perhaps one of the least important of all of the two hundred and eleven branches of the great Inter-City Trust Company was the small branch which the firm maintained a couple of blocks off the main business section in New Rochelle. Its principal activity was the handling of the checking and savings accounts of the small businesses and residents of its immediate neighborhood. In a good many ways, maintaining the branch was really a waste of good money. Except for one fact.

The Inter-City Trust Company used its New Rochelle branch not to show a profit, but as a training ground for the large number of personnel it was constantly hiring to staff its many other branches. The New Rochelle branch was a perfect place to try out beginners and neophytes, being completely unimportant in itself and handling no large accounts. If anything went amiss, nothing really serious would result.

File clerks, tellers, guards, automatic business machine operators, and even stenographers and secretaries—all of them served an apprenticeship at the New Rochelle branch. If they failed to make the grade there, it was quite obvious to Personnel that they would fail in the more significant branches of the big banking house.

Literally hundreds of young bank employees had started at the branch and there was a constant turnover of people. Clarence Pachel himself had worked a few weeks at the New Rochelle branch, having been connected with the Inter-City when he took his first job. Later he had changed companies, but he still remembered those early days of his apprenticeship.

Clarence didn't know any of the present personnel, but he did know something about them. He had opened a very small savings account a couple of weeks previously, in order to refamiliarize himself with the organization and to case the current setup in preparation for Donovan's plans.

Clarence didn't know the name of the young, red-faced Irishman who looked like he had just gotten off the boat and who was very obviously being given a tryout as a bank guard. But he had been very quick to detect that the man—who was actually little more than a boy, being, Clarence guessed, in his early twenties—was extremely nervous. He probably didn't feel that he would make the grade and was trying a little too hard.

Clarence had attempted to warn Donovan about the guard. But Donovan never seemed to listen to anyone but himself.

And Clarence had been absolutely right about young Dan Durrell. Durrell certainly did not have the emotional make-up necessary to become an experienced bank guard. If there had been any question about it in Durrell's own mind, it had certainly been dissipated that very morning. For on Tuesday at ten-thirty, Durrell was informed by the manager of the bank (who actually was connected with Personnel in the main office) that his services would no longer be required as of the end of the working week.

Dan Durrell was reviewing, for about the twentieth time within the past couple of hours, his conversation with the bank manager at twelve forty-five when the doors of the branch bank swung open and the two men in trench coats entered the lobby of the building. He failed to pay them any heed; he was too busy at the moment wondering how he would break the news of his failure to his mother when he got home from work that evening.

Barker, behind the steering wheel of the Caddie, waited only until Donovan and Jo-Jo stepped to the pavement in front of the bank before gently pressing the gas pedal and pulling away from the curb. Automatically, his eye went to his wrist watch as he pulled out again into the stream of traffic. He had exactly three minutes to circle the block and return once more to the spot in front of the bank marked off by the twin "No Parking" signs.

If everything went according to schedule, in three minutes Donovan and Jo-Jo would be crossing the threshold and heading for the curb. They would be carrying somewhere between six and seven thousand dollars in currency.

Once more it was exactly as Clarence had described it. Donovan took in the entire room at a glance. It wasn't a large room and he barely had to turn his head. There were two tellers' cages and one was closed up. A slender, short man in a camel's-hair topcoat was standing in front of the teller who was on duty. The man was wearing a fedora pulled down over his eyes, which were concealed behind dark sunglasses. Behind the cage, the teller was counting out a sheaf of bills. He didn't look up.

The two clerks were busy, one using a typewriter and the other a calculating machine, off to one side and behind a low railing. Two large flat-top desks faced the lobby, also from behind the rail, and the swivel chairs behind each were vacant.

The uniformed bank guard stood over near the far wall, opposite the tellers' cages. The gun belt containing the holstered pistol was strapped around his waist. He was staring moodily at the floor.

Jo-Jo moved over to the teller's cage in front of which the man with the camel's-hair coat stood, as Donovan crossed to the guard. They acted simultaneously, in concert, the way they had planned it.

The guard looked up, his face curious but polite, as Donovan came up to him.

Donovan said, "Could you tell me ..."

And then, in mid-sentence, he pulled the forty-five out and, before the guard could move, struck him across the forehead with the barrel. As the man fell, Donovan reached down and took the revolver from its holster and skidded it across the marble floor.

Jo-Jo reached the man in front of the teller's cage as Donovan opened his mouth to speak to the guard. Without so much as looking at the man, Jo-Jo reached out and shoved, pushing him a half dozen feet away and to his knees. And then the gun was in Jo-Jo's hand and his hand was thrust through the cage.

"Just don't move, buster," Jo-Jo said. "Don't move one single inch."

The girl who had been working the calculator looked up and her mouth opened. She was a rather large girl with an unattractive face, and when she opened her mouth, she slightly resembled a fish coming up for air.

Donovan by now had leaped across the counter and he lifted his gun.

"One sound," he said, "one sound and you are dead. Get down on the floor. Both of you—on the floor and lie on your stomachs."

As the two girls dropped to the floor, he turned quickly to where the customer Jo-Jo had shoved was beginning to struggle to his feet.

"You," he said, "over here. Get over here and lie down before—"

The sentence ended in mid-air and for a second he stared unbelievingly at the man in the camel's-hair coat. And then his eyes narrowed and his jaw went very hard and firm.

"Stay just as you are. Stand up, face the teller's cage, the empty one there, and stay just as you are."

He turned to Jo-Jo and saw that Jo-Jo was staring at the man, wide-eyed.

Jo-Jo had also recognized Clarence behind the dark glasses and the fedora pulled down over the top part of his face.

"Get to the door," he told Jo-Jo. "And watch them. First one makes a move, shoot him."

Donovan dropped the revolver into the pocket of his trench coat and then pulled out the large paper bag. A second later he was behind the teller's cage, stuffing in sheaves of loose bills. If his hand shook just slightly as he worked, it wasn't because of nervousness or fear. It was because of anger.

So Clarence had disobeyed his orders. Clarence hadn't been able to resist getting in on the act. He'd had to come and watch the proceedings, even if he didn't participate in them.

Clarence was a damned fool. Worse. He was jeopardizing everything they had planned. Taking a stupid, insane risk. Donovan couldn't believe that Clarence was going to be crazy enough to stay on after they left and try and brazen it out when the police came. Just pretend to be another customer. Such a course would be bound to attract the police to the boarding house. On the other hand ...

He was still stuffing the money into the sack when he heard Jo-Jo's soft whistle. He looked up quickly and saw Jo-Jo step nimbly to one side. A moment later the bank door opened and a middle-aged woman entered. Some sixth sense must have told her at once that something was wrong, and she hesitated, just inside the door. Her eyes went to the fallen guard who lay at the far side of the room.

She opened her mouth to scream.

Jo-Jo moved like lightning, throwing his arm around her and pulling her to him. The woman's tongue suddenly protruded from her open mouth and her face became a brick red. Jo-Jo held her for another half-minute and when he felt her body go slack, he dropped her so that she fell to the ground like a half-filled sack of flour.

Donovan had turned back and was continuing to put stacks of bills in the sack. Out of the corner of his eye, he saw Clarence make a move. Looking up, he stared at Clarence and saw Clarence swing his eyes to the fallen bank guard. The man was twitching, obviously regaining consciousness.

Donovan's eyes went to his wrist watch. In exactly forty seconds Barker would be back in front of the bank with the Caddie. Quickly he pulled the rest of the money into the bag. He turned then and reached out, pulling the teller off his stool, where he had sat through the entire operation, open-mouthed.

"On the floor," he said. "On your stomach. And don't move. Not for five full minutes, don't move."

He jumped across the low counter and started for the door. Jo-Jo waited until he was almost even with him, and then he too turned quickly to leave.

It was then that Donovan heard the sound at the rear of the room. He started to swing around and had just turned far enough to see that the fallen guard had risen to one knee.

And then the crash of gunfire split the air.

Danny Durrell never knew what hit him.

First there was the man walking over to speak to him. Starting to ask him something. And then the next thing he knew it seemed that the very walls had fallen in on him.

He must have been out for several moments, maybe a minute or more. But slowly, painfully, consciousness returned. He knew at once that he was lying on the marble floor of the bank and that someone had struck him down. His hand reached for his gun, but the gun was gone. And then, through a sort of dull haze, he saw the man behind the counter, cleaning out the money from the teller's cage. He saw the other man standing at the door, looking like a veritable giant as he held the gun in his great fist.

It wasn't until they were about to leave that Dan fully regained his senses. Regained his senses and saw his gun where it had been, thrown some twenty feet away.

He knew he would never be able to reach it. Never in this world. For a second then, he thought, why should he even bother? Why should he care what happened? Let the bank get robbed. They'd fired him, hadn't they? They would deserve everything that happened to them. Why should he risk his life?

And then he thought once again of what he was going to have to tell his mother when he got home that night. Break down and cry out his defeat. Couldn't even hold down a job as a bank guard.

Again Danny's eye went to the gun.

But it was hopeless. Hopeless. He would never have a chance.

It was then he noticed the heavy brass and marble ashtray on the small table, less than a foot away.

He had reached up, was on his knees, his hand less than six inches from the ashtray, when the man pointed the gun directly at his face. Fired the shot that killed him before his body even fell back onto the marble floor.

Dan Durrell died in a state of complete bewilderment. In that one instant when he had seen the gun there, pointing at him and not three feet away, he had had just time to understand that the man who was about to kill him was not one of the bank robbers.

It was the customer who had been standing in front of the teller's cage when the robbers had entered the lobby.

EIGHT

Barker was edging the Caddie slowly to the curb in front of the bank when the crashing explosion of the revolver shot reached his ear. He knew at once that the sound had come from within the bank.

Instinctively, his hand on the steering wheel made a move as he started to cut the car back into the line of traffic. His foot automatically pressed on the throttle. In that split second, while his mind subconsciously registered the shot, he began to pull away from the curb and it was only with a strong effort that he forced himself to slow down. His eye went to the doors of the bank and he could see them begin to open.

He came as near to panicking then as he ever had in his life. Every instinct told him to jam the gas pedal to the floor boards and get away as fast as he could. He had, of course, no idea at all of what was happening. But he knew that it was trouble. Bad trouble.

In that flashing moment, as he made his decision, the full realization of the desperate course upon which he had embarked when he'd decided to throw in with Donovan came to him for the first time.

But there was no time now for thinking, no time to weigh the moral or practical values. He had to do one thing or the other. He must either swing the wheel of the car sharply and put as much distance between himself and trouble—himself and Donovan—as he possibly could. Must run and never look back. Or he must stay and see it through.

He braked the car sharply, simultaneously reaching across the seat for the door handle.

Jo-Jo reached the car first and leaped into the back and a second later Donovan had tossed the paper bag on the seat next to Barker and was crowding into the car. It was then that Barker saw the third man leaving the bank. A man with a gun in his hand. A small, slight man in a camel's-hair topcoat and wearing a soft hat pulled over his eyes, which were shielded by dark glasses.

Barker at once assumed that the man was the one who had fired the shot; assumed that the shot had been fired at Donovan and Jo-Jo. He only had time to quickly wonder why neither Jo-Jo nor Donovan was returning the fire as he pulled away from the curb.

"Wait," Jo-Jo cried from the back seat. "Wait for him."

Barker thought Jo-Jo must have blown his top.

"Keep going!" Donovan yelled into his ear.

Barker pushed down on the gas pedal, swerving on two wheels as he made the first corner. He drove for half a block and then cut into a narrow alley, the way they had planned it. At the end of the alley, he turned right, slowed down to a normal speed and continued on for another two blocks, before again cutting to the right.

He concentrated on his driving, concentrated on following the route they had planned and established in advance. Donovan was talking rapidly into his ear and he heard the words, but none of it made any sense at all.

"Clarence—Clarence, that bastard," Donovan said. "That was Clarence."

"What happened?" Barker said. "What happened back there?"

"Careful," Donovan snapped suddenly. He had spotted the police patrol car coming from the opposite direction. Barker was aware of Jo-Jo ducking to the floor boards behind him and saw out of the corner of his eye that Donovan had removed his hat and glasses. He drove with a nerveless hand as he passed the police car, going at a normal speed. A quarter of a block further, he suddenly heard the scream of the siren and, looking into the rear vision mirror, observed the patrol car as the driver suddenly stepped hard on the throttle and it moved off fast, going toward the bank.

"What happened?" he repeated. "What happened back there?"

"It was Clarence," Donovan said through gritted teeth. "He was there in the bank when we arrived. Waiting. He blew up at the last minute and blasted the guard."

"Good God! They'll get him sure. We should have waited."

"The hell we should have waited," Donovan said. "He had no right being there. He wanted to come along and I told him not to. Any trouble he is in now he asked for."

"What do I do now?" Barker said. "Should we ditch the car and—"

"Play it just the way we planned," Donovan said. "The back road into White Plains. You remember what to do, don't you?"

"I remember," Barker said. "But what about Clarence? They'll get him for sure."

"I hope to God they do," Donovan said. "I just hope they do."

"But after we meet Carol?" Barker said. "What then?"

"We'll be lucky if we make the meet, after that play by Clarence," Donovan said. "But there is nothing else to do but try. Later on, we'll see. We'll have to play it by ear."

The moment the Caddie swung into the parking lot next to the supermarket, Carol knew something was wrong.

Instead of pulling up several spaces away, as had been planned, Barker continued on, stopping just long enough to let Donovan alight. She was pressing the starter as Donovan walked over to the convertible, but he didn't hesitate as he passed beside the car. He spoke out of the side of his mouth.

"Get going," he said. "Drive around the block and pick me up in front of the store."

He didn't wait for an answer, but continued on, entering the market by the side entrance. She was quick to notice that he was not carrying anything.

In the meantime, Barker drove on out of the lot and continued for another block. He pulled to the curb and the last thing he did as he got out of the car was to strip off his gloves and leave them on the seat.

Jo-Jo got out of the back. He carried a large briefcase into which he had transferred the stolen money. Everything else had been left behind in the car—the guns, the dark glasses, the trench coats and hats Jo-Jo and Donovan had been wearing.

Barker spoke quickly to Jo-Jo before he started walking rapidly away.

"Do just as he said," Barker said. "Get to the railway station and take the first train to New York. And be where he told you to be at six tonight. Without fail."

Jo-Jo grunted and walked off.

The movie house three blocks away was just opening its box office to sell tickets for the afternoon show when Barker reached it. He bought a ticket at once and went inside.

When Clarence pressed the trigger of the revolver and then, almost in the same instant, saw the bank guard lurch and fall back, it gave him the greatest thrill he had ever had. It was like no other feeling in the world—a sense of supreme power. He felt like God.

He had shown them—shown Donovan and Jo-Jo! Once and for all. They hadn't thought they'd need him? Yeah, they hadn't wanted him. But it had been he, Clarence, who had saved their necks for them. He was the one who had seen the guard reach for the ashtray; he was the one who had stopped him. If it hadn't been for him the guard would have flung the heavy object at their retreating figures and then, as they were momentarily shocked and startled, the guard would have had time to reach his gun and all hell would have broken loose.

Even as he thought about it, and experienced that terrible sense of power and achievement, Clarence turned and started after the others for the doors of the bank. He was strongly tempted to hesitate for just one moment and turn and fire at those others who were cowering in the back. He even halted for a split second, waiting to see if either Jo-Jo or Donovan did so, but when they rushed on without looking back, running for the door and the car which they knew would be waiting outside with Barker at the wheel, Clarence rushed after them.

He'd saved the day for them and this time Donovan would have to admit that his being there in the bank had made the difference.

Clarence still had the gun in his hand when he left the bank and started across the sidewalk.

By then Jo-Jo had piled into the back of the car and the front door was closing. The car was pulling away from the curb, its engine roaring.

Clarence screamed.

"Wait! Wait for me! Goddamn it ..."

But the car was several yards away and gathering momentum. For a moment then, he just stood there, his mouth wide open and his eyes popping.

God, they couldn't have made a mistake. They had recognized him back there in the bank. They knew it was he. They knew that he had fired that shot and saved them.

And the dirty rats were leaving him. Deserting him. For a moment he felt a great lump come into his throat, felt the tears rushing to his eyes.

He looked down and saw the gun in his hand. He lifted his arm, suddenly, wanting to throw it as far as he could. But some sixth sense must have warned him, and instead, he quickly pushed it into his coat pocket. He turned and looked desperately about him.

A man was walking toward him, almost running, coming from the store next door. The man had his mouth open, yelling a question.

"Quick," Clarence cried. "The police! Call the police. The bank has been robbed!"

For some reason the man continued coming toward him and then spoke, a foot or two away.

"You say the bank has been robbed?"

"Right," Clarence screamed. "Call the police."

The man nodded, his face pale, and then, oddly enough, hurried on to enter the doors of the bank.

Three or four people had stopped by now and a car was pulling up to the curb.

Once more Clarence yelled the alarm. And then he rushed to the car at the curb. He grabbed the door and opened it.

"Bank robbers!" he yelled. "They went that way. Hurry. We may be able to get the license number."

He pointed straight up the street.

The man started to say something, started to protest. While he was still speaking, there was a scream from inside the bank and then a series of long wails.

Clarence figured it must be one of the women clerks.

"Hurry, man," he said, and the driver of the car, apparently unnerved by the scream and unable to think for himself, put his car back into gear.

He was not more than a hundred yards away when Clarence rammed the muzzle of the gun into his side.

Twenty-five minutes later the man was lying dead in a culvert near an overpass over the Bronx River Parkway, with two forty-five-calibre slugs buried in his head.

Mamma still had a hangover when the telephone rang. For a while she let it ring, not much caring who might be calling. When finally it occurred to her that it might be one of the boys—that something might have gone wrong—she pulled herself off the day bed, went downstairs, and picked up the phone in the hallway. It was Donovan.

"Don't ask any questions," Donovan said. "Just answer yes or no. Have you heard from Clarence?"

It took her a second or so to come to and then she quickly spoke.

"What's the matter, Donovan? What's happened? Did everything go all right—"

"I said no questions. Have you heard from Clarence?"

"Clarence? What are you talking about? Just tell me—did

everything go off all right?"

Donovan swore and spoke sharply into the phone. "Everything blew up. We got what we went after but everything blew up. I asked you, have you heard from Clarence?"

Mamma shook her head to clear it and sputtered. "What's Clarence got to do—"

"Answer or I'll hang up."

She hesitated a moment and then said, "No."

"O.K. Get into your coat and hat. Go down to the tavern on Warburton Avenue. You know the one?"

"Yes."

"Be there in fifteen minutes and be sure you aren't being followed."

The phone clicked in her ear as she started to answer and she took the receiver away and held it out in front of her for a moment, looking at it in bewilderment. And then she slowly replaced it and turned to the hall closet for her hat and coat.

Carol was waiting, sitting in a booth in the back of the tavern, when she entered.

The waiter came over and Mamma ordered a whisky sour. When he looked at Carol, the girl shook her head. As soon as they were alone, Carol spoke in a low, guarded voice.

"All hell broke loose," Carol said. "Donovan is on a bus on his way to New York. Barker and Jo-Jo are lamming, but I don't know where. Here's what happened."

She proceeded to repeat what Donovan had told her minutes before. Mamma sat by, her face stolid and without any trace of expression as she listened. She only said one thing when Carol finished.

"So they left him," she said. "Left him there alone in front of the bank."

Carol nodded.

"Donovan said that if Clarence gets away, he will, without doubt, get in touch with you. You have to get back to the house at once and wait. The others, they are going to hide out until they hear something."

Mamma nodded, and laughed bitterly.

"Fine," she said. "That's just fine. They let Clarence take the rap after they desert him and now they are going to hide out. Why was Clarence there? What was he doing on the job in the first place? Why did Donovan take him with him? I can't understand ..."

"Donovan can't understand either," Carol said. "He told me he almost dropped dead when he and Jo-Jo saw him at the bank. Donovan said that Clarence tried to talk him into letting him go along and that he had definitely said no. But he went there anyway."

"The fool. The damned stupid fool," Mamma said, and Carol didn't know whether she was talking of her son or of Donovan. "Donovan should have told me about it."

"Well, in any case, Clarence hasn't been picked up yet," Carol said. "I heard a radio report less than five minutes ago. So I guess he must have made a successful break. But Donovan says he will be bound to get in touch with you sooner or later. If he does, Donovan says you should warn him to stay away from the house. If Clarence discarded the gun he was carrying, it can be traced. It's bound to be."

"Clarence isn't that big a fool," Mamma said. "Or maybe he is. Good God, what could have gotten into the boy? And what should I do if he calls?"

"Donovan said to have him phone Kurwitz. Kurwitz will tell him what to do."

Mamma stood up.

"I'll be getting back," she said. "By the way, who has the money?"

Carol shrugged.

"I don't know," she said. "Donovan just said they got it."

"Where are you going now?" Mamma said.

"I'm going to a movie to meet a man," Carol said.

Mamma stared at her coldly for a moment and then lifted her small shoulders in a disdainful shrug.

"Little bitch," she said, and quickly walked off.

Abe Kurwitz took his time and read every word. When he was finally through, he carefully folded the late edition of the New York *World-Telegram*, which had contained the news story he had been reading, and laid the paper on the side of his desk. He lifted heavy-lidded eyes and looked over at Clarence, who was buried in the big leather chair at the side of the desk.

"Nothing about finding the car," he said. "You say you left it in the Bronx?"

Clarence nodded, saying nothing.

"And they haven't turned up the body either," Abe said. "But of course they will. Where did you say you got the gun from?"

"Stole it from the locker of one of the guards at the bank where I work."

"Was it reported stolen?"

"No. If it was, I never heard about it."

Abe grunted and took time out to light a cigar.

"All right," he said at last. "Then here's the way it stands. At this point you are safe. You can probably go on back home, so long as the others got away clean. That is, if you still have the gun. If you haven't—" He hesitated, waving Clarence silent as the other man started to interrupt. "Don't tell me," he said. "I don't want to know. But I'm telling you. If you have been crazy enough to get rid of the gun and it is ever found, sooner or later it can be traced to you. Remember that. It can be traced. I hope you haven't been stupid enough to throw it away. But sooner or later you got to get rid of it. Permanently and everlastingly rid of it. Now you are sure you left no prints, on the car or at the bank?"

"I'm sure."

"And no one recognized you?"

Clarence nodded.

"All right, go on home then. But before you go, I got something to say."

The lawyer hesitated then and finally stood up, staring down at Clarence.

"You aren't my client. Tell your mother that I said so. And if Donovan or your old lady takes you in on anything from now on out, they aren't my clients either. Get it? I don't want you; I don't want any part of you now or forever. If it wasn't for your mother, believe me, I'd have my girl putting in a call to the cops right this minute."

He stepped back as Clarence suddenly paled and started to his feet. His hand flicked to the partly opened desk drawer in front of him and came up with a snub-nosed thirty-two.

"Sit still," he ordered. "I'm not through yet. You don't have to worry; you're safe enough with me. I told you, because of your old lady, I am not doing anything—just giving you some heartfelt advice and sending you home. The advice is this—go to some good psychiatrist and turn yourself in. You're crazy. I handle criminals, but I don't handle psychopathic murderers. At least not until after they get picked up. You'll be picked up one of these days and I might or might not handle your case. It will all depend on how big a fee Mamma wants to put up. But in the meantime, get one thing straight: I want no part of you, no part at all. So far as I'm concerned, you're a mad dog. It's what I told Donovan when I saw him this afternoon and it's what I'm telling you. A mad dog. You want to kill to prove you're a man. Well, all it does is prove you never will be a man. Now get the hell out of my office and stay out."

Clarence was shaking when he stood up.

"Listen," he said, "you listen to me. You've defended plenty of guys who've pulled triggers. So get off that high horse. Anyway, what could I do? You think I should let that guy go after he saw me? I'd already knocked off the guard."

"I don't want to hear about it, boy," Kurwitz said. "You came to me, I didn't send for you. You told me your story and you asked for advice. I'm giving it to you. Get lost. Drop dead or do anything you want. I want no part of you. I defend professional criminals—I'm not running an institution for the criminally insane. You can tell Mamma I said so."

He sat down behind the desk as he finished speaking, but was careful to keep the snub-nosed revolver in his hand.

Clarence stared at him for a long minute and then slowly turned and, without a word, left the office, not bothering to close the door behind him.

Fifty minutes later he was on the Staten Island Ferry. Halfway across the channel, between Manhattan and the Island, he dropped a newspaper-wrapped parcel into some eighty feet of water, from the upper deck.

He had dinner in a seafood place on the Island and took a return ferry back to New York around nine o'clock. He caught a late train to Yonkers and was home just before midnight.

The producer had spent more than seven million dollars on the picture, using the latest multi-camera, wide-screen process and starting with a script from a top Broadway musical. He had spared neither imagination nor money and as a result had ended up with not only a box-office smash, but a really first-class bit of entertainment.

So far as Bill Barker was concerned, he might as well have saved both his money and energy. Bill sat through it from beginning to end and saw nothing. His eyes followed the action on the screen, but his mind was a thousand miles away. His mind was on the events which had taken place at the bank in New Rochelle.

One thing kept coming back again and again. The sound of that pistol shot and then, a few moments later, the sight of Clarence running from the bank. He didn't like to think about it. He tried to take his mind off the whole thing, tried to concentrate on the expensive entertainment he was paying to see. But it kept coming back.

One other thought also bothered Barker. He was wondering if Carol was going to keep the appointment they had made the day before—the appointment to meet late that afternoon in the lobby of the motion-picture house where he was now just hanging around killing time.

If Clarence had been picked up, and it seemed to Bill that there was every chance he would be, then none of them would be safe. Clarence would be insanely mad because they had driven off and left him. He'd figure it for a double-cross, and under those conditions, he'd talk. He'd tip off the police to the whole thing. If he did, then Carol right now might very well be under arrest. Carol and Mamma and perhaps even Jo-Jo and Donovan.

Clarence must have been insane to have shown up at the bank. Yes, stark, raving mad.

But he didn't want to even think of Clarence. He wanted to think of himself. Think what he must do now, in case anything had happened. Thinking of himself, however, was not pleasant. The idea kept creeping into the fringes of his consciousness that he too must have been a little insane to go along with Donovan's plans.

It had all sounded so easy in the beginning. Even after the job last week, it had seemed easy. But now things were different.

He tried to imagine what would be happening if the others were already under arrest. What would they be doing with Carol? Would they have her in the back room of some precinct house? Beating the truth out of her?

Again he tried to concentrate on the picture, but without success. He looked down at the dial of his wrist watch, but was unable to see it. But he knew he had several hours at least to wait. There was nothing to do but sit it out.

He would have liked to have left the movie and gone outside somewhere so that he could sit in a bar and listen to a radio and find out what was happening. Or buy a late edition of the newspaper, or do almost anything but just sit and mark time. But he knew that the safest place was the movie. He knew that there was nothing he could do but wait.

At four-thirty he got up from his seat and went into the smoking room. He settled down and had two cigarettes and then, noticing that the attendant was beginning to look at him peculiarly, he got up and left. It was four forty-five and Carol had told him she would be there at five. He decided to spend the next fifteen minutes loitering near the entrance.

The white convertible was just pulling into a parking place, several yards down the street, when he walked outside. Carol spotted him at once and tapped lightly on her horn. Barker hurried to the car and climbed in.

He noticed at once that the girl seemed unusually pale.

"What's hap—" he began, but she quickly cut him off.

"Talk later," she said. "I want to get away from here."

Neither spoke then and Carol wheeled the car around several corners and at last found the parkway leading north.

"Where to?" Bill asked at last.

"Killing time," Carol said. "We'll find some place up in the northern part of the country and have dinner. I don't suppose you know what's been happening, do you?"

"No."

"Then I'd better tell you," Carol said. "I'd better tell you, Bill. I don't think you are going to like it. To begin with, that guard in the bank is dead."

There was a long silence and Carol drove looking straight ahead. At last Bill spoke.

"I was afraid," he said. "Yes, I was afraid. After I heard that shot and Donovan told me that it was Clarence who had been there and followed them outside, I seemed to know...."

Carol nodded. "Now you know for sure, Bill," she said.

"But, Carol, it wasn't part of the plan. It wasn't—"

"Nothing is ever any part of a plan when a man takes a loaded gun in his hand," Carol said. "But that isn't all of it. As far as anyone knows, Clarence made a getaway. This part I can't be sure about. But on the latest radio bulletin, police say that there were four men in on the job—the driver of the car and three in the bank. They know that one man was left behind. A man who a few minutes later kidnapped the driver of a passing car."

She hesitated a moment and took her eyes from the road and looked quickly at Barker.

"They found the driver a few minutes ago," Carol said. "He was dead and his body was in a culvert. He'd been shot twice. I don't know whether the car has turned up or not."

"Oh, my God!" The words escaped from Barker's lips in a whisper. "He must have gone crazy—kill crazy," he said.

"Are you surprised?"

Bill shook his head. "I don't know," he said. "I just don't know. What has happened to Donovan? And Jo-Jo?"

"As near as I know, they are some place in New York. You are supposed to meet Donovan, aren't you?"

"Later tonight," Bill said.

"Is it someplace you can phone?"

"Yes."

"Phone then."

Barker nodded. "O.K. But what now? What will we do now?"

Carol didn't answer and again there was a long silence. Finally Bill spoke again.

"Pull over to the side of the road." he said at last. "Pull over. I want to talk to you."

Carol shook her head. "I'll keep driving," she said. "Talk while I drive. If we stop, some nosy cop may spot us and start asking questions. You are in no position to be asked questions."

Bill nodded. "O.K.," he said. "O.K. But listen to me. Carol, I never bargained for this. I didn't bargain for murder. God—two men dead and we haven't even started on the big job. No, that's not the way it was planned at all. It's too late to have regrets now, but it isn't too late to stop. I can't do anything about that bank guard or the other man Clarence shot down, but there is one thing I can do. I can quit. Right now. And I want you to quit too."

Carol looked at him and for the first time it seemed that some of the subtle antagonism left her face.

"You should quit, Bill," she said in a low voice. "You should quit— you're not like those others. Not like Donovan or Jo-Jo or that insane Clarence. No, you should quit."

She was silent again for a long time and then she spoke, a note of determination in her voice.

"I can drive you up to Albany tonight," she said. "From there you can get a train or a bus. Head west."

"A train? No, why not take the car? Donovan paid for it. It isn't hot. But, on the other hand—" He hesitated, thinking. "Yes, on the other hand, we can just leave the car in Albany and mail Donovan the key. It would be better not to have any connection ..."

Carol partly released her foot on the throttle and turned to him with surprise on her face. "We? What do you mean, we? What have I got to do with it? What have I got to do with where you go and what you do?"

Barker stared straight ahead when he answered.

"Listen," he said. "Get something straight in your mind. You've got nothing to do with me or where I go. Nothing. But we're in this together. We are both going to be on the lam and we might just as well stick together until we get in the clear—if we ever do. That's all I want."

Carol's mouth was grim when she answered.

"I'm going back, Barker," she said. "I'm going back and I am going through with the thing. I've gone this far and I'm not going to be cheated now. I didn't kill that bank guard and I didn't kill that other man. There's no reason I have to quit. I want that money—want it more than anything in the world."

Barker turned and looked at her in amazement.

"Are you nuts?" he said. "For God's sake, Carol! You tell me I should quit, should run out, and yet you want to go back!"

"It's different with you," Carol said. "You just got through telling me this is more than you bargained for. That you want to quit while you still can. You've taken one fall, don't forget. You can't afford another. Don't you see, with you it's different. You're a man. You can go somewhere and lose yourself. Get a job, learn a trade or a business. Amount to something. You don't have to be a thief."

Barker laughed bitterly.

"But you do?" he asked. "You have to go back, get mixed up with those others? With Jo-Jo, after what he tried to do to you? With Mamma, who wants to put you in a house? With Clarence—a psychopathic killer?"

"Clarence will be out of it after what happened today," Carol said.

"Don't be silly; don't be a damned fool. If they go ahead now, Clarence will have to be in. Are you forgetting he's the one with the plans, with the inside information? Are you forgetting Mamma? She'd insist, no matter what. And Donovan needs both of them if he's going to take the Needle Trades Bank. He has to have them."

"It doesn't matter," Carol said. "I've gone this far and I'm going through with it. If it's the last thing I ever do, I'm going through with it."

"You are a little fool," Barker said bitterly. "You can moralize for me; tell me to quit and get out. But you want to stay in yourself. So why don't you do what you preach? Why don't you go somewhere and lose yourself? Start over. Hell, you don't even have the handicap of a record, like me."

"No," Carol said. "No, I don't have a record. But I have a father. A father who will probably spend the rest of his life in prison. You should know what that means, Barker," she said, her words sharp with bitterness. "You should know. There's only one thing now which will ever spring him. Money. Big money."

Barker shrugged.

"So why not take an honest job and earn some money—like you suggest I do?" he asked.

"Don't be a fool," she said. "By the time I earned enough money to do any good, my dad would have been dead for years. You know it and I know it. No, there's only one course open to me. I'm going back and if the others are going to go ahead with the plans for a week from Friday, then I'm going to be in on it. Clarence or no Clarence. Now if you want, I can drive you up to Albany, or I can take you some other place. Wherever you ..."

"You'll take me nowhere," Bill said grimly. "I'm staying with you. If you go back, then I go back with you."

This time Carol did stop the car. She pulled over to the grass at the side of the road and set her brake, but didn't turn off the engine. Turning to him, she said, "You fool."

He looked away from her, his mouth a tight line.

"Yes, you are a fool. Just because I do something, it doesn't mean you have to. What am I to you, anyway? I don't much like you to begin with and I know that I don't mean a thing in the world to you. You've told me the kind of girl you want to find someday. Someone sweet and clean and innocent. Furthermore, when I get a man sometime in the future, if I ever do, it won't be a dumb lump like you. Understand? No one like you at all. Now use your God-given brain if you have one. Let me take you someplace where you can start out from. If you want, you can have the car and I'll take a train back to Yonkers. I've got—" she started to rummage through her bag—"I've got about seventy-five dollars. You can have that, too. But for once in your life, use your head. Get out while you can."

"But you are going back?"

"I'm going back."

Bill nodded slowly, still not looking at her.

"All right," he said. "Then let's get started. Just stop at the next place you see a telephone booth."

Carol put the car into gear.

"What do you want a phone booth for?" she asked.

"To call Donovan. To find out if the coast is clear," Bill said. "If it is, then we can turn around and head for Yonkers. Because, if you go back, I go with you. Understand? I go with you!"

NINE

The police commissioner of New York City sat at his desk and leaned back in the swivel chair, making a church steeple with the fingers of his hands. He didn't look at his chief deputy as he spoke.

"I don't know," he said. "I really don't know. The newspapers yell about teen-aged mobs. They scream about muggings and juvenile delinquency. And the Lord knows they are right. But in the meantime, look what's really happening. Some nice, gray-haired old lady walks into a branch bank and slips a note to the teller saying she has a bottle of acid in her handbag. She asks for five thousand dollars and what's more, she gets it.

"I don't blame the teller. Why should he take a chance? Then maybe a day or so later, some shriveled-up old bum goes into another bank and he shows a toy pistol and maybe he walks out with a few grand. And then the next thing you know, you have a regular rash of bank stickups, loan company robberies and payroll jobs. But this time it's the real pros at work. They read about the soft touches and they want in. They get in. Look what happened up there in New Rochelle this afternoon."

His chief deputy nodded.

"New Rochelle," he said.

"Damned right. New Rochelle, and last week it was in Queens and the week before up in the Bronx and three weeks before that it was Nassau and then before that there were a couple in Jersey. It's getting closer all the time. One of these days soon it's going to be right here. Not in our backyard, but right here in Manhattan. We've already had a few of them. Yes, some mob is going to get a little crazy or overambitious or something, and they're going to pull one of those jobs somewhere in midtown or downtown New York. Where they can really clean up."

Again the chief inspector nodded.

"Yeah," he said. "I know. Someday."

"That's just the point," the commissioner said. "But not someday. Any day now. And we have to be prepared for it. You can't expect much cooperation from the banks. They do as well as they can. But those tellers, those clerks getting starvation wages and a key to the john instead of a decent living salary, they aren't going to stick their necks out. No, the banks do what they can, but there is precious little most of them can really do. It is up to us, the police, to supply protection."

The inspector stifled a yawn. He'd been hearing the same lecture for a long time now.

"Well," he said, "we do everything we can. These things come in cycles. They are like an epidemic. The more often some gang gets away with it, and the newspapers publicize the fact, the more often they occur."

"That's just the point," the commissioner repeated. "Just the point. That's why, if we do have a big one, I want to see that they don't get away with it."

"Well, we are taking every precaution," his assistant said. "The banks are notifying us when they have large shipments coming or going, when they have unusually large amounts of cash on hand. I've had the precinct captains supplying extra prowl cars, making extra checks. We do everything which is humanly possible."

"Be sure that you do," the commissioner said. "I can tell you this," he added. "Just let one big job be successfully pulled and the man in charge of the precinct where it takes place will wish to God he'd never heard of the police force. And that goes for every man jack who is anywhere around at the time. I may not be able to control fifty thousand juveniles and keep them from shooting craps or raising a little hell, but I am not going to have this town overrun by professional mobsters and stickup gangs. You can let the boys all down the line know how I feel about it."

"I'll let 'em know," the inspector said.

Patrolman Gallagher spent Tuesday night at home with his wife, Allie, watching television. It was his night off and he would have much preferred to spend it at the bowling alley with the boys, but things had been a trifle unpleasant at home recently, largely because of Gallagher's frequent absence during the comparatively few leisure hours he was able to find each week.

Allie herself worked, holding down a job in the toy department of a Brooklyn department store. She was planning to have a baby, her first, in another four months, and despite Gallagher's pleas that she quit her job, she insisted on continuing as long as she could.

"We'll need the money when the baby comes," was her irrefutable argument.

It was a good argument and one with which Gallagher was unable to disagree; but the fact remained that there were far too few hours during which they were able to see each other, and Gallagher had made the situation worse by hanging on to a good many of his old cronies, men he had known before his marriage. It was hard for him to break old habits and, in spite of the obvious charm of his wife, he still liked a night's poker session now and then and an "evening out."

Allie had no objection to Gallagher's keeping up old friendships, and even a certain number of old habits. But because of her job and the fact that, about half of the time, Gallagher was off duty during the daytime when she herself worked, she saw mighty little of her husband.

Just that evening there had been quite a discussion about this very thing, and that was one of the reasons Jim Gallagher had turned on the television. At least while they were looking at the twenty-one-inch screen, following the vicissitudes of endless cowboy heroes, conversation was impossible. Arguments were impossible. And Gallagher hated arguments.

They had already had the argument in any case. Allie wouldn't quit her job until she had to; Gallagher still felt that she should do so at once.

"I'll be a detective soon," he had kept repeating. "With the additional dough, you won't have to work. So why not quit now? We can manage."

"I'll quit when I have to," Allie had said for the hundredth time. "Detective or no detective. But in the meantime, I think that we should be saving every dime we can."

She hadn't come right out and said so, but Gallagher knew that she was thinking of those nights when he went bowling with the boys, or sat around drinking beer in a tavern and chewing the fat, or maybe playing penny-ante poker.

"Lookit," he'd said. "It's just a case of time. Any day now. I'll go into plainclothes and ..."

"... And I'll quit my job and have the baby," Allie finished for him. "Now if only you could manage to spend a little more time at home until ..."

And so he had gone over and turned on the television. He'd been tempted to find a station with a mystery or detective-story program, but had resisted the temptation. Allie liked westerns.

They sat on the couch, holding hands and watching the set. Allie kept thinking, "I really shouldn't pick on him. I guess it's just one of those things. I'm nervous and a little tired, and expectant mothers are always irritable and upset."

Gallagher was thinking, "I really should spend a little more time with her. She needs me. And I'll get that promotion—I'm bound to get it."

The trouble was, he knew he wasn't at all bound to get it. A couple of more bad breaks like the last few which had come his way, and he'd be lucky to stay on the force at all.

"I'll get us a couple of beers," Gallagher said.

Allie looked at him and raised her eyebrows.

"What did you say?"

"A couple of beers," Gallagher said, yelling to be heard above the sound coming from the set.

"One beer," Allie said. "I'd rather have tea."

"Tea?"

"Tea."

Gallagher took his hand away and stood up.

"Since when did you ever drink tea?" he asked.

Detective William Leadbetter of the New Rochelle Police Department, attached to Homicide, sat on the edge of the desk and wiped the sweat from his forehead. He skimmed his hat across the room and it landed in the half-filled waste basket. Looking at his partner, Detective George Crofts, he spoke in a hard, grating voice.

"Dirtiest job I ever had to do. Every time, every damned time, I swear I'm going to quit and find some other kind of work. It always happens to me."

"You saw Mrs. Rothman?" Crofts asked.

"Yeah. I saw her. Just left her. They live out in the northwest section. Ranch house. The kids were in bed."

Crofts nodded, sympathetically.

"She take it pretty tough?"

Leadbetter looked at his partner and growled.

"What the hell do you expect?" he asked. "Of course she took it tough. Why shouldn't she?"

He spat, aiming at the waste basket into which he had thrown his hat, and missed.

"Yeah," he said, his voice softer, "she took it damned hard. No tears, no hysteria. Just sat there in the chair, saying she couldn't understand. That he was so 'gentle'. And that she couldn't understand."

"You tell her how it happened?"

Leadbetter shrugged.

"We don't really know how it happened. I told her what we thought happened. That that son-of-a-bitch just happened to come out of the bank as her husband was passing. That he was seen getting into the car. And then the next thing—her husband's body is found with a couple of lead slugs in it. There are three kids," he added, "aside from the one in the hospital. The one Rothman was on his way to visit when it happened."

Crofts nodded.

"Tough."

"Damned tough. Rothman must have been getting about eighty bucks a week. Night chef in a diner. And the kid dying of leukemia. His wife doesn't look old enough to have had four kids. Rothman—how old was he, did you find out?"

"Twenty-nine," Crofts said. "His boss told me that he wouldn't have fought back. Said he was the gentlest man he had ever known. Wouldn't hurt a fly."

"He won't now," Leadbetter said, anger filling him. "No, he won't ever hurt anyone now."

Again he spat at the waste basket and this time he didn't miss.

"That son-of-a-bitch didn't have to shoot him. Rothman would have let him have the car without an argument."

He slipped down from the desk and looked at his partner as though he was about to strike him.

"I'm telling you," he said. "I'm telling you—the next time someone else can do it. Someone else can go out and tell the family. I'd rather face a machine gun at twenty feet."

"I know how you feel, Bill," Crofts said. "I know exactly how you feel. I saw the boy's mother. Young Durrell, the bank guard. That was no day in the country either."

Leadbetter nodded sympathetically.

"If I ever get my hands on the son-of-a-bitch...."

Crofts shook his head as the other man hesitated.

"We probably won't," he said. "Right now we don't have a lead, not a lead in the world. Rothman's car had no fingerprints. None that couldn't be checked out. He'd just finished polishing and washing it before starting out this morning. No, we probably won't catch up with him. But brother, somebody will! Somebody has to. A guy like that! A guy who will murder a man in cold blood, without a reason, when he doesn't have to...."

"Yes," Leadbetter said. "Yes, somebody will. Someone will catch up to him sooner or later. The only thing is, it isn't going to help Mrs. Rothman. Isn't going to help her at all."

Donovan looked across the kitchen table at Mamma, his eyes like ice. He twisted his head, glancing up at the ceiling.

"And believe me, believe me for your own good," he said. "Someday, and probably soon, he's going to get it. Get it for keeps. I know he's your son and I know how you feel about him. But he's nuts. Kill crazy. If I could back away from this thing now, I would. I'd walk right out of here and keep on going. But I'm staying, staying and seeing the job through. No one is going to cheat me out of it. I want that money and I aim to get it!"

Mamma shrugged.

"So what are you crying about?" she said. "What's the beef? I admit the boy was out of line. Admit that he shouldn't have been there. But that's water under the dam."

"Water under the dam?" Donovan looked at her sourly. "Killing two men, water under the dam? You're as crazy as he is."

"I'm not crazy," Mamma said. "Don't worry about me—and don't worry about Clarence. I've already said it and I'll say it again. You want to quit and get out, go ahead."

Donovan pounded his fist on the table.

"You listen to me," he said. "When Clarence killed that bank guard, he put my neck right square in the noose. You know it and so do I. You think I'll quit now? Not on your life. I'm just telling you—you control that sick bastard until this is over and finished or he'll wish to God the cops did get him today."

"He may be sick," Mamma said, "but next week you may be damned glad to have him along. Next week you may need someone who isn't afraid to kill when he has to."

"Sure," Donovan said. "When he has to. He didn't have to today. I'd kill also, if I had to. So would Jo-Jo."

Mamma sneered. "Yes? And Barker? I suppose he would, too?"

"Barker will be driving," Donovan said shortly. "You know that. Don't worry about him—he can handle his end all right."

Again his eyes went to the ceiling.

"What's he doing now?" he asked.

"He's sleeping," Mamma said. "He was tired."

Donovan laughed sourly.

"He should be tired," he said. "He's had a busy day. Anyway, I don't want to even look at him. You can talk to him when he gets up in the morning. Talk to him and tell him what I've said. In the meantime, go get the others. I want to see them. We're going to get this straightened out right now."

Mamma stood up and butted out her cigarette. "And you don't

want Clarence in on it?"

"I don't want Clarence," Donovan said. "I've told you already. He can be in on the job itself. But until then, I don't even want to see him. Not at all. If you are smart, you'll keep him locked up. Call the bank in the morning and tell them he's been taken sick. Make any excuse you want to. But he has got to stay out of sight. Completely. If you are smart, you'll get him out of the house altogether."

"He stays in the house."

"All right. That's all right, too. But keep him away from me. Until we are ready to pull the job."

"How about the warehouse—the other things he was supposed to do? Who'll do it now?"

"One of us will handle it," Donovan said. "Let him stay in his room. He and Jo-Jo—we keep them both in solitary until we pull it. And I can tell you this, once it is done and we have the dough, we'll come back here as we planned. But only long enough to cut it up and then I split out. Fast."

"That's fine with me," Mamma said. "Fine. I'll bring the others down now. Unless you'd rather wait until tomorrow. It will be daylight in another hour."

"Now," Donovan said. "Bring them down now."

He thought, God, I must be a little crazy myself. He closed his eyes, leaning on his elbows on the table. He could use some sleep.

He thought, Jesus, I must be a little crazy myself. Ten days away from the biggest job in my life; ten days away from better than half a million dollars. And what have I got, what have I got on my hands? An evil old woman who would steal the pennies from a dead man's eyes. A puny, psychopathic sadist who likes to kill for the fun of it. A punch-drunk moron who by all rights should be in a side show. A college boy who hates the world because he figured he took a bum rap. A girl who isn't dry behind the ears yet and who only wants to go for the ride because she thinks she'll get enough money out of it to spring her old man out of the clink.

Donovan laughed out of the side of his mouth.

Crazy? Yes, it was crazy, all right. It was so completely crazy that it might even work. But if it did, there was one thing he was sure about. The minute he got his, he never wanted to see any of them ever again. Except the girl, of course. He'd be able to handle the girl.

But the hell with all that. Right now he had to plan, had to talk to the rest of them and get them straightened out and he had to make his final arrangements.

With Jo-Jo out of action, and Clarence no longer trustworthy, he had to make the last-minute changes. It was going to mean there would be a lot of extra things for him and Barker to take care of. And a lot of extra risks to run. But it was going to be worth it. Well worth it...

Barker lay on the narrow single bed, hands folded behind his head as he stared, wide-eyed, at the ceiling. He had been lying there, in almost exactly the same position, since just shortly after midnight. Since he and Carol had returned to the house in Yonkers. He was fully dressed, but he had removed his shoes and loosened his necktie. He had heard the taxi arrive when Donovan and Jo-Jo returned to the house, but he had not gotten up. He didn't want to see anyone, talk with anyone. He just wanted to lie there and think.

He kept the light on and the ashtray on the night table was filled and overflowing with the butts of half-smoked cigarettes.

It was like it had been during those endless, restless nights he had spent lying on his cot in prison, unable to sleep and yet hating to stay awake and think. And like then, his mind concentrated on the past rather than the present or the future.

He could remember almost everything; back until the time when he had been a very small child. He even recalled incidents which had occurred when he was no more than five or six years old. He could remember his father's funeral, which had taken place when he was seven, but for some strange reason, he couldn't recall how he had felt. He knew that he must have been sad, but he couldn't remember. It was like that about so many things, a clear visual recollection of what had taken place, but no ability to recapture his emotions or his feelings.

It was odd how his life had been shaped by incidents rather than by feelings. His father's death. And then his mother's, some three or four years later. The years with his aunt and uncle, in the small railway apartment on the Upper East Side. Grammar school and high school. The three years in college and then his boredom and his desire to join the air corps. Get his military service out of the way.

And then the fight which had led to his prison sentence.

He had never cared for his aunt and uncle and they had cared little about him. They raised him because it was their duty. He had been a better than fair student, skipping a few grades, but they hadn't encouraged him. If it hadn't been for the scholarship, he never would have made college. The scholarship and the money he made boxing. The money he made during the summers as a swimming instructor.

He had never had friends. He liked very few people, and he had always been too busy to form any close attachments. There had been a few casual girls, but they had never amounted to much. The girls were like everything else. He didn't have the money and he didn't have the time.

He had read a lot and that was his recreation. He knew a thousand things, but he had had almost no real experience. And then, of course, he had gone to prison and he had met Donovan.

Donovan had opened up a whole new world to him. Donovan had formed his thinking and given some point to his life. Donovan had taught him how absolutely essential money was, taught him that without it he was licked and had been licked and always would be licked.

When he had gotten out, at the same time Donovan was freed, it was only natural that he had gone along with Donovan. Only natural that he had decided to throw in with the older man.

Lying there, remembering and thinking about it, Bill Barker for the first time really thought about Donovan. Was Donovan right? Was it true that the only way to get anything in this life was to take it?

He tossed nervously on his pillow and lighted another cigarette.

What, essentially, was the difference between Donovan and a man like Clarence? Clarence also thought that the only way to get anything was to take it.

God, he never wanted to be like Clarence. The truth was, he didn't even want to be like Donovan. He had just wanted to get money, to get paid off for those precious years he'd spent behind bars. He wanted to be compensated for what he had missed and for the handicap that a prison record was going to give him for the rest of his life.

He smiled wryly. Stupid? Yes, it was stupid. Wasn't that what he criticized Carol for? Wanting to be paid off for the years her father spent in jail? Wanting something for nothing and not being willing to work to get it?

Lying there, thinking about it, Barker for the first time really regretted that he had ever known Donovan or gotten mixed up with his plans. The thing to do was cut out—now.

And then he remembered the last few days. Sticking up the bank on Long Island. Going along on the New Rochelle job.

No, he couldn't pull out now. It was too late. Way too late.

There was something else. Carol. She would be mixed up in it and she would be alone. Alone with Donovan and Mamma and Clarence and Jo-Jo. Somehow the very thought of it sent a chill down his spine.

He tried to analyze his feelings about the girl; tried to discover if he was falling in love with her.

He whistled softly under his breath. It was a brand new idea and had come to him for the first time.

At that moment there was a soft knock on his door and Mamma said Donovan was waiting downstairs.

TEN

Friday, the Friday they had all been looking forward to, fell on April second, exactly ten days from the Tuesday on which they had pulled the bank job in New Rochelle. It had been in many ways a frantic, tense and nerve-wracking ten days.

The first big argument was about the Ford, the English Ford which would be in actual use for less than fifteen minutes. Mamma and Clarence argued that to buy the car was a needless expense and involved unnecessary risks.

Donovan thought otherwise.

"You seem to miss the point," he explained. "The length of time doesn't matter. What does matter is that the car will be parked in front of the bank for several minutes—the most important minutes of all. If we steal a car, there will be a report—even if we steal it out of state. Sure, I know we have different plates on it, but the point is, I don't want the police looking for a stolen English Ford. There are too few of them. I'll admit that it would be a long chance a cop might see it and get nosy, but I'm taking no chances. No chances at all."

Donovan had his way, and two days later Mamma and Carol took a bus up to Bridgeport and bought a year-old imported Ford. Mamma made the purchase, paying for the vehicle in hard cash. She showed the salesman false identification papers and said she was taking the automobile back to Boston, where she lived, and where she would register it. He loaned her a set of dealer's plates and Carol drove the car to Boston, substituted the New York plates which Donovan had supplied and mailed back the dealer's set. They then returned to Yonkers and the Ford was parked in the garage behind the house.

Barker at once went to work on the machine. It didn't take him long to do what he had to do.

Obtaining the big truck with the moving-van body was less complicated. This time there was no attempt at subterfuge. Barker had already located the vehicle in a used-truck lot in the Bronx and had already thoroughly examined it. Clarence made the actual purchase, buying it in his own name, making no effort to hide the transaction. He explained to the seller that he and Barker were going into the moving business in a small way. The registration plates were thoroughly legitimate, and Mamma even went out of her way to explain to neighbors that her son was backing a small venture for one of her boarders.

Barker drove the moving van home and put it in the garage. For the next three days, he made a point of driving it out each morning very early and returning later in the day. They wanted people in the surrounding houses to get used to the idea of seeing it.

Barker would leave and take the old Post Road down to Broadway and on into New York. Fighting Manhattan traffic, he would go south along Broadway, through the midtown section of the city, and cut east when he came to the thirties. Then he would drive down to the loft which Clarence had rented on Eighteenth Street.

Raising the big overhead door, he would drive into the building and park. The next couple of hours he would stay there, killing time listening to a portable radio. At ten-thirty exactly he would again raise the overhead door and drive out.

Each day he followed the same route on his return to the house in Yonkers. The legend, Trans-Boro Moving Company, had been carefully painted on the side of the van and if anyone bothered to notice its periodic departures and arrivals, he would have merely assumed that the firm was engaged in a healthy business.

Mamma picked up the tape recorder during the week and brought it back to the rooming house. Donovan and Barker both tested their voices on the machine and it was decided that Donovan had the better voice for their purposes. With Barker helping him, he spent a number of hours locked in the basement of the old house, taping and retaping until he had what he wanted down to perfection.

He used a stop watch when he made his final tape, timing each part of it to the second.

The tear-gas bomb gave them the most trouble. There had been no problem in obtaining it—the Kubric Novelty Company had taken care of that. The problem was in setting the device which would trigger it, setting it so that the timing would be precise.

Once more Barker's keen mechanical knowledge came into play and, after a number of trials and errors, he had his timing device down pat.

The six wrist watches were identical. They were not expensive watches, but each had a sweep hand and they wore them day and night, winding them at the same time and checking them every few hours. Donovan himself would make the infinitesimal adjustment until none varied from the others by more than a few seconds each twenty-four hours.

The guns were another matter. There was no difficulty in picking them up—they were delivered by a messenger service to a hotel room in midtown which Donovan had rented overnight, and he himself was there to receive them. The trouble was that he had no opportunity to test them.

"It would be better, of course," he explained to the others, "if Jo-Jo and I could get off a few rounds. The revolvers I don't worry about, but a submachine gun should be sighted in. I only hope to God that it won't matter. Hope that we won't have to find out how accurate they are."

Jo-Jo took the sawed-off shotgun up to his room and spent hours oiling and polishing it.

"A baby," he would say in his guttural voice. "A sweet baby." He fondled it as though it were a child.

At ten o'clock on Saturday morning a man showed up from Clarence's office. He told Mamma when she answered the door that the bank had wanted to send up Clarence's weekly pay check and also the salary to cover his two weeks' vacation. He wanted to know how Clarence was doing and if he had been operated on as yet.

Mamma knew at once that the bank was checking up on the story she had told them about the appendix attack. She took the man upstairs to Clarence's bedroom, where he was still in bed, reading a paper-backed novel. She spoke loudly as she approached the half-open door.

"... And the doctor thinks an operation can be avoided if he gets a good rest and just takes it easy for a week or so," she explained.

Clarence had time to duck the book, pull the covers up to his chin, and feign sleep, before his co-worker entered the room.

Donovan made it a point to spend an hour or so every day with each of the others. He wanted to keep them as contented as he could until the crucial day arrived. His conversations with Jo-Jo never varied; they would discuss plans for the future, Donovan mentioning Frisco, Mexico City and other towns which he had told Jo-Jo they would visit.

"But mum is the word," he would tell the big man. "Say nothing to the others. It will be just you and me, Jo-Jo, just you and me. We'll be taking off within a day or so after we get our hands on the loot."

"Just you and me," Jo-Jo would repeat. "Just you and me."

"Right, Jo-Jo. So take it easy. Get plenty of sleep and take it easy. Once we have it made, then you can have what you want, Jo-Jo."

Donovan knew what Jo-Jo wanted. What Jo-Jo was dreaming about.

With Barker he used a different line.

"I'm not asking what you are going to do, Bill," he would say. "I'm not telling you my plans. But kid, take my advice. Get as far from here as you can. Take your dough and run. Don't leave the country—you haven't got the right identification for that. But duck down to New Orleans, or someplace like that. Get a new name, a new personality even. Don't spread money around carelessly. Live simple. Buy into a gas station or some small business and get yourself settled. Build up a rep. Then later on you can spread out a little. But use the dough you are going to get as a stake. Don't squander it. If you play it smart, then this will be the last job you will ever have to pull. This will be the last chance you'll ever have to take, Bill."

Bill would nod, but was noncommittal. He knew what he was going to do and he wasn't telling any of them, not even Carol, although the girl figured large in his future plans.

Donovan only discussed the future once or twice with Carol. She tried to pump him about the hideout he had hinted at, but he was evasive.

"Don't worry, kid," he told her. "Just don't worry. I have everything set."

And, as he had done with Jo-Jo, he warned her to keep a closed mouth about the future. "Just let Mamma go on thinking you are planning to stay on with her and Clarence," he told her. "Let her think what she wants. But forty-eight hours after we pull the stickup, you and I will be on a plane."

Mamma and Clarence spent hours in secret conference. Clarence, beginning to worry at last about his part in the New Rochelle robbery and increasingly aware of the danger he had run, tried to convince his mother that their best bet would be to leave the Yonkers place as soon as they were able. But Mamma argued endlessly that to do so would be stupid.

"We'll stay on. Stay on until everything has quieted down and been forgotten," she would say. "We have the perfect hideout right here and no one will ever suspect anything. The rest of them will be gone and we'll be safe right here. Later on, when the danger is past, then we can leave. Just the two of us."

"And Carol?"

"I have plans for Carol," Mamma would say laconically, but would not go further.

Clarence had plans too, and he wasn't telling even Mamma about them.

The only two who made no effort to conceal their feelings or to, deceive each other were Carol and Bill Barker. Carol had explained to Barker about Donovan.

"Let him think what he wants to think," she told Barker. "Let Donovan make his plans. But I know what I am doing. I know very well. I'm getting out of here and I'm leaving alone. Taking my share of the money and going. The rest of you can do what you want. But I have my own private plans."

Barker tried to warn her of the danger of trying to fool Donovan, but Carol shrugged it off.

"I don't mean anything to him," she said. "It's just an idea he has."

"Idea or no idea," Barker said, "you are running a risk. A big risk. There's only one thing to do. You and I break out together. At least I can take care of you."

"I don't need anyone to take care of me," Carol told him. "No one at all. That's what Donovan wants to do—take care of me."

Barker blushed and looked angry.

"This is different," he said shortly.

And so they would argue about it, back and forth, not getting anywhere. Finally they reached a compromise. Carol agreed that she would leave with Barker, that they would take off secretly together.

"But understand," she said. "Understand one thing. Only until we get away. Until we are safely away. I'll go with you, but I won't stay with you. What I want to do, I'm going to do alone. But we can be together when we leave."

They worked together then, planning how they would do it. It was agreed that they would disappear at the very first opportunity, Carol leaving first and then Barker. The moment that each had his share, they would go. They would arrange to meet at the airport and go as far as Kansas City together and that Barker would leave her there and continue on by himself.

Barker reluctantly agreed to this scheme.

"You are right, of course," he said. "You will be safer alone. There will be far less danger of your ever being picked up that way. With me, there is always the chance ..."

"It isn't that, Bill," Carol quickly said. "You know it isn't that. It's just that what I want to do and what I have to do must be done by me alone."

Barker looked at her closely.

"Has it ever occurred to you," he said, "that something may happen next Friday? That maybe it isn't going to go as smooth as Donovan says it will? That maybe there will be a rumble and that—"

"It has occurred to me a hundred times," Carol said. "That's why I have pleaded with you to get out, to quit while you still can."

"How about yourself?" Barker said quickly. "How about you? Why don't you quit while you can?"

"It's different with me," Carol said. "I won't be there. I won't be at the bank, or in the loft building. I'm the only one who will be able to get free if anything happens. The rest of you are the ones who are taking all of the chances."

"You're taking a chance, too," Barker said. "You know that—you're taking a chance. Maybe not on next Friday at ten o'clock, but every minute and every hour and every day of your life after ten o'clock on Friday."

"Skip it, Bill," Carol said. "Skip it. I've made up my mind. And leave me alone now. I've agreed to do what you wanted. Agreed to leave with you. Let it stay there."

Barker made his last trip to East Eighteenth Street on Thursday morning. He opened the door of the loft building from the outside and backed the truck in and then closed the door. He edged the vehicle as far back as he was able to and cut off the motor. For the next twenty-five minutes he was busy making final arrangements. He wanted everything in readiness for the following day; wanted to be sure nothing was left to chance.

Leaving the place a little after nine-thirty, he walked east for a block and a half and reached the corner of Second Avenue just as Carol pulled over to the curb, driving the small Ford. Carol said nothing as she parked and moved over in the seat. Bill climbed behind the wheel. He looked at his wrist watch.

"On the button," he said.

He drove slowly, arriving at Fifth Avenue and Eighteenth Street at ten minutes to ten. He circled the block several times and then drove past the Needle Trades Amalgamated Bank, going south. He didn't stop at the bank; he merely slowed down for a moment and again checked his watch.

It took him exactly five and a half minutes to get back to the building where he had parked the truck. Again he failed to stop, but satisfied himself by merely rechecking his watch.

"The one variable," he said. "It can be anything from four minutes to twenty, according to traffic. But barring unforeseen jam-ups, it should be between four and seven minutes. More than seven will be dangerous."

Carol nodded.

"Very dangerous."

"The chance we have to take," Bill said. "How about you? Have you gone over your end of it?"

"A dozen times," Carol said. "I'll have no trouble."

"God, I hope you don't. Well, let's head back home. Driving this thing makes me jittery."

"Pull over and let me take it," Carol said. "I have the identification."

Bill slowed the car and a moment later stopped and got out and walked around to the other side.

"Twenty-four hours," he said in a low voice. "God—twenty-four hours! A half a million, maybe three-quarters of a million!"

Carol said nothing.

That night, Donovan took out the drawings and the maps for the last time. The six of them sat around the kitchen table for final rehearsal. Jo-Jo dozed through most of it, but Donovan was not annoyed. He knew that Jo-Jo would do what he had to do.

Before finally folding up the papers and taking them to the fireplace to set the match to them, he turned to Mamma.

"Now, if everyone has it straight," he said, "there is one final thing I have to say."

He looked over at Clarence.

"If anyone goofs, anyone at all, they are going to have to answer to me. Get it? I was never more serious in my life. If you get trigger-happy tomorrow, Clarence, I want you to know something and I want Mamma to know it. I'll open up with the chopper and you'll be the first one to get it. This whole caper depends on everyone doing what they have to do and no one blowing his top.

"We don't want a shot fired in that bank unless it is necessary. We don't want to panic ourselves and we can't afford to have one of the bank people or the customers panicking. Understand?"

Mamma nodded, staring at him.

"Clarence won't panic," she said. "Just be sure—"

"O.K.," Donovan said, cutting her off. "It's up to you and Clarence to see that he doesn't. We are shooting for something too big to let it get away from us. Now I think we should all go up and get some sleep. We gotta be fresh and on our toes the first thing in the morning."

He got up then, carrying the papers, and went into the living room. He stayed until the last of them had turned to ashes in the fireplace.

Three minutes later he carefully closed the door behind him in Jo-Jo's room. "Jittery, kid?" he asked.

Jo-Jo grinned and shook his head.

Donovan took a half pint of whisky out of his pocket and held it out.

"Take one big, long slug and go to bed," he said.

Jo-Jo looked at him with surprise, raising his eyebrows quizzically.

"One and no more," Donovan said.

Jo-Jo reached for the bottle.

Mamma waited until all but Clarence had left and then turned to her son.

"Well," she began, but he quickly interrupted her. "That son-of-a-bitch," he said. "He meant it. Where does he get off ..."

"Listen, son," Mamma said. "You listen to me. Donovan was right. Nobody can afford to screw this up. So don't get itchy. Just watch yourself—don't get itchy."

Clarence stood up and turned to the door.

"Go to bed, old woman," he said. "Go to bed. Don't worry about me. I want that dough as much as anyone wants it."

By twelve o'clock the four of them were sound asleep—Mamma, Clarence, Donovan and Jo-Jo.

Bill Barker took a magazine to bed with him. He knew that sleep would come hard. For more than an hour he tried to read, but he found it impossible to concentrate on the pages. At last he turned off the light and pulled the covers halfway over his head. For the next hour he tossed and rolled in the bed, trying desperately to make his mind a blank. At three-fifteen he finally got up and found his bathrobe and slippers. He didn't turn on the hall light, but crept down the stairs in the dark.

Opening the kitchen door, he was startled to see Carol sitting at the table, leaning on her elbows and staring into space. There was a half-filled cup of coffee in front of her.

He smiled at her wryly.

"You too?"

"Me too, Bill."

He took a crumpled package of cigarettes from his pocket and tossed them over on the table. And then he poured himself a cup of coffee and pulled up a chair.

"You suppose," he said, "you suppose it will be like this afterward? Not being able to sleep?"

She looked at him and didn't smile.

"I wish I knew," she said. "Bill, I only wish I knew."

Marvin Kelley reached for the package containing the one hundred single dollar bills and began counting them. He had done it so many times over the course of the last twenty years that he had developed the unusual talent of being able to carry on a conversation while keeping track of his figures. He didn't look at young Grayman when he spoke.

"So your brother-in-law or whoever it was decided not to give you the job driving the truck," he said, smug satisfaction in his thin, creaky voice.

"I didn't say that," Grayman said. "I just said I decided to stay on at the bank."

"In spite of this overtime, eh?" Kelley said.

"Despite this overtime," the younger man answered. "By the way," he said, "I was just wondering how many millions of dollars you have thumbed your way through in this last half-century. What would you say, a million, a hundred million?"

"I never think about it," the old man said.

"Did you ever think what you might do if maybe you had just one night's total? Say a night like tonight. Thursday night. Suppose, just for the hell of it, you were able to take home every cent you've counted out and put into envelopes this evening. Since we got back from dinner. What would you do with it?"

Kelley looked up at him, his face blank.

"What would I do with it? I don't know. It ain't mine, so why should I think about what I'd do with it?"

Grayman shook his head in annoyance.

"You could think about it," he said. "You could think about it, even if it isn't yours. There must have been at least a half million bucks put in pay envelopes in this place this evening. Suppose it was yours? Just suppose ..."

"Silliest damned thing I ever heard of," Kelley said in a petulant voice. "Plain damned silly. Why should I want to think about what I'd do with money that don't belong to me anyway?"

Grayman sighed and shook his head.

"That's the trouble with you, Pops—no imagination. Are you

satisfied to sit out your life counting other people's money? Haven't you ever wanted ..."

"All I want to do is finish up here sometime tonight and get home and get to bed," Kelley said. "Anyway, I have no time for thinking silly things. And I'd advise you, my boy, not to speculate about what you would do with money that you don't own. It isn't healthy."

"Healthy?" Grayman laughed. "You think it's healthy sitting here fondling hundreds and thousands of dollars? Placing the money in neat little piles and stuffing it in envelopes? You think that's healthy?"

"I think that's what the bank pays me to do," Kelley said. "They pay you to do it too, but you just sit here daydreaming. It would have been better if you had taken that job driving a truck."

"Maybe, maybe," Grayman said, his voice vague. He suddenly looked at the old man across the table and laughed.

"What's so funny?"

"I was just thinking," Grayman said. "Just thinking that sometime tomorrow all this dough is going to be passed out. Maybe a thousand, or I guess maybe even ten thousand people, are going to get their little hunks of it. Wouldn't it be funny as all hell if something happened—the damned bank burned down or an atomic bomb hit New York or something and not a damned one of those wage slaves got a nickel?"

Kelley stared at him and shook his head.

"Boy," he said. "Boy, you are sick. This bank ain't going to burn down. It's fireproof."

"Yeah," Grayman said, not listening to the other man. "It would sure be something. Not a damned one of 'em gets a nickel after working all week. Can't you see it? Ten thousand guys going home and explaining to their wives that they didn't get their dough. Ten thousand wives explaining to the grocer or the landlord or somebody that they didn't get the pay envelope. Ten thousand—"

"Listen," Kelley said, "will you just shut up and get back to work? It's after midnight. We got to get this work out. We don't get finished here and, by God, those ten thousand guys won't be getting their pay checks."

"Not checks," Grayman said. "Cash. Hard cash. Boy! A half million bucks—maybe more. What I could do ..."

The telephone on the night stand in the hallway, midway between the bedroom and the kitchen, began ringing just after one o'clock on Friday morning.

The sound reached Allie Gallagher's ears, but at first it didn't mean anything at all. She shifted in her sleep and turned on her side, subconsciously trying to shut out the noise. After a while the ringing stopped and Allie smiled in her sleep and again turned over.

The phone started again.

It wouldn't go away and at last one blue eye opened. It took her a half-minute or more to realize what it was, but when the knowledge finally came to her sleep-drugged mind, Allie leaped up and quickly reached for her dressing gown. A moment later and she was struggling along the dark hallway, a peculiar, nameless fear at the pit of her stomach.

It was always like that, every time. The phone would ring in the middle of the night, long after she had gone to sleep, and she would wake up suddenly and even as she went to answer it, she would have that sinking sensation at the pit of her stomach. Lately, since she had been pregnant, it had been much worse.

Allie wouldn't even admit it to herself, but she knew what that fear was. It remained nameless only because of an even greater fear—a fear of admitting to it.

It was a sensation experienced by thousands of other women when they were awakened late at night by the ringing of a telephone. Of women who were married to policemen, or airline pilots, or firemen— to men who risked their lives daily in the pursuit of their living.

Allie picked up the receiver, hating, as she always hated, that first moment after she said hello.

She breathed a sigh of relief, which she quickly choked back, when she heard Jim's voice at the other end of the line. She wouldn't for anything in the world have had him know how she felt. Of course, she could have asked him not to call, but that would have been even worse. She wanted him to call. It was just that late at night, well, somehow there was something almost evil in the sound of the telephone ringing.

Allie lived in constant fear of the night she would pick up the receiver and it would be some voice other than her husband's. A voice which would tell her ...

But quickly she forced the thought from her mind. Tonight it was Jim's voice and that was the all-important thing.

"Allie?" he said, the moment she answered. "That you, Allie?"

She was half smiling and half ready to cry, as she always was, when she spoke.

"Who did you think it was, you oaf?" she asked. "And what are you doing waking me up in the middle of the night?"

"Listen, Allie," Jim said. "Listen, old lady, I'm celebrating. I'm having a drink!"

She choked back her annoyance.

"Jim Gallagher!" she said. "Jim—what in the world? Have you taken me out of a sound sleep just to tell me ..."

"I'm celebrating, honey."

"James Gallagher, you are drunk," Allie said, now fully awake and suddenly quite forgetful of the happiness and relief she had felt only a moment before when he had spoken into the phone. "How dare you ..."

"Listen, honey," Gallagher said. "Shut up and listen. I'm here with Sheldon Greenbaum and we are ..."

"With who?"

"Greenbaum, honey. You know, Detective Greenbaum of the ..."

"I don't care who you are with. I need my—"

"You didn't ask me what I am celebrating, honey," Gallagher said.

"I don't care what you are celebrating, my friend," Allie said. "Now you listen to me. If you think for a minute that I—"

"The promotion," Gallagher said. "The promotion, Allie."

"I said I don't care ... What did you say, Jim? Darling! Did you say that the promotion—"

"That's right, baby. I got it! Honey, I really got it. It came through tonight and the Captain gave me the good news when I got off twenty minutes ago. Just think of it, kid, just think of it. Tomorrow is my last day on the beat. After tomorrow I put this damned uniform in mothballs and from then on it's James Francis Gallagher, Detective Third Grade."

"Jim," Allie said. "Oh, Jim—I'm so glad. Listen, darling, you come right on home this minute. You can bring your friend, Detective Greenbaum, with you. I'll put that bottle of champagne we were keeping for when the baby came, on ice, and—"

"Honey," Gallagher said. "Listen to me. I can't come home now. That's why I called. That and to tell you about the promotion, of course. The thing is, tomorrow will be my last day as a patrolman and the captain asked if I wouldn't take an extra tour of duty. Sort of a favor. We're pretty short-handed, with a half dozen men off sick. He wants me to report back at four in the morning."

Allie tried to keep the disappointment out of her voice when she answered. She didn't want to dampen his enthusiasm. "But, honey," she said, "you could come on out for an hour or so and we could still ..."

"No, baby," Gallagher said. "No, you have to get your sleep, even if I don't get mine. You have to go to that silly job tomorrow." He hesitated a moment and then said quickly, "Say, Allie, why not just call them up in the morning and quit. I got the promotion now and—"

Allie quickly interrupted him.

"No, dear," she said. "No. I'll quit, like I said I would. But I have to do the decent thing. I'll give them notice when I go in tomorrow. But you should come and get some rest if you have to be back early ..."

"I've just ordered supper," Gallagher said. "Greenbaum came over, to join me and we're eating together. Then I'm going to go back to the station house and get a couple of hours of shut-eye. There's no point in coming all the way out to Flatbush this late when I have to go right back ..."

"I know, honey," Allie said. "Yes, you have something to eat and try and get some sleep before you go back on. We can have our celebration tomorrow night."

"You bet your life we will, honey," Gallagher said. "Now you go back to bed and—"

"Jim?" Allie cut in. "You and that Detective Greenbaum have a nice supper. And have a bottle of champagne, anyway. Have two of them. But do try and get some sleep."

"I will, baby."

Sheldon Greenbaum looked up when Gallagher returned to the table, his eyebrows raised.

"Get her?"

"Yep."

Gallagher had a smile a mile wide on his plain, rather ugly face. "Yeah, I got her. She's happy as a clam. Said for us to have a bottle of champagne. Two bottles."

"On me," Greenbaum said.

Gallagher shook his head as he sat down, not looking at the other man.

"Boy," he said. "Boy, what a break! I didn't think it would ever happen. Not in a million years. I just can't get over it. Another few hours and no more uniform. How lucky can a guy get?"

ELEVEN

Releasing the spring lock from the inside of the large, double glass doors, Ronald Schlagel, who for thirty-two years had worn his bank guard's blue uniform, followed the routine he performed each weekday morning at exactly nine o'clock; he shouldered open the doors of the

Needle Trades Amalgamated Bank as the large financial institution prepared for its normal transactions with the public at large.

On this particular Friday morning, there were some twenty-eight employees behind counters and seated at desks in the main lobby of the bank. Half a dozen were junior officers, and they sat behind a low railing at the back of the room. The remainder of the lobby was lined with tellers' cages from which, following modern-day banking practices, the grillwork and glass had been removed. The Needle Trades Bank liked to give its customers a feeling of friendly intimacy. In pursuing this policy, most of the clerical staff had been removed to quarters on the second floor, and the ground floor of the structure was used almost exclusively for the taking in and paying out of hard money.

As was usual, this would be a busy day. A line of impatient clients had already formed outside the building, waiting for business to begin. Friday was payday in the garment industry and, for the first three hours of the banking day, the institution would be putting out a lot more money than it took in. A half dozen windows were allocated to the task of handling payrolls, and it was one of the little extra services of the bank to make up the payrolls in advance so that the persons picking them up need spend no extra time in waiting.

Later in the day, of course, more money would flow into the coffers of the bank than would go out. This would be the cash banked late in the afternoon by the many small firms in the neighborhood, firms disinclined to keep large sums of money in their own safes over the week end.

Mr. Schlagel, immediately upon opening the doors, stepped back and took up his usual position a few feet from the entrance, slightly to the left. He stood there, rather straight and somewhat military in his bearing, with his gun in a prominent position in its holster at his side. He greeted more than half of the customers by name as they entered the bank.

Some forty feet further on in the building was the second guard, also uniformed, but differing from Schlagel in that he wore no service hashmarks on his sleeve. His job was to keep an eye on the tellers' booths and to answer questions of anyone who might slip past Schlagel and still need information.

During the first hour that the bank was open, a great deal of routine business was transacted. A number of payrolls were picked up, now and then by carriers who were accompanied by armed guards. But in spite of the money which left the bank, a great deal more remained. The bulk of the payrolls would be called for between twelve and one o'clock.

Not much ever varied a great deal in the normal procedures on Friday morning. There was that first big rush of early-morning customers and then, along about a quarter to ten, things began to slow down a good bit and the air of hurried tension would become relaxed. By ten, business would have reached a temporary low ebb and then would gradually pick up to the peak for the day, which would come around the noon hour.

On this particular morning, when ten o'clock rolled around, there were not more than eight or nine clients in the lobby of the building. And it was exactly as the hands of the clock over the large square booth in the center of the lobby reached ten that two things happened which were certainly out of the ordinary, so far as the Needle Trades Amalgamated Bank was concerned.

One happened inside the bank and one just outside, beyond the doors opening to the street.

The thing which happened outside was the loud blasting of an automobile horn—a horn which apparently had suddenly become shorted somewhere in its electrical circuit and refused to stop blaring its raucous message.

The thing which happened inside was the sudden clear sound of a voice, an eerie voice which seemed to come from no exact place. A very clear, precise voice. A commanding voice, which said:

"Attention! Attention, everyone! Please do not move—stay where you are and be quiet! This is a stickup!"

Mamma and Carol were the first to leave the house on Friday morning. They left in the white convertible and Carol was driving. She was dressed in sport clothes and carried a small pocketbook in which she carried her wallet. She had been very careful to see that the wallet contained her driver's license, the registration papers for the car and other identification. It also contained five fifty-dollar bills, as well as a few other bills in smaller denominations. Everything was straight and in order.

Mamma was dressed as usual. In her bag was a key which fitted the small door at the side of the big overhead door, which gave entrance to the old building on East Eighteenth Street where the moving van had been left.

Wrist watches had been checked and Carol glanced at hers as she drove into town. They would have plenty of time.

She found a parking space on upper Broadway and she and Mamma left the car and went into a restaurant and had a leisurely breakfast. At half-past nine they were back in the car, and Carol had again come to a stop, near a fire plug on Third Avenue. She stopped only long enough for Mamma to alight, and then quickly put the car into gear and continued on. She had time to kill and spent it driving around the neighborhood, never getting very far away from the place where she planned to be at nine minutes after ten.

Mamma herself proceeded at once, on foot, to Eighteenth Street. She had no difficulty letting herself into the building. The moment she entered she climbed to the second floor and went to the front where she was able to see out of the windows facing the street. She found the chair which Barker had left for her and then picked up the long wire lying on the floor beside it. There was a small, switch attached to the end of the wire.

Turning the switch activated an electric motor which would raise the big overhead door just under her.

By straining her neck slightly, she was able to see for several hundred yards west on Eighteenth Street. She would be able to see the small English Ford almost as soon as it turned into the block.

Mamma took the wrist watch off and held it in her lap. She wasn't at all nervous. She had plenty of time. It wasn't yet a quarter to ten.

Donovan and Jo-Jo took the New York Central into New York from Yonkers. They caught the same commuting train, but they traveled separately. Each was weighed down with a large parcel.

Donovan carried the submachine gun in a leather-bound trombone case and he wore a gray trench coat and a felt hat. The steel-rimmed glasses on his nose were of clear glass.

Jo-Jo was dressed in a messenger's uniform and he had the sawed-off shotgun in a large flower box, carefully tied with ribbons. He also carried an airplane zipper bag. Except for the uniform, Jo-Jo had made no effort at disguise.

The train arrived at Grand Central at nine-thirty-one. Donovan was the first to alight and he didn't look at Jo-Jo or speak to him as he passed the other man on his way to the downtown subway.

They arrived at the Needle Trades Bank at almost the same moment, one minute before ten o'clock. Jo-Jo came by taxi.

The English Ford was pulling up in front of the building as they started for the entrance. Clarence, dressed in woman's clothes, was stepping from the back seat. The door was being held open for him by

Barker, in a chauffeur's uniform. Barker reached inside and handed Clarence the leather case containing the tape recorder as Clarence started to turn toward the entrance to the bank.

Clarence took short, mincing steps. He was wearing shoes with medium Cuban heels and they bothered him considerably. Mamma herself had made up his face and adjusted the wig under the floppy felt hat with the feather. He wore a tweed box coat, which fell below the line of the dress. His legs were encased in silk stockings. It hadn't been necessary to shave his legs.

Clarence had decided to discard the thick-lensed glasses he usually wore. They gave his face a grotesque appearance which made him ugly almost beyond belief and so he had sacrificed them for the sake of appearance.

Clarence found it difficult making his way across the crowded sidewalk. The big case holding the tape recorder was very heavy and he had to be careful in carrying it. The last thing he had done before the car had stopped at the curb was to set the mechanism starting the machine. He knew that the sound would start coming in exactly sixty seconds.

The revolver and the two tightly folded-up shopping bags were in the large leather pocketbook Clarence carried on his free arm.

The moment Clarence had entered the bank, Barker turned back to the car. He saw out of the corner of his eye that the policeman standing at the corner of Twentieth and Fifth Avenue, kitty-corner from where he had parked the car, was watching him. He was in a no-parking zone.

Moving unhurriedly, he rounded the car and climbed inside. For several seconds he fumbled with the starter, at the same time noticing that several people had entered the bank and that a couple had exited.

Barker looked at his watch and saw that the policeman was starting to cross the street and come toward him. He waited another ten seconds and then reached down to the switch he had installed several days before. He flicked the switch and the high-pitched horn began to blow.

Barker pushed several times on the horn rim, played with the ignition key. He saw that several people had stopped and turned to stare at the car.

Still moving unhurriedly, he opened the door and got out. He was raising the hood as the policeman approached. Several people had gathered around, smiling and making amused remarks. The policeman was at his elbow now. He tapped him and Barker looked up.

The policeman just shook his head, looking sad. He said something, but Barker was unable to understand his words above the sound of the horn.

The policeman shrugged and turned away as Barker began to feel around the wires under the hood. He looked at his wrist watch.

Two minutes and thirty seconds to go.

Donovan saw Clarence out of the corner of his eye as Clarence crossed the marble lobby to the center of the floor and slowly set the leather case containing the tape recorder on the floor, just under the edge of the counter which held the writing materials and the blank checks and deposit slips. Clarence pushed the case a little with his foot, getting it out of the way. He put the heavy alligator bag he had been holding on the edge of the counter and reached for a pen.

Donovan moved over to the uniformed guard, who stood just within the doorway. The man looked up at him alertly, questioningly.

Before speaking, Donovan's eyes crossed to the other guard. Jo-Jo was standing next to him, speaking, and the guard was shrugging his shoulders.

And then the voice came from the tape recorder.

"Attention! Attention, everyone! Please do not move—stay where you are and be quiet! This is a stickup!"

Jo-Jo and Donovan moved simultaneously. Jo-Jo was the fastest, and the blackjack which he had been concealing in his right palm sprang out like a snake. It made a soft, plopping sound as it crashed into the side of the skull of the bank guard.

Donovan was more careful—his blackjack caught Ronald Schlagel, the guard he faced, over the forehead. The blow didn't break the skull, but it was sufficiently hard to knock the old man unconscious.

Jo-Jo had been faster with the blackjack, but Donovan was faster with the trombone case. He had the gun out and cradled in his arms and had neatly sidestepped so that he was out of sight of the street entrance before Jo-Jo had completely torn open the flower box.

Clarence went on writing at the counter.

"Every man and woman in this room is being covered."

Once more the eerie voice came from the tape recorder. There was a sudden soft scream somewhere in the back and the sound of the shorted horn outside was very loud.

"The first person who makes any attempt ..." The voice stopped and there was the sudden sharp blast of a revolver shot.

A woman in the back of the room moaned and fell in a dead faint to the floor.

"You were told not to move," the tape recorder continued. *"A dozen guns are pointed at you."*

Donovan stood stock still, holding the gun, his eyes slowly circling the room. He was unable to withhold a thin grin of satisfaction. The taped gunshot, coming as it did between stretches of dialogue, had had the psychological effect he had known it would have. No one in the bank, aside from the three of them, could be sure who was a member of the gang; no one would know but that his nearest neighbor might have a concealed weapon and be waiting for a false move in order to use it.

Jo-Jo by now had the sawed-off shotgun in his arms and he too slowly looked over the people surrounding him.

Clarence opened the large alligator bag and took out the revolver. He pushed it into the belt holding his tweed coat together and then he took out the two shopping bags. Walking swiftly on his Cuban heels, he crossed the room and went to the first teller. He shoved one bag across the counter.

"Fill it!"

The man stared at him, temporarily paralyzed.

"The man in the back, at the desk," the tape recorder said. *"Make another move toward that alarm button and you are dead."*

Twenty pairs of eyes went toward the back of the room, but everyone was careful not to move more than his head.

Clarence took the revolver from his belt and the teller in front of him paled and began reaching for the empty shopping bag.

"Just the payroll envelopes," Clarence said.

The guard who had fallen at Donovan's feet stirred and Donovan quickly reached down and took the revolver from his holster. He didn't speak, but the voice continued to come eerily from the tape recorder.

A man and woman entered the bank and suddenly stopped in their tracks as they saw Donovan cradling the machine gun.

"Remember, no one else will get hurt if you don't try to be heroes. We will be leaving in less than a minute now—one by one. You won't know when we have all left until I stop talking. Until then you will stay exactly as you are. No one moves!"

Clarence was at the third teller's booth now and the first shopping bag was full. He went on to a fourth window, dragging the heavy sack and throwing the empty one at the man opposite him. Again he muttered his instructions. Donovan looked swiftly at his watch. A minute and fifty-five seconds had gone by.

The sound of the auto horn from the street suddenly ceased. Donovan moved forward, nodding at Jo-Jo.

Clarence turned and, taking a shopping bag in each hand, started for the entrance. He had left the revolver on the floor at the last booth he had stopped at.

Donovan stepped aside to let Clarence past and Jo-Jo began backing toward the doorway.

"We are getting ready to leave. Stay exactly where you are. Your life will depend on it for the next three minutes."

Jo-Jo was even with Donovan now, and he leaned down and put the sawed-off shotgun on the floor. He reached into the zipper bag which held the tear-gas bomb. Taking it out, he laid it next to the shotgun.

Donovan stooped down and picked up the trombone case and opened it with one hand. He began putting the machine gun inside as he moved to the door.

"Everyone will now face the back of the room. In another minute and a half..."

The voice coming from the tape recorder was suddenly drowned out as the tear-gas bomb exploded with a heavy thud.

Donovan and Jo-Jo were halfway across the sidewalk when the sound came and the shock made them stumble. A thick cloud of smoke suddenly began to seep from around the doors of the bank.

Clarence was in the back seat of the English Ford. Donovan climbed in beside him as Jo-Jo got in next to Barker, and then Barker had the car in gear and it was pulling away from the curb.

Out of the corner of his eye, Barker saw the policeman, who had wandered several doors down the street, turn suddenly and start running toward the bank.

He moved the car quickly into the line of traffic. He knew that he would have less than five minutes now. Five relatively safe minutes.

Behind him, back in the Needle Trades Amalgamated Bank, the tape recorder continued speaking in a precise but authoritative tone, and some three dozen persons suddenly found tears streaming down their faces, but not because they were aware of the fact that the financial institution had just suffered the largest single withdrawal of funds at one time in its more than thirty-two years of doing business.

On the second floor of the bank, young Mr. Grayman, quite unaware of what was happening below, would have been very amused to know that those thousands of employees in the dress industry, about whom he had been talking several hours previously, definitely would not be getting their pay envelopes on that particular week end.

Patrolman Jim Gallagher swung the wheel of his patrol car and turned into West Twenty-second Street. His eye went to the rear vision mirror and he saw the white convertible.

It was very odd; he had spotted the same identical car now twice within the last fifteen minutes. He could almost have sworn that the girl was deliberately following him. And yet the idea was a little too bizarre to really believe. He figured that he was as attractive to women as the next man, but he just couldn't quite believe that a beautiful young honey-haired girl was really going out of her way to follow him around New York City.

And yet he was sure it was the same white car. Patrolman Gallagher slowed down a little and again looked in the mirror. The white convertible also had slowed down.

He grinned to himself and stepped on the gas. He would go as far as Fourth Avenue and then turn south and see what she did. He looked at his watch (which was a minute or so off) and saw that it was just ten o'clock.

At Fourth Avenue, Gallagher swung his wheel, made the corner and again looked into the mirror. He was a little disappointed to see the convertible going straight on.

He had been wrong, of course. The girl had not been deliberately following him. She had continued driving east.

Two more hours and he would be taking the car back to the precinct house and checking it in. And then he would be signing out and it would be the last time he would ever sign out as Patrolman Gallagher. After that, it would be Detective Gallagher. He considered that a very pleasant thought.

Nothing much was happening and he decided to go as far as Seventeenth Street and then head west again. It was his usual route, which he varied only now and then. He knew that he could expect things to be pretty quiet now for the next couple of hours. Traffic wasn't too bad and everything seemed to be moving along fine. That was the trouble with his job—nothing ever did seem to happen.

He cruised along slowly, watching each side of the street, and saw nothing which was at all out of the way. The sound of his radio crackled now and then, but the calls were not for him. Nothing, in fact, had come his way now for more than an hour and a half. Nothing probably would. He was pretty tired, not having had any sleep to speak of, what with the doubling up of the shift, but he made a conscious effort to remain alert. He didn't want anything happening on this, his last tour of duty in uniform.

Carol turned into Nineteenth Street and looked at her wrist watch. It was exactly four and a half minutes after ten. Her body tightened a little with tension and she pressed down on the gas pedal. She saw, as she neared Fourth Avenue, that the light was against her. No pedestrians, fortunately, were crossing the street.

Out of the corner of her eye, she saw the police patrol car coming from the north, on her right. Her foot hesitated a fraction of a second and then she shot the convertible past the red light and out into the line of traffic.

There was the sudden scream of brakes as Patrolman Gallagher tried, too late, to swing his wheel and avoid the crash.

A man standing on the far curb opened his eyes wide and then opened his mouth as though to yell. But before he could even utter a word, the crash drowned out all other sound.

The nose of the white convertible caught the police car in the center of the left side and the momentum carried both vehicles halfway to the curb. Carol's head cracked sharply against the windshield and the blow stunned her for a split second, but not enough so that she didn't have a chance to pull on the handbrake as she slid across the leather seat and crashed into the door with her body.

Patrolman Gallagher was equally lucky. His head struck the rear vision mirror, but it was a light blow. It merely dazed him for a moment. Even so, before the vehicles had come to a full halt mortally locked together, he was opening the door on the side opposite him and leaping to the street.

He was rounding the tangled wreckage, hurrying to the side of the girl who had been driving the convertible, when he had to suddenly step back to avoid the small English Ford which was racing past at better than fifty miles an hour.

He stopped suddenly, staring at the receding rear end of the car. He was reaching for his police whistle as the driver swung sharply at the next corner, tearing into Eighteenth Street on two wheels.

It was at that very moment that the general alarm first came over the radio of the wrecked patrol car.

Mamma spotted the English Ford from her vantage point in the second-floor window of the building less than four seconds after it had swung into the block. She would have seen it even earlier if it hadn't been for the large garbage truck hogging the center of the street. Her hand automatically began to press the electric switch it held, but then suddenly she released the pressure.

The garbage truck had halted directly in front of the building, completely blocking the street from both directions as well as blocking the driveway from the street to the garage.

Mamma said something under her breath and it wasn't nice.

Barker jammed on the brake just in the nick of time. The Ford came to a stop with its bumper not more than two feet from the back of the truck.

Quickly, Barker put his head outside and looked behind him. A large delivery truck was turning in at the end of the block. He swore under his breath. He knew that the policeman getting out of the wrecked car had spotted them. He doubted that the alarm was out yet, but he had been speeding and the cop had blown his whistle. If the cop decided to follow on foot, it wouldn't take him more than a couple of minutes at the most to catch up to him.

Donovan looked to the rear and saw the delivery truck bearing down on them. He started to open the door to get to the street, but as he did, the garbage truck slowly began to move. He pulled back into the car as Barker released the clutch.

The garbage truck passed the garage and Donovan held out his hand to signal. As he did, the big overhead door of the one-time stable began to raise.

Ten seconds later the small English Ford was inside the building and Mamma again worked the switch. The four of them tumbled out as the heavy overhead door came to a rest against the concrete floor.

Barker was the first to reach the rear of the moving van and, by the time he had opened the double doors, Jo-Jo was at his side. Jo-Jo leaped into the back and a second later Donovan joined him. Moving with a precision that wasted no time or energy, they pushed out the two long, foot-wide planks with the iron hooks on the ends. When they were in position, they formed a ramp leading to the interior of the van.

Barker, still without a word, returned to the small English Ford. Putting the car in low gear, he slowly approached the ramp. Donovan, standing inside the van, directed him as the Ford began to ascend.

Mamma stayed on at her post upstairs, watching her wrist watch.

Barker was quickly stripping out of his clothes and getting into the gabardine uniform and the truck driver's black leather jacket and peaked cap as Donovan and Jo-Jo removed the makeshift ramp. He leaped to the ground as Jo-Jo held down his hand to haul Clarence into the back of the van.

Donovan spoke for the first time.

"O.K., kid," he said. "So far, so good. Now for God's sake, drive careful!"

Barker nodded, saying nothing. He closed the double doors of the van, locking the other three inside. Donovan began taking the submachine gun out of its trombone case.

Mamma heard the sound of the double blast on the horn below her and once more she pressed the switch in her hand.

Slowly the overhead door once more rose and the van edged out into the street.

A taxicab, with the figure of a uniformed policeman hanging half out of the front seat opposite the driver, was rushing past and Barker had to brake the van to avoid a collision. He waited until the cab was well past and then again released the clutch. The door began to descend behind him.

When he came to Third Avenue, he waited for the light and then turned north.

The neighborhood was suddenly alive with the sound of wailing police sirens.

TWELVE

Later on when he thought about it—and he thought about it a great deal—Jim Gallagher never could quite pin-point the exact time when he became aware of the words coming over the police radio. Things seemed to have happened just a little bit too swiftly and the chances were he was still in a daze from the blow he'd gotten when his head had struck the rear vision mirror.

As he tried to recapture the events in their proper sequence, it seemed to have all taken place like this:

First he was driving along Fourth Avenue, minding his own business. And then, just as he came to the intersection of East Nineteenth Street, he caught sight of the white convertible again, approaching on his left-hand side.

His first reaction was one of pleasure. That sensation certainly hadn't lasted very long.

He'd expected the honey-haired girl behind the wheel to pull up and stop for the red light; in fact, he *knew* that she would stop. Everyone stopped for red lights, or at least certainly everyone did when they could very obviously see a police car about to pass in front of them.

But this girl didn't stop. She not only didn't stop, she seemed to literally step on the gas and head directly toward him.

Gallagher thought as fast as the next man and usually his physical reactions were as fast. But he didn't have a chance. He swung his steering wheel and grabbed for his handbrake and jammed down his footbrake. But it was all a waste of energy.

She got him anyway.

He knew the second that he climbed out of the car that he was not really hurt badly, and at that moment he wouldn't have much cared if he had been. There was but a single thought in his mind—the captain wasn't going to like this. Not at all.

However, his duty allowed no time out for idle speculation. There had been an accident and the driver of the other car might be injured. Could be badly hurt. Gallagher started to go to the car and see just what had happened, and that was when the small black Ford sedan raced past, narrowly missing him as it swerved out to avoid the tangled wreckage of the police cruiser and the white convertible. The Ford was obviously breaking all speed limits.

For one split second, Patrolman Gallagher repeated his mistake of a moment before. He assumed that the Ford would immediately stop. Everyone stopped when they came upon an auto crash.

But the small black Ford didn't stop. Instead, the driver seemed to add coals to his fire and a moment later was taking the corner of Eighteenth Street on two wheels. The thought came to Gallagher at once that the driver was fleeing and a fleeing driver is usually a criminal driver.

Almost without thinking, Gallagher turned back to his patrol car, perhaps with some vague idea that it was still ambulatory and that he would take out after the other car. And it was probably then that he first became aware of the words coming over the police radio. He wasn't in time for the beginning, but what he heard was plenty.

"... Members of the mob are believed to be escaping in a black English Ford sedan. All police cars in the vicinity of the Needle Trades Bank at once ..."

He didn't need to listen to anything more. He knew what he had to do.

He was turning, seeking some means of transportation, when he became aware of the uniformed policeman rapidly turning toward him from the far side of the street. He yelled at his fellow officer as he approached.

"Stay here," he said. "See to the girl in the car. I'll be back."

Even as the other man stared at him, Gallagher leaped into the middle of the street, waving his arms like a lunatic. He was searching for a passing car to commandeer when he became aware of the tugging at his arm. He turned, furious, expecting to face his fellow officer.

It was the honey-haired girl, her beret askew over one eye and with a tiny spot of blood on her chin. She had both hands on his arm and was pulling for all she was worth.

"Don't you dare go away!" she said, screaming the words. "You've wrecked my car and don't think you can get out of it."

"Now see here," the other patrolman said. "What's this all about, anyway? Who did what to ..."

"Listen," Gallagher said, a little desperately. "Listen to me! There's been a bank robbery. I just saw the getaway car. Now you," he stopped, pushing Carol's hands away from him, "you just stay right here. I'm going after ..."

"You're going nowhere," Carol said, again grabbing his arm. She turned to the second officer.

"He ran me down and now he wants to—"

"Damn it," Gallagher said, "I told you there's been a bank robbery. I just saw the getaway car. It just passed by. Now you—"

"He's trying to get out of it," Carol said, turning to the second patrolman.

For a moment the second officer looked bewildered and then, quickly, he stepped back and took out his service revolver.

"Everyone will stay just as they are," he said. "We'll soon see what this is all about."

"Listen, you lunkhead," Gallagher yelled. "Listen to the radio in my car. They're broadcasting the alarm now. Just go over and listen."

For a moment his fellow officer looked at him coldly, and then spoke.

"Don't call me a lunkhead," he said. He nodded curtly at the police car. "All right, you, get in front of me."

"I demand that you arrest—" Carol began, but the patrolman cut her short.

"You stay out of this," he said shortly. Pushing Gallagher in front of him, he went to the side of the police car.

"... The Ford sedan is believed heading east, somewhere in the Twenties. The fleeing bank bandits are believed armed with a machine gun and every precaution ..."

"You say you saw that car, Mac?" the patrolman said to Gallagher, pocketing his gun.

"That's what I've been trying to tell you," Gallagher said. "Now stay here and watch the girl."

He turned then, looking desperately for a vehicle to commandeer. It was then he first became aware that traffic was tied up for a block in each direction by the crowds that had gathered.

By the time he made his way to Eighteenth Street and found the Checker cab which he took over, almost ten minutes had passed. He knew in his heart then that he was too late, but he made the try nevertheless.

Gallagher wasn't even aware of the moving van when his cab went by it. Gallagher was looking for a small English Ford.

Halfway down the next block, between Third and Second Avenues, he spotted the garbage truck. He had the cabbie stop while he questioned the driver.

The driver admitted that he had been on the two blocks of Eighteenth Street, picking up waste, for at least fifteen minutes. He categorically denied having seen anything of an English Ford.

"But it would have had to pass you," Gallagher said, trying to avoid yelling.

The garbage truck driver shrugged.

"Sure, officer," he said. "Sure—that's what you say. I say I didn't see it. If it turned into Eighteenth Street in the last ten minutes or so, it would have had to pass me. But I'm here telling you it didn't."

Gallagher stared at him for a moment and then turned helplessly back to the cab.

"Nineteenth and Fourth Avenue," he told the cabbie in a broken voice. "There's been an accident."

Donovan took off the ear phones which were plugged into the short-wave set and pulled open the small window separating the body of the van from the driver's compartment. He spoke in a hard, quick voice to the back of Barker's head.

"Where are we?"

"Third, coming up to Forty-eighth."

"Have to change plans," Donovan said. "Someone back at the bank must have phoned in the alarm just as we left. The police are forming a cordon and they'll have the whole of Manhattan sewed up tight as a drum any minute now. Cut back around to Second Avenue and we'll try to make the tunnel to Long Island."

"But," Barker said, speaking over his shoulder, "don't you think—"
Donovan didn't let him finish.

"Damn it!" he yelled. "Do what I tell you!"

Barker turned at the next corner.

The van was the next to the last vehicle to pass the toll booth at the Midtown Tunnel before the two patrol cars screamed up to form a blockade. The police were still looking for an English Ford, but they were taking no chances. They were going to keep the bank bandits confined to Manhattan Island if it were humanly possible to do so.

Following Donovan's orders, Barker drove east on Long Island, taking the throughway as far as it went and then cutting over to Route Twenty-five and still going on east.

Several times Donovan opened the window separating them to give him directions. After Barker had been driving for more than two hours, Donovan spoke to him once more.

"Nothing at all now on the short-wave," he said laconically. "But the regular news stations have picked it up. They say we got a half million dollars and I hope they are right. That must have been a riot after we left. Tear gas knocked out about half the people in the bank, but someone managed to get to the phone anyway. They are looking for a mob of six or eight men."

Barker grunted.

"So what now?" he asked. "Where the hell are we headed? We got to come to the end of this thing sooner or later."

"We're headed for Orient Point," Donovan said. "The Orient Point Ferry. To New London, Connecticut. If we make it, we'll be in the clear. Once across the Sound, we'll circle back and pick up the road to Yonkers. No one is going to look for us coming down from Connecticut."

"But the ferry? How about ..."

"That's the chance we got to take," Donovan said. "There are no guarantees, but it's the best bet. According to the radio, the police figure we are holed up somewhere in Manhattan. Can't figure how we could have gotten off the Island."

"They'll find that Eighteenth Street place sooner or later," Barker said.

"Sure, but it will be some time before they put two and two together. They'll still be looking for an English Ford."

When Barker finally arrived at the ferry slip, he discovered that he would have an hour and a half to wait. He told the others, after he had parked the van, and then he settled back, not leaving the driver's seat.

He had a bad minute or two, sometime later, when a state police car pulled up alongside the van and the state trooper who was driving it got out and strolled over. The man nodded at Barker and Barker asked him how long the ferry trip took.

The trooper told him, and then asked where he was headed.

"Load of furniture to be delivered to New Haven," Barker said. "Sure would like to get it out of the way before dark."

"You'll make it," the trooper said. A few minutes later he climbed back in his car and drove off.

Barker stopped once, on Route One, south of New London, and gassed up. While the man was putting the fuel into the tank, Barker got out and purchased a half dozen candy bars. Later he passed them through the window to those in the back of the van.

At eight-fifteen that evening, Donovan pulled up for the last time at a gas station on Route Nine, just north of Yonkers. There was a telephone booth several yards from the pumps and he went to it, after making sure the door of the cab was locked.

Mamma answered the telephone.

"Where in God's name—" she began, but Barker cut her off short.

"Can we make delivery? Yes or no."

"Yes."

Barker hung up the receiver.

Twelve minutes later the truck turned into the driveway and entered the garage behind the rooming house. Barker cut the engine and got out and locked the garage doors. And then he opened the back of the moving van.

When Captain Francis Huron replaced the receiver on the telephone, the perspiration was dripping from his forehead and his collar was wilted. He moved carefully, very slowly, like a man in a slow-motion picture. Turning his swivel chair so that he faced Patrolman Gallagher, he stared at him with unseeing eyes for a second or so, and then slowly exhaled his breath. When he spoke, his voice was deceptively soft.

"I want you to listen to me, Gallagher," he said. "Listen to me very closely. That was the commissioner. The commissioner himself."

"Yes, sir," Officer Gallagher said.

"Shut up!" the captain said. "I told you I wanted you to listen. Not to speak. Just listen."

He sighed and sat forward on the chair.

"I want you to understand something, Gallagher," the captain continued. "I want you to know that so far as the Police Department of the City of New York is concerned, you are dead. Get it? Dead!"

His voice suddenly cracked as he raised it to a scream. He stood up and pounded his fist on the desk.

"If it is the last thing I ever do in this life," he said, "I am going to see to it that your promotion is rescinded. I am going to drum you out of the department. I want you to know that after what happened today, you have probably ruined my own career. But I am not going down alone."

He stopped for a moment and took out a handkerchief and wiped his forehead. When he spoke again, his voice was soft and almost sad.

"God!" he said. "My God! Some twenty thousand men on the New York Police Force and you had to be the one who saw that getaway car. You. And what were you doing at the time, Gallagher? I'll tell you what you were doing. You were wrecking a patrol car. Understand— you were wrecking a patrol car. You were putting the kibosh on the one single patrol car in the entire city of New York which might possibly have intercepted the bank robbers. And you had to do it in my precinct."

"But, Captain," Gallagher said. "The girl had already run into—"

"Gallagher," Captain Huron said, again standing up and shouting, "Gallagher, I said, shut up! Don't try to explain anything to me. I swear to God if you say another word before I finish talking I will personally tear off your right arm and beat you to death with it!"

Again he hesitated, trying to control himself.

"Yes," he said at last, "you have an alibi! You always have an alibi. It never fails. Something happens on your beat and you are having your private troubles. The hell with the precinct, the hell with the whole police department—you are busy having your own problems. Well, let me tell you this, my boy—you don't know what a problem is yet! You have no idea. By the time I get through with you ..."

Gallagher shrugged, looking desperate and started to open his mouth, but again the captain shut him up.

"So the girl ran into you, eh? I suppose you are going to try and make me believe it was all planned? Just a great big plot to mess you up. I suppose that girl knew that the getaway car was going to be passing by at exactly that moment and chose it only so that you would be in trouble? I suppose—"

"I didn't say that," Gallagher began. "I only said—"

"Don't say anything, Gallagher. Listen. Listen to me. We will just go by the facts. It is bad enough when a patrol car has an accident with a civilian vehicle. It is bad enough. But you weren't satisfied with that. Oh, no. You have to pick your time. You have to have *your* little accident at precisely the moment that the biggest bank robbery that ever occurred in midtown Manhattan is taking place. You have to take the car out of circulation right at that moment. You even go out of your way to see that the accident takes place on the escape route of the getaway car. You see the car; you see it speeding by. But what are you doing, Gallagher? Why, you are standing around picking your nose and discussing a bent fender."

"But the radio alert wasn't—"

"Don't tell me, Gallagher. Don't tell me," the captain said. "I know all about the radio alert. You saw the car; you heard the alert. You even took off after the car in a commandeered taxi. You have told me once and you have told me a dozen times that the Ford couldn't have gotten away. But it did, Gallagher, it did. The Ford got away and the bandits got away. You say it was just another bad break.

"Well, let me tell you something, Mister Gallagher. You have had your last bad break in this precinct. If I could do so, before a departmental trial comes up, I'd take that badge and gun away from you right now. This very second. I can't. But there is one thing I can do. I can tell you to get out of my sight. Now—this very second! Before I really lose my temper."

The captain again stood up. His eye went to the clock on the wall.

"It is exactly seven o'clock in the evening," he said. "In one more minute it will be seven-oh-one. If you are standing in this room by then, I swear to God I will ..."

He suddenly sighed and shook his head.

"Get out," he said in a weak voice. "Please—just go."

Detective Sheldon Greenbaum was waiting at the cafeteria on Sixth Avenue, some twenty minutes later, when Jim Gallagher walked in. Gallagher, seeing his friend, nodded, looking sick. He went to the counter and got a cup of black coffee. He crossed to the table where Greenbaum was sitting alone.

Greenbaum looked at him and shook his head. "You call Allie yet?"

"I called her. It was great. She told me she quit her job."

"And you—you tell her anything?"

Gallagher shook his head.

"What in the name of God could I tell her?" he asked. "That I'd blown the whole thing? That I had goofed again? That this time I had really done it?"

He sighed and pushed the untouched coffee away.

"I can't understand it," he said. "By God, I just can't understand it. Why that particular car happened to be running that particular light, at that particular time ...”

Greenbaum looked at him keenly for a moment and then spoke slowly.

“Maybe,” he said, “maybe it wasn’t just a coincidence. Maybe ...”

Gallagher put up his hand and shook his head.

“No,” he said. “No, it was a coincidence, all right.” He pulled a slip of paper out of his pocket.

“‘Carol Jane Hardin, twenty-one years old, residing at 1986 Morgan Avenue, Yonkers, New York,’” he read slowly. Looking up, he added, “Dumb blonde. In town shopping. Had purchases she had made this morning. Oh, I checked the registration and everything. She knew where she was going, or trying to go. Some antique shop down on Lower Broadway. Just got confused in New York traffic and was trying to find the address. Registration was O.K. Driver’s license O.K. Even her story was O.K. Screwy as it may sound.”

“But you say she deliberately ran that stop light and ...”

“She says she put on her brakes and they didn’t hold. It could have happened. Yes, we examined the car and it could have happened. The brake fluid was almost completely gone.”

“So what did you do, give her a ticket?”

“I did more than that. I arrested her. Right there and then. As soon as I returned to the scene. I lost my head, I guess, and threw everything in the book at her. Reckless driving, resisting arrest, interfering with—”

“She gave you an argument?”

“Plenty,” Gallagher said. “I probably can’t make the resisting arrest thing stick, but I was so sore I took her in anyway.”

“And where is she now?”

“She made bail. I held her as long as I could. But she had some money with her and she pleaded not guilty and was held in two hundred dollars. She made it. Got out about half an hour ago and I suppose she’s on her way home now. She’ll probably even beat the rap when she comes up. But it won’t make any difference to me. The captain said—”

“You don’t have to tell me what old Huron said,” Greenbaum interrupted. “Remember—I used to work under him. The tough part of it is, he probably meant every word of it.”

“You can bet he did. I tell you, Greenbaum, I’m licked. This is one time I’m not going to end up on top. My goose is really cooked now—but good.”

“There’s one thing you could do,” Greenbaum said. “Turn up those guys who knocked over the bank."

"You kidding?" Gallagher said, staring at the other man. "Every cop, every dick in New York looking for them and you want me to find them? Great!"

Greenbaum shrugged his heavy shoulders.

"It's a chance in a million," he said. "But you got no option, kid. You have to take chances."

"And where do I start? Huh? Where do I start?"

Greenbaum shook his head.

"I don't know," he said. "I really don't know. Maybe the girl. You sure that girl couldn't have ..."

"I'm telling you, Greenbaum," Gallagher said. "I talked with her. I spent an hour or more with her. I checked her. She's nothing but a dizzy blonde. A school kid. There isn't a chance in a million she could have been mixed up with a bunch of heisters."

"Well, that's what the odds are, kid," Greenbaum said, getting to his feet. "A chance in a million. I got to be getting back. They got all of us working on this baby tonight."

"I know," Gallagher said. "I know. Every damned cop in New York. Everyone but me. The captain told me to drop dead. To disappear. I don't think if I took the mob single-handed, he'd even let me bring them in."

"Well, you can try it, kid," Greenbaum said. "Anyway, seriously, you better go home and get some sleep before you pass out on your feet. Maybe things will look better tomorrow. Maybe ..."

He turned then and left. He knew that nothing would look better in the morning—or any other time.

Gallagher sat there, staring at the untouched coffee. He still held the slip of paper on which he had written the vital statistics concerning the girl whose car had crashed into his own at just the precise moment designed to wreck his career.

THIRTEEN

Clarence read the headline aloud, slowly pronouncing the words. He looked up at the others, over the piles of bills spread out on the tablecloth.

"The lying sons-of-bitches," he said softly, and then tore the newspaper across the center and dropped the pieces to the floor. "Seven hundred and fifty thousand dollars!"

Donovan stared at him coldly.

"The papers aren't the only liars," he said, his voice like a knife. "You were the one who told us there was bound to be at least a half million, maybe a lot more."

"Don't jump Clarence," Mamma said. "The boy did his best. We still have a couple of hundred thousand here. We should be getting to it, starting to divide it."

"It's too late to cry over spilt milk," Barker cut in. "Anyway, two hundred thousand isn't peanuts. It's silly to waste time now. I for one want to be getting out of here. The police know too much."

"They know a lot too much," Donovan said. He turned to Carol, who sat next to Barker. "You should never have crashed that patrol car. That wasn't what you were supposed to do. You were supposed to merely let your car go out of control as you passed him. Just get him out of the car long enough for us to get by if he was in the neighborhood. You weren't supposed to run into him."

Carol glared at him.

"I did what I thought best," she said. "If I had waited for the light, he would have gone on and I couldn't have caught up. The only way to put him out of business was to run into him."

"Sure," Clarence said, his voice sarcastic. "Sure—run into him! And pretty soon someone is going to start putting two and two together and then they'll have a dick coming out here just to check up and—"

"Listen," Mamma said. "Let's all stop the bitching. We got the money, even if it wasn't what we figured. Everyone got away. Carol says they had no suspicion at all. Now let's start dividing it. Once each of us has his split, we can do what we want. Anyone who is worried can take off. So far as I can see, we are in the clear. The cops don't even know what they are looking for. They have the tape recorder and the tape, but they can't trace it. By the time they do, I for one am not going to be any place around New York. What else have they got? A couple of guns? They can't trace them. They don't even know what they are looking for. Or where to look. So let's get on with the business."

Donovan nodded shortly.

"Right," he said. "Let's get on with it. Now here's the way I see it. The original plan was, we were figuring on around six hundred grand. Me and Mamma were to take a hundred thousand apiece off the top. That's about a third. Then the rest splits into six equal parts. Right?" The others nodded in agreement.

"So we end up with about two hundred thousand. Mamma and I take a third of that off the top. Comes to about thirty-three thousand apiece. We split the rest six ways. Any squawks?"

Clarence looked quickly at his mother, and she nodded her head almost imperceptibly.

"How about you, Jo-Jo?" Donovan said.

"Fine with me, boss."

He looked over at Barker.

Bill in turn looked at Carol. Then he turned back to Donovan, doing some fast mental calculating, and slowly shook his head.

"I don't like it," he said.

"You don't like it?"

"No. It means my cut comes to about twenty-three grand. I don't like twenty-three grand out of two hundred thousand. Not when I was figuring on something like seventy-five or eighty."

Donovan stared at him and Jo-Jo moved slightly in his chair. He kept his eyes on Donovan.

"I put up expense money," Donovan said. "Me and Mamma both."

Mamma grunted in agreement.

"Not all of it," Barker said. "Carol and I worked on the two first bank jobs. It comes out we are averaging only about eight grand a job, or maybe less."

Donovan nodded slowly.

"I see," he said. "I see, kid. What would you suggest we do, then?"

Barker thought for a moment before answering.

"Everybody's disappointed," he said. "Everybody gets hurt a little bit. Suppose you and Mamma each take ten off the top for your expense dough. We cut the rest six ways."

Donovan slowly pushed his chair back. His right hand fell into his jacket pocket.

"Bill's right," Carol suddenly spoke up. "He's right. It isn't fair that we should be risking our necks for less than twenty-five thousand dollars."

"Keep quiet, girl," Mamma said. "Keep out of this."

Donovan stared coldly at Barker and spoke in a soft voice.

"Kid," he said. "This is not the time to have an argument. Not at all. Not an argument you can end up losing. I started this thing and I've been running it all along. What I say goes. We do it my way. A third off the top which me and Mamma cut up. The rest divided six ways."

"The boss is right," Jo-Jo said. "That satisfies me."

"You shut up too, Jo-Jo," Donovan said. "Now how about it, Bill? You seem to be outvoted."

For a second Barker stared at him and then he looked slowly over at Jo-Jo. His eyes went to Clarence and then to Mamma. He shrugged.

"O.K.," he said. "Let's get on with it." He looked down at his wrist watch. "It's after ten already. Clarence, you're the banker. Suppose you start dividing it up."

Clarence looked at his mother and then reached forward.

"Sure," he said. "Why sure. I—"

The loud ring of the doorbell stopped him in mid-sentence and his face went pale. Barker shoved his chair back quickly and Jo-Jo opened his mouth to say something.

Donovan, however, was the first to recover. Even as the second ring came, he spoke in a low, harsh voice.

"Keep your goddamned wits," he said. "Stay where you are. It isn't the law. The law don't ring first. They just come right on in. You, Mamma. Go see who it is. Get rid of them."

As Mamma slowly stood up and started for the door leading into the living room, Donovan took the thirty-eight police special out of his pocket.

"The rest of you stay put," he said softly. "Just don't move."

He crept over and stood listening at the crack in the door.

Mamma's voice reached them, and then the deep voice of a man. By straining their ears, they could barely make out the words coming from the other room.

"I am looking for a young woman named Carol Hardin," the stranger's voice said. "Does she live here?"

"She does," Mamma said coldly.

"Well, I'd like to speak to her."

"At this time of night? Say, who are you and what do you want with her?"

"Are you her mother?"

"I am not, if it is any of your business. But Miss Hardin is my ward and I am responsible for her. Just what do you want?"

"I would like to talk to her."

"And who might you be?"

"Well, if you will let me in ..."

"You can tell me from outside," Mamma said.

"I'm from the insurance company," the man said. "Miss Hardin's car was in an accident today and I would like to speak to her—"

"She ain't here," Mamma said.

"Could you tell me when—"

"I said she ain't here. I don't know—"

"Is there some reason you don't *want* me to talk to her?" the man asked. "Maybe ..."

Mamma quickly interrupted him. The light suddenly came on in the living room and Mamma said, "We have nothing to hide, young man. But you can't talk to Miss Hardin. She's gone to bed. She's had a bad day, as I guess you know, and the doctor has ordered her to bed. You can come in and I'll answer any questions that I can. But please make it as short as possible. I was just on my way to bed, myself."

The others heard the front door close. Carol stood up and, walking on tiptoes, crossed the room and looked over Donovan's shoulder. Her face suddenly paled and she poked him in the ribs.

Donovan softly closed the door leading into the living room and turned to her, holding his finger to his lips.

"He's no insurance investigator," Carol said in a whisper. "He's no insurance investigator. That's the cop whose car I ran into!"

Jo-Jo moved quickly, but Donovan waved him back. He again held his fingers to his lips, indicating that the others were to stay frozen where they were. A second later and he had slipped noiselessly out the back kitchen door.

Clarence stood up, his face white.

"I'm getting out of here," he said. "I'm—"

Jo-Jo's thick arm shot out and his hand went over Clarence's mouth as he pulled him half off his feet. He was holding him, a foot off the ground, when the doorbell rang for the second time.

Barker was on his feet now and he had crossed to Carol, taking her by the arm. The four of them held the tableau for a few brief seconds after the second ring of the doorbell and then there was the sound of the door being opened. A moment later a sharp cry came from the other room and then the sound of a dull thud as a body hit the floor.

Jo-Jo dropped Clarence to the floor and started for the door. It opened quickly and Donovan came into the room, dragging the slack body of a man.

Mamma followed him in, closing the door swiftly and locking it.

Donovan heaved the figure of Patrolman James Gallagher into a broken Morris chair, then lifted up Gallagher's chin and stared at him wordlessly.

Clarence quickly scrambled to his feet.

"Mamma," he said. "Mamma, come on. Let's get out...."

Donovan turned to him quickly.

"Shut up, you fool," he said. "Shut up."

"Maybe there's more of 'em outside," Jo-Jo said. "You want I should—"

"Be quiet, Jo-Jo," Donovan said. "Keep still, all of you, and keep your heads. This one came alone. He's doing this on his own hook. Don't you understand? If he'd had a partner with him, he'd have sent the partner in to say he was an insurance agent. He wouldn't have taken a chance on being recognized. Yeah, he was on his own. We're safe for the time being, anyway."

"Safe for how long?" Barker suddenly said, bitterly. "Safe till he comes to? Safe until ..."

He stopped speaking as Gallagher suddenly groaned and opened his eyes, staring around for a moment, vacantly. And then his eye lit on the money on the table and he moved quickly forward in the chair.

Jo-Jo reached down and grabbed the back of his coat collar, pulling him down.

Donovan stared at him a moment, the gun still in his hand.

"Yeah, copper," he said. "Yeah, the bank dough. Isn't that what you came to find? The money from the Needle Trades Bank. Well, there it is. Look at it. It's going to be your last look."

Clarence had scrambled to his feet and as Donovan spoke, Clarence too moved over to the table.

"Watch him, Jo-Jo," Donovan said, indicating the policeman. He laid his revolver on the table and pulled up a chair.

"This means," he began, but his voice suddenly stopped in mid-sentence. He moved, like lightning, but was just a second too late.

Clarence had the gun in his hand and he quickly pressed the trigger.

Patrolman Gallagher jumped as the bullet went into his right upper leg.

"You fool!" Donovan yelled. "You damned fool!"

He knocked the gun from Clarence's hand, at the same time striking him a smashing blow with his other fist. "Are you trying to draw every cop within miles to—"

Mamma had leaped at him, screaming, as he struck Clarence, and Jo-Jo just as quickly grabbed her, pulling her away.

In the sudden melee, Carol moved over beside the semiconscious policeman in the chair. Her hand slipped under his jacket and she found the revolver in the shoulder holster. Quickly, she stepped back, holding it behind her. In the next few seconds, as Donovan tried to make himself heard, she found Bill Barker and slid the gun into his hand.

Mamma, held tightly by Jo-Jo, was still.

Donovan spoke. "You are all making damned fools of yourselves," he said. "This is no time to blow up. We've got to think. I just hope no one heard that shot. If they did, we have damned little time. We have to move fast, and we can't leave him behind.

"Now listen," Donovan said. "Jo-Jo and I are taking off. We are taking half of the money. Like it or not, that's the way it is going to be. Half of the money. The rest of you can do what you want with what's left. But before we go…"

He stopped and looked at Jo-Jo.

Jo-Jo released his hold on Mamma and slowly reached into his pocket. He was holding a switch-blade knife in his hand when he drew it out.

Carol stared at him with wide, frightened eyes.

"Oh, God," she said. "Oh, God, no. You can't. You can't just kill him in cold blood."

"He's probably dying anyway," Clarence said, and laughed.

"Of course you have to kill him," Mamma said. "Go ahead, Jo-Jo. Go ahead. Now!"

Jo-Jo took a step forward.

Barker turned and looked at Carol and for a moment their eyes held.

Jo-Jo took another step and lifted the hand holding the knife.

Barker moved then, moved like lightning. He raised the gun with one hand and with the other he shoved Clarence off balance. The gun spoke twice and each heavy lead shot found the center of Jo-Jo's thick neck.

Mamma screamed an obscenity and stooped to where Donovan's revolver still lay on the floor, but Carol moved swiftly to intercept her.

Mamma went to her knees as Carol pushed her and Clarence started across the room, yelling. The third bullet from the gun Barker was holding stopped Clarence dead in his tracks and he slowly crumpled and fell.

Donovan stood dead still, staring at his ex-cellmate. "Me next?" he asked, his voice suddenly very quiet. "Me next, Bill?"

"Yes, Donovan," Barker said. "Yes. You next. If you make a single move. You next."

Mamma had thrown herself on the body of Clarence and was softly moaning.

"Carol," Barker said. "Carol, give the officer the gun. Then go to the telephone. Call the cops. Hurry, baby."

Gallagher weakly raised his hand as Carol crossed over and stood in front of him. She held out Donovan's revolver and he took it, complete consciousness coming back into his face.

Donovan stepped back and Barker spoke again.

"I said don't move. Carol, go ahead. Get on the phone."

"You fools," Donovan said. "You fools—do you realize ..."

"We realize, Donovan," Bill said. "Yes, we realize everything. For the first time."

"You're insane," Donovan said.

"Wrong, Donovan," Barker said. "For the first time in a long while, I'm sane. And Carol is sane. Get on the phone, kid. Call the police. This one here doesn't look in too good shape."

"I was never in better shape in my life," Gallagher said, his voice wavering a little. "Never in better shape in my life. But you better keep that gun in your hand until help comes. I *am* just a little bit tired."

Carol crossed the room and went into the hallway.

A moment later they heard her voice.

"Operator," she said, "operator, get me the police. This is an emergency."

THE END

THE BIG CAPER

- - - - - - -

Lionel White

Chapter One

1.

Kosta arrived on Tuesday.

Frank had already left for the gas station, over in town on Route Number 1, two blocks from where the principal street of Indio Beach intersected the four-lane north-south highway. This main street, Orange Drive, continued on east for another three or three and a half miles, through the better residential section of the town. It then crossed the new, state-financed concrete bridge spanning the river, ultimately terminating in a dead end at the public beach on the Atlantic Ocean.

Kosta came in a taxi, driven by a colored man, at eight-thirty on this Tuesday morning, the last week in January. Kay was alone on the flagged patio, sitting there with her third cup of coffee and her seventh cigarette and postponing what awaited her in the large, rather old-fashioned kitchen.

What waited was the collection of dishes from their breakfast, along with the dishes from the night before, when they had entertained the Loxleys, the young couple that lived a quarter mile down the narrow sand road and ran the laundromat on Coral Street.

The Loxleys, like themselves, were fairly new in town.

In a community such as Indio Beach, population 4,351 in the summer and 9,332 in the winter, there are three distinct and separate groups of people. There are, first of all, the "natives," those that have lived there for a long time. A long time, in Florida, is anywhere from ten years to a generation or so. There are the newcomers, that group which has almost doubled the static population of the town within the boom years since the war. And there are the winter residents and tourists, who come down to spend anywhere from a week to four or five months, and whose money keeps the economy of the town on a very level and very prosperous keel.

It was to the middle group that both the Loxleys and Frank and Kay belonged, and from this same group that they had drawn most of their friends.

According to the instructions that Flood had emphasized, they had circulated with the "natives" as much as possible. They also had hoped to form friendships with some of the winter visitors, particularly the more gregarious ones. But the wealthy Northerners who came down for the season were not exactly hobnobbing with the proprietor of a gas station and his wife, even if the wife was a slender, attractive blonde with nice manners, and the old residents formed a tight little clique of their own and were extremely reserved, if not downright cold.

A taxi pulled up on the hard-packed sand in front of the house and Kosta backed out of the rear compartment, hauling a cheap, imitation leather suitcase after him. He handed the driver a bill and waved the change away and then turned toward the semi-enclosed patio on which Kay sat sipping her coffee.

She knew who he was at once, although she had never laid eyes on him before. Flood had telephoned Sunday night to warn them that he would be arriving on Tuesday.

Kosta was the arsonist.

She observed with an almost aloof curiosity his slow, labored approach up the long path that circled in and out among the worn-out orange trees, the heavy suitcase banging against his short legs and impeding his progress. The house sat well back from the road in the center of what had once been a fairly prosperous citrus grove, but which, through the passage of years, had been allowed to degenerate until the fruit was no longer salable.

It was an old house, for Florida, where any house more than twenty or twenty-five years old is considered a landmark. Built during the boom years in the twenties, it was a large frame and stucco monstrosity showing neo-Moorish influence.

Flood himself had found it. It suited his purposes very well, being at once outside of the town proper and in an isolated section; having as it did more than a dozen rooms; and, possibly most important of all, being available at an extremely reasonable rental.

Kay was standing, holding open the screen door, as Kosta approached. She noticed that the short walk had brought large drops of perspiration to his forehead. He looked, she judged, about forty.

He hesitated as he reached the door, looking up at her. "Flood's girl?" The voice had a high, thin quality, and he spoke barely above a whisper.

Kay nodded and he passed her without another word and stepped onto the patio.

She stepped around him and opened the second screened door, which led into the square, sparsely furnished living room. He followed her, dropping his suitcase the moment he was in the room. He went at once to an oversized rattan chair and slumped into it. He removed his hat, and, taking a handkerchief from his inside breast pocket, carefully wiped his forehead. His breath made an odd, wheezing sound.

"We weren't expecting you until this evening."

He said nothing as he fought to regain his wind.

She was at once aware of his eyes. Unusually large, they were of an odd russet brown and they bulged out from their sockets in a manner that she realized must be the result of a chronic thyroid condition. They were extremely expressive eyes, but at the same time she couldn't guess exactly what it was they expressed. They reminded her somewhat of the eyes of a very sick person or a sick animal. They didn't ask for sympathy, or even understanding. They merely seemed to reflect the inner misery of the person that owned them.

His eyebrows were so white as to be almost invisible, although his untrimmed hair was a deep yellow. There was no sign of a beard under the dead white skin of his face. He was only five feet, five inches tall, nearly two inches shorter than Kay. His obesity made him appear even shorter.

"I took a bus," he said. "Jesus, what a trip!" His voice held a faint trace of a lisp. "He wanted me to fly," he went on, "but the hell with that. I started two days early and took a bus."

She nodded and reached over to an ash tray and crushed out her cigarette.

"No damn sleep," he said. "Not a wink."

Kay looked at him and tried to feel sympathy.

"Your room's made up and ready," she said. "Wouldn't you like to wash up? I'll call Frank and tell him you're here."

He wiped the back of his neck with the handkerchief, which she couldn't help observing was very dirty, and then bunched it up and blew his nose into it loudly.

"Did you have breakfast?" Kay asked.

He looked up at her as though he didn't quite understand her question. Slowly he shook his head.

"Breakfast!" He got to his feet, using both hands—tiny little fat hands, like those of a baby—to pull himself up from the chair. "I could use a drink," he said.

Kay nodded. "Come on out to the kitchen."

He followed her from the living room, through the bare, unused dining room, and down the long hallway to the kitchen, at the rear of the house. There was a long trestle table in the center of the room with a half-dozen armless, straight-backed chairs pulled up around it. He made a wobbling beeline for the nearest chair.

Kay went to the drainboard, which still held the dirty dishes from the previous evening's party. At one end stood half a dozen partly filled bottles of assorted liquors, several empty soda bottles, and an ice bucket in which the cubes had been allowed to melt.

"Any particular drink?" she asked.

"You got gin?"

Kay said that she had and asked him how he wanted it.

"Straight."

She found the half-filled gin bottle, which she had neglected to cap last night after making the Collinses, and poured out a double shot in a Martini glass. She went to the brand-new refrigerator and took out the bottle of spring water and poured a glassful and then put both glasses on the table in front of him.

She couldn't help noticing the odor of stale perspiration that lay about him like a dank miasma.

Back at the drainboard again, she poured herself a Scotch and mixed it with soda. She did it almost automatically, at the same time subconsciously censoring herself for drinking so early in the day. But special occasions called for special measures.

When she turned to lift her glass and drink with him, she saw that he had already swallowed the gin. He didn't touch the water.

"Another, if you please," he said.

She put her own drink down untouched and walked over and took his glass. When she brought it back refilled, she brought the remainder of the bottle of gin with her.

He looked grateful.

He swallowed the second glass of straight liquor without a grimace, and then looked up at Kay.

"You alone?"

She nodded. "I'll go phone Frank that you're here," she said.

He reached for the bottle as she left the room.

The telephone was in what had originally been designed as a sewing room, off the hallway between the dining room and the kitchen. She dialed the number, standing beside the small table on which the instrument rested. She heard the sound of the buzzing as the bell rang at the other end of the line. It would ring three times and then there would be a short interval before it would start ringing again.

She waited several minutes. She wasn't impatient. She knew that Frank could very well be busy, out in front by the pumps, waiting on a customer. Ham wouldn't have arrived yet and Frank would be handling the service station alone.

She waited almost four minutes before he picked up the receiver. "Harper's Service Station!" He spoke in a crisp, businesslike voice. "Frank? Kay. Your uncle has just arrived."

It was a private line, but still she didn't take any unnecessary chances.

They hung up simultaneously, neither having said another word.

2.

Frank Gerald Harper placed the receiver on the hook and was turning away when a bell rang sharply. It was the bell actuated by the rubber hose that ran from the front door of the small office to the curb, giving warning that a car had been driven up to the gas pumps.

It was a blue Cadillac convertible with the top down and there was a large, red-faced man behind the wheel. A girl who could have been his daughter, but looked like something else altogether, sat close at his side, and they were talking quietly to each other.

Frank passed behind the car, absently noticing the New York plates, and approached on the driver's side.

"Fill her up and check the oil." The man didn't bother to look at him and he gave the order in an indifferent, almost insolent voice.

Frank reached for the hose attached to the pump marked "Special," smiling wryly. Six months ago he would have taken exception to being spoken to in that careless, offhand manner. Now he cared only that something like four or five dollars would be rung up on the cash register.

What made it funny was that he was getting a kick out of it—and it didn't mean a thing to him. Not one damned thing.

Almost without thinking about it he lifted the hood, checked the oil—the Caddie didn't need any—then checked the radiator and the water in the battery. He sprayed the windshield and wiped off the collection of dust and dead bugs. The car took fourteen gallons and two tenths, and Frank took the ten-dollar bill from the red-faced man and went in and rang up the sale on the register. He brought back the change and said thanks and stop back soon.

The Caddie pulled out, the back wheels once more ringing the signal bell.

Frank went back into the station. He wasn't thinking about the Caddie or the red-faced man or even the pretty little brunette who had been with him. He was thinking about the telephone call from Kay.

"So he's here," he said in a voice just barely above a whisper. It was a habit he had formed lately, this talking to himself half aloud.

Harper, tall, thin, and in his early thirties, had the broad shoulders, narrow hips, flat stomach, and tanned, healthy complexion of a man who had always kept himself in top physical condition. His hair was a little too dark to be called true blond, and he had large, rectangular blue eyes in a lean, high-cheekboned face. His mouth was possibly a little too generous, but his chin, which needed shaving, was square and firm.

Slouching into the battered, one-armed chair facing the scarred desk, he looked up at the electric clock on the wall. It was just nine o'clock, and, once more speaking in a barely audible whisper, he swore softly.

"That goddamned Ham," he said. "He would be late again today."

The words were hardly out of his mouth, however, when he heard the unmistakable rattle of the old Ford service car as it pulled in beside the gas station and came to a creaking halt. A moment later he heard Ham Johnstone slam the car door. He had the usual apologetic grin on his wide, black face as he rounded the building and entered.

"Mawnin', boss," he said.

Frank stood up. Again he looked at the clock.

"Damn you, Ham," he said, "you're late again."

The colored man kept nodding his head as Frank spoke.

"Save it," he said. "I've gotta run out to the house for a few minutes. Uncle of mine just got in for a visit. You take care of things. There's a couple of tires have to be changed, and watch those pumps. And goddamn it, don't try to use the cash register. I'll leave the change drawer open and you just make change and mark it down."

The colored man kept nodding his head as Frank spoke.

A minute later Frank was outside and hurrying to his parked Chevvie. He was about to open the door when a police car pulled in and stopped just short of the pumps. Frank looked up and smiled.

"Morning, boy."

"Hiya, Waldo," Frank said.

He strolled over and leaned against the door of the tan sedan. There was a large red spotlight on the top of the car, a tall, sturdy radio antenna at the rear, and a chromed siren mounted on the right front fender. Otherwise it was a stock Ford, except for the racks behind the front seat that held the automatic rifle and the tear-gas bombs.

Sergeant Waldo Harrington yawned and stretched. He was alone in the patrol car.

"Goin' be hot," he said.

Frank nodded.

"I'm gettin' off at noon," the Sergeant said. "Thought we might go over to the beach and do a little surf castin'. Hear they're gettin' a few blues."

Frank shook his head. "Like to, fella," he said, "but I can't make it today. My uncle just got in from the North and I have to run out and get him settled."

Harrington stepped on the starter. "Too bad," he said. "Well, some other time." He pulled out of the station, still yawning.

Frank got into the Chevvie. He drove two blocks north and then turned west on Orange Drive. He crossed over the Florida East Coast tracks, continued on another couple of blocks, and found a parking space a few yards from the entrance to the Ranchers and Fruit Growers Trust Company. He cut the engine and climbed out of the car, at the same time reaching into his pocket for some change. He stopped in front of the car and put a couple of pennies into the parking meter. Then he crossed the sidewalk and entered the bank.

The Ranchers and Fruit Growers Trust was the only four-story structure in the town. It stood, an imposing monument to the prosperity of Indio Beach, at the intersection of Orange Drive and Seminole Avenue, in the very heart of the business section. Capitalized at $12,000,000, and a member of the Federal Reserve System, it was as strong as the Rock of Gibraltar. Its reputation and its soundness were beyond question.

On this Tuesday morning, a few minutes after nine, the pseudo-marble lobby, recently redecorated and air-conditioned, was crowded. There was a preponderance of tanned, dungareed ranchers from the Glades, wearing wide-brimmed Western hats. There were half a dozen men whom Frank recognized as orange and grapefruit growers from the eastern end of the county, a few housewives, and perhaps half a dozen sunburned, sport-shirted men with well-developed paunches whom he immediately placed as visitors from the North.

Hal Morgan, the bank's vice-president, was sitting at his desk in the enclosure just beyond the entrance and was talking to a tall, gaunt woman who stared at him with glazed and skeptical eyes. Hal looked up and smiled as Frank passed. Frank nodded and waved.

Frank went to the row of high desks in the center of the lobby and, taking a wallet from his rear right pocket, extracted three checks. He endorsed them on the back and then made out a deposit slip. They were small checks, one for three dollars and fifty cents, one for ten dollars, and one for twelve dollars and thirty cents.

He passed the half-dozen tellers' windows until he came to the last window on the north side of the room. The gold lettering on the sign said, "Miss Simpson."

Miss Simpson was the chief teller. Forty-six years old, thin to the point of emaciation, with a leathery, bony face hiding behind gold-rimmed glasses, Miss Simpson was an exceptionally competent person.

But for the accident of the Second World War, Mary Lou Simpson would probably never have been anything but a stenographer, or possibly a saleslady. But the war came along and the Ranchers and Fruit Growers Trust, like banks all over the country, suddenly became aware of an acute manpower shortage.

Miss Simpson had been hired and from the very first had proved to have an amazing adeptness for the work. Now, after a dozen years, she was an institution within an institution, and there was even talk of putting her on the board of directors someday.

It was only the second time that Frank had approached her window, but she remembered him at once. She greeted him with a thin but friendly smile.

"Mr. Harper," she said. "Nice to see you."

Frank smiled back and pushed the checks and the deposit slip under the grille. He was through in less than a minute and a half and turned to leave the bank.

For three months now, since the first week he had leased the run-down gas station, he had been making it a practice to stop by at the bank at least two or three times each week. He chose a different day of the week each time, a different hour of the day, a different teller's window. By now he knew the routine of the bank as well as was possible for the casual layman to know it.

Leaving through the double glass doors of the bank, which opened and closed through the use of an electric eye, he saw Sam Loxley about to enter.

"Some night!" Sam, a small, wiry, dark man in his late twenties, was smiling broadly.

"Sure was."

"Don't forget," Loxley said, "our house on Friday. And this time we'll really show you how to play canasta."

"Gee, I don't know, Sam," Frank said. "Kay and I may have to call that off. My uncle got into town this morning. Fact, I'm on my way out to the house now. Don't know what it'll do to our plans."

Sam Loxley shrugged. "Hell, boy," he said, "bring 'im along. The more the merrier."

Frank hesitated for a second. "Well," he said, "I don't know. The old boy's been a little under the weather, from what I've heard, and I don't just know …"

Sam stopped smiling and looked serious. "That's too bad," he said. "But we'll hold it open. Anyway, Kay and Alice can get together on it."

He said good-by then and turned to enter the bank. Frank walked over to the curb, opened the car door, and climbed behind the wheel. He had to wait for the stop light, the only one in the center of the town, and then headed west on Orange Drive until he came to the city limits, some thirty-five city blocks out.

He cut over a lateral throughway to the south and drove another mile, then turned west once more and continued for about ten minutes. On this last road he passed few houses and no cars. Once more he turned left. This was a dead-end road, of hard-packed sand, extremely narrow and little used. He drove by several groves without seeing a house, then passed the small, neat, modern one-story bungalow that the Loxleys had recently built.

Alice Loxley was hanging clothes in the yard; Bitty, the three-year-old golden-haired baby, was playing in the basket at her feet. Alice waved.

He waved back and then drove another quarter of a mile and turned into the driveway circling around in back of the rambling old house where he and Kay lived, in complete respectability, as Mr. and Mrs. Frank Gerald Harper.

Kay was standing in the driveway by the back porch.

Her long legs were bare and she wore a pair of pale-blue shorts. She had a halter, also blue, around her high, full breasts. In between, the skin was bright gold, and it had an almost iridescent quality. Her long straw-colored hair was turned under at the ends. The bangs failed to cover her wide forehead completely, and they were ragged, but very attractive.

Her eyes were blue with a strong greenish tinge. Her face was just a trifle too long and thin to be considered beautiful in the classic sense, and possibly her well-formed, full mouth was a bit too large. But she was the picture of health. Even women considered her attractive; men found her completely stunning.

She looked exactly like what everyone that they knew in Indio

Beach believed she was—the young, extremely attractive wife of a nice-looking ex-Marine who was establishing himself in business and was about to settle down and raise a fine, healthy family, which would be an asset to the community.

Kay spoke as Frank braked the car to a stop.

"Well, he's here," she said. "And drunk as a pig."

3.

Kosta stood at the window, his round, fat body naked except for shorts. He was not drunk; he was never drunk. Liquor did many things to him, but the one thing it never did was to interfere with the clarity of his mind.

Kay had directed him to a bedroom on the second floor, and the moment he'd closed the door, he'd stripped off his clothes. He wanted to talk with Frank, but that could wait. Right now his main wish was to lie down and rest. The gin had relaxed him, temporarily relieved that strange tension under which he always moved, especially when he was physically exhausted.

He had gone to the window to pull down the shade so as to darken the room, and that was how he happened to look out and see Kay and Frank walking along the path leading to the garage, sixty or seventy yards to the rear of the house.

Frank had his right arm around her waist in a half-careless, thoroughly familiar manner, and, watching them, Kosta sensed a strong intimacy between the two.

His normally phlegmatic expression suddenly changed and there was a peculiar, almost avid look in the bulging eyes.

"Flood's in for a surprise," he muttered under his breath.

He turned then and left the window, falling on the bed without bothering to remove the spread.

In another moment he was once more in that strange, exciting half-dream world in which he spent the greater part of his life.

4.

Sam Loxley, who had sat in a canvas deck chair and spent most of his time opening cans of cold beer, and Jim Dexter, the local carpenter whom Frank had hired to help him do the work, had got a big kick out of the garage.

"You're like all those crazy Northerners who come down here," Sam had told him. Sam himself had been in Florida a little more than a year. "Just like the rest of 'em. Think you have to build like you do in the North. Hell, you don't need nothin' but a roof."

Jim Dexter was being paid for his work, and so he didn't say much one way or the other, but it was obvious that he thought Frank was wasting his time.

Frank had tried to explain it.

"You see," he'd said, "I'll probably get a little repair work now and then, and hell, the gas station just isn't big enough for it. I figure I can bring a car or two out here and this old barn will be a nice place to work on them in my spare time."

"But why bother to close it in?" Sam asked. "All you gotta do is keep the rain off of 'em."

Frank told him that he'd just feel safer if the cars were locked up when he wasn't around. And so he had gone ahead, following the plans that Flood had given him, and rebuilt the ramshackle barn into a tightly closed garage that would hold three cars and a good-sized workbench. There were double overhead doors and only one small window, high up in the back. Even Jim squawked about that.

"Boy," he said, "you'll roast to death working in here. You gotta have air in this country. Wait till you try and come in here in the summer."

But Frank had gone ahead anyway and let them think he was stupid. Flood wanted the garage in back of the house, and what Flood wanted he was going to get.

Kay and Frank passed the doors of the garage and then circled around the left side of the building. There were two folding lawn chairs and a weather-beaten redwood table under a large rubber tree a few yards from the building, and they sat down there.

"No," Frank was saying, "I've never met him. But I know all about him. He's the best torch in the business. Flood wouldn't have him if he weren't the best."

"But Frank," Kay said, "you should see him. Doesn't look as though he could get out of his own way. And his eyes. He looks insane. There's something sick, unhealthy, about him. He gives me the creeps."

"Look, kid," Frank said, "of course he gives you the creeps. What the hell, the guy's a maniac. If Flood wasn't paying him to do it, he'd do it anyway. That's how he gets his kicks. He likes to see 'em burn."

A shiver went through her and she shook her head. "Well, thank God, he's your problem," she said. "But you better get him sobered up and out of those smelly clothes before you start taking him around town. The way he looks and smells, he could be locked up on general principles."

"Don't worry about him," Frank said. "He'll be all right. I'll let him rest up and take him around this afternoon. It'll have to be this afternoon. Paulmeyer gets in tomorrow and I'll have to drive down to Fort Pierce and see him. I want to take him the plans and go over the details."

"Paulmeyer?" Kay said. "He's the ..."

"He's the dynamiter," Frank said.

Suddenly he turned in his seat so that he was facing her. His face was very sober and there was a petulant expression in his eyes.

"Goddamn it, baby," he said, "I wish you didn't have to go to Palm Beach. I wish you didn't have to see Flood tomorrow."

She reached quickly for his hand and squeezed it. She tried to be easy and casual about it, to keep the undercurrent of worry out of her voice.

"Don't worry about Flood," she said. "I can handle him all right."

"Nobody can handle him," Frank said. "I know. My God, I've been around him enough."

He looked down at the ground between his feet, his eyes half squinted and worry lines around his mouth.

"What I still can't get is his sending you down here with me. He might have figured—"

"Not Flood," she interrupted. "You know how he figures. Nobody would ever have the guts to take anything from him. He's not used to losing."

"I know," he said. "He keeps 'em until he's tired of 'em and then he throws 'em out."

She took her hand away suddenly and her eyes held a hurt, unhappy look.

"We weren't going to talk about it, Frank," she said.

"O.K. O.K., we won't. But I can tell you one thing: The second this job is over and done with, I'm through. Through for good. Then we cut and run."

She looked over at him and again her hand found his.

"That's right, Frank," she said. "We'll both be through. So don't worry about him. It won't be long now. Just until Saturday. Nothing can happen until then. You know Flood. He won't let anything, anything at all, interfere with this one. This is his pet, the big one. The job means more to him than anything else."

He leaned over and kissed her lightly.

"I still wish you didn't have to see him," he said. They stood up then and started back toward the house. They held hands as they walked.

"I'm going up and see Kosta," Frank said as they reached the porch. "Drunk or sober, he's got to get up. I want him out and around the town this afternoon. I want him to go over the maps."

"I've got to get those damned dishes done," Kay said. "Alice is bringing the kids over this afternoon and I promised I'd go to the beach with them."

She pulled him to her suddenly and her arms went around his waist and she lifted her mouth to his kiss.

"Don't ever worry about Flood again," she said.

Chapter Two

1.

Nothing suited him. The warm, indolent climate, the second-floor room in the tourist home that he had rented for a week, the restaurant two blocks away where he had his meals—he hated them all, the same as he had hated the long ride down on the train.

He was an old man, well past seventy, and he was set in his ways. Never married, with any memory of family long faded, with neither friends nor companions, he was a man who had always lived alone and who had become intolerant of change. No human being in the world meant anything to him, and the few persons with whom he was forced to deal in the course of his solitary life he accepted only grudgingly.

The ones whom he would be working with on this job he neither knew nor wanted to know. He had no curiosity about them, no interest in them.

Flood had hired him and Flood was the only one who meant anything at all to him. Flood meant fifteen thousand dollars in cash—the money he was being paid to do what he had to do.

There were only a very few like him left and he knew it. He knew his value. That was one reason he had been able to drive the bargain with Flood when he had been approached. That's why he had told Flood to take his percentage and shove it; that his price was fifteen thousand, paid in advance.

And he had had his way. Flood had been forced to agree.

For Flood he held a certain degree of respect, if not liking. Flood was an expert in his field. Not a specialist, but at least an expert.

This old man with his faded blue eyes, his veined, gnarled hands, his sunken chest, and his gaunt, stooped frame was a specialist. He knew his business backward and forward. He'd started out in Bavaria as an apprentice in a toolmaking shop and he'd been several years learning his trade. What he had learned he'd learned well, and it had always stayed with him.

When he had first come to the United States he had worked in a shipyard, and then later he had worked for a safe and vault firm. That's where he had obtained the second part of his education.

Years later, long after he had finished his first stretch in the penitentiary, he had taken up explosives, and he had mastered the delicate technique of handling them with the same thoroughness that characterized his mastery of his other crafts.

He never forgot anything and he never lost the amazing dexterity that had made him an artist in his field. Not even the last long stretch, the fifteen years in the federal penitentiary, had made him lose it.

He was one of the very last of an old school. In his entire career he had never carried a gun or found the necessity for using one. He didn't understand or approve of the current crop of burglars and hoodlums. He was a criminal and that he freely admitted, but he belonged to a different generation and a different time, an era that no longer existed.

And now he was an old, old man and this would probably be his last job. With what he already had saved and safely invested in government securities, the fifteen thousand dollars would see him through until he died.

When it was over he'd just get on the train and go back up North to the little town where he owned the tiny bungalow, and he'd sit on his porch in the sun and know that he was all through and that there was nothing else left to do but wait for death. No worries, no fear of ending up in the poorhouse.

He had a tremendous pride and he'd always had it. He wanted to be dependent on no man.

His needs were simple: a roof over his head, plenty of the kind of food that he liked to cook for himself, a glass of schnapps now and then for his stomach's sake. And the music.

He'd go down to New York when they had one of the Wagnerian operas or a Beethoven concert. Those he loved. And in between times he had his own Capehart and his fine collection of records. It was his only indulgence, the only thing beyond the bare essentials of existence on which he spent money and on which he squandered the diminishing fund of his desires.

In the meantime, he sat here in this room that he had rented, his feet thrust into a pair of worn bedroom slippers, his old tired body wrapped in a faded dressing gown, and waited.

Flood had said Wednesday, and today was Wednesday. Today the other one would come and give him the information he had to have. He knew no curiosity about the man who was going to meet him; he only hoped that he would be intelligent and able to answer his questions. He hoped that he would have competent floor plans of the building, a layman's knowledge of the vault and its location, and, if possible, its make. Anything else would be fine, but that was all he expected and that was all he would really need. And of course the tools.

Those and the protection that Flood had guaranteed him for the few minutes it would take him to do his work.

He understood the risks. He had been taking risks like this all his life. Sometimes he had won out and sometimes he had lost. When he had lost he had paid for it. Usually it was because of someone else's carelessness. Once it had been just a bad break. That was the time the nitro had been poor and something had gone wrong and he'd had to take a half hour longer than he'd counted on. The patrol car had returned before it was expected and then everything had happened at once.

Old Jonesy, who had worked with him on half a dozen jobs, had been killed in the first blast of gunfire, and he himself had been hit in the leg. He still limped from the wound. That was the job that had drawn him the twenty-year stretch in the federal can; the stretch of which he had done fifteen years before he'd finally got out.

He hoped this one would be different.

One thing had impressed him: Flood himself would be present on this deal. And Flood wasn't one to take any chances at all. Not where his own freedom was concerned.

He lay back in the armchair and his withered hand reached for the pipe on the table at his side. He lighted the dottle that had been left in the bowl from the last time he had smoked it and then coughed an old man's hacking cough.

He hawked and spat, aiming at a wastepaper basket in the corner of the room. And just then he heard the knock on the door.

2.

Kosta didn't get up on Wednesday morning, and Kay and Frank had breakfast together on the patio at seven o'clock.

Both were tired and both looked worried and nervous.

As the time approached, the tension was beginning to tell.

Tuesday afternoon, Frank had driven Kosta around the town. He'd shown him the beach first, feeling that maybe Kosta would like to see it, but then, when the dumpy little man had expressed no interest or curiosity, they'd driven back to the main section of the village.

Frank had shown him the courthouse and the public park where the shuffleboard courts were and the old couples from the tourist camps and trailer courts playing in the sun. Later they had driven out past the school, a large sprawling collection of buildings, five blocks to the west of the business district.

Kosta had expressed keen interest in the school auditorium. It was a large frame structure with a great deal of glass, and it contained an indoor basketball court, an enclosed amphitheatre where the high-school students held their rallies and put on amateur theatricals, and several smaller meeting rooms.

This was the building that Flood had picked out as the principal target.

Later he had driven by the warehouse along the railroad tracks and then circled around past the two-story department store at the east end of the business district. Kosta had looked at the block-square building and shaken his head.

"Never do at all," he said. "Flood should have known. All steel and concrete. It would take forever to get started."

Frank hadn't commented. This was not his part of the business. All he was supposed to do was show the other man around. It was up to Kosta—and Flood himself, of course—to select the spots.

Frank had stopped at the drugstore to get a pack of cigarettes and he'd met Waldo Harrington again, this time in civilian clothes.

"Thought you were going fishing," Frank had said.

Waldo shrugged. "Wife got ahold of me before I could start," he said, smiling. "Wanted me to take her shopping, and so here I am. She figures my day off is her day off."

"With your connections you should get her locked up on your day off," Frank told him, and laughed. He'd brought Harrington over to the car and introduced his companion.

"My uncle," he'd said, not bothering with a name. "Want you to meet Waldo Harrington. He's the guy you'll see behind you in the patrol car if you're going too fast." And again he laughed.

They had shaken hands and Harrington said he was glad to know Frank's uncle.

It was a nice break. He wanted to establish an identity for Kosta, just in case.

Later they had stopped by the gas station and Frank had spent a little time with Ham Johnstone checking up on the day's business. As usual, Ham had tried to operate the cash register, and things were all fouled up. But Frank didn't worry about him. He knew the money end of it would work out all right. Ham was honest.

They'd gone out to the house then and Kosta had spent the night drinking straight gin. He hadn't talked at all, just drunk and stared at Kay until she had at last got up and gone upstairs. Sitting there, with his bulging eyes watching her, had not only made her nervous; she'd felt a sense of nausea.

And now it was Wednesday morning and they were having a hurried breakfast. Frank had already stopped at Kosta's room and told him that they'd both be gone for most of the day.

Without opening his eyes, Kosta had said, "Go ahead. I'm staying in bed. Don't feel good."

And then, as Frank had been about to shut the door, he'd spoken again, lying there half nude and obscene and not opening his eyes.

"Tell the girl to say hello to Flood for me," he said. "Have her tell him that everything is fine. I'll take the city hall and school auditorium."

He'd started to snore by the time Frank had the door closed.

Frank was pouring the coffee. He still had the petulant, worried look that his face had worn yesterday afternoon when he and Kay had talked out in back of the barn.

"Honey," he said, "suppose I were to go on down and see him after I get through with Paulmeyer. I could tell him you're sick or something."

"No," she said. "No, it wouldn't do. You know Flood. He'd know at once that something was wrong. He'd come back with you. We don't want that. It's best if I go. Don't worry about me. I won't be staying. I'm only going to see him for a few minutes. I doubt if I'll even be alone with him. We have to do it this way. It's what he's expecting and there's no point in risking trouble. After all, he can't know anything."

"It isn't that," Frank said. "It isn't that I care if he did know. It's only ... "

She reached over and caressed the side of his face with the soft palm of her hand.

"Baby," she said, "stop worrying. I've told you. He was through with me a long time ago. Everything was over. He was just hanging on, waiting for something else to come along. He doesn't care anymore. Anyway, I can handle him."

"Nobody can handle him when he wants something," Frank said. "You know that. And you know that the minute he sees you it's going to start all over again with him."

"It may start with him," she said, "but it won't start with me. Let me worry about it, honey."

They left the house together just before eight o'clock.

Passing the Loxley house, Kay turned to him and put her hand on his arm.

"How about Friday night?" she asked. "You think we better stop by and call it off?"

Instinctively his left foot went to the clutch, and then he took the pressure off and continued on.

"No," he said. "No, we better go along just as we planned. We don't want to do anything at all out of the way. We said we'd show up for dinner and we better do it. It won't make any difference."

"Yes," she said, "I know. But don't forget. They'll all be here by then."

"Let 'em," Frank said. "Let 'em. We'll still go."

They stopped in town for a minute and Kay left a grocery order at the chain store. She said that they'd be in late in the afternoon to pick it up.

A few minutes later they stopped at the gas station. Ham had already opened up. He smiled widely when he saw Kay, exposing two rows of large white teeth. He thought Kay was a fine woman. Frank was the best boss he'd ever had and he sure hoped that the gas station was going to work out all right and make money. Like most people in Indio Beach, both black and white, Ham knew everyone's business. He knew that Frank Harper had rented the gas station and taken over the franchise some three months back. He even knew that he was paying two hundred dollars a month on the lease.

Ham had worked for the man who had previously leased the station, and more often than not he'd gone home on a Saturday night with either no pay check or at best a partial pay check. The man had been a drunk and didn't much care whether he made a go of it or not.

But this fellow, this Frank from up North, he was different. He was a plugger. Look at the business they were doing already, after just three months.

Frank didn't waste any time. By nine-thirty he was driving south toward Fort Pierce.

Once there, he parked a couple of blocks from the place where he knew that Paulmeyer was staying. He sat for a while behind the wheel without moving while he and Kay had a final cigarette together. At last he opened the door at his side and stepped to the street.

"Take care of yourself, baby," he said. "I'll take the two-thirty Greyhound back and you come on home as soon as you can get away. Tell Flood everything is under control."

She leaned out of the car on her side and kissed him good-by.

"Don't worry about a thing, honey," she said. "Nothing. You know whose girl I am."

Frank turned without a word and stared down the street.

Kay shifted over in the seat and started the engine.

Ten minutes later she had left Fort Pierce behind her and was starting the sixty-odd-mile drive to Palm Beach. Her eyes were very sober and her mouth was set in a hard straight line.

It wasn't going to be easy.

She tried her best not to think about it. Thinking about it only reminded her of those other months and years when she had been in truth Flood's girl.

The very thought of it made her a little sick. God, she wondered how she had ever been able to do it.

She shook her head and again tried not to think about it. She tried to think only of Frank, and the difference these last three months had made in her life.

3.

Frank knocked and waited until he heard the old man's voice. Then he reached for the knob and opened the door and entered the room.

He'd been hearing about Hans Paulmeyer for years. The man was a living legend. But he'd never actually met him before. As he closed the door behind himself and turned and saw him sitting there, hunched down in the chair, a dozen swift thoughts passed through his mind.

Lord, he thought, so this is him. This ancient relic of a man who looks like he should be in an old soldiers' home or in a county poorhouse. This is the man who has stolen more than five million dollars in his day. The biggest and the best of them all. It was almost impossible to believe.

"I'm Frank," he said.

The old man nodded. "Sit down," he said.

Frank pulled up a chair and sat down.

"Can we talk here?" he asked.

"Yes," Paulmeyer said. "We can talk, but keep your voice down. Ain't no one on this floor but me. Nobody else would be crazy enough to live in the goddamned place. Why anyone wants to come down to this Godforsaken country in the first place is more than I'd know, anyway."

He stretched and pulled himself out of the chair and Frank was surprised to observe that in spite of a pronounced stoop, he stood well over six feet.

Walking to the bureau, Paulmeyer pulled open a drawer and took out a pad of paper and a stubby pencil. "Let's go over it," he said, moving back to the chair.

Frank nodded.

It was the strangest sensation, but he felt almost like a schoolboy in front of a stern teacher who was about to give him an oral examination.

"First," the old man said, "the acetylene."

"Got it," Frank said. "Also an electric arc job."

Paulmeyer nodded and made a check mark on the paper.

"Won't need the electric," he said. "Hope I don't need the other. Next, the hand drill."

Frank nodded.

"What kind?"

"Master brand," Frank said.

The old man shook his head.

"Light," he said. "Too light. You should have got a regular professional make. But we'll have to make it do."

"I can borrow a bigger one," Frank said.

Paulmeyer looked at him out of cold, bleak eyes.

"Don't be a fool," he said. "Borrow! Suppose we have to leave it? Never borrow. Where'd you get the one you got—and the other stuff?"

"Miami," Frank said. He wondered why he'd been stupid enough to suggest borrowing a drill. Hell, he knew better without being told. "Bought them at a secondhand tool place in Miami. No chance of their being traced."

The old man stared at him for a second or two and then lowered his eyes to the paper again.

"Drills?"

"A couple of dozen, from a sixteenth to a half. The very best."

Paulmeyer grunted and continued down the list. He mentioned ball-peen hammers, chisels, hack saws, crowbars, and a half-dozen other assorted items, checking them off as Frank told him that he had them ready.

"Not," the old man said, "that I hope I haf to use all this junk. May not use nothing but the soup. But we gotta be prepared. I know how these goddamn tank-town boxes are. Never know for sure what you run into. All right, let's see the floor plan."

"I can explain ..."

"Explain later," he said. "Let's see the plans."

Frank took a folded paper out of his wallet and handed it over. He stood up and stepped to the side of the chair, so that he could see over the other's shoulder.

"It's a little rough," he said. "Had to pace it off a little bit at a time, whenever I got a chance. And there were always ten or twenty people around. I had to be careful."

The old man studied the rough drawing for several minutes without saying anything and then he nodded. He looked up at Frank out of his bleak, faded eyes.

"All right, son," he said. "Now explain it."

Frank reached down as he talked and pointed out various features of the floor plan. He explained about the double plate-glass front doors, the alarm system, the ceiling-high bars three quarters of the way back in the huge lobby that shut off the vault department from the banking floor proper. He had carefully marked in partitions, windows, and every possible detail of the inside of the building.

The architects who had planned the interior would have been surprised how complete and accurate the plan was.

The old man studied it for a long time. At last he grunted once more, coughed, and spat into the corner of the room. He carefully folded the plans and put them into the pocket of his bathrobe.

"Damn good thing," he said, "that Flood's going to knock out the power station. Never could do this job otherwise. My God, the damn place is built like a greenhouse. Any sonofabitch and his brother can stand across the street and see right into the guts of the place."

For a moment Frank was tempted to tell him that at the time the job was pulled there wouldn't be any so-and-so and his brother around to look. Everyone would be too busy in another section of town, watching something a lot more spectacular.

But he said nothing. He didn't know just how much Flood had told the old man about the plans. Flood never took anyone completely into his confidence. When he blueprinted a job, he allocated certain phases to certain people, and half the time one group didn't even know who the others were or what they'd be doing. Flood considered this the safest plan. It had a double advantage. It kept the members of a mob from gossiping among themselves before a job was pulled, and it avoided any chance of jealousies and clashing personalities. And then later, in case someone was picked up, he couldn't spill too much because he didn't know too much.

So Frank said nothing.

He and Kay were the only ones outside of Flood himself who had a pretty fair idea of the whole general setup. Frank had to know. He not only was fingering the job and supplying the hideout, but was also, to a great extent, the coordinator, the contact man.

He had to know a lot of things, but even he didn't know who else would be in on it. There would be Flood himself, of course. And he'd probably want at least two others with him at the bank itself. Then there'd have to be a couple of boys to take the powerhouse out. Somewhere in the background, probably in Miami, would be a lawyer and a bail bondsman waiting for possible trouble.

There might be others.

A job of this size, involving a figure that well might run close to a million dollars, was complicated and tricky. It took real teamwork. It took brains.

Flood had the brains, all right.

Frank spent another half hour with the old man. He told him a little about the town, a lot of incidental information about the bank. He got a street map and explained exactly how far the railway station was from the bank.

Frank knew that old Paulmeyer was planning to take the twelve-fifty train, which came up from Miami and went on through to New York. Whether the job was completed or not, the old man was going to be on that train.

That had been the agreement he had made with Flood and nothing was going to interfere with it.

The old man was pleased that it was only a three-block walk. He was going to get in and out as fast as he could.

"I'm going to be on that platform when she blows," he said. "An' if I time it right, the train will just about be pulling in."

Frank finally got up to leave. Paulmeyer didn't offer to shake hands with him, just nodded. He didn't know whether he'd ever see Frank again and he didn't care.

He was reaching again for his pipe as Frank left the room.

4.

Leaving the rooming house, Frank walked into the main section of town. He made a point of stopping at a wholesale auto-parts place and putting in a small order for a few supplies for the gas station. He wanted to have a legitimate excuse for his visit to the town in case it should ever be questioned later.

The bus wasn't very full and he had no trouble finding a seat. It was only a short ride, less than an hour, but he was dozing as they came into Indio Beach. The bus station was on Route 1, just a little past the Orange Drive intersection and only a few blocks from his gas station. He woke up as they growled to a stop and he knew at once that something was wrong. He sensed it even as he shook himself awake and started for the door.

He was stepping down to the pavement, suddenly conscious that the bus station was virtually deserted, when he happened to look up, over toward the town, and saw the smoke.

There was a colored man in a chef's hat and white apron standing in the doorway of the restaurant that served as the bus depot. He too was looking toward the south, where great billowing masses of black and purple smoke rose up like huge flowers into the blue sky. His thick-lipped mouth was half open and his eyes were big.

Hurrying around in front of the bus, Frank heard the sudden wail of a siren, and he quickly stepped back off the highway as a state police car roared by.

Frank knew that it was a patrol car, probably out of the substation twenty miles north of the town. He began to run south on the highway. As he ran he watched the smoke and saw the sudden yellow flames shoot up out of it some seventy or eighty feet high. A moment later there was the dull roar of an explosion and then nothing else again but the smoke.

It took him less than three minutes to reach the fire. He had known at once what it was that was burning. It was the long line of warehouses just south of the Florida East Coast station.

There must have been more than a thousand persons already gathered there when Frank arrived. He saw that the three local fire engines were on the scene. The two police patrol cars were also there, and officers were trying to keep the crowds back.

The town had a volunteer fire department, with only three hired professionals and the rest of the membership made up of merchants and citizens of the town.

There was a good deal of yelling and confusion and the men on the big pumper were apparently having trouble making a hose connection. Among them Frank saw Sam Loxley, and he remembered that Sam was a volunteer fireman. Loxley had on a white helmet and had stripped to his waist. His thin, wiry body was sooty and dripping with sweat.

At the far edge of the crowd he suddenly spotted Ham. Quickly he went to him. Ham's eyes were wide and he was so excited he could barely talk.

"All of a sudden, boss," he said. "Jus' all of a sudden! One big bang and then she took right off."

He managed to tell Frank that the fire had started less than a half hour ago.

Frank asked him who was taking care of the station and Ham merely shrugged. The fire had his total attention.

"Well, get the hell back there," Frank yelled at him. "Somebody's gotta be there. Go on, now, get back, and I'll be along in a few minutes."

"But, boss," Ham said, "de whole town's heah!"

"Get back, Ham," Frank said. "Hell, one of them sparks lands on us, we'll be on fire too."

Ham nodded then with quick understanding. He hurried away.

The entire east wall of the warehouse suddenly burst into flames and the crowd surged back as it fell. The driver of the hook and ladder quickly climbed behind the wheel to get the truck out of the way, and Frank heard Waldo Harrington yelling for the people to clear the road. A moment later he reached over and tapped Waldo on the shoulder. He asked if there was anything he could do.

The police sergeant turned, his face angry, and then he recognized Frank. He smiled tightly.

"Hell, boy," he said. "Ain't nothin' anyone can do. That damn warehouse was filled with furniture and building material. Tar paper, from the looks of all that smoke. No chance saving it. Only thing the boys can do is try and keep her from spreading."

Frank watched for another ten or fifteen minutes and then turned and walked to the gas station. Ham was standing in the driveway, looking over toward the fire, when Frank arrived. He was still excited.

"Listen," Frank said. "I'm going to take the Ford pickup for a while.

Want to run out to the house. Be back later."

Frank had just remembered something. Something very important.

It took him the better part of a half hour to get through the traffic jam in the town. He was amazed at the number of cars that had suddenly converged on the scene.

Reaching the house, he pulled the car around the drive and parked in front of the garage. He climbed out and started for the back door. Entering the house, he went directly upstairs and to the room in which he had left Kosta.

The room was vacant.

He took his time and made a thorough search of the house and the grounds. There was no sign of the other man.

Frank finally went into the kitchen. He went over to the cupboard, opened it, and took out a bottle of rye. He got a glass from the dish shelf and poured it a third full and then added water. He drank it standing up.

He needed a drink.

There was no doubt in his mind at all. He knew what had happened.

This was it. When Flood found out, he'd kill Kosta. There was no doubt about it, he'd kill him. And he'd blame Frank. Flood always blamed someone.

Frank poured another drink, carrying the glass out to the patio. He didn't know what was going to happen and he wanted to think. He wanted to plan. He got up once, half tempted to go to the phone and call Palm Beach, but then he changed his mind. In the first place, calling Palm Beach would be too damned risky. And in the second place, what could he say?

He knew in his own mind what must have happened, but there was still a lot he didn't know. He still didn't know where Kosta was.

He suddenly realized that he was silently hoping that Kosta was in the center of that warehouse, right at this very moment.

He was out in the kitchen, making himself another drink, when he heard the car pull into the drive and stop. For a second he had an almost irresistible urge to turn and run. But he shrugged his shoulders and, a grim look about his mouth, left the room and walked to the front of the house. He reached the door in time to see Waldo Harrington get out from behind the driver's seat. Waldo saw him and beckoned.

He set the drink down on a table in the patio and opened the door and walked toward the driveway. Waldo was opening the rear door of the patrol car. "Better give me a hand here, boy," he said.

Looking over the police sergeant's shoulder, Frank saw Kosta in the back seat of the car.

The little fat man was sitting straight up in the seat, his bulging eyes wide. His mouth was half opened and his face was a sickly greenish white. He looked as though he were in a trance; there was no movement in his face or body. He was staring straight ahead and it was obvious that he was seeing nothing.

"Found him like this, leaning against a building over in town," Waldo said. "Does he have these seizures often?"

Kosta smelled of stale gin. Frank said something about his having been sick.

"Remember you said he wasn't well," Waldo said. "He shouldn't be wandering around alone." His voice was disapproving.

Together they got him out of the car and carried him into the house. They didn't try to move him upstairs, but laid him out on the couch in the living room. Frank went into the kitchen and got a glass of water and put a little brandy in it. In the meantime the policeman loosened his clothes. When Frank came back, they forced some of the liquid down his throat, and Kosta mumbled something and for a moment seemed to be recovering. But then his head fell back and he breathed heavily. His eyes remained wide open.

"Guess I better call the doc," Waldo said.

Frank shook his head. "No," he said. "No, it isn't necessary. This happens now and then. We had a little party last night and he drank a bit too much. He shouldn't drink at all. And then I guess he went out and started walking around in the hot sun and it hit him. Happens now and then. We know what to do for him."

Waldo stood up. "Must of been quite a party," he said. "My God, I could use a shot myself. First the goddamned fire and then this."

He followed Frank out into the kitchen and they had a drink together.

"Better keep an eye on the old boy," Waldo said as he was leaving. "He's in no shape to be wandering around."

Frank asked him how the fire was coming along.

"About burned out," the Sergeant told him. "I was back in town trying to clear up the traffic mess when I spotted your uncle. Lucky."

Frank thanked him again and in a few minutes Waldo left. Frank went back into the living room. The other man hadn't moved. For several minutes Frank stood there, staring down at him.

"You insane sonofabitch," he said at last in a tight, hard voice. "Flood should have known better. He might have guessed."

He turned and started again for the kitchen.

Thinking of Flood made him think of Kay. Right now he didn't want to think of Kay. He had too much on his mind as it was.

He decided to call the gas station and tell Ham he wouldn't be able to get back.

He didn't dare leave the house alone. Not with Kosta in it.

Chapter Three

1.

U.S. Highway 1 stretches south from Fort Pierce for the better part of a hundred miles before entering the northern suburbs of West Palm Beach. For the most part it is single-laned each way, although it is one of the most heavily traveled arteries in the state, and, in fact, the entire Eastern seaboard. It is an almost straight and, for the most part, flat road; dull, uninteresting, and without character.

The dullness and the scenic monotony of the highway are the cause of innumerable accidents, as drivers frequently find their passage over it so tiring that they tend to doze.

Kay had made the trip three times before, and each time she found it difficult to keep awake. But this time she was wide awake. Kay had plenty on her mind to keep her awake. Kay was thinking of Flood.

She had known Flood for four years; for most of them she had been his mistress.

She had never been in love with him.

Contrary to generally accepted conventions, Kay was neither more nor less moral than thousands of other young women her age. She was, however, a great deal more attractive than most other girls, and circumstances had had a lot to do with the establishing of her destiny.

Her full name was Katherine Jane Garner, and she had been born into a middle-class family in a middle-class sort of town in Ohio. She was an only child, and her father, a linotype operator, had died of lung cancer when Kay was ten years old. He had, thoughtfully, left fifteen thousand dollars in insurance, and that sum, plus what her mother was able to earn as a part-time trained nurse, enabled Kay to obtain the proper high-school education and attend business school for two years. It was during the week that she was to be graduated that her mother was struck by a hit-and-run driver and killed.

Kay stayed on in the Ohio town long enough to see to the funeral, and then, feeling lost and unhappy, she had decided to go to New York.

She hadn't much liked the business school and she had no desire to be a secretary. What she had wanted to do was to become a dramatic actress.

Kay arrived in New York City on her nineteenth birthday, and she took a small apartment in Greenwich Village. She also enrolled in a dramatic school that guaranteed to teach radio and television techniques, as well as stagecraft. It was several months before Kay realized she was learning nothing of value and paying far too much for the experience.

Disillusioned, she concluded that all schools were rackets and decided to seek practical experience. Because of her beautiful figure and her spectacular good looks, she found no difficulty in finding work in a night-club chorus line. The pay was not much, but she still had several thousand dollars left from her mother's estate, and so money wasn't any problem.

In her second year in New York, Kay discovered two things. The first and perhaps most important was that New York was not really much different from any other place, including her small home town in the Midwest.

Most of her friends also came from small towns. Some of them had jobs; some were in New York studying and living on money sent from home.

It is true that she was in theatrical work of a sort, but it was, for the most part, hard, tedious, and uninspiring. She was just as far from being a real actress as she had been when she started out.

It wasn't that she was actually disillusioned; she was merely becoming bored and beginning to wonder where it was going to end. She couldn't see any particular future for herself.

The second discovery was Artie.

Artie Monroe was a couple of years older than Kay and he was a musician. He too was from a small town in the Midwest and he had come to New York to study music. He had ended up at the end of a year playing with a small orchestra in a place on West Fifty-second Street. He had an apartment in the same building in which Kay lived.

Artie was a tall, dark, good-looking boy with a nice face, long eyelashes, and a weak chin.

Kay never analyzed her feelings about Artie. She knew only that she liked him from the very first, that he was kind and attentive, and that he offered companionship. It wasn't until she'd been going with him for about six months that she found out he was also married and the father of a child.

By that time it was too late to do anything about it. She was already pregnant.

They had been planning on getting married, or at least she had, and Kay had taken the few thousand dollars she still had left and put them into a joint bank account with Artie. The day she found out that he was already married, she found out too that Artie had gone to the bank and drawn out every penny from the joint account. She never saw him again.

Kay went to work that night in the spot up on the East Side where she had a walk-on part in the floor show. She was four months pregnant and the shock of having found out about Artie was just too much. She fainted in the dressing room, about ten minutes before she was to go on, and when she failed to come out of it, one of the girls had called a doctor.

That was the night she'd met Flood.

Flood owned the night club, or a big interest in it, and he'd come in with the doctor to find out what was wrong. From the doctor he found out part of it, and from a couple of the other girls he found out the rest.

He'd had her sent home in a cab; later on he'd arranged for the abortion. He saw to it that her salary was continued while she was at home recovering. He even sent her flowers every couple of days.

At first Kay had not known that Flood was a racketeer. She knew nothing about him except that he had been kind to her and helped her when she'd needed kindness and help; that he had taken care of her when she desperately needed someone to take care of her.

She never did go back to the floor show. Within a month she was living with Flood in an East Side apartment.

Actually, it was more her apartment than it was his. He merely paid the bills and spent a day or two a week in the place. He was neither good to her nor bad. They never had made any actual verbal arrangement; the thing had just gradually developed. She had learned very early never to ask him questions, never to make demands.

During the four years in which he had kept her in the apartment and taken care of her, she had never known whether he was married or where he spent his time when he was away from her.

Until some six months ago, she had just drifted. She'd spent her own time, except on those occasions when Flood took her to the track or to night clubs or out dancing, doing almost nothing. She window-shopped, bought clothes now and then. She read a good deal, mostly popular novels and magazines. She went to movies and occasionally to plays. She had few friends, and Flood never brought any of his friends or acquaintances around.

Then, six months ago, Flood had stopped coming to the apartment, though he'd gone on paying the rent and sending her a few extra dollars every week. At the end of about six weeks he had finally come to see her, and he'd laid it down to her without any preliminary sparring.

The time had come when she was going to have to do something for him. The something had been to come to Florida with Frank Harper, ostensibly as his wife, and to set up the background for the bank robbery. She had met Harper only once before and she was under the impression that he worked for Flood.

By this time, of course, she knew that Flood was mixed up in rackets; that he was, in short, a crook.

When he had given her the story, outlining his plans for robbing the bank and explaining the part she was to play in the scheme, she had been as much surprised as she had been shocked. The fact that he was dishonest, that he was a criminal, she had more or less taken for granted. The fact that she herself might ever become involved had never occurred to her.

But Flood had been smart about it. He'd given her no chance to protest.

"I'm broke, see," he said. "Wiped clean. I'm putting every last buck I've got into this one. And you're helping me with it. For four years now you've been living on my dough. It's time you paid back. This is your chance to do it."

Two weeks later she and Frank had left for Florida. They'd come down by bus, because that was the way Flood had it planned. He had everything planned. He even knew about the house that they were to rent; he knew about the gas station that Frank was going to lease. He'd made all the arrangements. He'd given Frank the background and the stories to tell and enough money to set it up.

Flood had talked to her alone the morning she and Frank left. Frank was waiting outside in the taxi.

"Just remember one thing, kid," he'd said. "You're going down there as Frank's wife. In public you're going to act like his wife. Right up to the hilt. But after dark you're going to remember you're my girl. Don't, ever forget it. My girl!"

He hadn't kissed her good-by.

It was a strange thing, but now, just three short months later, as she drove south on Route 1 and thought about it, she found it almost impossible to remember what Flood had really looked like. She couldn't, to save her life, even recall the color of his eyes. The whole thing, that entire four-year interlude, had faded into the background of her mind. It seemed never to have really existed at all.

It was incredible that three months could have made so much difference. It was exactly as though now, for the first time in the twenty-five years of her life, she were really living, were really an actual human being.

As she thought about it, one strange thing suddenly occurred to her. She had never been aware of it during the four years she had lived with Flood, but she must have been frightened to death of him during the entire interlude. For the first time she had the clarity of understanding to realize it. It was as though she had been mesmerized, and the very intensity of her fear had kept her from consciously recognizing it.

2.

Roy Cluney sat on the edge of the day bed and shook a cigarette out of the pack and lifted it to his cupid-bow lips. He was nineteen years old and he had the round, half-formed face of a baby. His large, agate-blue eyes seemed perennially startled; his small ears were set close to his head.

He was dressed in gray slacks, tennis shoes, and a striped polo shirt; he didn't wear socks. His blond hair was carefully combed and parted on the right side of his spherical head. He was watching Wally and Wally's girl, Doll, where they sat across the room having breakfast, which had been sent up from downstairs.

Roy, Wally, and the girl had been in the hotel for two days now and they were thoroughly bored. They wanted to get out, to go down to the beach, or to a bar, or almost anywhere away from the hot, airless hotel room. But they didn't dare leave. Not until they heard from Flood. When he'd call or come, they didn't know. All he had told them was to go to the hotel, check into the rooms that he'd reserved for them, and stay there and wait.

So, on Wednesday forenoon, they were still waiting.

It wasn't so bad for Wally. He had Doll, and Doll was enough to keep anybody from getting bored. If Wally wasn't such a selfish sonofabitch, Doll would have been enough to keep Roy from being bored also. But Doll was strictly Wally's girl, and Wally was going to keep it that way.

Wally was ten years older than Roy, a tall, broad-shouldered, dark-browed man with a surly disposition. He had a short, unfriendly way of speaking, and he had the reputation of being plenty tough.

This last didn't bother Roy at all. Roy, in his own way, was also plenty tough. But he knew that it would never do to mix it with Wally. Not now, certainly. Flood had laid it down for Roy and he knew what he had to do. He wasn't afraid of Wally one bit, but Flood was another matter altogether.

And so he sat there, smoking the cigarette and watching Wally and Doll from across the room.

They had just about finished their late breakfast and Roy was opening a new pack of cigarettes when the phone rang. Wally reached it first.

He said yeah a couple of times and then listened for a while. Finally he said yeah again and hung up. He ignored Doll and turned to Roy.

"The boss," he said. "He's in Miami, tied up. Said he won't be in till late. Said someone's on the way to meet him here; someone from you know where. We're to tell her to hang around until he shows."

"He say who it was?" Roy asked.

"Nah. Just said 'she'."

Roy looked interested.

"It'll be good to see somebody around this dump for a change," he said.

Doll looked over at him, her red mouth petulant.

"Just whattaya mean by that crack?" she asked.

Wally glared at her. "Shut up," he said. He sat down and poured himself a second cup of coffee from the silver serving thermos.

"I mean," Roy said, "that I'm gettin' damned tired of sitting around here doing nothing. Damned tired."

"You'll be doing plenty before long," Wally said.

"Yeah?" Roy looked over at him. "I guess I will. You too. And you'll be doing a little explaining to the boss when he shows."

Wally stared at him. "I don't explain nothin'," he said.

"Oh, yes, you do," Roy said. "You explain why we ain't in this room alone. You know damn well Flood told us to come down here and check in alone. You know he—"

"I know that what I do is none of your business," Wally cut in. "There's no goddamn reason I can't have Doll along with me. What she don't know ain't hurtin' anyone, and Flood knows she's my girl."

"Listen," Doll said, her small pert face angry, "what the hell—"

Wally's right hand went out and he slapped her across the cheek. "Keep out of it," he said.

He turned back to Roy. "Don't you worry about me," he said. "When Flood shows, I'll do my own explaining. In the meantime, me an' Doll are going out for a while. Long as the boss will be late, there's no use the both of us hanging around. You can wait for whoever's coming."

"That's all right with me," Roy said. "It's fine. Go right ahead. But when Flood comes an' he asks me, I'm tellin' him you went, see? I'm tellin' him."

"Tell him any goddamned thing you want," Wally said. "Come on, kid."

He and Doll got up and left the apartment.

Roy was glad to see them go. He was getting damned sick of sitting around with them. Jeez, the way they acted, you'd think they were on a honeymoon. You'd think they were alone in the place.

He got up and crossed the room and looked down at the dirty dishes. He spotted a half of a piece of toast that hadn't been touched and he reached for it. Going back to the couch, he pulled a comic book from his rear pocket and opened it and began to read. His lips moved as he laboriously spelled out the words.

He was still reading when the knock came on the door.

He got up slowly, stuffing the folded book back into his pocket. He crossed the room with all the subtle litheness of a large cat. He stood at one side of the door and carefully reached out and jerked it open.

Kay stood there and looked at him.

He said nothing, just stared at her.

"I'm sorry," she said then. "I was looking for Mr. Flood's room. I guess I've made a mistake." She started to turn away.

Instead of speaking, he half jerked his head back, opening the door wider.

When she still hesitated, he said in a half whisper, "No mistake."

She entered the room and he carefully closed the door behind her. He turned and for another second stared at her and then quickly spoke as Kay herself suddenly blushed and started to open her mouth.

"You're expected," Roy said. "He called from Miami and said he was going to be late; that he got tied up. Said you'd be coming along and to tell you to wait."

Kay nodded and went over to a large overstuffed chair and sat down. Roy went back and sat on the couch. For another three or four minutes neither spoke. And then Roy coughed and stood up.

"Want me to get you a drink?" he asked. "I don't drink myself, but I'll get you a drink if you want."

Kay looked up and half-smiled.

"Yes," she said, "I guess I could use a drink."

3.

At exactly the same moment that Roy Cluney was mixing a Scotch and soda in the hotel apartment in Palm Beach, George Candle was mixing a gin and tonic with a couple of ice cubes in the front room of the efficiency apartment a couple of blocks from the beach at Indio. He was mixing two of them, in fact, one for himself and one for Shorty, who lay sprawled out on the day bed, his hairy body flaming red with sunburn and glistening with lotion. He was stripped down to a pair of gaudy nylon swimming shorts.

Candle was wearing a gray linen suit, a gray shirt, gray socks, and gray suede shoes. A big man, well over six feet two, he was heavy across the chest and had arms and legs that bulged with strength. His face was hard and rugged; he was a man who kept himself in top physical condition. The collar of his shirt was tight and he was sweating.

"Damn fool," he said. "Sittin' out there in that goddamn sun. You might have known."

"Just mix it, chum," Shorty said. "Just mix it and don't talk. You ain't got no idea how I feel."

Candle looked over at him and smiled. He had a pleasant, friendly smile. In spite of the almost meticulous care with which he dressed, there was something open and casual in his manner.

"We were supposed to make like a couple of goddamn tourists," he said, half laughing, "but that didn't mean you had to go out and get yourself broiled, kid."

He finished making the drinks and carried them across the room and handed one to the man on the bed. Shorty pulled himself up, groaning, as he reached for it.

He lifted the glass and they drank together.

"How'd you make out?" Shorty asked.

Before answering, Candle went to the door and closed it. On the way back he snapped on the electric fan, then went to the wide jalousied window and looked out. He came back and pulled a nylon-seated aluminum chair up next to the day bed.

"Well, we'll be earning our dough," he said. "It's both bad and good."

Shorty looked at him, not concealing his curiosity. "Tell me about the bad first," he said.

"Bad this way," Candle said. "They got two men on at night. Shift changes at six o'clock and the night crew stays until two, and then one guy comes on and takes over for the next shift."

"Two men," Shorty said. "Hell, that ain't bad."

"It isn't that that worries me," Candle said. "Just the general setup. You saw where the place is. Over past the tracks, not more than a half mile from the police station. One private road leads into it from a dead-end street. There's the big door in front, one at the side, and one at the back.

"Once we get in, we could have a little trouble getting out. We'll have to leave the car parked outside on the street and walk in. Otherwise we might find ourselves trapped. That's the part I don't like, leaving the car out on the street. Never know who might come along and spot it while we're in the place."

Shorty looked thoughtful. "Only one thing to do," he said at last. "We don't use our car."

"I thought of that," Candle said. "But a hot car could be too risky. They could spot a hot job and be waiting for us." He hesitated a minute or two and then went on. "Only thing I can see to do is run down to the next town, or maybe West Palm or Miami, and rent a job."

Shorty thought about that for a while and again nodded his head. "We ain't got too much time. Saturday isn't very far away."

Candle agreed with him.

"The good thing," he continued, "is the inside layout. It's a cinch. One of the guys is an old duck and he won't be no trouble at all. The other's a kid. He may get a little flighty, but he'll be all right. The main thing is the phones. We got to be sure to keep the old guy in line so he answers and says the right thing. The machinery itself is a cinch. I can fix that in no time at all. It's a big double job, and I can have it out within five minutes after we start to work. They won't be getting juice through for at least twenty-four hours the way I'll fix it."

He got up again, reached for Shorty's empty glass, and went to the kitchenette, where he mixed two more drinks. When he was back in the chair and had handed Shorty his refilled glass, he continued talking.

"Of course," he said, "a hell of a lot of it is going to depend on Flood. He told me that we definitely don't have to worry; that every cop in town will be busy as hell taking care of something a lot more important."

"Didn't tell you what, did he?" Shorty asked.

"No, he didn't. And I didn't ask and I don't want to know. The less we know about what's going to happen Saturday night, the better I like it."

"Yeah," Shorty said. "Yeah—maybe. But I'd feel a little better if—"

"Listen," Candle said. "Don't worry. We're gettin' paid and we're gettin' paid good. Twenty grand and it's already in the bank up North. What we don't know can't hurt us. After all, what we got to do is simple enough. We go in and we put that light plant out of commission. Then we get out and we leave. Either we come back here, if that looks like the best bet, or we take off and blow the town altogether. Either way, all we done is a little sabotage job. We ain't robbed nobody and we ain't killed nobody. We won't have nothing on us—not even the guns—by the time we're through."

"That's the thing that makes me wonder," Shorty said. "Twenty grand is a lot of dough. A hell of a lot of dough. For that kind of money, this caper is going to be awful important to Flood. Whatever it is he's going to do, it must be big."

"I still don't want to know about it," Candle said. "Nothing at all. The only thing we got to worry about is taking care of our end of it. We got to see that those lights go off promptly at eleven o'clock and that they stay out for at least four hours. That's all. Meanwhile, you better get that damn sunburn fixed up. When we do start moving, we're going to have to move plenty fast."

Shorty suddenly slapped at a fly that had landed on his heavy thigh. His big hand came down hard on the raw, sunburned flesh, and he howled. Then he looked over at Candle again.

"You got the route all figured?" he asked.

"I got everything figured," Candle told him. "And tomorrow I think I'm going downstate and pick up that rented car. If it turns out we have to make a fast getaway, I want to be able to use our own car and I don't want it hanging anywhere around that powerhouse on Saturday night."

"I don't want to be hanging around there myself a damn minute longer than I have to," Shorty said with a distorted smile.

Candle took the last drink out of his glass and then put it down on the table at the end of the day bed.

"I got a little news for you," he said softly.

"Yeah?"

"Yeah. Get this. When I stopped over in town early this morning I went into a gas station, an' who the hell you suppose was running the joint and filled up the car for me an' wiped off the windshield?"

"Well, who?" Shorty said. "Who? What is this, a goddamn quiz show?"

Candle smiled slyly. "A guy named Harper," he said. "Frank Harper."

"An' who the hell is Frank Harper?"

"I guess maybe you never knew him," Candle said. "Harper's a young guy who worked for Flood up in New York. He came out of the Marines and he took a job driving for Flood. He wasn't exactly a chauffeur—he was more of a bodyguard."

Shorty whistled softly under his breath.

"You don't say," he said. "You don't say so. Well."

"I guess," Candle said, "we'll be seeing some other old familiar faces around town in the next day or two. I wouldn't be at all surprised. Not at all."

"Look," Shorty said suddenly. "Did this Harper guy spot you? Did he—"

"No," Candle said. "Never gave me a tumble. No reason he should. I never knew him personally; never even met him. But I used to see him around now and then. I knew who he was, all right."

"We'll probably see him again sometime before Saturday night is over," Shorty said.

Chapter Four

1.

Ed Morningside telephoned the Harper residence at six-fifteen.

Frank was sitting in the living room at the time and he'd been on edge for more than an hour, hoping to hear the sound of a car pulling into the driveway. It had been a rough day and he was tired and nervous, and when the bell in the phone box jangled, he jumped up from his chair, startled, and for a moment was unable to associate the sound with the other sound for which he had been anxiously waiting.

In a second, however, he recovered and hurried to the table holding the instrument. There was a sudden relieved expression about his grim, tight mouth.

It was probably because he was so sure it would be Kay that he was abrupt almost to the point of insult when he heard Ed's voice.

"Yes, goddamn it," he said into the mouthpiece, "this is Harper. What do you want?"

"This is Ed," the voice at the other end of the line said. "Ed Morningside, down at the supermarket."

"Sure, sure," Frank said. "How are you, Ed? Sorry I yelled. I was expecting someone else. What's on your mind?"

Ed sort of half laughed and he spoke in the soft Southern drawl that he'd brought along to Florida from Georgia when he'd settled in the town some five years back.

"Well, I tell you, boy," he said. "Your missus stopped by this mawnin' and she left an order and said she'd pick it up sometime this afternoon on her way by, but she hasn't showed up yet and we're closin' shop. Guess maybe she forgot, but anyway, she ordered some hamburger and some milk an' some other stuff an' I just thought maybe she was plannin' on it for supper and so I thought I better call you about it. I can stay on a while if y'all want to stop by an' pick it up."

Frank started to say that he'd be right along. But then he remembered Kosta.

"Why, I tell you, Ed," Frank said, "she had to run down to West Palm Beach and I guess she got tied up. You know how women are when they shop."

Ed said he knew.

Frank went on to say that he'd like to pick up the order but that he had to wait for a phone call. That if it would be all right, he wished Ed would just put the stuff in the refrigerator, and then he or Kay could get it first thing in the morning.

But Ed cut in before he was through. He said that probably Mrs. Harper was counting on the food for supper, and that he'd be only too glad to drop it off on his way home.

Frank started to protest, but either Ed didn't hear him or he didn't want to. Anyway, he said he'd stop by in a half hour and then hung up.

For a moment, as he put the phone back in the cradle, Frank Harper stopped thinking about the thing that had been bothering him for the last two hours: Kay and Flood. Instead he was thinking that it was damned nice of Ed. Hell, back in New York something like this just couldn't happen. You left something in a store up there and the damned clerk would likely enough take it home and eat it himself.

As he turned, his eyes went at once to Kosta.

The bloodshot russet eyes were open and watching him, although the man's pudgy body had not moved since Frank and Waldo had placed him on the couch.

Frank walked over and stared down at him. He sensed that the man was conscious at last and could understand him.

"Get up," he said, his voice harsh and low. "Get up, you crazy bastard, and get up those stairs and into your room. Don't give me any trouble at all. Get into bed and stay there. Hear me? Stay there! One goddamned peep out of you and so help me God ..."

Kosta half rolled off the couch and came to his feet. He weaved slightly, but at last turned and wordlessly shuffled toward the staircase in the hallway.

Frank turned his head and followed him with his eyes. A moment later he heard the door of the room on the second floor slam shut. He turned and went out into the kitchen. Without thinking about it he began to put the partly filled rye and brandy bottles back in the cupboard and the dirty glasses into the sink.

Ed had said half an hour, but Frank knew that as likely as not he would come any time now. He wanted the place to be looking neat when Ed showed up.

He tried not to think again about Kay as he cleaned up and emptied out the ash trays. Thinking about Kay was getting him nowhere. She should have been back long before this. He cursed himself for ever having let her go down to meet Flood. He should have been firm about it. He should have gone himself. At least, he should have gone down with her.

He was still thinking about it when he heard the sound of the car as it pulled up in front of the house.

His ears told him that it wasn't their car. Hell, he could tell the sound of the Chevvie's motor without even trying. He'd done enough work on the old car to recognize its wheeze in his sleep. But in spite of himself, he half ran toward the front door.

It was Ed Morningside in his Ford station wagon. Ed was already walking up the path through the worn-out fruit trees, a large brown paper bag in his arms.

Ed followed Frank out into the kitchen and he allowed that he just would have time for one quick one before he had to be getting on home.

"The old lady'll have my supper waitin'," Ed said, "and she raises all hell when I'm late."

Ed lifted the straight rye and smiled and winked. He drank it, and then Frank poured a second glassful for him.

"So Mrs. Harper went down to West Palm to do a little shoppin'?" he said. "Well, boy, I know how it is. She probably won't be back for hours. Probably buyin' out the goddamn town. Yeah," he said, his face wrinkled with good nature, "probably buyin' out the town. That is, course," he added slyly, "if she hasn't run into one of them rich old city boys from New York and decided that she's just been wastin' all those good looks on an ol' no-good grease monkey like you."

He laughed at his own joke and slapped Frank on the back and then downed his drink.

Frank walked with him to the door. He was trying to grin, to make a joke out of it, too.

"Yeah," Ed said. "Couldn't blame her, a real beauty like Mrs. Harper. Probably got herself a real live one—Caddie roadster, probably a yacht or so. Real live dough."

He was still laughing as he turned and waved before climbing into the station wagon.

Frank turned back and entered the house.

Christ, he thought. Jesus Christ! If Ed only knew. That's just what she had done—got herself a real live one. Caddie, money, and all. Flood. James Xavier Flood. Frank slumped into a wicker chair and his long, narrow eyes stared sightlessly down at the floor between his feet. He was thinking of Flood, of the first time he had ever seen Flood.

It had happened about a year and a half ago, less than two months from the time he had been discharged from the Marines.

The Marines. Well, he had no squawk about the Marines. Korea had been tough, almost unbelievably tough. But he'd joined up because he'd wanted to and because he'd felt in some vague way that it was his duty to do so. Some of the finest guys he'd ever known had been his buddies during those terrible days when he'd fought in the hills and in the valleys of that barren, dismal country.

No, he had no squawk about that, in spite of the fact that he'd ended up with a chunk of a land mine in his left leg.

Flood had come along a couple of months after his discharge, after the series of incidents that had swiftly embittered him and had almost made him despise himself for ever having been in the service in the first place.

It had started right after he'd been released from the hospital and been given his honorable discharge. He'd been taken for better than a thousand dollars by a couple of con men on the train somewhere between Chicago and Detroit.

He'd still been weak and wobbly. Otherwise the liquor wouldn't have hit him the way it had; otherwise he just wouldn't have been such a sucker.

It wasn't exactly that the police had laughed about it. They'd just shrugged and said that there wasn't much they could do. Returning servicemen who carried around a wad of dough and got drunk were constantly being rolled. They didn't have time to baby-sit with every soldier who didn't have enough sense not to get drunk and play cards with strangers.

And then the business in Cleveland when he had gone back to the construction company to see about his old job. It wasn't as though someone else had taken his job. No, it was merely that things were not quite so good at the time and they just didn't have a spot for him.

But big Hal Mefford, his old foreman, had felt sorry about it and had insisted on loaning him a hundred dollars.

So he'd gone to New York, still wearing the uniform, still limping with the pain that had been left over after the wound had healed.

Maybe he had been a fool, maybe he had been weak and disillusioned and sorry for himself. But this time he didn't even look for a job. He just drifted around for a few days and then he ended up that Saturday night in Harlem. He'd picked the girl up in a dance hall. A pretty, slender, olive-skinned girl who had smiled up into his face and caressed his cheek and suggested that he come home with her.

The attack had taken place while they'd been walking down the street, one of those dark side streets somewhere off St. Nicholas Avenue, very late at night.

He knew now that the girl had been a part of it.

There were at least five or six of them. Short, too sharply dressed little men, with felt hats in which they wore feathers. On minute he and the girl had been walking along, his arm around her waist, and then in an instant she had seemed to slip away from him and there were the others.

They came at him wordlessly, seemingly without anger and without any particular feeling. He saw the flash of a knife, felt an arm circle his neck, was conscious of fists beating against his face.

He never could remember whether or not he was conscious of the car that pulled to the curb. Dimly he seemed to recall the other one wading in, his arms flailing. Of course he didn't know anything about the blackjack in the other's hand or the deadly precision with which he used it.

Moments later he was aware of the man leaning over him and pleading with him to get up.

"Quick!" The face was close to his own and he was remotely conscious of the urgency in the voice. "They'll be back, soldier. We only have a second or two. Try and help yourself."

He struggled to get up and he knew that the other's arms were under him and helping him.

And then he was in the car, slouched over in the corner of the front seat, and he knew that the powerful engine had come to life.

Later he'd turned and looked at his companion, at the man who had risked his own life to save him, a complete stranger, from what might have been a fatal mugging.

He had looked over and for the first time had seen the face of James Xavier Flood.

They'd gone to a hotel and a doorman in a braided uniform had helped Flood get him through the lobby and into the elevator. A doctor had come, and although Frank hadn't realized it until much later, the doctor had gone to work on him and patched him up and made him comfortable and only then turned to Flood and taken the ten stitches to sew up the long gash where the knife had cut into his left arm.

Flood listened to his story the next day while they had breakfast from a tray that had been sent up by room service. Frank tried to thank him, but Flood cut him short. Flood was more interested in hearing about Frank than he was in listening to any expression of gratitude. He was interested in knowing how Frank had got himself into the spot in the first place, and in knowing what his plans were now that it was over and done with.

When Frank thought back on it, it didn't seem that he'd really had a lot to do with it. Flood had started taking over at the very moment when he'd been driving by and had seen the attack. He continued to take over.

He'd had him patched up, given him a place in which to rest and recover; and then he'd given him the job.

It was a hard job to define. A sort of combination chauffeur, companion, and secretary. Actually, more of a glorified messenger boy.

Not, certainly, that Frank had minded the office boy part of it. The way he felt about Flood, he'd have done anything for him. He'd have been a hell of a lot more than a mere driver and messenger boy. And he wouldn't have worried whether he got paid for doing it or not.

And that's the way it was until three months ago. Until the day Flood called him in and told him what he wanted him to do; about Florida and the Ranchers and Fruit Growers Trust Company, and Indio Beach, and Kay.

2.

Roy handed her the drink and she noticed that his hand was small and pudgy with very clean, polished nails. It looked like the hand of a child. She looked up into a pair of guileless, large blue eyes.

He was a child, or almost a child. For a brief second she wondered if, after all, she wasn't in the wrong place. What in the world would Flood be doing with this boy who looked as though he still hadn't quite lost his baby fat?

Roy didn't smile back; he just handed her the drink and stared into her face without expression. For a second their eyes met and held, and then Kay quickly looked away. He was no baby.

"I'm Roy," he said, still without expression. He turned then, tossed the comic book into the seat of a chair, and crossed the room. He sat down in a second chair, facing her, and once more his eyes went to her face and stayed there. He watched her, unblinking, as she lifted the drink and sipped it.

In spite of herself, Kay felt the blood creep into her face.

For the next five minutes neither of them spoke a word.

Kay finished the drink and reached over and put the glass down on the end table next to the couch. She leaned back and then at once sat straight again. She was suddenly conscious of the fact that she had been sitting with her long slender legs crossed and that the thin skirt she wore left her knee exposed. It was the sort of position that she had assumed upon a thousand occasions, in front of friends and strangers alike, and it had never before made her feel self-conscious. But suddenly she uncrossed her legs and placed her feet closely side by side, sitting straight on the couch. She looked up again at Roy.

"Did he say how long he'd be?" she asked. "When I might expect him?"

For a minute she didn't think he was even going to bother to answer. He just sat there and stared into her face. At last the cupid-bow lips opened and he spoke. He had a high, thin voice, the voice of an adolescent.

"Naw. Just to wait. You want something or other while you wait?"

"Want something?" She didn't know what he meant.

He shrugged. "Yeah. 'Nother drink—or anything."

"Nothing, thank you," she said.

A half hour went by and neither moved. Kay finally looked down at her watch and saw that it was getting on toward four o'clock. She looked up at Roy, who still sat in the same position, his eyes never having left her face.

"He's sure late," she said, and smiled weakly.

"I don't drink and I don't smoke," Roy said. His face remained without expression. "Don't smoke the weed, I mean," he added. "Don't take no junk at all, and I save my dough. I can get plenty of girls. Any time I want. Plenty."

For a moment she just stared at him. She didn't know whether he expected her to say anything or not. She found herself wishing that Flood would come soon, in spite of her fears and in spite of the way she'd been feeling about him these last few weeks.

"That's nice," she said at last, and at once felt like a complete fool.

For the first time Roy smiled. It was a thin, almost sickly smile that seemed more like some painful contortion of the facial muscles than an actual, smile.

"Sure," he said. "Nice. Mr. Flood trusts me, you know," he added, completely irrelevantly. "He understands me and he trusts me."

"I'm sure he must," Kay said.

Roy got up and turned to the other room.

"Get you another drink," he said. He was mumbling something about girls as he left the room.

He was gone for at least ten minutes, and Kay was feeling uneasy when once more he appeared in the opened doorway between the two rooms.

He had stripped to the waist, exposing a broad, thick, very white, and completely hairless chest. He had taken off his shoes and was in his bare feet.

There was no drink in his hand. Instead, he was whirling, in long slow arcs, a slender, long leather belt, which he held by the buckled end.

For what seemed like hours to Kay, they held the tableau: Roy standing there in the doorway, whirling the belt; she sitting wide-eyed, on the couch.

And then there was the quick tattoo of the triple knock on the door.

"That will be Mr. Flood," Roy said, and suddenly he smiled. Once more he looked like an innocent youngster from some prep school.

3.

He disliked Miami for the same reason that he disliked Hot Springs; for the same reason that he disliked Las Vegas, Los Angeles, Saratoga during the season, Chicago at any time. You never knew for sure who you might run into, but the chances were a little better than even, in any of those towns, that it would be some hoodlum or racket guy. Or perhaps a detective, which could be even worse.

It wasn't that he objected to hoodlums, or, as far as that went, to detectives that worked on the racket squads. It was merely that living the way he did, and doing the sort of things he did, it was a lot healthier to stay clear of them.

He had never been mixed up with the syndicates, with organized crime. He'd never messed around with prostitution or drugs or even professional gambling. In fact, he had been, for the most past, completely legitimate. There had been the night clubs, there'd been the booze, 'way back in the old prohibition days, when he'd still been a kid. And, of course, on very rare and exceptional occasions, there had been a few far more questionable things. But he'd always played it alone; alone as far as the organized underworld was concerned. At times he'd brought in others on jobs, but the others had worked for him, not with him. He always selected them with extreme care.

He went out of his way never to move in on anyone else's territory, and he'd been equally cautious, in selecting those that worked for him, to pick the odd ones, the loners, the eccentrics who, for one reason or another, weren't tied in with the regular mobs.

There had been, of course, disadvantages. When things had gone sour, such as the recent New York operation, and he'd been hard pressed for money, he hadn't been able to call on any of the regular so-called underworld sources. It was during these times that he'd been forced to light out on his own and temporarily forget his preoccupation with being a legitimate businessman, and take an exceptional risk in doing something highly spectacular in order to recoup.

The only possible compensation lay in the fact that he'd never had to depend on the others; and so had been able to keep the big money for himself. Once he'd made a new stake, he was free to return to more legitimate and safer fields of commercial endeavor.

Consequently, when he'd alighted from the United airliner that morning, he had at once checked into a middle-class, rather obscure hotel in Miami, rather than one of the top-flight spots over at the beach. Before checking in, he'd gone to the automobile agency at the airport and, using the false identification papers he carried with him, rented a Cadillac convertible.

His luggage carried the proper initials to fit the identification papers and was as conservative and unostentatious as the well-tailored clothes that he affected. There had been no difficulty about leaving the airport, as none of the several detectives assigned to check incoming travelers had recognized him.

The first telephone call had been to Feeney, the lawyer. He arranged to meet him at the golf course at eleven, and the only thing discussed over the telephone was the fact that they would try to get in eighteen holes.

Although the sole reason for his having come to Miami instead of going directly to Palm Beach was to see Feeney, and leave with him what he had to leave, he still looked forward to the eighteen holes of golf as much as he did to taking care of the far more important thing that had brought him to Miami in the first place.

Clarence Feeney was waiting on the porch of the clubhouse when he arrived. Feeney was a man in his mid-sixties. His hair, which he wore long, in the style of an old-time Southern politician, was patrician white; he was a heavy-set, rather stout man with a very red face, which was completely without lines or wrinkles. He looked exactly like what he was; a very expensive, very respectable attorney who sometimes took on a criminal case, but more often confined his practice to routine corporation and estate matters. He had been, at one time, a state senator; later he had been a municipal court judge. A family man of conservative habits, he was well known throughout Florida and several other Southern states and enjoyed a reputation for, if not outstanding legal brilliance, at least thorough honesty and integrity.

Feeney walked to the three steps leading down to the patio as Flood pulled the car into the driveway in front of the clubhouse, braked it, and handed his keys to an attendant. He reached into the back and took out his golf bag, at the same time smilingly waving a second attendant away. A moment later he was standing in front of Feeney, his right hand outstretched.

"Well, Senator," he said, "nice to see you."

"And you, my boy," Feeney said. "Very nice, very nice indeed. It certainly looks like we have a perfect day in front of us."

It wasn't until the fourth hole that they had a chance to get far enough from the caddies to talk.

"You told me damned little when you called from New York," Feeney said, his rather pompous, heavy voice holding a petulant note.

Flood hesitated and then stopped, taking a package of cigarettes from his pocket and extracting one. They were midway between holes and there was no one in sight.

"Senator," he said, "you really wouldn't want me to tell you anything much, would you?"

Feeney smiled. "Nothing much," he said. "Naturally not, my boy. But still and all, I gather you are here for something besides golf?"

"Right," Flood said. "I'm here to give you something." Reaching into the pocket of his linen jacket, he took out an envelope and handed it to the Senator.

"There are ten one-thousand-dollar bills in this," he said. "Five of them belong to you."

Feeney took the envelope without hesitation and put it unopened in his inside breast pocket. He nodded slowly.

"Should I ask for what? And should I ask about the other five bills?"

Flood smiled thinly and shook his head.

"It will not be necessary to ask, Senator," he said. "If you don't know by next Sunday or Monday, you are merely to keep your five and return the other five to me at your convenience. On the other hand, I feel quite sure that should the other five have to be used for some more important purpose, you will know about it. You will, without doubt, read about it in the papers."

"You plan to be in Florida long?" Feeney asked.

"The five thousand is to guarantee that I am not," Flood said. "That is, of course, unless something should come up to delay my return North this weekend."

"And in case you might not be able to get in touch with me, should something come up to delay that departure, just where ..."

"Somewhere between Palm Beach and Jacksonville on the east coast," Flood said. "I am quite sure, should anything happen, and I am not able to reach you, you will know where to reach me."

Feeney nodded.

"Will there be anyone else who might need help leaving—in case, as you say, anything might happen?"

"No."

They walked on for a few yards without further words and then Flood asked, "And Goldfarb?"

"Simon is fine. Still doing the biggest bail-bond business in town."

"Just thought I'd ask," Flood said.

That was all of it. They finished five more holes and went into the clubhouse and had a light lunch. Feeney insisted on picking up the tab. Flood saw that it was well after one o'clock by the time they were back on the course, and he told Feeney that he had an appointment around three and asked if Feeney thought they'd have time to get in two or three more holes before he'd have to pull out.

Feeney told him they would.

Flood was back at the hotel at exactly three, and that's when he called the apartment in Palm Beach. He made the call from a public phone booth in the lobby. Then he went upstairs, took a quick shower, changed his clothes, and packed a one-suiter. He left his golf bag and the other suitcase in his room, and stopped at the desk in the lobby and explained that he'd be away visiting friends in the Keys for several days and asked that his mail be held, in case any arrived during his absence.

Then he went out, carrying his light suitcase, and got into the rented car.

Driving north, he took the cutoff route to avoid traffic and kept the needle of the speedometer at an even sixty. He didn't want to waste any time; on the other hand, he was taking no chances on getting a speeding ticket.

He wasn't a bit worried about how things had been going at the other end. He had complete confidence in each of the others. In fact, it was their very eccentricities that had been responsible for his having selected each one for his individual part in the over-all scheme.

Flood felt very much like a Broadway producer who starts out with a perfect script and then, luckily, is able to hire the perfect actor for each part in the drama. Only a completely unforeseen accident could possibly mar the perfection of the end result.

4.

With a backward flip of his wrist, Roy Cluney tossed the belt on the bed in the room behind him. He walked to the door and opened it and then stepped back.

Flood entered.

For just the fraction of a second he stood still, a couple of feet inside the doorway. Then he turned and carefully closed the door and snapped the lock. He looked over at Kay and there was no expression at all on his face. But his right eye closed in a slow wink. Then he looked at Roy.

"Where's Wally?"

Roy shrugged.

"There's something I got to tell you, boss," he said. His eyes went to Kay and then back to Flood. It was obvious he didn't want to speak in front of her.

Flood said nothing. He walked across the room and entered the bedroom. A moment later Roy followed him and the door slammed behind them.

Roy stood next to the dresser. He looked nervous. "Jeez, Mr. Flood," Roy said, "I told him not to go out. I told both of them—"

"Both of who?"

"That's what I wanted to tell you about," Roy said. "Wally's got a dame here with him."

For a moment Flood just stared at him.

"Jesus Christ," he said at last. "What dame? Who is she? Where'd he get her? Come on, stupid, talk up."

Roy backed away a little.

"I don't know who she is, Mr. Flood," he said. "Some bum he picked up in New York before we left. She met us at the railroad station. Name's Doll."

"Doll. My God!" Flood looked disgusted. Suddenly he whirled on Roy and his face was white with anger. "You punk," he said. "You dumb punk. Why the hell didn't you get hold of me and tell me about it?"

"You told me not to call you, no matter what," Roy said. "Anyway, you said I was to take my orders from Wally. You—"

"All right. All right," Flood said. "You did right. But who the hell is she? And what has Wally told her?"

"I think they're old friends," Roy said. "Anyway, they sure act like it. My God, he spends about half the time in the saddle."

"The hell with that," Flood said. "Just tell me how much she knows."

"She knows we're down here on some kind of job. Nothing else, or at least I don't think anything else. Just that Wally and I are down here for some sort of caper. That's about all."

"That's plenty. More than plenty. All right, where are they? I told Wally to sit tight; not to go out. So where are they?"

"They went to the beach, I think," Roy said. "Anyway, after you called and said you'd be late, they left. And then this dame came."

Flood looked at him coldly, slowly nodding his head.

"O.K.," he said at last. "All right, Roy. Now let's take up the next thing. What the hell are you doing prancing around with half your clothes off?" I

"I was just getting ready to take a shower," Roy said. He looked at Flood blandly.

Flood sat on the edge of the bed. He didn't look at the boy at all and he spoke in a low, controlled voice. He spoke very slowly and distinctly.

"You have apparently forgotten how I happened to pick you up, Roy," he said. "But I haven't forgotten. No, I haven't forgotten at all. Maybe you were about to take a shower. And then again, maybe you weren't. Maybe you were about to do something else."

He looked up now at Roy, and he picked up the leather belt that Roy had tossed on the bed. He doubled it over and gently slapped his hand with it several times. Then he stood up.

He was facing the window, his back to Roy, and he still spoke in a low, casual voice.

"You want to remember things, Roy," he said. "You want to remember what I told you that other time. Remember that I told you the next time it happened—well, I'd just toss you to the wolves and that would be that."

As he finished speaking, he suddenly wheeled and lashed out, loosing one end of the belt. It caught Roy full across the face, just under the eyes, and it struck with a vicious slap. The blood began to seep from the red welt almost at once.

Roy sat down in a chair and started to cry. It wasn't a loud cry; it was more a low, sick moan.

Flood dropped the strap.

"Now get dressed and go out to a movie and be back here in exactly four hours," he said. "Four, no sooner."

Without another word he walked over to the dresser and picked up the bottle of whisky there and poured something less than an ounce into a glass.

He left the room, walked through the living room, never once looking at Kay, and went to the bathroom. He found a second glass and filled it half full with water.

Once more he returned to the living room, this time sinking into a large upholstered chair directly facing Kay. He lifted the glass with the whisky, looked at her, and smiled slightly.

"Hello, kid," he said.

Chapter Five

1.

He was a stranger. It was as though the four years had never existed; as though these last three months had, by some strange magic, enabled her completely to erase those other months and years.

Looking across the room at him, she saw the familiar lean hardness; the blue-black hair graying at the temples; the almost black eyes, shaded by the heavy brows; the lean, hard-boned face, fine nose, squared chin. For a moment the thought crossed her mind that she hadn't the faintest idea what his age was. He could have been anywhere from thirty-eight to fifty-eight. She couldn't guess.

Four years. Of course she knew him. She couldn't have forgotten. And then a second thought crossed her mind. It was true that she knew every inch of his body, but underneath the surface of that finely kept exterior, beneath the skin and the flesh, he had always been a stranger.

And now, after these last three months, he was a dangerous stranger; a stranger who had it within his power to wreck her and to wreck that which she loved.

He was smiling at her, the casual, indifferent smile that she remembered so well; the smile that wasn't really a smile at all, because it had nothing of laughter or even of humor about it. It went no farther than his thin lips and the perfect even white teeth.

"Glad to see me, kid?" he asked, making it a question that demanded an answer.

"How are you, Flood?" she said. She tried not to be nervous. And even as she asked, it struck her for the first time as being odd that she had always called him Flood. He'd hated to be called by his first name, and he'd told her he never had had a nickname. Somehow, in spite of the intimacy of the years, she had never been able to use any of the more familiar and endearing terms that other women used with their men.

"How are you, and how are things in New York?"

He ended the smile with a short laugh. He nodded slightly toward the closed door behind which Roy was dressing. She knew that he did not want to talk until the boy had left the apartment.

"A drink?" he asked.

She nodded.

He looked for ice and there was none, and so he went to the telephone and asked that some be brought up. He also ordered a couple of bottles of soda and some quinine water. He drank almost nothing himself, possibly one or two ounces of whisky a day at the very most. The rest of the time he drank the quinine water; in a glass with an ice cube, merely to be polite.

The bellboy came with the ice as Roy was leaving. Kay noticed the nasty red welt across his face, but Roy studiously avoided looking at her. He started to say something to Flood, but then, looking into the uncompromising eyes, he merely nodded and left the room.

Flood handed the bellboy two dollar bills, and then they were alone together in the room.

He made her a drink, and as he mixed it she found it impossible to keep her eyes from watching him. Immaculate in his inevitable gray sharkskin suit, spotless white linen shirt, conservatively patterned tie, black silk socks, and polished black oxfords, he was as coolly imperturbable as he always was. Nothing had changed about him; nothing would ever change. And yet he was a stranger.

She felt like a bird under the hypnotic spell of a snake as her eyes followed his quick, light movements.

He handed her the drink.

"You've been happy?"

For a moment she almost lost the thin edge of her control, and she knew that the blood rushed to her neck and face. But at once she realized that the question was probably without meaning, like all of the questions he had ever asked her concerning how she felt, or what she had done, or what she wanted to do. It was merely one of Flood's odd mannerisms, his peculiar habit of selecting words that had a definite personal meaning, but uttering them in a tone that canceled out all emotion and all significance.

He didn't wait for an answer, but went on talking as he poured his quinine water over an ice cube.

"Better tell me what's been happening," he said, "before Wally gets back."

She told him that Frank had contacted Paulmeyer and was giving him the information he would need, and that he had purchased the tools and materials that would be used. She told him about Kosta's arrival and about the garage Frank had built out of the old barn. She told him everything they had done while they had been in Indio Beach setting up the job.

That is, she told him almost everything. About Frank and herself, of course, she said nothing.

He asked a hundred questions. Questions about the town, whom they had become friendly with, whom they knew, about the neighbors, the streets, the weather, even where they stopped and how the gas station was doing. He wanted to know everything.

She sat in the same position on the couch that she had assumed when she first entered the room. Her slender hands played nervously with each other in her lap and her body was still and tense, but her eyes constantly moved, following him as he paced back and forth across the room.

He was never still, never relaxed. A driving nervous force seemed to activate him constantly. He seemed utterly controlled, calm, and poised, but never still; never at peace with himself.

Once, passing in back of her, he dropped his right hand and casually stroked her shoulder. In spite of herself she felt the fine skin go taut under his touch and she knew at once that he reacted to the gesture and understood it.

The next time he stood in front of her and looked at her, she saw the odd, half-quizzical expression in his gray eyes.

He repeated his questions endlessly. He was particularly anxious to know about Frank. Finally, once more standing in front of her and looking down into her face, he said, "Sounds like Frank likes the town. Is *he* happy?"

"Happy?" She didn't understand him.

"Yeah," he said. "Happy. Is Frank happy? He should be, you know. It isn't every young fellow who finds himself a ready-made wife."

She opened her mouth to say something and then quickly found that there was nothing she could say.

She realized suddenly that he was all through asking questions about the job. He'd found out everything he needed and wanted to know about that. Now it was something different; something personal.

"Yes, Frank," he said, once more stepping back a foot or two and beginning again to pace. "He's a good boy. I just wanted to be sure he's happy."

"I guess he's happy enough," she said, and she knew that her voice was no longer natural.

He swung back toward her suddenly. "Stand up," he said.

Slowly she got to her feet, her eyes wide. She tried not to look startled. She knew something was coming, but she didn't know what. For a moment the thought occurred to her that she was experiencing a feeling of guilt. She hated herself for it, but she couldn't control it. She felt as though she had done something wrong; that in some way she had betrayed him. Well, in a way, she supposed that she had.

He wheeled quickly and stood in front of her, close, so that the buttons of his coat brushed the thin fabric of her dress. He made no effort to touch her.

"You haven't kissed me," he said. His voice didn't change. It was a casual remark, seemingly in context with the previous pattern of his conversation. But the words struck her like a slap across the face.

She started to open her lips, to form the words of a reply. But once again she found it impossible to say anything. Once more that strange, unpleasant feeling of guilt overcame her.

He didn't give her a chance.

It wasn't at all like the old familiar gesture to which she had long ago grown accustomed. There was nothing casual about it this time. Quickly one arm reached behind her and he pulled her close to him. At the same moment his other hand went under her chin and tilted up her face. He leaned forward and his mouth was hard and cruel against the softness of her lips.

She couldn't help herself.

She knew that she shouldn't; that it was both foolish and dangerous. She knew that she should give herself to him, answer his passion and desire with a matching enthusiasm, or at least passively submit to him.

But he had never been like this before. He'd never approached her with this almost sadistic fury of feeling. And so, in spite of her intelligence and in spite of realizing the danger, she was unable to help herself and she instinctively struggled to pull her face away.

His hands were tearing at her then and he was pushing her toward the couch. She was able to take her mouth from his for a brief moment, and she looked into his face. She half cried out.

As suddenly as he had reached for her, he released her. He stood back and, suddenly freed of him, she fell back on the couch.

He laughed. The sound was hard and metallic against her ears.

"You hurt me, Flood," she said.

It didn't work.

He took a cigarette from the pack on the mantel and then turned back to her. His face was again perfectly controlled.

"Something has changed," he said. "What is it, kid? Don't tell me you've forgotten me in three months."

"It isn't that, Flood," she said. "I haven't forgotten you. Only—only you surprised me. And you were rough. You hurt me."

"So nothing's changed?" he asked.

She looked up at him and found that she had to drop her eyes. "Nothing's changed," she said, her voice barely audible. "It's just ..."

"O.K.," he said suddenly, the voice now soft. "O.K. Nothing's changed. So go on in the bedroom and get yourself ready."

"But Flood," she said, speaking quickly and knowing that she wasn't fooling him at all, "the others will be back any second now. We don't want to ..."

"Maybe you don't," he said. "I do. You say nothing's changed? All right, kid, let's go inside and prove it. Let's find out."

He smiled at her as he spoke, but the smile was completely without humor. She knew him; knew what he'd do if he was crossed. At the same time she realized instinctively that it wasn't that he really wanted her. He never had cared much about their sexual relationship. But it was his innate cleverness. He knew. There was no doubt that he knew.

It was the one thing she had feared.

She knew what she had to do. She'd have to allay his suspicions, because unless she did, Frank would be the one that would be hurt. Flood wasn't the man ever to let someone else take something away from him.

She knew that she should start at once to make him forget the thing that had begun working in his mind. She would do anything for Frank, anything in the world to keep him safe.

Flood didn't give her a chance.

Reaching down, he pulled her quickly to her feet.

"Nothing's wrong?" he said. "Nothing's changed? All right. Give." Again he pulled her to him and again the cruel hard mouth found her own. She tasted the blood from her bruised lips.

2.

Wally made two mistakes.

He opened the door without knocking. And then he started to laugh.

Flood was standing almost in the center of the room, his broad lean back to the door. Kay was held close in his arms and he had bent her head far back and he was forcing it back even farther as his lips pressed harshly against hers. The window was behind them, so that their blended figures were a dark silhouette against the afternoon sun, and it is doubtful if Wally recognized Flood at all. What he saw was a man kissing a girl, obviously against the girl's will.

It was the sound of Wally's laughter that made Flood realize that the door had opened. He pushed Kay away from him as he swung around.

Doll, seeing the expression on his face, and neither knowing Flood nor understanding the danger, giggled. She was the first to speak.

"Gee, Wally," she said, "you suppose Roy's rentin' the room out for a—"

She didn't get any further.

Wally had recognized Flood. He also recognized and correctly evaluated the expression of pure fury that had torn the suave mask from Flood's face. Without a word he reached out and slapped Doll across the mouth.

"Shut up," he said.

"You louse!" she said, her voice high and breaking with sudden anger at the blow.

Flood moved like some large cat, silent and swift. Doll felt the steel pressure of his hard fingers as they dug into the soft flesh of her upper arm. Her mouth was still half open as Flood propelled her violently across the room. She brushed against Kay as she passed her and then stumbled and fell as she came up against the couch.

Flood slammed the door and swung around to face the room. Wally took a couple of backward steps, staring at him, his eyes wide.

Kay froze into immobility as she watched the scene.

Flood just stood there and stared. He made no movement at all. Doll's childish, spoiled mouth started to open, but then in a moment even she caught the drama of the situation. Her mouth remained half opened and her large blue eyes went wide as she saw Flood's right hand slowly start for his left armpit.

Wally broke the silence.

"No," he said. "No, Mr. Flood. Wait. Let me explain." His low, narrow brow was corrugated and the muscles of his jaw worked nervously as he spoke. The tanned skin of his face was bloodless and his heavy square fingers played hide-and-seek with each other at his sides. He knew the temper of the other man, understood the fine, tenuous thread upon which his nervous system was strung.

Flood continued the movement of his right hand and then a moment later he had taken a white square of handkerchief from his inside breast pocket. Seemingly unconscious of the gesture, he wiped it across his lips.

It was as though the room had been a vacuum and then suddenly someone had opened a window and it had once more filled with air.

Kay turned and went to the couch and sat down beside Doll, and Wally took a long breath that ended in a half sob. Without a change of expression, Flood spoke. His voice was low and expressionless.

"Kay," he said, "stay here and keep an eye on that little tramp." He turned then and started for the bedroom. Wally followed him and a moment later the door closed behind their backs.

Doll took a compact from the leather bag that hung on a strap from her shoulder. She extracted a powder puff, squinted into the tiny mirror lining the cover of the compact, and carefully began to make up her face. She finished with the powder and then went to work with a lipstick, accentuating the cupid bow of her lips. When she was finished, she neatly put the make-up back in the bag and then turned to face Kay.

"My God," she said, "that's the first time I ever saw Wally scared. Scared stiff. Your boy friend is some guy!"

Kay forced a weak smile.

"Yes," she said, "some guy."

3.

Fingers interlaced behind his head, Frank lay on the rattan day bed out on the screened porch. His lean body was stretched out straight and he lay on his back without a pillow. He had stripped to a pair of shorts and nothing covered him, but nevertheless there was a thin layer of sweat on his skin as he lay there. The air was dead still, heavy with moisture. The temperature had barely dropped since the sun had gone down.

He had extinguished the last light in the house shortly after nine o'clock. The porch too was in darkness now. He had been lying there, staring sightlessly at the ceiling, for a long time. He guessed that it must be close to midnight.

A dozen times he had been tempted to get up and look at the clock, but each time he had resisted the temptation. There was no point in finding out how many hours had passed, no point in torturing himself.

He didn't move until he heard the sound of the car approaching far down the narrow dirt road.

Even before the twin headlights slanted into the driveway leading to the house, Frank knew that it was Kay. He had recognized the chronic knock in the car's engine; it was unmistakable.

And yet, despite the fact he had been nervously awaiting her return for hours, he made no attempt to get up as the car pulled in beside the house and he heard the engine die out. It wasn't until the screen door slammed shut and he heard the soft soles of her low shoes as she crossed the porch that he spoke.

"I'm here," he said. His voice was listless.

Kay stopped. She said nothing for a moment. And then she reached over and turned on a shaded floor lamp. He was staring up into her face as she looked down at him.

"You startled me, honey," she said. "What in the world are you doing out here?"

"Too hot to sleep," Frank said. He swung to a sitting position. "You're late. Did everything go all right?" He tried to make it sound casual and disinterested. He took his eyes away from her face as she started to answer.

"For me, yes," Kay said. "But there was a little trouble. I'll tell you about it."

Frank got all the way to his feet. He still avoided looking at her.

"You sit down, baby," he said. "It must have been a hot, tiring drive. Take it easy for a few minutes and I'll go in and get us each a drink. I had a little trouble up here, too."

"Trouble, Frank?" Kay couldn't keep the worry out of her voice.

"Nothing too bad," Frank said, moving toward the door. "Nothing to worry about. I'll get the drinks and then we'll talk."

"Make mine a Coke, or something soft," Kay said. "I've had my quota for one day."

"So've I," Frank said. "But I think I'm going to have another anyway. You better have one too." He didn't wait for her answer.

Kay had kicked off her shoes and was lying back on the day bed when he returned. He'd taken time to slip into a pair of slacks and a sport shirt. He handed her a Scotch and soda.

"Tell me what happened," he said. He sat beside her, not touching her, but staring at the floor between his feet.

Kay gave it to him in short sentences. She told him about everything, everything except about Flood's attempt to make love to her. Frank waited until she was through before he spoke. He sensed that she had glossed over something, and he thought he knew what.

"Well, what took you so long?" he asked at last.

"I had to stay with the girl, while Flood was in with Wally. He was there for a long time. And then later, after Flood had decided that things had gone too far and that it was no longer safe to throw the girl out, there was another long discussion about what to do with her. At first they thought I should bring her back here to stay with us."

"And why didn't you?"

"Flood finally decided against it. Afraid it might look bad, her coming back with me. She's not exactly the type.... "

"He was right," Frank said.

"Anyway," Kay went on, "I think he wanted her where he could keep an eye on her. They'll all be here by tomorrow night, in any case. But anyway, tell me what's been going on here."

"In just a minute, honey. There's something else. How was Flood? I mean about you. Did he ..."

He didn't want to ask her; didn't want to know. But he couldn't help herself. He had to know.

"He was all business," Kay said quickly. "All business. Wally and the girl came in right after he got there. We didn't hardly have a chance to speak before they came in. And then he was so damned mad about the girl that there still wasn't any chance for us to talk to each other alone."

Frank nodded. "And you don't think ..."

Kay reached out and took one of his hands in her own.

"Listen, Frank," she said. "You know Flood. You probably know him even better than I do. I don't know what he thinks. Right now he's completely involved in the job. He isn't thinking of anything else at all. But there's no point in fooling ourselves. He's going to know sooner or later. He's got to know. Even if he doesn't figure it out for himself, he'll still have to know."

"Yeah, he's got to know. As far as I'm concerned, I'd just as soon tell him right off—the second he shows up."

Kay looked at him with sudden alarm.

"No," she said. "No, not when he shows up. You know Flood. He'd go crazy. There's no telling what he'd do. You, know"—she hesitated a moment, looking directly into his face—"if it wasn't for this job, we could just leave now. Take off and get away."

"Are you suggesting that we give up ..."

"No," she said. "No, I guess we're in too deep now for that. The only thing is, I just wish it had never started. I wish we'd never heard of the job in the first place."

Frank smiled at her suddenly.

"If we hadn't heard of the job, we wouldn't have found each other," he said. "Anyway, forget about it for now. I said I'd see this thing through, and I'm going to. No matter what else I may think of Flood,

I promised him I'd see him through on this deal. I owe him that, at least. I owe him a lot more than that. But let's not talk about Flood anymore tonight. I want to tell you what's been going on around here today."

He told her about the fire at the warehouse, about Kosta. He told her about seeing Paulmeyer earlier in the day. It was almost two o'clock before they finally left the porch and went upstairs.

Chapter Six

1.

Sunrise was at exactly five-twenty-six on Thursday morning. It was a large, hot, yellow sun, and even as it slowly hoisted itself over the horizon where the still Atlantic blended into the cloudless sky far to the east, the day began with no promise of release from the heavy sub-tropic heat that lay over Florida.

Old Paulmeyer had been awake for at least three hours before daylight and he welcomed the first dim light of dawn. He pulled himself out of bed and went into the bathroom at the end of the hallway and filled the tub with lukewarm water. He lay quietly in the water until it had become the temperature of the room, and then he scrubbed himself and stepped out of the tub and rubbed his lean old body dry with a rough towel.

After that he shaved, using a straight razor, which he frequently stopped to hone on a double leather strap that he'd anchored to one of the faucets in the sink.

Returning to his room, his gaunt frame encased in the faded bathrobe that he had worn for years now, he meticulously put his shaving things away in a dresser drawer and then began to dress.

He made no compromise with the sultry heat. He started with his usual knit underwear, gartered up heavy wool socks, and then climbed into a blue serge suit and a white shirt. He buttoned the collar and put on a thin black tie. Before getting into his coat, he pulled on the congress shoes that he had worn for years over his bunion-distorted feet.

Carefully brushing the lightweight felt hat that he wore winter and summer, he slanted it across his forehead and then left the room, carefully locking the door behind him.

It was almost seven o'clock when he stopped at the newsstand in the bus depot and bought a Miami morning newspaper. Then he found a restaurant and went in and ordered breakfast.

Although he knew that he would only pick at it, he ordered a breakfast of fruit, cereal, two eggs and bacon, buttered toast, and a pot of coffee. He liked to linger over his meals.

Today he had plenty of time. Time to kill. There was nothing to do now but wait. He had nowhere to go once he left the restaurant, except back to the rooming house. He wanted to postpone that as long as possible.

Had he happened to look up at about the time he was pouring his second cup of black coffee, he would have seen the car waiting at the corner just outside the restaurant window. It was waiting for the traffic light to turn from red to green at the main intersection of the town, where Route 1 passed the restaurant on its way south to Palm Beach and Miami.

But it would have meant nothing to him. He had never met its occupants. He had never met Candle, who was driving, or Shorty, who was sitting next to him.

Shorty sat on the extreme edge of the upholstered seat, careful to keep his heavy shoulders from rubbing against the back. Perspiration rolled down his face and neck and he was extremely uncomfortable.

The light changed and Candle shot the car into gear and eased it forward, at the same time sneaking a glance at his companion.

"Still bothers you, eh, kid?" he said. His voice was sympathetic.

"Not as bad as yesterday," Shorty said. "Jesus, I didn't know the sun got this damned hot. Didn't hardly feel it while I was lying there on the beach."

Candle grunted. He was wheeling along at sixty now, south of town.

"Maybe you should have stayed back at the beach," he said. "Rested up."

"Rested up, hell!" Shorty said. "One more day in that dump and I'd have been ready to flip my lid."

"Look," Candle said. "Millionaires spend thirty-five to fifty bucks a day to stay there."

"Millionaires are nuts," Shorty said. "Otherwise they wouldn't work so damned hard to become millionaires. Anyway, as long as you'd decided to run down and pick up the rented car, I figured I'd come along."

"You must like to suffer," Candle said.

Shorty smiled. "You don't know why I decided to come," he said. He laughed. "While you're out renting the car, I thought you might just as well drop me off at the track."

Candle nodded and his mouth turned up at the corners.

"You think that's news? Hell," he said, "that's why I started early, chum. We'll pick up the car in Palm Beach, leave this one in the parking lot, and then drive down to the track together. We can stop and get the car out of the lot on the way back. You can drive this and I'll take the rented job."

"You suppose the millionaires down here go to the track too?" Shorty asked.

"No. Only the poor guys go to the track. If the millionaires went to the track, they wouldn't be millionaires."

"After this weekend *we'll* be millionaires—at least for a couple of weeks," Shorty said.

"We'll go out to Las Vegas and lose our money honestly then," Candle said. "The hell with the track."

"We'll go back to New York and sink it into a Columbus Avenue barroom," Shorty said. "Like we planned. A Columbus Avenue barroom. I'm getting too old for these kind of jobs."

Candle drove on in silence. He was thinking of the bar and grill that he and Shorty planned to buy when they returned to New York. He certainly hoped there'd be no foul-up on this job. He didn't think there would be. He'd had a pretty good chance to look over the police force at Indio Beach the afternoon before, when he'd been downtown during the fire and they'd all been out. No, he figured everything would go smoothly enough. Flood always had top people working with him. People that didn't make mistakes.

Kosta was running the water in the bathroom and it was the sound of the water that woke Frank Harper just after seven in the morning. He climbed out of bed noiselessly and, pulling on a pair of shorts, left the room and went downstairs. He had finished putting the coffee on and was squeezing orange juice when Kosta entered the kitchen.

Aside from slightly bloodshot eyes, Kosta looked as normal as he ever looked. He had shaved and the razor had nicked his chin, but he'd pasted a piece of adhesive plaster over the cut and it had stopped bleeding.

He still wore the trousers of the suit in which he had arrived, but now he wore a wildly patterned, flowered sports shirt, opened at the throat and with the tails hanging outside of his trousers. His small feet were encased in tennis shoes. There was a trace of color in his pasty, fleshy face, and his hands were steady as he went to the matchbox over the stove, took out an old-fashioned kitchen match, and lighted his cigarette.

He didn't say good morning, gave no sign that he was aware of Frank's presence. He went to the kitchen table, pulled out a chair, and slumped into it, leaning his elbows on the table.

Frank spoke out of the side of his mouth without looking at the other man. "Breakfast?"

Kosta stared up at him. "Like a drink," he said.

For a moment Frank stopped dead still, and then he swung around.

"A drink, huh?" he said. "So you'd like a drink, would you, you slimy, foul sonofabitch?"

Kosta stared at him with neither fear nor surprise. "I'd like a drink."

"What would you do," Frank said, "if I gave you one? Go out and set the whole damned town on fire this time?"

"I don't know what you're talking about," Kosta said. "You must be nuts."

Frank turned away and shrugged. "You're insane," he said. "Insane. Flood should have guessed it." He reached for the gas cock under the percolator and turned it down. "I'll give you one shot with your coffee after you've had breakfast," he said. "And God help you if you go nuts on us again today. God help you. Flood's coming tonight."

2.

It was the sound of the dishes clattering in the kitchen, directly beneath the room in which she slept, that awakened her. For a long time she just lay there, her eyes still closed. She lay on her right side, her long legs slightly bent and one arm thrown out across the white sheet, half caressing the hollow, warm place next to her. She always awakened very slowly, gradually becoming aware of where she was and who she was. It took her a little time to identify the kitchen noises coming from below, but once she did, she quickly opened her eyes, staring at the gray-white wall of the room.

For a moment then, as she realized that Frank was already up and that it must be he downstairs preparing breakfast, she felt a twinge of guilt that she had let him get up first and do the work that was normally hers. Back in New York, in the apartment, she hadn't bothered to cook or prepare food, except for odd snacks and sandwiches, and she had almost forgotten how until she had come down to Florida and Indio Beach. But in these last three months she had once more got into the habit of working in the kitchen. It was a part of the plan, a part of the act they played. She had been told that she must pretend to be the young, happy bride, and the business of buying groceries and preparing meals was a piece of the general pattern.

Quickly she had discovered that it was something that she liked to do. What had started out as a chore had soon become a pleasure and something she looked forward to each day. She wasn't a very good cook because she had never really learned how, but she tried very hard and she had a great deal of enthusiasm.

Frank had been a perfect partner in the game of make-believe domesticity. He himself had almost forgotten what it was like to eat home cooking, to have someone wait on him and try to please him. And so they played the game, and before long it was no longer a game, but had become a part of the fabric of their life together. Before either of them realized it, it was no longer an act. She couldn't have tried harder or been more deadly serious if they had actually been married and starting out in a real home of their own.

So she felt slightly guilty and turned quickly, shaking the long blonde hair out of her eyes, and began to sit up.

It was then that she heard the mumble of voices from the room beneath her, and she at once realized that Kosta must also be in the kitchen. She sank back on the pillow. She couldn't face Kosta just yet, not after what Frank had told her. She didn't think Frank would mind if she waited a while before going downstairs; Frank understood how she felt about the man.

So she lay back on the bed and for a minute or two she closed her eyes, thinking that perhaps she might once more fall asleep. But sleep didn't come.

In trying not to think of Kosta, she found that her mind returned to Flood, who would be arriving that evening.

She shivered. She didn't want to think of Flood, either; she wanted to think only of Frank. But thinking of Frank meant that she had to think of Flood.

It was then, for the first time, that a sudden consciousness of the last four years swept over her, and she became acutely aware of what they had meant to her. And for the first time she sensed a deep, bitter regret for those wasted, pointless, inane years.

Her body trembled and she stifled a sob and turned her head and buried it in the pillow as her shoulders shook. It was as though she had been half dead for the whole four years, and now she was suddenly fully alive, fully aware of everything that had taken place.

She didn't like to think of it; but the years had happened and the things she had done had also happened, and there was no wiping them out. God, she thought, if only they had never been, if only she had never met Flood, never even gone to New York at all. But then, almost at once, she reflected that if she hadn't gone to New York, hadn't met Flood, she would never have found Frank.

She took her face from the pillow and turned on her back and stared up, dry-eyed, at the ceiling.

With the quick, clear logic of a woman who has found love, she at once dismissed the four years and the regrets and the memories, and she began to think of herself and of Frank and of what lay ahead for them. Suddenly, from nowhere, a new idea crossed her mind.

What in the name of God, she thought, are Frank and I doing here? Frank is no criminal, no bank robber. Neither am I. Perhaps we have done some unconventional things, perhaps we have even done things that are not legal. But neither of us is a criminal. How did we ever get into this? I certainly don't care about the money, and I'm sure Frank doesn't, either. All we want is each other. Each other and a chance to start a real life together. To be let alone and allowed to live.

Suddenly she tossed the sheet aside and slid from the bed. She went into the bathroom for a quick shower.

She wanted to get downstairs as soon as she could and talk to Frank. She wanted to tell him about it. She must tell him, now, right away, before it was too late.

The thing was at last clear in her mind.

3.

Roy knew that Wally, lying flat on his back in the twin bed next to the one on which he himself was sprawled, was awake. He had listened as the other man turned and tossed, breathing heavily through his mouth. He had heard him cough and clear his throat. He knew that Wally was awake, but still Roy couldn't help laughing. Just thinking about it made him laugh, and although he made an effort to muffle the sound, he realized that Wally heard him and knew that he was laughing. So what? Let the sonofabitch hear him.

It was certainly funny, although he doubted if Wally appreciated the humor of it. No, Wally wouldn't think it was funny at all. Wally had been so tough, so damned sure of himself.

Well, Mr. Flood had certainly shown him how tough he really was. Roy wished he had been there the afternoon before when Wally and Doll had walked in on Flood. That must have been something. The real action, of course, had been all over by the time Roy had returned to the apartment. From the looks of Wally's face, it must have been good.

Roy chuckled again as he remembered the scene when he had knocked at the door and entered.

Wally—beetle-browed, tough, dangerous—had been sitting over on the couch with his face in his hands and the blood still running from the corner of his mouth. And Doll, who had never given Roy the time of day, had been sitting on the edge of a chair just staring wide-eyed at Flood. Flood, apparently, had just finished telling her off.

Flood had looked up when Roy entered the room and then had sent him down for sandwiches and some soft drinks. Later the four of them had sat around and had a sort of light supper together. Flood hadn't said anything until they were all through. That was when he had handed Wally the news. He had talked just as though the girl hadn't been in the room with them.

"So you got only yourself to blame," Flood had said, staring at Wally. "You did the one thing you knew you shouldn't do. You brought this dizzy broad along with you. She may not be smart, but she knows we're down here for something. She knows too damned much."

Doll had been scared stiff. There was no doubt about that. Doll didn't have many brains or much imagination, but she knew the spot she was in.

She had started to say something, but Flood had merely looked over at her and she shut up quick. Wally hadn't even tried to talk.

Flood said, "If I had a little more time, I'd let Roy here take her out someplace for a date. His kind of date. I might even make you do the job yourself, Wally. But we haven't time and I don't want to take any extra chances at all. So there's only one thing to do. She stays with us until the whole thing is over and done with."

He had hesitated then and Roy could hear Wally draw a long breath of relief. Even the girl had sat back in the seat and started to look a little less frightened. But Flood had continued to speak.

"Afterward," he said, "I don't know just what we'll do with her. It will all depend. In the meantime, she's getting out of here. You and Roy are staying in this place alone, the way we planned it. Tomorrow, late in the afternoon, you're going to check out of here and drive up to Indio Beach. You got the map and the directions. You know where to go. I may not be there when you arrive, but that part doesn't matter. Just don't make any more bad plays; don't get yourselves in any sort of trouble. Don't drink, don't drive too fast. And try to get there without calling attention to yourselves. Above all, remember, if there are any cars around the place, when you get up to Indio, outside of the Chevvie, don't stop. Come back later."

Wally looked over at Doll then.

"Roy and me," he said. "What about ..."

"About her?" Flood said, turning toward Doll. "Don't worry about her. You've already worried too much. From now on, she isn't your problem anymore."

He took his coat from the back of a chair.

"Pack up, sister," he said. "You're coming with me."

Yeah, that had been something. Roy laughed again, a muffled, mean little laugh, as he remembered the expression on Wally's face when Flood and Doll had walked out of the room. Flood hadn't offered to help her with the suitcase and Doll had looked sick with fright as she had passed in front of him while he held the door open.

Wally's voice cut into his thoughts.

"What's so damned funny?" Wally asked. But he didn't sound tough anymore. His voice was a whine as he spoke.

"You are," Roy said, turning over. "You're funny. You and that Doll of yours."

"The hell with her," Wally said. "Who wants her?"

"I don't, that's for sure," Roy said. "But I can't help wondering what the boss is doing with her. I never thought he'd be the kind of guy to take a wet deck from anybody. I never—"

"Don't be a sap," Wally said. "Flood just figured she might be dangerous. The chances are he took her outta here and—"

"Don't you ever think it," Roy said. "Not Flood. If he wanted her bumped, he'd have me do it. Flood isn't the kind to take care of his own dirty work. He'd never soil his lily-white hands."

Wally grunted something and sat up and reached for a cigarette. "Well, the hell with Doll, and Flood, too," he said. "We got a day to kill and we're stuck with each other. So the hell with them. Let's forget it. You feel like sending down for something to eat, or should we go out?"

"Let's get dressed and go out," Roy said. "We can eat and maybe hit a movie."

"Movie my fanny," Wally said. "Where the hell you think you are, New York? The movies in this dump don't open till afternoon. Let's see if we can't find a poolroom, or anyway go over to the beach and get in a swim."

"Make it a poolroom," Roy said. "Breakfast and then a poolroom."

He yawned, stretched, and then slipped out of bed.

"I still wonder what the hell he's doing with her," he said as he started for the bathroom.

4.

It was shortly after nine-thirty on Thursday morning when Mrs. Carrie Emerson Gillette checked Cabin 9 to make sure that Hettie had changed the sheets and towels and swept under the desk. She also carefully inspected the blankets and counted the ash trays, to be certain that the occupants hadn't taken anything when they had checked out an hour earlier.

She smiled grimly as she noticed that one of the hand towels was missing, as well as the light bulb from the lamp over the double bed. She made a mental note to have Hettie replace them, and then closed the door of the cabin behind her and turned toward Cabin 10.

She saw that the black Cadillac convertible was still in the drive beside the cabin. She knew at once, from the number on the Florida plate attached to the rear of the car, that it was a rented car.

She shrugged and started back to the office. She knew what a rented car meant. Probably they'd stay until noon. Mrs. Gillette's tourist court was on the main road just outside of town and she very rarely got anything except overnight transients. People who came down to Florida for several days or a week always went over to the beach, or else they checked into one of the fancier roadside motels, one of those places with swimming pools and restaurants and such.

Well, the day hadn't come yet when she'd put in a swimming pool, thank God. She'd rather put up with the overnighters. After all, she didn't have much trouble getting her share of the business, and she'd be darned if she'd spend a nickel more than she had to. She did wish, though, that people would have the decency to get out early in the morning so she'd have a chance to get the rooms cleaned up and get her work out of the way. It was nothing less than criminal the way people slept half the day away.

Back in the tiny office, she yelled for Hettie, and then, not waiting for an answer, walked behind the desk to check the registration book.

It was just as she thought. A Mr. and Mrs. George Harvey, from

Miami.

Humph. Mr. and Mrs. Harvey. She just bet. Probably some potbellied businessman with a wife and five kids, sneaking out for a night with his secretary. She knew the type. She yelled again for Hettie.

It didn't matter to her, one way or the other. At least there was one thing about the ones that showed up in the rented cars and spent the night with their secretaries or girl friends: They weren't any trouble. They never stole anything and they didn't make a lot of noise. All they wanted was to be left alone.

It was the sound of Mrs. Gillette's shrill voice, calling Hettie, that awakened Flood.

He reached over automatically and picked up his solid-gold wrist watch from the night table. The Venetian blinds were closed but there was enough light seeping through to allow him to read the face. He replaced the watch and started to stretch. His right hand struck the breast of the girl that lay beside him and for the first time he remembered where he was and how he happened to be there.

He twisted his head so that he could see her face. The shoulder-length red hair was disarranged and covered her closed eyes. The carmine-smeared mouth was opened and she was breathing heavily and Flood noticed that she had surprisingly white teeth. But her almost childlike face was streaked and dirty and she hadn't bothered to remove her make-up before going to bed. She lay on her back, her legs stretched wide, and there was a gentle movement of the thin sheet across her nude body as she breathed.

Looking at her, Flood suddenly thought, Jesus, it's fantastic how completely unfastidious a man can become once he finds himself in a double bed. His mouth twisted in self-disgust and he moved to get out from under the sheet.

The movement disturbed her and she grunted in her sleep.

Getting up, Flood went at once to the bathroom and turned on the shower.

He hated the idea of having her on his hands for the rest of the day. Thank God, at least when he had checked in the night before there had been no one around except the colored boy in the office. If there was one thing Flood had never done, it was to allow himself to be seen hanging around with an obvious tramp. And this Doll was just about as obvious as they came.

He wondered why it was that these silly, stupid little pushovers didn't at least learn how to dress, how to do their hair and make up their faces so that they didn't look so exactly like what they were.

In spite of the night he had just spent with her, Flood cursed the girl and the necessity of being seen with her in public. He hated the idea, but he knew there wasn't much he could do about it. He was damned if he was going to let her out of his sight until everything was all over.

Then? Well, then he guessed he'd turn her over to Roy. Get them a couple of tickets on a plane to Cuba or the Virgin Islands or someplace where they wouldn't need passports. He could count on Roy to take care of her. He wouldn't even have to tell Roy what to do.

He smiled as he stepped under the shower. No, he wouldn't have to say a word to Roy. Roy would do it without being told, without even caring whether Flood wanted him to do it or not. Flood only hoped that he might be doubly lucky and that Roy would get himself picked up after he'd done to the girl what Flood knew that he would do.

The chances were that, without Flood around to take care of him and to advise him, Roy would be picked up. With Roy it was just a case of time. Sooner or later, somewhere or other, they'd get him. There would be a girl and Roy, and then they'd have Roy.

Flood hoped that the girl would be Doll.

By the time he was through with his shower and was standing in front of the mirror and shaving, he had stopped thinking of Doll. He was thinking about Kay.

"The little bitch," he said under his breath. "I might have known what would happen."

His thin lips twisted and his eyes half closed as he leaned forward to scrape the blade across his jaw.

She didn't really matter; he was tired of her, anyway. It was only that no one, no one at all, was going to put anything over on him. He could have handed the girl over to Frank and never given it a second thought. But he'd be damned if he'd let them make a sucker of him. Well, once this caper was over, he'd tie up the loose ends. There were several that would need tying up. Roy, Doll, and Wally. Frank and Kay.

The others, old Paulmeyer, Candle, and Shorty, he didn't have to worry about. Or Kosta. Kosta was like Roy; sooner or later he'd take care of himself. It was just a matter of time.

Christ, the people a man had to do business with in order to make a decent living!

5.

By late Thursday afternoon, a sudden high wind had come up from the north, bringing sheets of rain. Storm warnings went out and weather prophets up and down the coast closely watched the barometers, preparing to issue hurricane warnings. It was very late in the season for hurricanes, but one could never tell. The weather in Florida did some funny things. One thing was certain: It was going to be cold—cold for Florida. Already the thermometer had dropped almost a dozen points.

Hal Morgan had spent the morning at his desk in the bank. At noontime he drove out Orange Drive and across the Indian River to the beach and parked his Pontiac sedan in front of the Atlantic Grill, where the Rotary Club met once each week. Hal attended these meetings for two reasons. First, it was good business to mix with the merchants and small businessmen of the town. The second and more important reason was that it gave him a perfect excuse for taking the rest of the afternoon off and getting in nine to eighteen holes of golf.

As Hal explained it to old R. P. Matthews, the president and biggest stockholder in the bank, lunching and then later playing a few holes of golf with the bank's customers put things on a sort of casual, informal basis and tended to make firm friends of old as well as potential clients. Old Matthews had, of course, built the bank up from nothing, without ever having learned to play golf and without as much as ever splitting a ham sandwich with a customer, but he was broad-minded about the thing, and he knew that competent vice-presidents who would work for little more than you'd have to pay a good bricklayer were hard to come by. So he had merely nodded sagely and told Hal that it was all right if he felt it necessary. Take an afternoon off each week, he said, but remember, the important part of the job was behind the desk. That's where the depositors showed up—the ones that gave money to the bank instead of taking it away.

The wind was already blowing at about twenty miles an hour when Hal parked in front of the Atlantic Grill, so he carefully wound up the side windows of his car to keep the sand out before going inside.

He stopped at the bar, said hello to Eddy, the bartender, and pulled up a stool. He was the first one to show up, and Eddy, without asking, mixed him a Martini. Hal always had two Martinis before the Rotary group sat down in the dining room at the rear. He had learned a long time ago that a Martini was the best buy for the money, and as long as he felt it necessary to limit himself to two drinks, he wanted to get a bang out of them if possible.

He was halfway through the first drink when the door opened and Paul Turner, who owned the smaller department store over in town, came in accompanied by Big John Reardon, the local dairyman. Big John clapped Hal on the shoulder with a hand like a small steam shovel, while he nodded to Eddy. Eddy said hello to John and reached for the Scotch bottle. He ignored Turner. Turner didn't drink and he didn't buy.

Eddy liked Big John. The dairyman, who also had an interest in cattle and citrus, was just about the only local businessman who drank Scotch. He was also the only one who ever thought to leave a tip.

Big John was telling them about a football game that he had driven up to Georgia to see over the weekend when Sam Loxley entered. Sam didn't leave tips either, but he never ordered a drink without offering to buy someone else one, and he always asked Eddy to have one too. Eddy didn't drink, but each time he'd religiously take a cigar and put it into his inside breast coat pocket.

Sam was talking about the previous day's fire when Eddy got around to serving Hal Morgan his second Martini.

"Damnedest thing," Sam was saying, "but I was talking with Waldo a few minutes ago. Said that the railroad people were around and they suspected arson. Said they figured someone must have set the blaze."

Morgan looked over at him, startled. "Set it? Who the hell would have set it?"

"How do I know?" Sam said. "I'm just telling you what Waldo told me."

"Doubt it," Big John said in his slow Texan drawl. "Doubt it, boy. No insurance angle."

"That's what I told Waldo," Sam said. "No insurance, so why the hell would anybody want to set a warehouse on fire? A railroad warehouse. Only stuff in it was some furniture and building materials that hadn't been delivered yet. Railroad would be responsible for all of that."

Eddy was shaking a cocktail and he looked up. "Could be one of those fire bugs—you know, whatever they call 'em."

"Pyromaniacs," Morgan said. "But we don't have that kind of people in Indio. Hell, we got the tourists and God knows they're crazy enough, but we don't get criminals or maniacs. Not in this town, we don't. This isn't Miami."

Big John laughed and told Eddy to pour another round.

"All tourists are crazy," he said. "For my dough, boy, they could be maniacs and criminals, too. We just been lucky so far. Only drunks and a few queers an' a coupla crazy artists and writers, but you never know, boy, you never know."

"Not in this town," Morgan said. "Not in Indio Beach. Why, we haven't had a major crime here in twenty years. Outside of a couple of stabbings over in Black Town, of course."

Chapter Seven

1.

Had it not been for the fact that a certain Millie Hartman, a hairdresser who worked without enthusiasm and certainly without ambition for the Bijou Coiffeurs of Indio Beach, was thinking of her boy friend, a married women's-wear salesman working out of Jacksonville, rather than of her profession late on that Thursday afternoon, Roy and Wally probably never would have encountered two other men whose destiny was closely related to their own.

Alice Loxley visited the beauty parlor once each month to have her hair done. On this particular Thursday, her regular day, she had been forced to miss her appointment, as she had been unable to get her steady baby-sitter. And so she had arrived at the beauty salon at ten minutes to five, just as Millie was about to quit her job for the day.

A smile and the expectation of a good-sized tip had combined to persuade Millie to stay on and take care of Mrs. Loxley's corn-silk tresses. The only trouble was that Millie's mind was more on her gentleman friend than it was on perfecting Alice Loxley's already almost perfect beauty. As a result, Millie picked up the wrong bottle from among the numerous lotions on the glass shelf that held her aids to charm, and instead of establishing a soft sheen in Mrs. Loxley's fine head of hair, ended up by leaving a long blueish-black streak over that lady's left temple.

Mrs. Loxley finished with the hairdresser, not realizing what had happened to her, left the expected tip, and returned home.

It wasn't until an hour and a half later, when she was preparing dinner for Sam, at the same time feeding three-year-old Bitty and six-year-old Sammy, that she became aware of the damage. Sam arrived home hungry, as usual, and reached for her to give her the nightly kiss and hug. He got the hug in and was starting to work on the kiss when he suddenly released her and stepped back, his eyes wide.

"My Gawdamighty," he said. "What the hell have you done to your hair?"

Alice stared at him for a minute and then went to the mirror in the bedroom off the kitchen. She was gone some time and when she returned she was almost in tears. She wasn't quite sure just what had happened, but she was pretty sure Millie probably had something to do with it. She tried to get the beauty shop on the phone, but it was closed.

She turned to Sam. "That girl!" she said. "She must have put something on it."

"Well, hon," Sam said, "don't let it worry you. A lot of women with dark hair fake in white or gray streaks."

Alice wasn't amused. She said that as soon as supper was over, she'd run down the road to the Harpers'. Maybe Kay would have something to take the streak of color out.

"You do that, sweetie," Sam said, and finished the kiss he had started before.

2.

Kosta was back upstairs in the bedroom, lying with all his clothes on, covered to the chin by a thin blanket and staring sightlessly at the ceiling. Frank and Kay had just finished dinner and were having a cup of iced coffee before getting up from the table. They had eaten alone. Kosta had refused to join them when Frank had refused him a drink before dinner.

Frank was the first to hear the car pulling into the driveway and he was out of his chair and halfway to the window by the time Kay got up. Kay was pale and nervous and she almost spilled her coffee in leaving the table. She knew that Flood and the others were due at any time, but she prayed that they hadn't come yet.

The sense of relief as she recognized the Loxleys' old station wagon was immense.

The minute Alice Loxley opened the screen door of the back porch and entered the kitchen, Frank knew that he would have to get rid of her as quickly as possible. The one thing that Flood had insisted on was that the coast be clear when he and the others arrived.

Frank knew what he had to do, and yet, for some perverse reason that he was unable to figure out, he heard himself welcoming the girl and then telling her to sit down while he made her a drink.

"It's too soon after dinner for a drink," Alice Loxley said, "but I'll take one anyway. The shape I'm in, I need one," And then, before anyone could say anything else, she turned to Kay and started telling her about the hairdresser.

Kay looked nervously across at Frank, but Frank only winked. He walked over to the cabinet above the sink, opened it, and took out a bottle of gin. He knew that Alice liked gin and Coke.

"The hell with the iced coffee," he said over his shoulder to Kay. "This calls for stronger medicine. We'll join Alice in one of those cracker cocktails she and Sam like."

"But shouldn't we be getting dressed and ready?" Kay said. Alice couldn't have misunderstood. It was obvious that Kay didn't have any time to spare, that she and Frank had something to do.

Frank knew that Kay was right. They had to get rid of her. But even while he was admiring the way Kay was handling the thing—doing it so that Alice wouldn't be offended—he again felt that odd sense of perverseness that he was completely unable to understand.

"We've all the time in the world, baby," he said. "Relax. Plenty of time for a drink."

Kay weakly backed him up, and in another couple of minutes the three of them were sitting around the table with drinks in their hands, listening to Alice on the subject of hairdressers. The first drink was followed by a second round, on Frank's insistence. He went so far as to suggest that they give Sam a ring and ask him to join them.

"Sam has to stay with the kids," Alice reminded him. "Anyway, you'll be at our house tomorrow night and Sam can make up for it then."

They drank the second round and the clock over the stove showed eight-thirty. It was almost completely dark in the kitchen and Frank got up and turned on an overhead light. He walked over to the window to look out at the trees bending in the high wind. He started to comment on the weather, but stopped speaking suddenly as he caught sight of headlights coming rapidly down the road.

He turned and, muttering an excuse, left the room.

Frank was out on the front terrace, standing at the door, as the car slowed almost to a stop and then quickly surged forward again.

Frank felt a sense of relief as he returned to the kitchen. Alice was getting up to leave.

"Not on your sweet life," Frank said. "You don't leave this house on only two wings. I'll make one for the road."

Kay watched him in bewilderment as he reached over and playfully pushed Alice back down in her seat. A moment later he had gathered the glasses and was refilling them.

3.

Shorty had his usual luck. He was broke by the end of the fourth race. He had done what he always did when he went to the race track. He'd taken ten dollars for expenses, ten dollars for the daily double, and an additional ten dollars for each of the eight races. The rest of his money he had carefully hidden under the mattress when he and Candle had left the house that morning. In spite of having spent the major part of his life as a thief, Shorty always hid his money in the one spot where a burglar would look first.

He lost on the daily double and the first race, but hit a winner on the second and broke even on the third. And then, following an old pattern, he'd shot the bankroll on an even-money bet in the fourth. As far as anyone knows, the horse is still running.

Candle accompanied the five-dollar loans before each of the other races with a series of lectures. He also paid for the drinks that they consumed during the remainder of the afternoon. As for Candle himself, he ended up the day with a $280 profit. He kindly and laboriously explained his technique to Shorty as they left the track.

"You see, kid," he said, "I can't help but win, the same as you can't help but lose. You go out and buy all the goddamned tip sheets, you check the past performances, read the experts, figure the jockeys, go down to the paddock and look the nags over. You take a pencil and paper and figure the odds, the track conditions, the weight handicaps, the scratches, and God only knows what else. Then you pick your horse, and naturally you lose.

"Me, I'm stupid. I look over the entries, see a name I like, and I bet it—on the nose. So I win."

"Just don't talk," Shorty said. "Drive."

They picked up the other car and Candle followed Shorty up Route 1. They were in Indio Beach at eight o'clock after leaving the rented car in a roadside garage, Candle telling the attendant to give it a wash and a grease job and to change the oil.

"Better backflush the radiator, too," he added. "Take your time. Won't need it until sometime late tomorrow."

The attendant, relieved that he wouldn't have to work on it himself, said that he'd see to it. He'd leave it for the morning shift. Candle took the wheel when they left.

"Let's head out to that tavern just south of town," he suggested to Shorty. "Some guy said they have good steaks."

"As long as you're buying," Shorty said, "fine."

The Hillside Inn—there were no hills within miles—was a large, rambling, weather-beaten, and badly constructed frame building just off the highway some four miles south of town. It served good food and so it did a good business, in spite of its rather grim exterior, the bad taste of its interior decor, and the constant blaring of its gaudy jukebox.

By the time Shorty and Candle walked into the place on Thursday evening, the bar was crowded and about a third of the tables were occupied. The two men found a table just past the bar, neatly placed between the jukebox and the swinging door of the men's room. A tubercular-looking waiter in a soiled white jacket listlessly wandered over to take their order.

"Double bourbon, water on the side," Shorty said.

"Make it two," Candle added. "Now. We'll give the food order later." He stood up, reaching into his pants pocket as the waiter walked off. "Big night," he said. "Let's have music." He walked over to the jukebox and inspected the list of records for several moments. Then he inserted a coin into the slot. The machine had started to play by the time he had returned to the table.

"Recognize it?" he asked, sitting down.

"My God," Shorty said. 'Somebody Stole My Gal.' Where the hell did they ever dig that one up?"

"You should see the others on the list," Candle said. "Most of 'em go back before my time, even. By the way, you want to play that thing, you get two tunes for a quarter. Some racket."

"That's because the songs are old enough to be museum pieces," Shorty said. "You gotta pay for antiques, you know."

They were finishing their second drinks and had already ordered steaks, hash-browned potatoes, French-fried onions, and a salad when the swinging doors opened and Roy and Wally walked into the place and found two stools at the bar.

4.

Roy Cluney had started out the day feeling fine. True enough, Flood had given him a hard time the previous afternoon, but on the other hand, Flood had given Wally a lot harder time. It was enough to make Roy feel good by comparison.

They'd had their breakfast and then they'd walked around town for a while, finally finding a pool parlor that was open. They had the place to themselves most of the day. Wally began drinking beer, but Roy touched nothing but Cokes.

Roy kept buying beers for Wally, figuring that sooner or later Wally would get just a little edge on. Enough of an edge so that his pool game might be affected.

Wally hadn't disappointed him. He'd started out shooting his normal excellent game, a game that Roy was able to match but not to beat. But then, as he went on drinking beer, he became careless. At three o'clock in the afternoon he was still playing and still hoping to get even. Roy was running the table almost at will. Wally raised the stakes, hoping that that would help. Roy kept right on winning.

Wally finally went to the men's room. He went, however, not because of biological necessity, but in order to take inventory of his wallet. He discovered that he was better than forty dollars out. Returning, he suggested a final game for the forty dollars. Roy smiled and agreed. Roy won.

Wally threw his cue halfway across the room.

"Lucky bastard," he said.

"Well, you know what they say," Roy said, collecting his winnings. "Lucky in love, unlucky at—"

"Aw, shut up," Wally snapped. "Let's get going. We still have to pick up our stuff and we don't wanna be late."

Roy wanted to drive, but Wally wouldn't let him. He knew about Roy and cars. It was the way it was with girls. Once Roy got in a car and started going, he didn't know when to stop. The craziness came over him and he just had to put his foot down all the way. Flood knew about this and therefore he had instructed Wally to do the driving.

Wally waited downstairs while Roy went up for their luggage and paid for the room. He was feeling meaner every minute. Goddamn Flood, he thought. If it hadn't been for Flood he wouldn't have been stuck with this creep Roy, and he wouldn't have lost his money playing pool; he'd have been driving up to Indio with Doll.

He hated Flood, but for some odd reason, he didn't blame him—he blamed Roy. Roy was nothing but a goddamned freak. The car was a late-model Ford sedan that Wally had rented in Miami the previous week. In spite of his blazing anger and bad temper, Wally drove carefully, and he timed himself so that he arrived at the outskirts of Indio Beach just as the sun was sinking below the western horizon. Roy held the map that Flood had given him and they had no difficulty finding the turnoff at Orange Drive.

"Think Flood will have Doll with him when he shows up?" Roy asked.

"What the hell do you care?" Wally said. He continued on through town, carefully noticing the bank as he passed it.

"There's baby," he said.

"Damn thing's lit up like a Christmas tree," Roy said. "How the hell you think Flood ever figures to—"

"Don't worry," Wally told him. "You can be sure he's got an angle. He doesn't talk, but you can bet he has it all planned out."

"I sure hope so," Roy said. He sounded worried. "After all, you and I are going to be in there—an' I don't feel like playing clay pigeon for these country cops."

"Christ," Wally said, irritated, "what the hell are you doing? Getting chicken? You don't want to take chances, what the hell you come in on this caper for?"

"Let it lay," Roy answered. "Just drive, brother."

When the car passed the Loxleys' place, Sam looked out of the window curiously. He knew that the road ended a half mile beyond and that the house occupied by the Harpers was the only other place after his own bungalow. Well, at least Alice would be getting back if the Harpers were going to be having visitors.

But Alice didn't get back. Instead, Sam heard the car returning a few minutes later and again looked out at it curiously. Some dope made a wrong turn, he figured.

Wally was madder than ever.

"Goddamned fool," he muttered. "The guy knew we were expected. You'd think the least he could do was keep people away."

"Maybe the wagon belonged to Flood," Roy said, although he didn't believe it.

"Hell, no," Wally snapped at him. "Flood always drives a Caddie. You don't see him with anything that's second-class."

"He's with Doll," Roy said with a sneer.

Wally looked straight ahead and his mouth tightened. "Keep it up, you sonofabitch," gritted between his set teeth. "Just keep it up."

When they got back to town, Roy suggested that they hit a movie for an hour, but Wally ignored him. He turned south on Route 1 and drove until he came to the Hillside Inn. Viciously he cut the car into the drive and braked it to a halt.

"I'm going in for a drink," he said. "You can either stay or come with me. If I got to kill time, I'll be damned if I'll do it looking at some goddamned horse opera."

Roy shrugged and opened the door on his side of the car. Mario Padino, the Hillside Inn's owner, was behind the bar, and he was busy squeezing some fresh lime juice. He was conscious of the two men as they entered, but he was busy at the moment and so he went on with his work.

Wally waited less than a minute and then he reached into his pocket and took out a half dollar. He banged it on the mahogany.

Padino looked down at him, then went back to squeezing limes.

Wally's face suffused with blood. He spoke in a slow, normal voice, but the words carried clearly above the sound of the jukebox.

"You working this bar or not, ginso?" he said.

Padino stood dead still for a moment, half of an unsqueezed lime held in his right hand. Then carefully he put the fruit down, wiped his hands along the front of his apron, and walked over so that he was facing Roy and W ally.

"What you say?" he asked.

"I said, greaseball, that I want some service."

For a full half minute the old man stared at Wally. His heavy-lipped mouth was half opened and his big brown eyes were incredulous. Then his eyes narrowed in anger and his right hand slowly reached out toward the sawed-off baseball bat that rested on the ice under the bar.

"Go ahead and reach for it," Roy suddenly said, his voice soft, almost indifferent. "Just reach for it."

Padino's hand stopped as though controlled by an electric switch. His eyes went from Wally to Roy.

Roy stood there, completely relaxed, half grinning, almost friendly. He had spoken in a voice without anger, without threat. He looked like a friendly high-school kid, but as Padino watched him, the hot blood of anger retreated from the old man's face, leaving it pale and sick-looking.

"What'll it be, gentlemen?" he said. "Sorry, didn't see you come in."

Roy laughed softly.

"Rye and water," Wally said.

"Coke," Roy said.

"And shut that goddamned jukebox off," Wally said.

Without a word, the old man turned and walked to the end of the bar. He rounded it and went over to the jukebox. He reached behind the machine and pulled the plug from the wall socket. Then he started back to the bar to get the drinks.

Shorty looked up as the music stopped, halfway through "Somebody Stole My Gal." He saw Padino and then his eyes went to the electric cord lying on the floor beside the machine. He beckoned to the waiter.

The waiter waited until Padino had finished serving the drinks and then went to the end of the bar. When Padino walked over to him, they held a whispered conversation for a moment or two. The waiter nodded and went at once to the table where Shorty and Candle were sitting.

Leaning over, he explained to Shorty in a low voice.

Shorty looked over at Candle. Candle smiled at him and looked over at the bar.

Shorty stood up slowly. He walked over to the jukebox and studied the list of records for several minutes. Very deliberately he took two quarters from his pocket and put them in the slot. He pushed the number-twelve button, the one for "Somebody Stole My Gal," four times. Then he reached down and put the plug into the electric socket before he walked back to the table and sat down.

Wally had the drink half raised to his lips when the machine started playing. With the first bars of the music, he smashed the glass down on the counter so that the contents spilled and the liquid rolled in a quickly spreading puddle until it began to drip off the edge of the bar. His eyes went to the jukebox.

"The fat guy sitting at the table next to it," Roy said, smiling maliciously.

Without a word, Wally started for the table where Candle and Shorty sat. Both men were watching him. "Never could stand punks," Shorty said.

Candle glanced at Shorty for a quick moment and then his eyes went back to Wally.

Wally didn't hesitate. He'd been feeling mean all afternoon, mean and in a fighting mood. He was unconscious of Padino and the waiter, standing motionless at the end of the bar, blind to everything but Shorty, who had started the jukebox after he'd ordered it stopped.

He halted when he came to the table, leaned down, and spoke in a harsh, guttural voice. "You turned that goddamned thing on?"

Shorty stared at him, his expression indifferent. Then he looked away and over at Candle and winked. Candle started to get to his feet, and then two things happened quickly. Wally reached out with one hand and grabbed Shorty by the front of his shirt, at the same time doubling his right fist and pulling his arm back. Candle, seemingly without effort, hit Wally with a short rabbit punch that couldn't have traveled more than twelve inches. The blow caught Wally on the Adam's apple and he gave a short, almost soundless grunt. His left hand loosened its grip on Shorty's shirt and his other hand dropped to his side as he took a quick backward step. He seemed to be fighting for air.

Roy left the bar and started for the table.

At that moment a woman on the other side of the room screamed, and just then the wide double door of the place again opened.

Flood walked into the barroom.

5.

The second he pushed open the doors and entered the place, Flood knew something was wrong. Instinctively, barely glancing around, he caught the tenseness in the atmosphere, seemed to understand that something was happening. Whatever it was, he wanted no part of it. He started to swing around to leave the place, his eyes quickly circling the bar. He saw Padino and the waiter standing there motionless, staring. And then, a second later, he followed the direction of their gaze and took in the tableau at the table.

He didn't know what had happened, but he didn't have to know. The juxtaposition of the figures made the scene only too clear. It was obvious that Wally had just been hit; there was no doubt about what Roy, who was moving in, was planning to do. Shorty was reaching for the water pitcher and Candle's hands had found the back of a chair as he prepared to raise it over his head.

Flood moved with lightning speed. He was across the room and at the side of the table before Roy reached it. Flood didn't bother to look at either Shorty or Candle. He brushed Wally aside and turned to face Roy.

Almost without hesitating in his stride, Roy turned off at an oblique angle and went on into the men's room. A moment later, Wally followed him.

Candle showed no sign of recognition, but he quickly put the chair back in place and sat down. Shorty hesitated a second, and then he too sat down.

Flood said nothing, but swung on his heel and went to the men's room after the other two. Wally and Roy were alone in the place when he entered.

"Get out. Pay your check and get out!"

He spoke the words in a low, tense, bitter voice, finding it difficult to control his rising fury.

Roy started to say something, but Flood cut him off.

"Later," he said. "Just get out of here now—quick."

Roy left the room, and as Wally started to follow him, Flood gave him a shove between the shoulder blades.

Doll, sitting outside in the Caddie, looked up as the door of the place opened and Roy and Wally hurried down the steps.

"Well, I'll be!" she said. She leaned out of the car window. "Hey, Wally," she called.

Wally looked over at her, but kept on past the car without saying a word. A moment later he and Roy were back in their own car and Wally was pressing the starter button.

Candle waited only until he saw Roy and Wally leave the washroom. As the two walked past the bar, Candle got up.

Flood was washing his hands as Candle entered the men's room.

Candle went to the next sink and turned on the water spigot. He caught Flood's eye in the mirror behind the sink. He spoke, barely moving his lips.

"What do you say, boss?" he said.

"What was the rumble about?" Flood had to repeat the question a little louder before Candle could make out the words.

"Oh, just a couple of young punks who decided they didn't like Shorty," Candle said. "It wasn't serious. They came in looking for trouble. Asking for it."

Flood nodded grimly.

"That kind always does," he said. "Everything all right on your end?"

"All set," Candle said.

"I'll be seeing you," Flood said, turning from the sink. He left the room and bought two packs of cigarettes at the bar. Then he left the place without looking back.

"Well, I'll be goddamned," Shorty said when Candle returned to the table. "How the hell you suppose *he* happened to walk in just at that moment?"

"Don't be a sap," Candle said in a low voice. "Those punks were a couple of his boys, that's how. I thought they were local, but I shoulda known better. Didn't you see their faces when they saw him?"

Shorty nodded thoughtfully. "Yeah," he said. "You must have it right. A couple of his boys, all right."

"I wouldn't want to be in their boots when Flood gets them alone," Candle said.

An hour later they finished their dinner and left. They returned to their room at once and spent the rest of the evening playing gin rummy. Candle won, as usual.

Chapter Eight

1.

The minute Alice Loxley left, Kay started the thing all over again. They'd been batting it back and forth most of the day, whenever they had been alone and sure that Kosta was unable to overhear them. They had got nowhere.

"You've still got to make a decision, Frank," Kay said. "We haven't got much more time. They'll be here any time now. I heard a car pass only a few minutes ago and then go back down the road. It could have been them."

"It could have," Frank said.

"Well, what are you—"

"What can I do?" Frank asked, looking miserable. "Don't you see, I just can't quit now. We're in the thing too deep. If we walked out now, it might kill the whole plan. You know what Flood would do then, don't you?"

"What do you think he'll do after it's over and he finds out we're leaving together?"

"That isn't the point," Frank said, trying to keep the annoyance out of his voice. "I still think I owe him something. I agreed to go through with this and I just can't back out now."

Kay looked at him, her eyes sick.

"Anyway," Frank said, "this isn't murder. It's only robbery. And I've told you already that as long as you feel the way you do about it, I'll pass up taking my share of the money. At least I won't be getting anything out of it. But I have to see the thing through. Once it's over, you and I'll just disappear."

Kay stood up and walked around the table until she was standing in front of him. She reached out with both hands, putting her arms around his waist as she looked up into his eyes. She opened her mouth to speak.

Each heard the car coming down the road at the same moment. Even as Kay stepped quickly back, the lights cut across the window as the machine pulled into the drive. It continued on and through the opened doors of the garage.

The two of them were still standing there, waiting in stiff silence for the back door to open, when the second car pulled into the driveway and headed for the garage.

Frank nodded toward the other room. Kay turned without a word and left. Frank heard the sound of her footsteps on the stairs a moment later.

He was facing the door leading onto the screened back porch when Wally opened it and entered the room, quickly followed by Roy. A moment later the door again opened and Doll walked in. Flood was directly behind her.

Without a word, Flood went to the window and closed the Venetian blind.

"Haven't you enough sense to keep the shades down?" he said, turning back to Frank. He didn't wait for an answer, but went on speaking in a low, controlled voice. "Take this girl upstairs and have Kay stay with her," he snapped. "You two," he indicated Wally and Roy, "sit down there at the table. Where's Kosta?"

"Upstairs in his room," Frank said.

"Good," Flood said. "Bring him down as soon as you get the girl upstairs. Where's Kay?"

"She's upstairs seeing to the rooms," Frank said.

"Listen," Doll suddenly cut in. "I don't wanna—"

"Do what I tell you," Flood said, glaring at her.

She followed Frank out of the room.

Wally avoided Flood's eyes as he sat at the table. Roy sat across from him, staring at the floor. Flood pulled a chair up so that he half faced each of them.

"Didn't I tell you two to stay out of trouble?" he asked. He watched them coldly as they avoided his eyes. "Are you so stupid you'd take a chance on getting into a jam now? What the hell were you doing in that barroom?"

"Wally wanted a drink," Roy said.

Wally looked over at Roy with a mean expression. He spoke up quickly. "It wasn't that at all," he cut in. "We came out here. There was a car in the driveway, so we headed back toward town. I didn't want to be seen hanging around town, or just driving around, so we went in to get a drink."

"You went in to get a drink," Flood said. "Great! So why the hell weren't you at the bar having a drink? What were you doing starting a fight with the customers?"

"A couple of wise guys," Wally said, still looking anywhere but at Flood.

"You damned fool," Flood said. "God, what I ever wanted to tie up with a couple of punks like you for!"

He stood up as the kitchen door opened and Frank returned.

"Kosta will be right down," Frank said.

"You get the girl taken care of?" Flood asked.

"Kay's with her. Didn't expect her, so we didn't have a room ready for her," he added.

"She can stay with Kay in her room," Flood said shortly. "Sit down."

Kosta came into the room as Frank was pulling a chair up to the table.

Flood gestured to Frank. "Come out to the garage with me," he said. "Want you to help me bring in a couple of things. The rest of you stay here and be quiet. You hear a car coming, get upstairs quick. Kosta, you take the boys to your room if anything happens. And remember, no lights."

A moment later, he passed through the rear door, followed by Frank. They went to the garage behind the building and Flood stopped beside the Cadillac.

"Won't need a light," he said. "But close the overhead doors."

Frank closed the doors from the inside, and when he was through he went back to the Caddie. Flood was sitting in the front seat, dimly illuminated by the dash light.

"Come in and sit down." He waited until Frank was seated beside him. Then he said, "All right, what's been going on?"

"Plenty," Frank said. "We had a nice fire yesterday. Warehouse burned down. While it was still going, a cop picked up Kosta walking around the streets. He'd been drinking, but it was something more than that. He was in a complete stupor. The cop brought him out to the house."

"Good God," Flood said. His surprise was genuine. "Did the cop make any connection?"

"I don't think so," Frank said. "I'd already introduced Kosta to the cop as my uncle and said he'd been sick. Cop just thought he'd got a little too much to drink."

"The dumb bastard," Flood said bitterly. "That's the trouble with using men like him on a job. You never know when they might go nuts. But I didn't think ..."

"He'll be all right," Frank said, "as long as you don't let him out of your sight. But how about afterward? Is he going to be safe then?"

"As safe as guys like that ever are," Flood said. "I've been having a little trouble with the other boys, too," he added. "They picked up that girl I brought in with me and started spilling their guts all over the place. God, the people you can get mixed up with on one of these deals!"

In the darkness he looked over at Frank, his eyes veiled. "Thank the Lord for you and Kay," he said. "At least I don't have to worry about you two."

Frank sat very still in the seat beside the other man. He didn't want to look at him. He couldn't tell whether there was a double meaning behind those words.

"Outside of Kosta," Frank said, "everything else seems all right. I guess Kay told you about my seeing Paulmeyer?"

Flood grunted. "How was he?" he asked.

"Fine," Frank said. "Everything under control. He'll be no problem at all."

"No, he won't be a problem," Flood said.

Frank again wondered if the words had some hidden meaning.

"I don't want to leave the others in there alone together too long," Flood said.

"Well, everything is all right at this end," Frank said. "Should be a cinch if everyone keeps his head. Only thing worries me is the bank itself. It's lighted up like a Christmas tree at night."

"It won't be on Saturday night," Flood said. "Don't worry about that part of it. Just tell me about the rest. You set up all right here in town? No suspicions? Nothing unusual?"

"Nothing," Frank said. "Everything is fine. But I didn't think you'd be showing until tomorrow night. How come—"

"I didn't intend to," Flood told him. "But that damned fool Wally picked up this girl. I was afraid to leave her with him and Roy, and at the same time I couldn't have her hanging around with me. Nor could I just throw her out. There's no telling what she knows or what she may have guessed. So the only thing I could do was get her away from Wally and Roy before there was a battle over her, and bring her out here."

"What happens to her afterward?"

"Don't let it worry you," Flood said shortly. "Just worry about your own end of it. Anyway, I've had to change my plans. I'm going to stay here until it's all over. I want to keep an eye on the boys."

Thinking of Kay, Frank said, "I can handle them all right. Them and Kosta, too."

He saw Flood look at him curiously out of the corner of his eye.

"You got plenty to handle without them," Flood said. "No, I'll stay on now. The girl—her name's Doll—can stay with Kay. I want you to stick close to Kosta, and I'll stay with Wally and Roy."

Frank started to say something, but Flood went on talking.

"We've got to be very careful," he said. "Daytimes, I want you to keep right on doing as you've always done. Only thing is, try to keep everyone away from the house. I don't want anybody hanging around."

He opened the door of the car. Walking around to the rear of the Caddie, he inserted the key in the lock of the back compartment.

"The long canvas duffel bag," he said. "Handle it carefully. It holds the guns."

Frank took the canvas bag and hoisted it to his shoulder.

Kosta, Wally, and Roy were still sitting at the table, saying nothing and not looking at each other, when Frank and Flood returned.

"These are the guns," Flood said, indicating the bag as Frank carefully put it down on the floor. "Wally, you understand guns. I want you to go over them carefully. Check them."

"I'm not carrying any gun," Kosta suddenly said, staring at Flood with his opaque eyes.

"I wouldn't let you carry a gun," Flood snapped at him. "What you have to do doesn't call for a gun."

He reached down and unlocked the small padlock that held the thin chain drawn tightly around the neck of the duffel bag. The others were watching him. It was probably because they were watching him so intently that no one heard the sound of the car's engine. No one heard anything until the harsh noise of the horn cut the night air. It came from the driveway beside the house.

Flood was the first to recover after the shock of hearing the blast.

"Jesus!" he yelled. "Quick, Wally, take the bag! Get upstairs. All of you. Frank, give us half a minute and then get outside and see who it is. Whoever it is, get rid of them. Don't do anything suspicious, but get rid of them."

He was pushing the others from the room as he finished speaking. Wally stumbled under the weight of the bag and Flood swore softly.

Frank waited about twenty-five seconds and then went to the back door. The first thing he noticed as he stepped onto the porch was the red light on the top of the patrol car.

2.

Sergeant Waldo Harrington carried a half-gallon jug of whisky in his right hand as he stepped from behind the driver's seat of the patrol car. His wide, open face was very red and he was wearing a big smile. Walking over to the porch, he held the jug high in the air.

"Fella," he said, "just looky what I got!"

He crowded past Frank and went across the porch and into the kitchen, sitting the bottle on the top of the table. He took off his policeman's cap and wiped a thin line of sweat from the top of his forehead.

"Well, for God's sake," Frank said. He didn't know anything else to say.

"Just getting off, an' after a tough day," Waldo said, still smiling. "And what do you think? Passed a couple of old boys from out in the Glades. They were in a jeep, busted down by the side of the road. Well, I went over to see what was the trouble, and damn if they didn't have a load of booze. Stuff they made themselves."

Frank whistled under his breath.

"You take 'em in?" he asked.

Waldo looked at him in shocked surprise. "Hell, no," he said. "I did not. You think I'm some goddamn federal man? No, I just told 'em to get their damned ol' jeep going and get out of my county. So they gave me this little present to remember them by."

Frank laughed. "From what I've seen of bootleg stuff," he said, "you'd be better off if you never saw them."

"Don't you kid yourself, boy," Waldo said. "This is good straight corn likker. I know those boys and I know the stuff they been makin'. Hell's bells, Frank, you drink it more often than not outta phony bottles and don't even know it. Only difference is, this ain't been cut. Get us a couple of glasses and a little water."

Frank went over and took down two glasses from the cupboard. He filled a pitcher with water and threw in some ice cubes.

"Would the missus care to join us?" Waldo asked when he returned to the table. "I won't ask that uncle of yours," he added, and laughed.

"She's upstairs," Frank said, putting the water down on the table. "You pour and I'll run up and ask her."

Quickly he left the room. Waldo was unstrapping the holster that held his service revolver as he left.

Flood was standing in the doorway of Kosta's room as Frank

rounded the head of the staircase. He walked over to the room on tiptoe and Flood reached out and pulled him inside, closing the door softly. He spoke in a whisper.

"That's a cop's car outside," he said, his voice tense. "Who is he? What does he want?"

Frank quickly explained, speaking in an undertone. He ended by saying that the cop wanted Kay to come down and join them.

"Which room is she in?" Flood asked.

"End of the hall on the left," Frank said.

"Get back and I'll send her down," Flood said. "But for God's sake, get rid of him as soon as you can. Don't do anything to arouse his suspicions, but do it as fast as you can."

Frank nodded in the dark and left the room, not closing the door behind him. He sensed that the others, Kosta and the two boys, were also in that room, silent and alert.

He returned to the kitchen and told Harrington that Kay would be right down.

As they sat drinking and idly talking, Kay, Waldo, and Frank, two thoughts kept racing through Frank Harper's mind. One was that he had to get rid of Sergeant Harrington as soon as he possibly could. The second was that as long as Harrington remained in the house, Kay would be with them and not upstairs; that as long as he and Kay were together, she was safe from Flood.

Sergeant Harrington, more than half drunk, but still able to walk and think straight, left the house at a quarter to four on Friday morning. He'd had a swell evening and he thought Frank Harper was a great guy. Mrs. Harper was a darn good scout, too. He liked them both. Nice people. He liked to have people like the Harpers move into Indio Beach. Backbone of the goddamn country.

Within a minute of the time the sound of Waldo's car had blended with the sounds of the night, Flood was downstairs and standing in the doorway. He had taken off his coat and tie and his hair was disheveled. His mouth was a straight grim line and he had lost his usual urbane, sophisticated manner. He stood still and stared at Frank and Kay, slowly nodding his head. When he spoke at last, his voice was still low and controlled, but it was obvious that he was furious.

"What the goddamned hell took you so long?" he asked.

Frank started to say something but Kay quickly got to her feet. Frank was amazed as he noticed her stagger slightly. He knew that she had taken only three drinks during the entire evening.

"Sure shorry," she said thickly. "Guy wouldn't go home. Got no home, guess." She weaved slightly and reached for the table for support.

Flood's eyes opened wide. "Well, I'll be damned," he said. "You're drunk."

"Yep, drunky," Kay said.

Flood stepped forward suddenly and for a second Frank thought he was going to hit her. Instead he swung sharply toward Frank.

"Get her upstairs," he snapped. "Put her in with the other dame." He turned and stared at Kay, disgust on his face. "Great," he said. "You come down here to do a job, come down to play being a respectable little housewife, and you end up a lush. You even get slopped on my first night. Get her the hell out of my sight."

He went over to the table and sat down as Frank steered Kay toward the door.

There was a perplexed look on Flood's face as he reached over and pulled the three-quarter-empty jug across the table. He tipped it forward, removed the cork, and sniffed the contents. He wrinkled his nose in disgust.

"Good God," he said. "The people I get mixed up with."

3.

At three o'clock on Friday afternoon, Ham Johnstone finished putting a dry patch on a tire, placed the tire back on its rim, and filled it with thirty pounds of air. It was the last tire he had to repair, and he was glad. Not that he minded the work; it was only that he wanted to find time to clean up around the office.

He yawned when he was through, then shivered slightly. It was cold. He decided to go into the office. Ham had lighted the small kerosene stove and it was warmer in there. He opened the door and walked in.

Frank Harper was sitting in the swivel chair at the desk. He was leaning forward on his elbows. His eyes were closed and he was breathing heavily. He was asleep.

"Ol' boy sure musta tied one on," Ham said under his breath. He watched Frank sleeping and smiled. Ham didn't like heavy drinkers. They worried him. Heavy drinkers made a lot of trouble. But he knew Frank was no drunk.

Reaching over, he gently shook him. Frank awakened suddenly and looked up, startled.

"Tol' me to be sure you got to de bank," Ham said.

Frank looked at his wrist watch. "Damn it, Ham," he said, "it's after three. You know the bank closes at two. What did you wanta let me sleep for?"

"Ain't got no watch, boss," Ham said.

Frank concealed his annoyance and got up and stretched. He was starting for the door when Sam Loxley pulled up in his station wagon. Frank went out and reached for the gas hose.

"You must have had a brawl last night," Sam said. "I was up with the kid around three or three-thirty and saw a light on over at your place."

Frank nodded. "Yeah," he said, "Waldo stopped by. We killed a few."

"Well, get a little rest," Sam said. "Alice and I are expecting you over tonight."

For a moment Frank was tempted to beg off. But then he quickly changed his mind. He knew that it would be easy to convince Flood that they were expected, and that if they didn't show up the Loxleys might get the idea of coming over to get them. He could explain it to Flood easily enough.

"We'll be there," he said. "Warm up the ice cubes."

Sam talked with him for several minutes more while Frank washed off the windshield and checked the oil and water.

"Around seven-thirty," he said, as he started the car rolling.

Returning to the office, Frank sent Ham out to check the gas and oil in his own car. After Ham left, he reached for the telephone and called his house.

Kay answered almost at once.

"How things going, kid?" he asked.

"Everything under control," Kay said. Frank could tell by the sound of her voice that she was not alone.

"Sam Loxley just stopped by," Frank said. "Reminded me about the party tonight." He hesitated for a second, carefully considering the phrasing of his next remark. "I may be a little late getting home, so you be all set to go. I'll just grab a quick shower and change my clothes. I'll shave down here at the gas station."

When Kay failed to answer, Frank spoke again.

"We have to go, honey," he said. "They're expecting us. If we don't show, they'll want to know why. We definitely have to go." He hung up.

4.

Kay waited for the click at the other end of the line and then she too put the receiver back on the hook. She had heard the footsteps coming down from above. She knew that someone was standing in the doorway, watching. Slowly she turned around. It was Kosta.

His mild, hurt eyes were clearer than she had ever seen them before. His face even had a tinge of color, and the pudgy, hairless cheeks looked freshly washed.

"They want you upstairs," he said. Then he walked into the room. He came close to her and she couldn't help taking a step backward. He spoke in a high, thin whisper.

"Lemme have a shot of gin," he said. He looked at her beseechingly.

"Over the sink in the kitchen," she said. She turned at once and started for the stairs.

She hadn't seen Flood since he had sent her upstairs at four o'clock that morning, when he had walked in on her and Frank just after Waldo left. She had gone at once to her own bedroom, where Doll was sleeping. There were twin beds in the room and she had quickly changed to pajamas and climbed into the bed next to the other girl. When she had awakened the next morning around nine o'clock, the house had been quiet. She'd got up and gone downstairs. Frank had already left the house.

Around one in the afternoon, Wally had come downstairs. She had made a pot of coffee and some sandwiches and he'd taken them back upstairs with him. A little later Doll came down. Kay fixed breakfast for the girl, but neither of them had been inclined to talk. Then Doll too had gone back upstairs.

Flood was standing in the room down the hall from that occupied by Kosta. Across from it was the room that she had prepared for Wally and Roy. The room she and Frank had shared was at the other end of the hallway, opposite the one occupied by Kosta. Frank, theoretically, had used the fifth room on the floor, a tiny compartment next to the only upstairs bathroom, facing the stairway.

Flood beckoned to her. He stood aside and she entered the room. It was a large, square room and there were two double beds in it, one along the north wall and one along the south. In the center was a large round table, in one corner an open lavatory.

Doll, Wally, and Roy sat at the table. Wally had a disassembled submachine gun in front of him and he was greasing it. Lying next to the machine gun were an automatic pistol and a stack of ammunition.

Flood waited until she had entered the room before speaking.

"I want you to bring us up something to drink," he said. "Fix up some sandwiches and things. And make me a couple of soft-boiled eggs and some toast."

"Make mine a beer," Wally said, without looking up.

"Coke," Roy said.

"And bring up coffee," Flood said.

Doll suddenly stood up. "I'll go down and help you carry it up," she said.

Flood put his arm out. "You will not," he said quickly. "I don't want anyone going downstairs again. I don't want anyone taking a chance on being seen from now on. She'll get us anything we need."

"That other guy's downstairs," Roy said, looking up.

"He doesn't matter," Flood said shortly. "He's supposed to be here. But the rest of us aren't. So we stay up here until we're ready to pull out tomorrow night."

Doll had started to complain as Kay left the room and went back toward the staircase. A moment later she felt a hand on her arm. Flood was at her side and he had closed the door behind them. He said nothing, but steered her down the hallway and into her own bedroom.

"You and I," he said, "are going to have a little talk." He spoke in a natural voice, but there was something ominous about the words. "Right now, get the food and drinks up. And tell that rummy downstairs that if I find him taking a drink, I'll let the boys work him over." He stared into her face as he spoke, but he made no move to touch her. "I heard the phone," he said. "Who was it?"

"Frank," she said. "He called from the gas station. About tonight."

"What about tonight?"

"Well, we've been invited over to visit the people next door. We more or less had been planning the party for some time. Frank thinks we should go."

"Why should you go?" Flood asked quickly.

"They'd think it funny if we didn't," Kay said. "They might stop by and see what was wrong if we didn't show up."

"Who lives next door?"

"A man named Loxley and his wife. They run a laundromat. Have a couple of kids."

"All right," Flood said, after a moment's reflection. "If you're expected, you better show up. But just remember one thing." Suddenly he reached out and his lean, strong fingers dug into her arm above the elbow. He pulled her brutally to him and spoke in a low, hard voice. "No drinking, get it? No more goddamn lushing it up. Take one or two if you have to, but that's all. Since when did you start hitting the bottle?" He didn't wait for her to answer. Instead he squeezed her arm cruelly again and then shoved her away.

"And don't forget. You and I are going to have a talk. Now go down and get the food."

5.

At six-thirty Frank got back to the house. Kay was alone downstairs when he walked in. He started toward her but she gave him a warning look, indicating the second floor with a nod of her head.

"I have a pick-me-up in the icebox," she said in a low voice. "Go on up and change and then come down and we'll leave."

He noticed that she was dressed in a pair of shorts and a halter and was wearing low-heeled shoes without stockings. She had done up her hair and was wearing fresh make-up. She looked very fresh, very beautiful. He found it difficult to resist the temptation to go to her and take her in his arms. But he turned toward the staircase.

"Be down in a few minutes," he said.

Wally and Doll were playing two-handed casino with a deck of dog-eared cards when he entered the upstairs room. Flood lay on one of the beds, fully clothed. Kosta was nowhere around and Frank guessed that he'd gone to his own room. Roy sat at the table, ignoring the others as he read a comic book.

Doll was the only one that looked up as he entered the room.

"Pull up a chair, big boy," she said, "and sit in."

Flood spoke without moving. "Kay says you have to go out. How soon?"

"In about an hour or less," Frank said.

Flood pulled himself to a sitting position and then stood up. Frank noticed that he had changed his shirt and had shaved. He looked as meticulously neat as ever.

Without a word he walked to the door. Frank followed him out of the room. In the hallway Flood turned to him.

"Go down and get us a couple of drinks. Straight Scotch for me, if you got any. I'll wait in here."

He went into the room used by Kay and Doll.

Frank went downstairs and into the kitchen. Kay was at the sink, washing some dishes. She looked up quickly as he entered the room, but Frank shook his head quickly. He took a half-filled bottle of Scotch from the liquor closet, found a couple of glasses, and then opened a bottle of soda.

"You won't be long?" Kay whispered as he passed her on his way back upstairs.

"Not long," he said.

When Frank entered the room, Flood walked behind him and closed the door.

Frank poured two drinks and handed one to Flood.

Flood held it in his hand but made no effort to drink. He stared for several minutes at Frank and then at last spoke.

"What was the idea of letting Kay get tight last night?"

Frank hunched his shoulders. He knew what he had to say, how he had to play it.

"Hell, I got nothing to say to her," Frank said. "I'm not her keeper."

"No?" Flood stared at him coldly. "She been doing that little trick often?"

"No. Fact is, she hasn't been drinking any to speak of. Guess the cop coming by just got her nervous. She didn't get out of line."

"What made the cop hang around so long?"

"He's a friend," Frank said. "It was your idea I get friendly with the local law."

"That's right," Flood said. "My idea. But it wasn't my idea to have you get my girl drunk."

"She wasn't too drunk," Frank said.

"O.K. We'll skip it for the time being. About this party tonight. I don't like it. One of you should be around, just in case someone comes snooping around the house. Another thing, with you and the girl gone, it isn't a good idea to have any lights on in the place. I'll be goddamned if I like sitting around in the dark."

"Kosta will be here," Frank said. "He's supposed to be my uncle, remember?"

"Well, that's right," Flood said grudgingly. "Kosta will be here." He shrugged, a look of disgust on his face. "A great little evening," he said. "Wally and Roy, Kosta and that Doll broad. I'll love every minute of it."

"We'll be back early," Frank said.

"See that you are."

6.

It had been a swell evening.

At eleven-thirty Kay was out in the kitchen with Alice Loxley and the two men were still sitting at the cluttered card table in the living room, talking. Kay could hear their voices as she helped Alice with the late supper they were having before going home. Alice herself was over at the stove, stirring a Welsh rarebit. Kay was making the coffee, getting out the cups and saucers, and arranging the tray.

The words drifted in from the front room.

"Lucky," Sam was saying. "Really lucky."

"Not luck at all," Frank said. "Hard work. Yeah, I know it sounds like boasting, but a hundred and ten bucks ain't hay. That's what I cleared last week. And the important part is, it was more than half on service."

Kay, listening to Frank's words, detected the pride in his voice.

"Of course, I like the gas-and-oil end of it," Frank said. "That's the bread and butter. But the service part of the business is what I've built up myself."

"You're sure doing a lot better than the last guy who had the place," Sam said.

He's doing great, Kay thought to herself. And from nothing. Why, he'd taken the business when it was running in the red and in three months really made a going thing of it. There was no telling where he would end up at this rate.

And then, for the first time all evening, she suddenly remembered where he'd end up. For the first time in hours she thought about the house a half mile down the road—their house—and the people in that house.

These two, Sam and Alice Loxley, must have, in their simple way, some sort of magic, she thought. Here, all evening as Frank and I have sat playing cards and talking, I haven't thought of Flood or those others once. I haven't thought of tomorrow. And neither has Frank. He's been thinking about the garage business, or the laundry business, or the card game. It had been a brief and unexpected reprieve.

For four hours Frank hadn't been a member of a gang of criminals planning a desperate and violent crime; she herself hadn't been the ex-mistress of a racketeer and bank robber. No, she and Frank had been, in truth, what they had come down to Florida to pretend to be: a young married couple, starting out with a new business, in a new town with new friends.

Alice's voice quickly brought her back to reality.

"Honey," Alice was saying, "what in the world are you thinking about? You just poured a whole half pint of cream into the sugar bowl."

Kay stared blankly at the other woman, and then she smiled quickly and mumbled an apology.

"Just thinking," she said. "I guess I was dreaming. Getting a little tired. I didn't have much sleep last night."

"Well, you just go on in and sit with the boys," Alice said. "I thought you were a little peaked tonight. We'll eat and then you two go on home and get some rest. Sam and I have a big night tomorrow, anyway, and we should be getting some sleep too."

Alice playfully pushed her out of the room.

Frank looked up quickly. He must have seen something in her eyes, because he at once stood up and came toward her.

"Is anything—"

Before he could finish the question, there was a sudden sound of crying from the back of the house. The four of them quickly froze and listened.

It came from the rear bedroom and it was the cry of a child.

Sam and Alice rushed out of the room. In a moment Alice returned.

"It's Sammy," she said. "Nothing serious," she added at once, as Kay started forward. "Just that he woke up and was having a nightmare and became frightened. And now Bitty's awake, too. Honey," she said, turning to Kay, "will you go out and put some milk on to heat? I'll give 'em both hot chocolate and they'll be fine and go back to sleep. Sam's in comforting Sammy and I'll go in and talk with Bitty. You just yell when the milk comes to a simmer and I'll fix it." She hurried back to the children's room.

Frank followed Kay out to the kitchen.

It took only a moment for Kay to put the milk into the top of a double boiler and turn up the heat under it. Then she went to the kitchen door and very quietly closed it.

Frank, watching her, realized something had happened; something was on her mind. There was a subtle change about her, a change he couldn't quite understand.

Quickly she walked over and stood in front of him.

"Frank," she said, "there's something I must tell you. Right now. At once."

"Honey, let's wait until we get—"

"It can't wait, Frank."

He reached for her, but she quickly stepped away. She looked up at him and her eyes were oddly somber.

"I've come to a decision, Frank," Kay said. "I'm not going back. I'm never going near that house again. It's all through. When I leave here tonight, I'm leaving for good. I want you to come with me. But either way, I'm leaving. I can't go back. I love you and I want you. But I don't want you as a criminal."

Frank stared at her, his eyes wide.

"Baby," he said at last. "Baby, what's happened? What in the world's come over you? Are you sick or something?" He reached for her again, but once more she pushed him away.

"No, Frank," she said. "I'm not sick. But I must have been sick for a long time now. For the first time in months, perhaps in years, I'm normal and sane."

She shook her head slightly and her large eyes rapidly opened and closed as she tried to keep the tears back.

"Can't you see? Oh, darling, can't you see it? We've been mad—crazy! You're no bank robber, no thief. How could you be? How could I love you if you were? You're a decent, honest guy who's been pushed around. But now things are changed. You're like Sam, if you only knew it. A guy with a job, a business, a life ahead of him."

"You want me to walk out on Flood, just like that?" Frank asked.

"I want you to walk out," Kay said.

"Flood made the business possible," Frank said, stubbornness in his voice. "He made this life of ours possible. He made you possible."

Kay began to cry silently.

"Yes," she said, "he made it possible. And now he wants to take it all away. He wants to take it away and ruin us."

"But I owe him something. Very possibly I owe him my life. You, Kay—even you admit that Flood was good to you, and kind, when you needed kindness."

"Yes, yes, I know. And we've paid him back. Paid him back well. I'm not suggesting we turn him in. I'm not asking you to double-cross him or hurt him. I'm just asking you to stop, now. To leave, now, with me, before it's too late."

This time it was Kay that came to him. She put her arms around him and looked up into his face.

"It has to be that way," she said, and now she was no longer crying. "It's either us—you and I together—or it's them over there in that house."

For a long moment Frank looked down into her face. And then

suddenly his own face softened and he slowly expelled his breath.

"All right," he said. "All right, honey. You don't leave me any choice. It's you and I."

She tried to smile, but she couldn't.

"And we'll leave, leave here, now and forever?" Kay asked.

"As soon as we finish Alice's rarebit," Frank said. His head bent and his lips found hers.

"Well, I never!"

They looked up then and moved quickly apart as they saw Alice standing in the doorway.

"Of all things!" she said, smiling widely. "A couple of real lovebirds, if I ever saw any. And you two an old married couple! Why, it's hardly decent."

She came into the kitchen, laughing.

"You've let the milk curdle," she said. "But never mind, I'll take care of it. You children go in and sit around and Sam and I'll be with you in a couple of minutes. We'll eat and then you can go home to bed. Looks to me like that's where you belong, if I may be crude enough to say so."

Alice, however, was not with them when they sat down to their rarebit and coffee with Sam. She was still in with the children and didn't get back until they were almost through

She apologized as soon as she returned to the living room.

"That child," she said, irritation and love intermingled in her voice. "I really suppose I shouldn't blame Sammy too much, though. You see, he's all excited about tomorrow night and he was dreaming about the dragon."

"The dragon?" Kay asked politely.

"Yes," Alice said. "You see, Sammy's a shining knight, and tomorrow evening, in the play, he's going to kill the dragon. It's his first play, you know, and I guess he's been taking his part a little too seriously. He's worried now that maybe the dragon won't be killed after all. Sammy takes such things very seriously."

Kay smiled. "Sammy's a dear," she said. "I wish I had one just like him. And one like Bitty, too."

Frank looked over at her and smiled.

"What's the play?" he asked, getting to his feet. "I hadn't heard about it."

"You hadn't heard?" Sam said. "Well, I'll be! For the Lord's sake, fella, I gotta sell you a couple of tickets right now." He reached into his pocket and pulled out a sheaf of cards. "Where you-all been, anyway?

It's the big deal of the year. At the school auditorium. Tomorrow night. Why—"

His voice stopped suddenly and his eyes opened very wide. He was staring at Kay.

"For God's sake," he said, "what ..."

Frank caught her as she fell.

7.

The car was parked well off to the side of the road, a half mile from the Loxleys', in the opposite direction from their own house. They'd been sitting there with the lights out for more than fifteen minutes now.

She was still breathing heavily, but she was all right. She started to say something, but Frank quickly put his fingers to her lips.

"Not yet, darling," he said. "Just take it easy for another minute or two. Get your breath."

He sat back, his own breath coming short and hard through his clenched teeth.

It had been very tricky back there, for a moment or so, after she had fainted. Of course, Sam and Alice had been fine, almost too fine. They'd done everything. Brought the brandy, the smelling salts and all. They'd even wanted to help Frank take her home. Then when he'd explained about her being sick and needing the medicine that he'd left at the gas station, Sam had insisted on driving in to get it.

But Frank had finally outtalked him, and they'd managed to leave at last, after Frank had explained that it was nothing serious and that she needed a little fresh air more than anything else.

They'd been very concerned. Worried. They pretended to understand his explanations, but they really hadn't understood at all. However, he didn't believe that they connected her fainting spell with Sam's talk about the play at the school auditorium.

Gradually Kay's grip on his arm relaxed. He could sense her turn to him as she started to speak.

"Oh, God. Oh, God, Frank!" she said.

"Take it easy, baby," Frank told her. "Just—"

"Take it easy? Frank! Dear Lord, don't you understand? The school auditorium. Tomorrow night. It'll be filled with people. With children. Children like Bitty and Sammy. Tomorrow night. When Kosta ..."

She started to cry then and it took him several minutes to quiet her again.

"Frank," she said at last, "what are we going to do?"

He stared at the opaque windshield for several moments before he tried to answer.

"I don't know," he said at last. "I really don't know. There's only one thing I can tell you: We can't leave now."

"No, we can't leave now. We've gone too far to turn back. Oh, God, how did we ever ..."

"Never mind that," Frank said, his voice harsh and bitter. "Never mind that. This isn't the time for regrets."

"We'll have to tell them. Have to bring in the police," Kay said.

Again Frank was silent for a long time before speaking.

"No," he said at last. "No—not yet. I could have walked out on the whole thing, but I can't turn stool pigeon. Not on the man who saved my life."

"The man who's planning to set fire to a building filled with women and children? God, Frank, don't you see ..."

"He doesn't know about the play—about people being in the building tomorrow night," Frank said. "We didn't even know ourselves."

"But it doesn't matter," Kay said. "They'll be there, whether he knows or not."

"I'm not turning him in," Frank said. "Not yet. We'll just have to go back. We'll have to explain."

"And suppose, after you explain, he still wants to go ahead with it."

Frank reached over and pulled her close.

"Honey," he said, "just trust me. One thing I'll promise you: Kosta won't go near the school. If they want to rob a bank, if they want to burn up some broken-down, empty building—well, they can do it. But they won't touch the school. That you can be sure of."

Chapter Nine

1.

It was like a smoldering volcano.

All day the tension had been building up. The very atmosphere, warm, humid, oppressive, seemed a part of it. There wasn't the slightest breath of air, and by six o'clock on Saturday afternoon the mercury had risen to ninety-four. This was high for the time of year; but it wasn't the heat alone.

Mostly it was the people in the house, the expectancy, the fear. And, too, it was the subtle atmosphere of dislike and distrust that had begun to affect them all.

For Flood, Kay, and Frank, there was something else. It had started, likely enough, when Flood had first seen Kay down in Palm Beach. Swiftly his original suspicion had grown until now it flowered like some malignant tropical weed.

There had been that business of her drinking when Waldo, the police sergeant, had arrived. The very fact that the policeman had come at all had been enough to set aflame a fresh spark of suspicion.

And this last thing, this talk about the school.

It wasn't that Flood had said or done anything when Frank talked with him. No, he'd been reasonable enough. At least, reasonable enough for a man who was bent on robbery and possibly murder.

"No," he'd said. "No, I'm not anxious to have the responsibility for women and children, or anyone else, being killed."

Frank had noted that the moral aspects of the thing hadn't worried him. He'd been worried only about the possible results of the crime.

"I don't want that," he'd continued. "You were right to tell me about it. I'll see that Kosta leaves the building alone. He can set off the city hall just as well. It'll be empty."

He'd sounded reasonable enough about it. But there had been something about his expression, something in the look of his eyes, that bothered Frank.

"You've done your job," Flood told Frank. "You and Kay." He pronounced her name with distaste, almost bitterly. "You have nothing more to worry about. I can take it from here on in. All she has to do is sit tight—act natural. And all you have to do is the same. Except I'll want you to drive Kosta tonight. He doesn't know the town and he can't handle a car, anyway. I'll want you to drive him. And then you'll be through."

Yes, it all sounded fine, but it didn't add up.

And then there was the other thing: the way Flood never let him and Kay have a second alone together.

Of the others, Kosta would have seemed the most likely to start showing the strain and going to pieces as the zero hour approached. But oddly enough, Kosta became increasingly calm and self-contained.

He'd stopped drinking, partly through choice and partly because of Flood's constant surveillance. The bulging eyes cleared and became less hysterical and the general air of repressed excitement that had characterized his actions from the moment of his arrival abated.

Most of Saturday afternoon he spent alone in his room, working over the equipment he had carried with him in the heavy suitcase. Once, as evening approached, he had come out and called Flood aside and whispered with him for a few minutes. Returning to his room, he passed Doll, who was returning from the bathroom. Doll, intent on arranging her clothes as she came down the hallway, neither heard his soft tread nor saw him. She brushed against him as they passed.

She looked up quickly, started to smile, and then saw who it was. Kosta didn't look at her, but kept moving on to his own room.

"Bitch," he said in a whisper. "Bitch."

Doll stared at him, speechless. Back again across the table from Wally, she spoke in a whining wail.

"My Gawd, the people in this house!" she said. "That fat creep just damn near ran me down in the hallway—and then he called me a bitch."

Wally stared at her and said nothing.

"What's wrong with everyone around here, anyway?" Doll asked. "That blonde dame—who does she think she is? What's she so stuck up about?"

"Shut up," Wally said sharply. "Just sit down and shut up!"

"What are you getting so snotty about?" she asked.

Instead of answering, he reached across the table and slapped her. "I said shut up."

"Take it easy," Flood said. "I don't want any trouble. Not any at all." He looked at Doll. "Get back to your own room," he said.

Roy lay on his back on one of the beds and said nothing, just watching the others. He felt the excitement, the tenseness, and it made him happy. He watched Wally slap Doll and it made his blood run fast. He hoped that Wally wouldn't stop, that he'd really go to work on her.

Frank, following Flood's instructions, stayed at the gas station until four o'clock, and then returned to the house, leaving Ham in charge of the pumps. Flood had told him to make some sort of excuse and get home early. Kay herself spent most of the day in the kitchen, doing small chores, trying her best to keep busy. She had to prepare food for the others, had to do it carefully, so that in case anyone showed up at the house by accident, everything would look natural.

It was a bad day for her. She didn't know what Frank planned to do; didn't know what he could do.

At the same time, she didn't know Flood's own plans. She knew only that he would rob the bank, and that he'd return to the house to hide out if they weren't able to make a clean getaway. About Kosta—well,

Frank had promised her. She trusted him. But still she worried.

At seven-thirty Kay heard the faint sound of the Loxleys' car start down the road. She went a little pale, and Flood, who was sitting in the kitchen with Frank, raised his eyebrows. He started to get up, ready to leave the room in case the car came in their direction, but then sat down a second later as the sound of the engine retreated into the moist night air.

Finally, at half past eight, he stood up.

"All right, Frank," he said. "About time. I want you and Kosta to leave before nine. I'm going up to talk with him. You better start getting set."

2.

Old Hans Paulmeyer packed his suitcase at seven o'clock, and after tightening the leather straps that encircled it, he washed his hands for the last time, carefully wiped them dry, and then put on his necktie, his coat, and his hat. He hoisted the suitcase from the floor and carried it downstairs. He left it in the hallway while he knocked on the door of the rear ground-floor apartment.

When Mrs. Flagman answered, he handed her an envelope.

"This week's rent," he said gruffly. "Miss Ramsey said to give it to you if I should be leaving. I'm leaving."

Mrs. Flagman reached for the envelope automatically. "I hope everything is all right," she said. "I just hope ..."

The old man turned and stalked back down the hallway, leaving her hoping. He didn't bother to call a taxi, but went at once to the railway depot, carrying the suitcase and limping slightly as he walked. He went first to the ticket window and purchased a through ticket to New York. Then he went to the baggage room and asked to have the suitcase checked through to New York. The clerk told him he would take care of it.

From the depot the old man went to a restaurant across from the bus station. He entered and sat down, first buying an evening paper. He already knew the bus schedule and he took his time in ordering. He had pork chops, mashed potatoes and gravy, two vegetables. Later he ordered apple pie and coffee. He finished everything.

He looked over the headlines as he ate, and when he got up to leave he left the newspaper behind on the table. Walking across the street, he entered the bus station and purchased a one-way ticket for Indio Beach. The ticket agent said the next bus would be through at nine-ten. The old man grunted and went over to the long wooden bench in the waiting room and sat down. He just sat there, quiet and serene, an old, old man, staring at his shoes.

3.

Candle and Shorty left the tourist court sometime after dusk. They had already picked up the rented car, and Shorty drove it while Candle drove his own car. They crossed the bridge that separated the beach section of the town from the older part, and drove down Orange Drive until they had almost reached Almond Avenue. Almond Avenue was the dead-end street that went past the entrance to the power plant. There was a tavern a block down the drive, beyond Almond.

Candle parked just before they came to the tavern; Shorty stopped slightly past it. They entered the place together and walked on past the bar to one of the booths at the rear. Shorty carried the brief case and Candle the golf bag. When the waitress came over, they told her they'd have the regular dinner and a couple of bottles of beer.

The girl brought the beer while they were waiting for the food to come, and Shorty had to move the brief case over to make room for it. The brief case was bulky and very heavy and he handled it with care.

They didn't talk much during the meal.

4.

There was no moon as Frank walked out behind the house to the garage. Flood, who had been careful to look around and make sure no one was in the neighborhood and that no cars were coming, followed directly behind him. Kosta followed Flood, but only as far as Frank's Chevvie, which was parked in the driveway. He stopped there and opened the door and climbed in.

Frank entered the garage and pulled the cord of a single naked bulb that hung over his workbench. Flood was careful to stay away from the window. Frank took a key from his pocket and inserted it into the Yale lock that safeguarded a six-foot tool chest resting on small trestles under the workbench. Flood moved over to watch him as he worked.

Frank reached deep into the box and started removing the tools that he had described three days before to old Paulmeyer. He laid them out neatly on the bench, then reached back into the box and pulled out a pair of cotton work gloves. Using a soft Turkish towel, he methodically wiped off each tool and then placed it in the duffel bag that Flood had used to carry the guns.

When he was through, he lifted the heavy canvas bag and carried it across the garage to the Ford sedan that Wally and Roy had driven up from Palm Beach. He opened the back door and put the bundle on the floor.

As he removed the gloves, he turned to Flood and spoke in a low voice.

"You're sure now that Kosta understands about the school?"

"He understands," Flood said, his voice soft, almost friendly. "He knows what he has to do."

"Why wouldn't it be better for him to take the train out as soon as he's through?" Frank asked. "Why should he bother to come back here at all?"

"Because he's already been here," Flood said. "People know he's been here. You don't want him disappearing now, at the same time the thing happens."

Frank had to agree.

"We'll be pulling out at ten-thirty sharp," Flood said. "We pick up the old man at a quarter to eleven. It will take us about fifteen minutes to get inside the bank. We go in through the rear. But I'm allowing for up to half an hour in case any one's around or we have any sort of trouble. I don't expect trouble. Not if you and Kosta handle your end."

Frank had already gone over the plans with Flood a dozen times. He wondered why Flood was telling him about it again. A moment later, as Flood continued talking, he understood.

"The only change is this," Flood said. "When you and Kosta get through, don't return to the house at once. Wait until the fire has a chance to get well started and the alarm has been sounded. There's going to be enough traffic going out of here and I want to be sure that things are all set in town; that people will be running to the fire and that there'll be plenty of commotion. Then, when you return, you probably won't be noticed."

Frank thought about it for several moments.

"What do you think we should be doing?" he asked. "We'll have some time to kill."

"Do whatever you would normally do over in town on a Saturday night. Go to a bar, do anything that will be natural. Don't forget, that fire will be burning. The natural thing will be to go to it, the same as the rest of the people in town will be doing."

"All right," Frank said. "You want us, then, to wait until you have a chance to leave, before we get back here?"

"Right."

A minute later they left the garage and started back to the house. Frank went only as far as the Chevvie. Flood hesitated a moment, then reached out and patted him on the back. He continued into the house as Frank climbed behind the wheel.

Kosta said nothing as he pulled out of the driveway. It wasn't until they were halfway into town that he spoke.

"A drink," Kosta said. "I want to stop somewhere and get a drink before I do it."

Frank's first instinct was to protest, to remind Kosta that Flood had given strict orders against drinking. And then, he changed his mind. A drink would be the best thing possible. It would take time to get a drink; time that Frank himself needed.

At this particular moment Frank suddenly made the final decision, the decision he had been postponing all afternoon and evening; the decision that he had been gradually approaching since the night before, when he had driven Kay home.

There would be no fire. No fire at all. Not only would he prevent the burning of the school auditorium, but he'd keep Kosta from setting the city hall off as well.

The hell with Flood and the hell with all of them. If Flood wanted to take the bank, let him. But no fires. He couldn't call the police; he couldn't turn Flood in. But he could do this one thing. He could prevent Kosta from following through with his end of the plan.

He thought then of Kay, back at the house alone with Flood and those others, and, thinking of her, he felt an icy chill go down the back of his spine.

If there was no fire, Flood would know. He wouldn't leave the house at all. He wouldn't leave unless it was to make his escape. But before he escaped he'd take care of Kay. One way or another. He'd take her with him, or he'd leave her. But if he left her....

Frank needed time to think. And time was running out. The Tropical Bar was just ahead, on the outskirts of the business district, three blocks from the city hall.

Jerking the wheel to the right, Frank pulled in to the curb. He opened the car door and stepped to the street.

"Let's go," he said. "We got time for one quick double."

Kosta followed him into the place. The bar was filled with the usual Saturday-night crowd, but they found a deserted booth.

The waiter had to ask for the order twice. Frank looked up at him blankly for a moment, and then he brought his mind back. He ordered double Scotch for himself and Kosta asked for gin.

It was then that Frank saw the solution. The simplest, easiest way out. He had to give Flood and the others a chance to leave the house, to leave Kay, and they wouldn't leave until a fire started. And at the same time he had to prevent Kosta from setting the fire.

Preventing Kosta from acting should be easy. As for the fire, why not a false alarm? He could set a false alarm at exactly nine-forty-five and then another at ten-thirty, as Flood would be taking off. He'd hear the sirens; in a town like Indio Beach, everyone within a radius of five miles could hear the sound of the alarms.

Then, the moment Flood and the others were gone, he'd go back and pick up Kay.

If Flood wanted to go ahead with the bank, all right. Let him. That he wouldn't stop.

He was thinking about it, planning it, as he became conscious of the pressure against his arm. He looked up.

Kosta was staring at him and his pudgy, short little fingers were plucking at his sleeve.

"Over there," Kosta said. "Over there by the door. Isn't that man who just came in a cop?"

Frank looked up, but saw no one he knew. He shook his head.

"He stepped in back of the tall one," Kosta said. "The shorter one, in back of the tall one with the cowboy hat."

"So what if he is a cop?" Frank said, irritation in his voice.

"I want to know," Kosta said. "Please, stretch around and tell me. Tell me if you know him."

Frank shrugged. He leaned across the booth and still couldn't see the man. And so he stood up and turned his head, stretching.

If it hadn't been for the mirror behind the bar directly opposite the booth, he never would have seen it. As it was, all he caught, looking between the two broad-shouldered silhouettes that partially obscured his view of the mirror, was the image of the glass on the table and the hand slyly reaching over and dropping something into it.

He needed no more than the sight of the hand. He recognized the pudgy, babyish fingers.

As he dropped back into his seat, the thought flashed through his mind that this might be Flood's idea. Or was Kosta doing it on his own? It could be either way.

He spent no time in idle conjecture. He had no time, no time at all.

"Nobody I ever saw before," he said, and as he spoke he looked straight into Kosta's eyes and his hand reached out for his glass. But he didn't pick up the glass. Instead, clumsily, he knocked it off the edge of the table.

He jumped up quickly.

"Damn," he said. "Damnit, how can I be so clumsy!"

He didn't know whether he got away with it or not. He didn't much care. It didn't matter what Kosta thought. The only thing that mattered was to get the man out of the place, get him away to some quiet, secluded spot and make him harmless.

But he couldn't take a chance of knocking him out and leaving him. With Kosta he had only two courses. He'd have to turn him in or take him with them when they left. And you didn't turn a man like Kosta in, unless you were ready to have him talk.

There was only the other thing. A quick blow on the jaw, then tie him up, toss him in the back of the car, and do what he had to do.

Later he and Kay could drop him off somewhere out in the Glades. Somewhere far from Indio Beach and the city hall and the school auditorium.

Someplace where he'd be harmless.

Kosta insisted on another drink and Frank went along with him. He didn't want trouble if he could help it. The moment the drink came he raised it to his lips and downed it. Then he stood up and handed the waiter a bill.

He started for the door and there was nothing for Kosta to do but follow him. Once in the car, he headed up the street, and when he came opposite the city hall, he cut over to the right to circle the building. He made another right-hand turn and then stopped halfway up the block. They were on a dark, unlighted street, little more than an alley, behind the courthouse. Opposite was a huge vacant parking lot, used during the day by customers of the supermarket on the other side of it. There were no lights in the deserted city hall, and it loomed dark and brooding in the still night.

"The suitcase in the back," Kosta said. "Will you hand it to me, please?"

Frank turned and leaned over the back of the seat, reaching for the bag.

The fool, he thought. Trying to give me knockout drops. It was just the sort of thing he could have expected from a man of Kosta's type. But he'd been lucky, nevertheless.

It was the last thought that passed through his mind before the pistol butt crashed into the side of his skull.

5.

At ten-fifteen Alice Loxley stood in the wings just off the stage of the Indio Beach High School auditorium. She held Bitty in her arms. The child had fallen asleep with her rosebud mouth half open and the long dark lashes caressing her pink, rounded cheeks. Alice herself looked somewhat disheveled. It had been a tough night. Bitty had been irritable, and little Sammy, who had been too excited to take his afternoon nap, had grown sleepy along about eight-thirty and had had to be awakened and put into his homemade costume in time to go on stage.

Sam had tried to help, but Alice found that she could handle it better alone, and had shooed him out in front, where he sat with the other proud fathers.

And now at last the curtain had gone up and Samuel Loxley, Jr., had walked out across the stage, and in front of the outstanding citizens of Indio Beach was facing a dragon. The dragon consisted of three fifth graders partially concealed in a long, oddly bulging tube of velvet, which everyone in the audience recognized as a piece from the old curtain at the Bijou Theatre.

Alice put up a hand to wipe the perspiration from her forehead and at that moment the sound of the fire siren began its pulsing wail.

Hal Morgan, sitting two seats down from Sam Loxley—Hal's ten-year-old son, Dick, was the middle part of the dragon—was so intent on watching his offspring that for a second or two he didn't get the full significance of the alarm.

By the time he did, Sam was already trying to get past him. Torn between admiration for his offspring and his obvious duty—Hall was a lieutenant in the Indio Beach Volunteers—he quickly leaped to his feet and in a second was running down the aisle after Sam.

The children on the stage suddenly ceased all activity, thus prolonging the dragon's life for minutes on end after the time he was normally supposed to have succumbed to Sammy's lance. They stood frozen as they listened to the siren.

The main doorway of the auditorium was crowded with a dozen or more men and there was a general air of controlled confusion in the hall as volunteer firemen rushed for the doorway.

In the meantime, Jane Mellon, first-grade teacher who always played the background piano music for the school festivals, valiantly pounded the keys, her right foot pressing hard on the loud pedal.

The wail of the siren was suddenly interrupted by the sound of a terrific explosion, and for a brief moment, as the entire sky lighted up, the lights within the auditorium dimmed.

Waldo Harrington, who had been standing at the entrance of the auditorium, was already in his squad car and racing toward the center of town before the first carful of volunteers headed for the firehouse, a few blocks away.

A town the size of Indio Beach doesn't have a great many fires, and this, the second one within a week now, created a tremendous amount of excitement, even before most of the people of the town realized that it was their city hall that was going up in smoke.

6.

Ham Johnstone had followed the same procedure he had followed on Saturday nights for as long as he could remember. That is, the Saturday nights on which he received a pay check.

He'd closed the gas station after washing up, and then he'd climbed into the old service car and driven out about three miles north of the city to Black Town. He'd stopped in front of the general store and gone in and cashed his check, at the same time paying his weekly bill for groceries and sundries.

He stopped and talked for a few minutes with the storekeeper and his wife, and then he left and went into the gin mill a half block down the street. Fanny Smith, who ran the gin mill, was an old friend. Ham went to the end bar where Fanny sat in a huge old wicker chair. He took out his wallet and carefully removed a five-dollar bill. Then he handed the wallet to Fanny.

Each Monday morning he'd stop by and she'd return the wallet to him, its contents intact. Neither dynamite nor the fear of God would have forced her to part with it before that time.

Ham's next step was to return to the middle section of the bar and order a drink for the house. The house consisted of anyone that happened to be in the place at the time. This first drink, on this particular Saturday, set him back three of his five dollars. The rest of his evening would depend on the two remaining dollars, plus any casual drinks that might be forthcoming as a result of his initial generosity.

At ten o'clock, happy, hungry, half loaded, and cold broke, Ham left the gin mill and climbed into the old service car. He started the motor, threw the car into second gear, and headed back through town and out Orange Drive, toward the section past the city limits where he lived in a tiny shack in a deserted real-estate development. He kept the car in second gear all the way, realizing that he'd had quite a bit to drink and wanting to play it safe.

He had reached his turnoff, about a mile from where the Harpers lived, when he heard the siren. A moment later the sound of the explosion reached his ears. He stopped the car and looked back toward town in time to see flames shooting high in the air.

"Well, I'll be," he said. "I certainly will. I'll be."

He started the car again, suddenly and miraculously almost sober.

"Better go over and see if Mr. Harper wants I should get down to the gas station," he said, speaking aloud. "Yes, sir, I sure better."

He remembered Frank's sending him over to watch for sparks when they'd had the warehouse fire.

7.

The five of them sat there and waited. Doll asked Wally to play cards with her, but he didn't bother to answer. She turned to Kay, but Kay sat staring blindly out of the darkened window at the night, so Doll shrugged and kept quiet. Roy was busy with a penknife, cleaning his nails. Flood did nothing. He just sat and watched the others.

Finally, as the clock down in the hall struck ten, Flood stood up.

"Doll," he said, "go to your room."

She looked up at him, startled.

"I said go to your room."

For a moment she opened her mouth to protest, but then, seeing the expression in his eyes, she quickly got up and went out. As soon as he heard the slam of the door down the hall, Flood turned to Wally.

"All right," he said. "Go on in there. Tie her up. Tie her and gag her."

Wally nodded, his face grim.

"And you, Roy, you go along with him and see that he does a good job of it."

Roy put the penknife away and grinned.

"Don't hurt her," Flood said coldly. "I don't want any screaming."

When they had left the room, he turned to Kay. She was watching him, her face pale.

"We're leaving in a few minutes," Flood said. He stared into her face, his eyes bleak and expressionless. "You're to stay here with Doll. I had her tied up so that she couldn't possibly give you any trouble." He stopped and for a long minute was silent. "Maybe," he said at last, "you're wondering why I don't worry about you giving me trouble."

"Me?" Kay said. "Me give you trouble?" She looked at him, startled. She felt fear, but even more than that, she felt the strange sense of guilt.

Moving with the speed of a cat, he swung his right arm and slapped her hard across the face with his open hand.

"Yes, you!" he said. "What the hell do you think I am, stupid or something? Don't you think I can see what's been going on? Between you and Frank?"

He reached out and slapped her again, back and forth across the face, and the tears came to her eyes as she fell back. But he was careful not to hit her too hard. Then he pulled her to him, holding her with one hand twisted in the front of her light cotton shirt. He lifted her chin with his other hand and stared down at her, his mouth a thin, twisted, bloodless line.

"But you won't make trouble," he said. "You'll stay right here with Doll and do nothing. Not until I come back. And do you know why you will?"

She didn't answer.

"You will because your boy friend isn't coming back. Not for quite a while. He's staying with Kosta. He doesn't know it, but Kosta's keeping him with him until we're all through. I want you to remember it. Frank will be with Kosta. When we've pulled the job and come back here, if everything's all right and you've behaved yourself, then we'll let you see Frank again. Then everything will be fine."

For a second she thought of protesting, of trying to convince him that nothing had changed. But she knew that it would be no good. She couldn't fool him; he was too smart. Saying anything would only make it worse.

"Frank's loyal to you, Flood," she said. "You must know that. He's been loyal all along."

"Maybe he has," Flood told her. "Maybe you both are loyal. I don't know, and I no longer care. I only know one thing: Nothing is going to interfere with tonight. I'm taking no chances. You stay here. Keep your eye on that girl, and don't let her get away. If everything goes all right, you'll have nothing to worry about."

No, she thought, nothing to worry about. He knew about her and Frank. With his evil, quick mind and his sensitiveness, he also probably knew that they were planning to run out, as well. And they had Frank. He had suspected and somehow they had trapped Frank. There was nothing she could do now. Nothing at all.

He flung her away from him as the door opened and Wally and Roy came back into the, room.

"She'll hold," Wally said.

"O.K.," Flood said. "Let's get started."

They were downstairs then, in the kitchen, when they heard the distant sound of the fire siren. As though on signal, they all stood dead still for a moment and listened.

"That's it," Flood said. "Have you got everything?"

Wally, halfway to the door, suddenly stopped.

"Jesus," he said, "I forgot." He turned and hurried back upstairs. He was buckling on a shoulder holster when he returned. Roy had shoved his own .38 automatic down inside his belt. He buttoned his light sports coat over it. If Flood carried a gun, Kay didn't know where. She had never seen him with one.

Wally finished pulling on his own coat and then he reached for the submachine gun he had laid on the table when he'd first come downstairs. He and Wally started for the door.

Flood turned back once more to Kay.

"Don't forget," he said. "Just don't forget."

Wally had the door half open and Flood was about to pass him when they heard the sound of the car.

Roy quickly ducked back into the room. They stood there like that for the next half minute, like statues, Flood and Wally at the door, Roy tense and poised a couple of feet inside the room, and Kay over by the kitchen table.

There was no mistake about it. It was a car, all right, coming down the road toward the house.

"Kosta?" Wally asked in a hoarse voice.

"No, you fool," Flood said. "No, someone else. Quick, into the living room."

It was then that Kay learned where he kept his gun. He whipped it from under his left armpit as he swiftly ushered the other two into the hallway leading to the next room.

"Stay here," he ordered Kay in a low whisper. "Get rid of 'em quick."

The car pulled into the yard as Flood stepped through the door leading into the hall and closed it all but a couple of inches.

A moment later there was a quick knock on the back screen door. Before Kay could reach it, the door opened.

Ham Johnstone came into the room.

"Miz Harper!" he said, breathless. "Miz Harper, the boss heah? They's a big fire over town an' I gotta see the boss."

Kay knew that he must have been drinking, but she knew too that he was sober enough to know what he was saying and doing. And she knew that she had to get rid of him, at once.

"Why, Ham," she said, "you must have passed him on the road. Mr. Harper heard the siren and he's already left for town."

Instead of saying anything, Ham took off his cap and scratched his head, shaking it back and forth several times. Then he looked up and grinned.

"Well, well," he said. "Don't that beat nothin'? He's sure the fast one, that Mr. Harper."

"You'd better get on over," Kay said. "He may need you at the gas station, just in case the fire's nearby."

Even as she spoke she could hear a tiny rustle of sound at the door. She looked at Ham pleadingly. Oh, God, why didn't he leave while he could?

Ham still shook his head, as though he hadn't heard her. "Can't understand," he said slowly. "Just can't understand why I didn't pass him comin' in heah."

Kay stepped forward with her hands out, almost as though to push him from the room. Suddenly she stopped and stared at him. He was looking past her, over her shoulder, and his eyes were suddenly wide. His mouth had fallen open and he was no longer smiling. As Kay swung around, a shot exploded almost in her ears. She saw Flood standing in the doorway, the gun in his hand, before a tiny cry escaped from her lips and she turned back to the colored man.

But Ham was no longer standing there. He had lurched to one side and was down on his knees. As she watched, he fell slowly forward on his face with his arms outstretched.

"And that," Flood said, stepping into the room, "is what will happen to Frank if you get out of line."

She was leaning down over Ham, holding back the sob in her throat, but with her eyes still raised and watching them, as Wally and Roy and Flood went out through the kitchen door and crossed the back porch, heading for the garage.

Chapter Ten

1.

He climbed down from the bus at four minutes after ten. There were a half-dozen people around the lunch counter in the restaurant and they had all turned and watched the big blue and white bus as it pulled in and stopped. They stared at the three or four nondescript passengers that got off, but no one noticed him in particular.

He was just another old man getting off of a late bus. Old men were always getting off of busses in Indio Beach and no one ever paid any attention to them.

Instead of going into the restaurant, he walked over to the long wooden bench in front of the place. He sat down and took off his light felt hat and pulled a handkerchief from his coat pocket and wiped the perspiration from his forehead. He looked up and then turned so that he could see the clock on the wall inside the restaurant. He pulled the ancient railway watch from his vest pocket and checked it against the time.

Putting the watch back, he took out his pipe and lit it, smoking the remainder of the tobacco that he had packed in and partially smoked earlier. Ten minutes later he looked at his watch again, not bothering with the clock in the lunchroom. As he was putting the watch back in his pocket, he heard the sound of the siren.

He paid no attention to the people who rushed out of the restaurant and looked over toward the town. Not even when the explosion went off and the sky lighted up with swift yellow flames did he move.

The counterman came out then and the others started across the road, in the direction of the flames.

"By God," the counterman said, speaking to no one in particular, "looks like it's the city hall this time." He went back and took his apron off and then came through the door again and headed for the fire.

Twenty minutes later, the old man was still sitting there. Once again he checked his heavy gold watch. This time, after putting it back in his pocket, he slowly got to his feet and started walking south along the edge of the highway. He was two blocks from the station, having walked very slowly, when a car came up behind him. It passed him and then quickly braked to a halt.

When he was even with it, the rear door on his side swung open.

"Get in," Flood said.

He stumbled over the sack of tools as he crowded into the back seat. Wally, who was driving, ground the gears in his hurry to get going.

Three minutes later he pulled into the alley behind the bank. He parked in a dark recess between two large cement trucks, which were backed up to the loading platform of the town's leading lumber and hardware company. The trucks, as Flood knew, were always left there over weekends.

The moment the motor was cut, Flood turned toward the back of the car. "We'll wait here, Pop," he said, "until the boys open up. Then you and I go in."

As Wally and Roy left the car, Flood leaned out the window. The sky was dark, but now and then flames shot up from the city hall, a half-dozen blocks to the north. Even from where he sat, Flood could hear the shouts and the noise of the crowd, and now and then he detected the crackle of flames eating through wood. Several times he heard the sirens in the distance and he correctly guessed that the state police were arriving to help keep the crowds back and control traffic.

He stepped out then and, walking around the car, looked in the direction in which he knew the school lay.

He swore under his breath. Damn it, what was the matter with Kosta? What was taking him so long?

He got back into the car and spoke to the old man. "It will take the boys a few minutes," He said. "They're not going into the bank, but through the rear door of the millinery shop next to it. We follow them in and we climb upstairs. It's an empty loft up there. We have to break through a wall, which will put us in a bathroom over the private offices of the bank. There's a stairway leading down from the bathroom to the bank's offices. We go down and then we wait for the power plant to go out. When it does, you start to work."

"How about burglar alarms?" Paulmeyer rumbled.

"None in the millinery store and none in the loft. We don't hit any till we're in the bank lobby. By that time there won't be any electricity. The alarms work off the regular city power system."

Paulmeyer leaned back in the car and waited quietly. He'd allowed the pipe to go out and he made no further attempt to ignite it.

2.

Candle was looking at the clock over the center of the bar when he heard the sound of the fire siren. Quickly his eyes went to Shorty.

"Forty minutes to go," he said.

Shorty nodded, not paying much attention. He was watching the customers of the place as they began to stream into the street. A few moments later, when the explosion sounded and he heard the clang of the fire apparatus, he lifted his glass and spoke slowly.

"Better order another one. That bartender looks like he'll take off any minute himself."

Candle laughed. "These small towns!" he said. "They're something."

The bartender was still at the door as Shorty picked up their empty glasses and carried them over and tapped him on the shoulder. Reluctantly he returned and refilled them. He went back to the opened doorway at once.

A few moments later, as the siren continued to wail its macabre dirge and they heard the clanging of additional fire equipment, Candle once more looked up, his expression quizzical.

"Nice break for us," he said, in a barely audible whisper. "If this thing keeps up, it will keep every cop in town tied up. All three of them. State police, too, in case any're around."

Shorty nodded. "You don't suppose this is a part of it, do you?"

Candle looked at him curiously for a minute. Slowly he nodded. "Could be," he said. "It could be. You know Flood. Imagination. Plenty of imagination."

"But hell!" Shorty said. "He wouldn't go around setting fires, would he? Not fires."

Candle didn't answer, but once more looked at the clock. "Let's go," he said. "We'll drive past the fire first. Like to see what it is; how much law is around."

They took the rented car, leaving their own where it was parked.

Within a block, Candle realized it was a major blaze. The whole town seemed to have turned out to watch, and he knew that if he attempted to get any closer, he might find himself locked in traffic. So he cut down a side street and returned to Almond Avenue.

"You set?" he asked as he drove toward the entrance to the power company.

"Yeah. All set."

He passed the drive leading into the place and went to the end of the street, which stopped at the fence marking the railroad right of way. Carefully he backed the car around and then drove a few hundred yards and came to a stop. There was no one in sight.

Candle left the key in the ignition and cut the lights. He stepped out of the car and Shorty handed him the golf bag. Shorty sat in the car and opened the brief case. He took out a pair of .38 police positives. One he put in the side pocket of his jacket, the other he handed to Candle.

They walked up the drive toward the entrance to the power plant, Shorty in front and Candle following, lugging the golf bag. There was a single naked bulb over the small door leading into the place. Candle set the bag down on the ground and then reached up and unscrewed the bulb. In the dark, Shorty handed him the Halloween mask, after he had pulled his own over his face. And then they opened the door and walked inside.

The blackout hit Indio Beach at exactly eleven o'clock.

Over at the high-school auditorium, where the Saturday-night festivities had already suffered a serious casualty when most of the male audience had deserted to go to the fire, the curtain was just about to come down on the final sketch of the evening.

And in the Ranchers and Fruit Growers Trust Company, Flood, followed by Roy, Wally, and old Paulmeyer, walked from the executive offices toward the room holding the huge main vault.

In front of the city hall, Sergeant Waldo Harrington, his shirt half torn off and covered with soot, turned to State Trooper Menninger and Fire Chief Nixon and swore loudly as the street lights went out.

"Now what!" he yelled. "Jesus Christ, looks like every damn light in town is out. Get over to a phone and see what's happened, Menny."

3.

At first there was nothing, nothing but the pain. The shattering, splitting, throbbing ache. And then, as consciousness gradually returned, he identified himself as a person, as something human and alive and suffering.

He remembered who he was, but for the next few moments he couldn't recall where he was or what had happened to him. There was a sweet-sour taste in his mouth and he was next aware that something soft and warm was coursing down the side of his face. At last he realized that it was blood and that the pain was in his head.

He still couldn't figure out where he was or how he had got there. Trying to think about it, trying to bring some order out of the chaos of his mind, he understood at last that he had been hurt. And then he remembered Kosta, remembered leaving the bar and driving with him to the city hall. He remembered leaning over the back seat of the car.

He was still in the car, but it was moving now. He felt the regularity of the vibrations, smelled the familiar smell of an automobile. He was all crushed up, lying in Stygian darkness half on his knees and half on his side. The ringing in his ears abated then and he knew that he was hearing the sound of an engine.

There seemed to be a great deal of noise, and in his effort to clarify the confusion of sounds, he suddenly identified the shrill note of a police whistle. He heard yells and cries and then there was the rumble of a passing truck, and then a siren.

His mind went back to Kosta, and from Kosta to what Kosta had planned to do.

He groaned and tried to lift his head. At once conscious of his own groan, he shuddered and became still. He knew that he must not warn whoever was driving the car that he had regained consciousness.

The outside noises lessened and for a moment he tried to dismiss the awful thought of the school auditorium from his mind. There was a fire. Those other noises had told him that. But maybe there was still time; maybe it wasn't the school yet. In spite of the pain in his head, he made a terrible effort to think clearly. He had to think clearly.

He was huddled on the floor of a car. Under the front seat, from the nearness of the sound of the engine. It wasn't hard for him, now, to identify the place in the darkness. He'd worked under the dashboards of a lot of cars in the last three months.

He began to understand what had happened. Kosta had slugged him with something, probably the butt of a gun, as he had leaned over to get the bag. He had underestimated Kosta all along the line. He hadn't dreamed that Kosta even carried a gun. In fact, he remembered Kosta bitterly complaining when it had been suggested that he might go armed.

Yes, he had underestimated Kosta. He'd been a fool, a double fool, especially after the warning he'd had in the bar.

Kosta had slugged him, knocked him out. And he had set the fire. One fire?

Frank didn't want to think about that. God, he prayed that it was only the one fire. Frank knew what would have happened if that school auditorium were ever ignited with all those people in it.

He knew then a bitter moment of regret; regret that he had ever become involved in the terrible plot in the first place; regret for his stupidity in thinking that one crime could be committed without setting up a pattern of events that sooner or later would lead to violence and murder.

But it was too late now for regrets. He just hoped to God it was not too late for other things.

He knew Kosta. Even if he was lucky and Kosta had only set fire to the city hall, Frank knew he would go on to the school. Kosta would not rest now. Even if Flood had instructed him to pass the school up—and Frank wasn't convinced that he had—it wouldn't matter. Kosta was a madman. This was his night.

Carefully Frank moved his hands. He almost cried out in relief when he discovered that they hadn't been bound.

He understood then that Kosta was on his way to the school now. He'd set one fire and, convinced that Frank was unconscious and would remain so for a long time, he was going now to complete his evil task. The auditorium was to be his masterpiece.

Frank understood something of the queer, twisted mentality of a man like Kosta. An empty building blazing into the night sky would be fine, but it would act only as the first taste of blood. Kosta would want screaming, flaming death before his night's work was through.

But now there was no more time to think about it or to plan. The throb of the engine diminished and then he heard the crunch of sand under the wheels and the forward movement stopped. Frank heard the driver pull up the hand brake.

It was quiet now, quiet except for the low, harsh mumbling from the seat above him. There was a sudden flash of light and Frank closed his eyes swiftly as he felt the beam of a flashlight fall on his face. Then there was a sharp, dull blow, striking his face, and he knew that Kosta had drawn back his foot and kicked him. He had to exert tremendous self-control not to cry out.

He heard low, maniacal laughter, and then the man crawled across his body and opened the door of the car and stepped out. A moment later he heard the rear door as it was opened and he knew that Kosta was taking out his deadly equipment.

It was torture, but he lay there and waited until Kosta's muffled footsteps retreated into the distance.

His muscles were cramped and one leg seemed dead and bloodless, but torturously he forced himself up until he had his head above the window of the car door.

Off to the left was the school auditorium, and he knew at once that the car was parked in the playground in back of the building.

He half fell out of the car and staggered toward the auditorium.

He knew where to look. There was only one spot that lay in total blackness: the rear door of the building, the one leading into the darkened dressing rooms used by the athletic teams; wooden rooms with wooden benches and wooden lockers, fragile and inflammable.

The door was opened a crack when he reached it.

For a moment he thought wildly of seeking help, of sounding an alarm. But then at once he knew that he would have no time, that already it was too late for an alarm. Kosta would have the kerosene, he'd have the package of dynamite caps. Even if Frank could warn those in the building in time, the explosion would still take place before they could all get out.

He knew what would happen in that auditorium filled with women and children if they all started for the exits at the same time. He knew and he shuddered and threw caution to the winds and ran into the dressing rooms.

The candle in Kosta's hand guided him. He had time to see the other's yellow, pudgy face with the bulging, russet eyes staring at him like some devil's mask as he leaped. His left hand closed on the candle. That was all he was thinking about, the need to extinguish that flame. He wasn't conscious of the burning flesh as his hand closed over it.

The soft, baby hands were at his throat then, but they were no longer soft. The nails were like tiny daggers and he felt the skin of his neck tear.

He felt Kosta's flabby body press against his own and he dropped the already extinguished candle and both hands went to Kosta's wrist.

But Kosta had the strength of an insane man, and as the channel of his throat closed and he struggled for air, Frank suddenly knew that he would never tear those hands away.

It was then that he became conscious of the hard object pressing into his side, and he knew what it was at once: the gun in Kosta's jacket pocket.

His hands fell from the murderous wrists and he fumbled and then he had the gun in his right fist.

It was a glancing blow, but it struck, and for a moment the hands clawing at his throat relaxed. It gave him his chance and he lifted the weapon again and brought it crashing down on Kosta's head.

He fell on top of him as Kosta toppled to the floor.

He never did remember pulling Kosta back to the car. He couldn't recall why he had wanted to do it, unless some automatic protective instinct was at work and he had subconsciously remembered that Kosta would be identified with him and Kay should he be found there in the back room of the auditorium.

It was only when he was halfway out to the house that things began to clear up in his mind.

There was only a single thought now: Kay. Get back to the house and get Kay. Find Kay and leave.

4.

The thin needle of light wavered and for a moment the small, black hole was in darkness.

"Back," Paulmeyer muttered. "Back on the hole. Keep it steady."

Wally found the hole again and the old man went back to work.

"How long?" Flood asked.

"Soon," Paulmeyer said. "Don't rush me."

He worked for another five minutes and then got up off his knees. "Give me the light," he said.

Wally handed him the pencil flash.

"All right. Back. All of you. Get back."

They fell back then, the three of them, Flood, Wally, and Roy. Once more Paulmeyer stooped down and there was the flicker of a match. A moment later he too hurried away from the front of the safe.

When the explosion came, it threw the old man to his knees on the rug of the office where he crouched. Flood saw him fall in the blinding flash that followed within a split second of the terrific roar, but he made no effort to go to his aid. He didn't wait until the billowing clouds of smoke cleared, but rushed at once to the vault. He was like a madman as he plowed through the rubbish.

He didn't have to tell Wally and Roy what to do. They were already there at his side with the empty sack, scrounging in the debris.

Paulmeyer slowly got to his feet. He went first to watch the others as they worked in the dim light of the blackened oil lamp that Wally had set on the floor in front of the gaping vault. He watched for less than a half minute and then he grunted. He turned and walking with unerring instinct in the darkness, made his way back through the offices and upstairs. He coughed as the smoke reached his lungs, but kept on going. Soon he was in the building next door and then he was downstairs and in the alley.

As he reached the end of the alley, he heard the sound of a distant siren. He hurried toward the railroad station.

Far down the tracks, south of the town, the great round headlight of the Sunshine Special, running from Miami to New York, cut through the night air, and the engineer slowly began to release the throttle for the stop at Indio Beach. He thought it odd, as the train pulled into the outskirts of the town, that there was not a light in the entire city.

The Sunshine Special was already four minutes behind schedule and he had other problems on his mind. He was grateful that there was only one passenger standing on the platform. The stop took less than two minutes, and then the lonely whistle of the train cut the night air, as once more it started north.

5.

He was turning off Orange Drive into the lateral road when the street lights went out. At first he thought it was only that he had come to the edge of the town, but then almost at once he realized what had happened. He would have to hurry. Flood and the others wouldn't be long now.

Possibly it was because of this hurry that it happened, but he took the corner sharply and skidded. The rear wheel of the car slid off the road and into the broken coral-rock shoulder. The sound as the tire blew was like a pistol shot. Instinctively he let up on the gas, but he didn't stop. He attempted to keep going, to limp far enough to get the car home on the flat.

Quickly he realized that it wouldn't work. He would be able to make it, sooner or later, but he'd waste more time than if he pulled over and changed the tire.

He cursed as he came to a halt. It was necessary to move Kosta to get at the tools, but the man showed no signs of consciousness as Frank lifted his body and dropped it into the back.

It was difficult in the dark, but his practice at the service station during the last three months came to his aid, and after a certain amount of fumbling he had the wheel off.

He was almost finished when he heard the sound of a siren far down the road. He looked up as the car approached from the west, and as it went screaming past he knew that it was a state police car, called in by radio from somewhere in the center of the state.

Time was running out.

At last the spare was on the wheel and he'd pulled up the lug bolts. He didn't bother to take the jack down, but put his shoulder to the rear of the machine and rocked it free.

Seven minutes later the house loomed up like a great gray ghost out of the night as he cut the wheel and turned into his own driveway. He didn't stop in the yard, but drove through the open door of the garage. Then, before he had a chance to turn off the engine and switch off the lights, she rushed up to him, reaching for him with both arms through the open window at his side.

"Oh, God, Frank," she said. "Oh, thank God. You're here at last."

She saw the blood on his head and started to cry out, but he quieted her at once.

"I'm all right," he said. "All right, honey. But we've got to leave at once. Quick, now!"

But as she started to say something, to open the car door, he remembered Kosta.

"No," he said. "No. Go back to the house. Get what we must take."

He didn't want her there when he pulled Kosta from the car.

She stared at him, barely able to make out his features in the dim glow from the headlights.

"I can't," she said. "I can't go back. He's there."

"Who's there?" Frank asked, sudden new alarm in his voice.

"Ham," she said. "Ham Johnstone. In the kitchen. He's—he's dead."

He stared at her wordlessly for a moment, and then slowly he climbed out of the car.

"They killed him," she said. "For no reason at all, they shot him."

In a daze he left her and started for the back porch. Quickly she caught up with him.

"Frank," she said. "Frank, not now." Her voice was a pleading cry. "There's nothing we can do now. Nothing. If we're going to go we must do it at once. You can't help Ham now."

He kept going, stalking toward the house as though he didn't hear her at all.

He found the kerosene lantern on the back porch, lit it, and carried it into the kitchen. He leaned down beside the body of the fallen man. For minutes he was still, and then at last he looked up.

"Go to the telephone," he said, his voice a dull monotone. "Go to the phone and call the police."

"But Frank ..."

"I'm through running," he said. "All through."

She looked at him then and the tears slowly came into her eyes.

"Yes, Frank," she said at last. "I'll call them."

She started to turn away, and then stopped for a moment and said, "The girl's upstairs. Tied up."

Three minutes later, when he came downstairs, one hand behind him leading Doll, Kay was sitting in front of the telephone, the receiver at her ear. The kerosene lamp was on the floor beside her. She looked at Frank with frightened eyes.

"It's the operator," she said. "She says the switchboard is hopelessly jammed up. She can't get through to the police. There's no telling how long—"

"Never mind the phone," Frank said. "We haven't time now. You'll have to take the car and drive into town. Find the police. They'll be somewhere, probably around the fire. At the city hall. Find them and bring them back with you."

She started to leave and he remembered Kosta. He still didn't know whether Kosta was alive or dead.

Quickly he crossed the room, reaching the door before she did.

"Wait," he said. "Wait for one minute. I'll bring the car out."

He ran across the yard and into the garage. Opening the rear door of the car, he reached in, and his hand found the fabric of the man's coat. He jerked and pulled and Kosta rolled out on the cement floor. Frank pushed him to one side and then got into the car and backed it out. Kay was waiting in the side yard as he stopped.

"Frank," she said. "Oh, Frank, are you sure?"

"I'm sure," he said. "Dead sure. Hurry."

He was back in the kitchen as Kay swung out of the yard. Doll stood in the doorway, her horrified eyes staring down at Ham's body. She looked at Frank when he came into the room.

"You're crazy," she said. "Crazy!"

Frank went to the table and pulled a chair out and sat down. He didn't look at her.

"No," he said. "I'm sane. Sane for the first time in months. Maybe for the first time in my whole life."

6.

In spite of the bad breaks, of all the trouble, in spite of everything that had gone wrong, he'd pulled it off. He'd got away with it.

God, he felt great!

Riding in the back seat of the sedan, Flood nudged the bulky weight of the duffel bag on the seat at his side. A half million, maybe more!

Nothing had stopped him; not Wally with his stupid Doll, not Kosta, that mad, insane pyromaniac with his drinking, not Frank or Kay or any of them. He overcame everything, every obstacle.

In another half hour he'd be behind the wheel of the Caddie and on his way. Roy and Wally—well, he'd pay them off quick, once they were back at the house. And then they, and Doll too, could do what they wanted. He no longer cared. He had the money.

Kay? Kay and Frank? The hell with them, too. He no longer cared about them. The money was the thing, and he had the money.

Thinking about it, he was unaware of the car that passed them as Wally swung into the road leading to the house.

Wally himself hardly noticed the car. He was filled with his own excitement. He had no idea how much money they had taken, but it must be plenty. At least a hundred thousand dollars, he figured. Plenty. Flood had stacked it into the bag so he couldn't be sure, but it would be enough.

Roy was thinking of the money too. Thinking of the money and thinking of other things. He knew how Flood felt. He could tell. He could even guess that Wally was so excited about the success of the plan that he'd be thinking of nothing else. But Roy was thinking of something else. He was thinking of Doll. Doll, up in the bedroom, tied and helpless.

Roy would let the others stay downstairs, and while they were dividing the loot, he'd sneak up and pay a visit to that bedroom.

Wally dimmed the lights as he approached the house. "Stop in the yard," Flood ordered.

Wally followed instructions.

"You take the bag," Flood said. "Bring it in."

He climbed out of the car and started for the house. Wally and Roy followed, carrying the heavy duffel bag between them.

Possibly it was because of the excitement and his exalted state of nervous tension, or perhaps it was only that he was too preoccupied with the success of his scheme, but for once the subtle sixth sense that had always warned Flood of danger deserted him.

He entered the kitchen and the first person he saw was Doll. Then he saw Frank, standing over to one side. It is doubtful that he noticed the double-barreled shotgun in Frank's hands at all.

"We did it," he said, his voice shrill with success. "We did it, boy."

Before he had finished speaking, Wally and Roy crowded through the doorway behind him.

"Doll!" Wally said. "What the hell—"

Doll's shrill scream cut him short.

"He's got a gun," she said. "Watch out, he's got a gun. And he's tipped the cops. That girl—she's on her way to get the cops!"

As she yelled the words, she jumped toward Frank. He had started to lift the shotgun, but he had to leap back quickly. As he did so, Roy pulled the .38 from his belt. He started firing from where he stood, directly behind Wally.

Flood moved like lightning, grabbing the table and pulling it over and falling behind it. His own gun came out as he went to his knees.

Frank had no time to aim. The gun was pointed toward Wally and Roy and he pulled the trigger almost simultaneously with the crashing blast of Roy's revolver.

Frank never felt the bullet as it smashed through his upper right arm. He was already pressing the second trigger.

His first shot, from a distance of less than eight feet, virtually tore half of Wally's head off. The second blew a hole the size of a dinner plate through Roy's chest.

Flood fired only twice. The first slug entered the left side of Frank's chest, just over the sixth rib; the second one took him in the stomach.

7.

By the time Flood had dragged the duffel bag out to the garage and tossed it into the trunk, Doll was already in the car. He hardly was aware of her presence as he backed out of the double doors and swung around in the yard, barely missing the Ford sedan.

Far off to the east he heard the rising and falling sound of a siren.

Chapter Eleven

1.

He lay there on the clean white sheet in the white iron bed and his face was almost as colorless as the pillowcase on which his head rested.

They had all gone, the two doctors, the nurse, and the others. Gone and left him alone at last. All of them, that is, except this one man who sat in the straight-backed chair next to the cot where he lay.

He was just as glad that he was unable to move, that he was unable to talk; that all he could do was lie there and suffer as the morphine wore off and the pain surged through his body.

But he didn't have to move or turn his head to know who the man was that sat patiently at his side.

He was silent, this man, for a long time. But at last he spoke.

"And so," he said, "that's how it was, Frank. He was doing about eighty-five miles an hour, this guy in the Caddie with the girl. About eighty-five when it happened. You know that stretch of road, just north of Palm Beach. A dangerous stretch at best. But he was doing eighty-five and we weren't far behind him. He swung out to pass the car and there was the trailer truck, coming up from Miami. The driver tried to get out of his way, but there was nothing he could do. They hit head on. The truck driver was lucky; he'll pull through."

Again he was silent, but he finally continued.

"It was bad," he said. "So bad that when we finally pulled them from the burned wreckage, there was no chance of ever identifying him. Not him or the girl. It's strange that the only thing that didn't burn was the money."

He got up, lighted a cigarette, and he passed Frank's line of vision. He was wearing a fresh uniform and Frank inconsequentially reflected that Waldo Harrington always looked good in his uniform.

"Yes," he said at last, "that's about it. Wound it up. The whole gang of them except for the two that put the powerhouse out of business. We probably never will get them.

"But there's one more thing. The doctor didn't want me to tell you about it because he was afraid of any additional shock. But now he tells me you're going to pull through all right and so I think I better tell you. It's about that uncle who was visiting you. I hate to have to tell you, but apparently, when they missed their way and turned off on the dead-end lane and came to your house, he must have got in their way. So they killed him. Beat his head in with a pistol butt. I hate to have to tell you."

Harrington put out his cigarette and walked over and looked down at Frank. His face was cold and serious—not the face that Frank remembered at all.

"There's only this one other thing I have to say to you, Frank," he said. "Don't try to answer me. Just listen to me. You remember a few days ago, one evening, I stopped by your house? I had a jug of liquor. Bootleg liquor I'd taken off a couple of boys I know. Well, I'm a cop, and I think a good cop and an honest cop. Small-town cops, like we have here in Indio Beach, are a little different than your big-city cops. Perhaps a little more human. I don't know. But different. Anyway, a lot of people might think I was pretty careless about that bootleg liquor. Might think I wasn't doing my duty when I didn't arrest those boys. Even worse, that I was doing something criminal when I not only let them go, but drank some of the stuff myself.

"But me, I'm a small-town cop. I look at it different. Those boys were doing wrong, of course. On the other hand, I happen to know the facts. They sell that stuff over in Black Town to a bunch of colored boys who don't have the money to buy the high-priced stuff at the liquor stores. They don't sell much, just enough to get by. It means that those colored boys, who are trying to get by on starvation wages, are able to get a cheap load on now and then on Saturday night.

"And the stuff isn't bad. It isn't poison or anything like that. If it was, I wouldn't drink it myself.

"Anyway, they bootleg it and just make a bare living. So I just turn my back and pretend I don't know about it. They're doing wrong, but they're not vicious or mean or trying to hurt anyone.

"Well, anyway, that's the kind of cop I am. I let 'em get away with it."

He was standing directly in front of Frank as he finished talking, staring into his face and looking thoughtful.

"The next time I see them, though," he said, "I'm going to tell them they gotta quit. Quit before they get themselves into something that they can't get out of."

He smiled then finally and patted Harper's shoulder. He turned and started for the door.

"I'm sending your wife in," he said. "She's been waiting outside. She had a pretty rough time of it, but now that she knows you're going to be all right, she's feeling better. She's an unusual woman, Frank. A very unusual woman. It was lucky that it was me she found when she escaped from the house and went for the police.

"Yes, she's been waiting for you."

THE END

A Matter of Time:
Looking Back at Lionel White
by Cullen Gallagher

Lionel White didn't write action novels. Or mysteries. Or thrillers. Or suspense.

Lionel White wrote novels of tension.

Sure, there's always some action in there—fist fights, shoot-outs, maybe an explosion or two—but they are never the focal point. In fact, in White's second novel, *The Snatchers* (1953), the central kidnapping happens before the first chapter even begins. Most of the rest of the novel is like a fuse slowly burning as the conspirators pace around the hideout, biding their time until delivery of the ransom, and losing their patience with each passing moment.

And yes, there's usually an element of mystery in his novels—like, what's going to happen to the characters?—but White rarely withholds any crucial plot details from the reader, as in more traditional mysteries. There's no question of "whodunnit" in White's books—we know, because the criminals are frequently the protagonists. Recall the opening line of *The Big Caper* (1955): "Kosta arrived on Tuesday." Person, action, and time, all in four words. And in the next paragraph, another character is introduced, Frank, who "had already left for the gas station." The wheels of the titular caper are already in motion, and White is letting the reader in on everything that's unfolding step by step. We get to see first-hand who's doing what, where each character is located, and how they fit into the heist. In fact, White *wants* us to know these things; design and choreography is integral to the structure of his books. The opening paragraph of *Steal Big* (1960) similarly is designed not only for the reader to identify who the criminal is, but also in a Hitchcockian twist, to immediately identify with the criminal, inviting them to literally see the world through their eyes: "From where the car was parked, two doors down from the A & P and directly opposite the South Shore Loan Company office, Barker was able to look into the rear vision mirror and see the uniformed policeman as he turned into the tavern."

Despite featuring some genuinely thrilling moments, White's books are not really thrillers—at least not by David Corbett's definition from *Writer's Digest:* "thrillers are typically the most emotional [type of suspense novel], focusing on the fear, doubt and dread of the hero as she faces some form of what Dean Koontz has deemed 'terrible trouble.'" Not only do many of White's novels—such as the ones collected here—lack heroes, the protagonists don't always face "terrible trouble" because often they are cause of it. Consider *Death Takes the Bus* (1957), an ensemble novel about a group of passengers on a bus whose journey is interrupted when a prisoner being transported attempts to escape. Switching perspectives between the prisoner, his cohorts, and the innocent victims on the bus, there's no single main character to the story, and thus no single perspective. Is it a novel about a prisoner trying to escape, is it about an accomplice wrestling with his moral and conscience, or is it about the trauma of being hostage on a hijacked bus? Depending on which character White is inhabiting, it is a very different type of story. Perhaps, then, Lionel White's books are not traditional thrillers, but rather multiple different thrillers unfolding at the same time. This multi-dimensional aspect is typical of the way that White constructs his novels.

And while there's certainly suspense in waiting to find out what's ultimately going to happen to the protagonists of his stories—do they pull off the heist in *The Big Caper*, do the kidnappers get the ransom in *The Snatchers*, or does the prisoner get away in *Death Takes the Bus*—it's the "waiting" that is most important to White, not what happens to the characters (as often White's scenes can be quite mundane) but the tension of waiting for it to happen. Take, for example, *Hostage for a Hood* (1957), in which most of the novel takes place in a hideout while a character waits with a hostage for his accomplices to arrive, and once they arrive they wait for the money to arrive; meanwhile, the husband of the hostage is waiting for the police to figure out whether something bad happened to his wife or if she just ran away (their hypothesis). This is a book about waiting for things to happen. Waiting for things to go right, for things to wrong, for time to pass, waiting for anything except the unbearable eternity of the present moment.

This is why I say that Lionel White wrote novels of tension—and the building block of that tension is time. "I went back to my hotel room and I waited," narrates the protagonist of *The Mexico Run* (1974), White's antepenultimate novel about a Vietnam vet-turned-marijuana smuggler. "I waited for thirty-six hours. I waited through a quart and a half of bourbon. I didn't leave my room. I had my meals sent up. I didn't use the telephone. I had no one to call. And I began to wonder if I'd misplaced my confidence in Bongo's recommendations. I certainly hoped that I had not. If this one fell through, then it was very likely the one in Mexico would fall through, and that would spell complete disaster for all of my plans." The motif of waiting continues through the entire book—the protagonist is waiting in motel rooms for people to show up (or for them to leave), waiting for phone calls or letters to arrive, waiting for plans to start, waiting for plans to finish, waiting to see whether he lives long enough to wait another day.

Time is more than just a measure in White's world, however, it's a philosophy. An interior monologue from Barker, one of White's criminals in *Steal Big*, articulates just how time is seen as a guiding principle for one's life: "It wasn't the case of the half-minute, the thirty seconds. It was a lot more than that. It was a matter of the right way or the wrong way of doing the thing. A matter of precision and perfect timing. A matter of ultimate perfection. It was something you had to understand and believe in—just as Donovan had always insisted. The woods were filled with people who never did have that understanding. Woods, hell. The prisons and the ground out at Potters Field were filled with guys who had never understood."

White also uses time as a structural element, often organizing his chapters like an editor of a movie. There's a cinematic sense of synchronicity to White's work, and it's no wonder that he has been adapted to the screen many times: *Clean Break* (1955) *The Killing* in 1956; *The Big Caper* in 1957; *The Merriweather File* (1959) for the TV series *Thriller* in 1961; *Obsession* (1962) as *Pierrot le Fou*, directed by Jean-Luc Godard, in 1965; *The Money Trap* (1963) in 1965; *The Snatchers* as *The Night of the Following Day* in 1969; *Obsession* again in 1974 as *Karvat*, or *The Hair*, a Finnish production; and finally *Rafferty* (1960) as a Soviet television film in 1980. White's most recent credit is in 1992, seven years after his death, as a dedicatee of Quentin Tarantino's *Reservoir Dogs*. White's multi-character scenarios and violent, ruthless world is a clear influence not just on *Reservoir Dogs*, but on all of Tarantino's films.

The most famous film interpretation of White's work is indisputably *The Killing*, directed by Stanley Kubrick and adapted by Kubrick with the help of Jim Thompson, a contemporary of White's from the crime fiction shelves. It's an archetypical White story: a professional criminal enlists a group of men, mostly everyday average joes, to knock over a race track. The genius of the movie is all there in the original, the way that White cuts back and forth between each of the characters and their roles in the heist. *Clean Break* was published the same year as *The Big Caper* and, while both share a similar plot and structure, I'll go on the record that *The Big Caper* is a better example of White's orchestration of multiple characters and actions happening simultaneously. The Florida-set *Big Caper* involves multiple sets of conspirators working independently of one another, a safety measure that backfires and threatens to compromise the whole operation. Unlike *The Killing*, which instinctively understood White's characters and design, the movie version of *The Big Caper* (directed by Robert Stevens and written by Martin Berkeley) completely misunderstands its source material. Flood, the cut-throat and intimidating organizer behind the titular crime in the novel, is turned into a pushover, a mere figurehead who can be manipulated into pulling the heist. In the movie, the real muscle and brains of the operation is Frank, played to the hardboiled hilt by Rory Calhoun, a real life bad-boy who spent several years in prison for grand theft auto and brings a great deal of authenticity to the role. In White's novel, Frank was another of White's everyman characters, a jobless vet sucked into the crime by circumstance and opportunity; he's also a character of conscience who tries to make the situation right by foiling Flood's plans. By so drastically changing Frank's personality in the movie, however, the character dynamic of White's novel is totally lost. Furthermore, the film cuts back on the number of characters, thereby also losing the architectural design of White's original novel.

Time can be a cruel mistress, as many of White's characters learned. You can plan things down to the second, but in the end it doesn't matter. Ultimately, time runs its own course and chooses your destiny for you. Man is powerless in the face of time.

Such is the fate that White, himself, suffered.

For just over a quarter of a century, Lionel White was a mainstay of crime fiction. Between 1952 and 1978, he published 37 novels. That's upwards of a novel a year for just over 26 years. In 1955 alone he produced four novels: *The Big Caper, Clean Break, Flight Into Terror,* and *Love Trap*. He also managed to maintain a career in both hardcover and paperback at the same time, straddling a literary dichotomy that typically divided writers. Before becoming a novelist, he was a crime reporter, and an editor for true crime pulps. And his work was adapted eight times to the screen—more than Clifton

Adams, Gil Brewer, Bruno Fischer, Fletcher Flora, Dan J. Marlowe, Margaret Millar, Wade Miller, Vin Packer, Peter Rabe, and the list goes on. All in all, White had a career that many writers would have killed for.

But time was not kind to Lionel White.

Over the years, while many of his fellow crime writers were catapulted from obscurity into cult legends, White's literary legacy faded further into obscurity. When Zomba was publishing their Black Box Thriller omnibuses in the early 1980s of David Goodis and Jim Thompson, White's back catalog remained out of print. While *Clean Break* received one paperback reprint in 1988 under the original Black Lizard-Creative Arts line (under its filmed title, *The Killing*), the book did not remain in print when Vintage took over Black Lizard. Blackmaskonline did print bootleg editions of *Clean Break* and *Flight Into Terror* in the early 2000s, but those poorly proofread and slap-dash designed volumes were not a proper tribute to the works contained within their covers. Since their launch in 2004, Hard Case Crime has not republished one of White's works. And while the Library of Congress has included works by many of White's peers in anthologies (such as Dolores Hitchens, Dorothy B. Hughes, Thompson, and Charles Willeford), and even devoted an entire volume to David Goodis, White has been left out.

This makes the current volume you are holding all the more special, and all the more vital. This is the fourth collection of White's work that Stark House has republished, totaling eight novels. It marks the greatest effort to republish, and keep in print, the legacy of one of crime fiction's most unique voices. If you enjoyed *The Big Caper* and *Steal Big*, then I hope you continue your exploration into Lionel White's life of crime by picking up one of Stark House's other volumes. Maybe now, time is finally on White's side.

—February 2021
Brooklyn, NY

Cullen Gallagher lives in Brooklyn, NY. His writing has appeared in the *Los Angeles Review of Books*, *Paris Review*, and *Not Coming to a Theater Near You*, as well as in the anthologies *Cult Cinema: An Arrow Video Companion* (2016) edited by Anthony Nield, and *Screen Slate: New York City Cinema 2011-2015* (2017) edited by Jon Dieringer. His western fiction appears in the anthologies *Bourbon &*

a Good Cigar (2018) and *Time to Myself* (2018), both edited by Scott Harris. He blogs about noir and western fiction at *Pulp Serenade* (www.pulp-serenade.com).